MW00965236

The Red Wing Sings

Ron & Darlene,

I hope you both enjoy my
novel. There's a lot of
local content. ~ Thank you.

Tom O.

By Tom Omstead

Copyright © 2011 by Tom Omstead
First Edition – September 2011

This book is a work of fiction. Characters and events are either the product of the author's imagination or used fictitiously. Any resemblance to actual events or persons, living or dead, is entirely coincidental and not intended by the author.

ISBN
978-1-77067-511-7 (Hardcover)
978-1-77067-512-4 (Paperback)
978-1-77067-513-1 (eBook)

All rights reserved.

No part of this publication may be reproduced in any form, or by any means, electronic or mechanical, including photocopying, recording, or any information browsing, storage, or retrieval system, without permission in writing from the publisher.

Published by:

FriesenPress
Suite 300 – 852 Fort Street
Victoria, BC, Canada V8W 1H8

www.friesenpress.com

Distributed to the trade by The Ingram Book Company

I dedicate this book to the memory of my brother, Frederick William Omstead.

ACKNOWLEDGEMENTS
AND SOURCES

~

First and foremost, I would like to thank two extraordinary ladies in my life: my multi-talented wife, Sue, for her encouragement and tireless assistance as first editor, and my mother, Maeve Omstead-Johnston, for her life-long inspiration and encouragement and whose beautiful poem 'Did the Indians know it would end this way?' I've gratefully incorporated into Chapter 24.

My gratitude also goes to my Uncle Fred and Captain Kate for generously sharing with me their piloting expertise and suggestions.

Merci à mon ami Marc Germain pour m'avoir aidé avec la traduction.

Thank you to Nancy Belgue for her scholarly input and suggestions.

Thank you to Lanny Mann of www.twomanntent.com – photographer of the landscape photo used on the book's cover; Randy Roberts of www.randyroberts.wordpress.com – photographer of the red-winged blackbird; Patty Meuser-Kristy – for the image artwork; and Bill Underwood of www.underwoodwildlifestudio.com – for the feather artwork.

My gratitude to the 'The Project Gutenberg EBook of The Life and Correspondence of Sir Isaac Brock', edited by Ferdinand Brock Tupper (Major-General Sir Isaac Brock's nephew), for making their eBook available for the use of anyone anywhere at no cost and with almost no restrictions.

The Queen's speech in Chapter 15 is fictional; however, I have incorporated some words and phrases actually spoken by Queen Elizabeth II in speeches she has made on visits to Canada over the years.

The Lord's Prayer was taken from the Anglican Book of Common Prayer, 1662.

Finally, thank you also to my friends and family whose own lives and experiences have undoubtedly imparted some ideas and adventures into my subconscious and may have innocuously found their way into the story.

~

PREFACE

~

I wrote this story for myself. Before October 13, 2009, I'd never thought of myself as a writer. That morning, I woke with a scary storyline in my head. I got up and wrote it down. I'd dreamt about a witch's brew of events that catapults the current state of fear in America to paranoia and ultimately ends with the US armed forces occupying Canada.

With the encouragement of my wife and mother, I continued to write. The storyline set the course and destination of my journey, but the adventures en route were initially unknown to me. Those details slowly revealed themselves to me as though I myself was the reader. I found enjoyment and fulfilment in simply developing the story and inventing its characters.

Much of my story intertwines with the War of 1812. 2012 marks the bicentennial of that defining war. From it, I draw events and timelines as well as the unifying inspirations and exploits of the 'Hero of Upper Canada', Sir Isaac Brock, who was respected by both Canadians and Americans alike. 200 years later, this story pays homage to a man and the people who helped defend with their lives this land we have inherited.

Brock's exploits inspire the main character, Will. Brock's diary becomes Will's bridge to the past as the diary reveals to him time-less strategies for repelling the invaders.

All this was simply a figment of my overactive imagination. Or so I thought. The storyline inevitably led me to do some research. Imagine how pleased I was to discover that Brock's nephew actually published Brock's memoirs in 1845! These have been indispensable to me and helped bring depth to my story. I dug into the history of the US expansion across North America, the War of 1812, the Monroe doctrine, the expulsion and relocation of native Americans from their lands, the Underground Railway (when black slaves took refuge in Canada), the Alaskan Panhandle border dispute, War Plan Red (a secret continental war plan developed by the US in the 1930s to attack and capture Canada), the Canadian / US / British collaborative development of the atomic bomb (and its offspring, nuclear power plants) and most recently, the War on Terrorism.

The nature of the story requires that Canadians and Americans are enemies again. As in any conflict, there are good and bad characters on both sides. I do not intend for this story to be one-sided or anti-American. On the contrary, I respect and am inspired by America's founding philosophy and ideals.

I researched both sides of the debate concerning the plausibility of a future nuclear 9/11 and, if it happened, the likelihood that the US could blame Canada. I've perused news stories about other border security issues and trade tensions that continue to wear on Canadian and US relations today.

Lastly, to better buttress my storyline, I discovered words spoken by a number of prominent American historical figures about their desire to annex Canada to America. I'm chilled to discover this has actually been a recurring theme throughout American history. My story simply sets in motion events that result in the fulfilment of those aspirations. Scarily, my research only validated, at least in my mind, the plausibility of my story.

Regardless, this is still a novel and I have taken the liberties that only a novelist can take.

~

"Surgite brave York Volunteers! Push on, don't mind me... [Give] some token of remembrance to my sister."

— final words spoken by Major-General Sir Isaac Brock as he succumbed to a fatal bullet wound at the Battle of Queenstown Heights, October 13, 1812

~

CHAPTER I

By The Dawn's
Early Light

*The first step to preventing a nuclear 9/11
is imagining that it could happen.*

~

Pearson International Airport, Toronto Canada
6:45 a.m. Tuesday, June 19th.
Veteran pilot Max Ridley pulled back on the control column of
Can-Air Cargo flight 619. Clear of the ground, the plane climbed
smoothly into bluebird skies.

"Positive rate," called out First Officer Khurshid.

"Gear up," ordered Ridley.

"Gear up," acknowledged the F/O.

Next, Ridley scanned and re-scanned the instruments. Gears up
and checked, flaps up, lights out, ignition off, fuel pumps set, air
conditioning shutoff on override, hydraulic pumps off and low, flood
and logo lights at ten, and altimeter at five angels and climbing. All
appeared normal as he turned the aircraft away from the rising sun
to a southward heading of 190 degrees. Visibility was unlimited.

Toronto Air Traffic Control had cleared the flight to climb to and
then maintain a flight level of twenty-two thousand feet. Leaving
Toronto ATC's airspace, Can-Air 619 was passed onto Cleveland
ATC, which directed Captain Ridley to maintain flight level two-
two-zero because of traffic, but to expect to climb to flight level
three-eight-zero shortly.

Gradually Captain Ridley relaxed, handing control over to his
first officer, co-pilot Javed Khurshid. This was just another routine
flight of countless others Ridley had logged. At the pinnacle of
his career, he'd flown CF-18 Hornets in the air force. Now he

flew heavy cargo planes. By comparison, the Boeing 767-200ER freighter drove more like a bus than the nimble fighter. Still, any plane demanded respect and he took his job seriously.

"Can-Air six-one-nine, climb and maintain flight level three-eight-zero, turn right, heading two-six-zero," directed Cleveland ATC.

"Climb and maintain three-eight-zero, heading two-six-zero. Can-Air six-one-nine heavy," Captain Ridley acknowledged. Then, turning to the F/O he said, "I think I smell something funny."

"Me too," confirmed the F/O. "Should I go and check the cargo compartment?"

"Yes," answered Ridley, taking back control.

Moments after Khurshid left the cockpit, a BOOM sound came from the cargo compartment.

Right away, the cargo compartment fire warning bell sounded in the flight deck. Ridley pressed the master warning light to cancel the fire bell. Suddenly, a cold fine mist appeared in the cockpit, indicating a rapid change in cabin pressure, and then the altitude warning horn sounded. Captain Ridley turned off the warning horn.

Seconds later, Khurshid stumbled back into the cockpit.

"What the hell's going on back there?" Ridley demanded as they donned their oxygen masks.

"THERE WAS AN EXPLOSION! WE'RE ON FIRE!" shouted the panicked first officer.

"Calm down, man," ordered the captain as he switched his transponder squawk code to 7700 transmitting to ground radar that they had a problem. "What exploded and what's on fire?"

"One of the cargo pallets exploded and we're burning! WE'RE GOING TO CRASH AND BURN!" Stressed by the situation, Khurshid had reverted back to his heavy foreign accent.

"CALM DOWN DAMNIT! I can barely understand you! Now, what exactly is on fire?" the captain repeated.

Gathering himself, Khurshid reported more clearly, "One of the cargo pallets exploded setting a number of other pallets on fire, Captain!"

"Understood," replied Ridley, realizing that his own composure was the only thing keeping his first officer from totally losing it. Calmly, he asked for the Emergency Descent Quick Reference Checklist and then turned his attention back to flying.

"You better send out a Mayday and request an emergency descent to flight level eight-zero," he advised Khurshid.

"Roger, Captain," and then into the radio, "Mayday, Mayday, Mayday, Can-Air Cargo 619 heavy is declaring an emergency and wishes to do an emergency descent to flight level eight-zero," he advised Cleveland ATC. "We've had a small explosion causing a fire."

"Can-Air six-one-nine, confirm you wish to descend to flight level eight-zero," replied the controller at Cleveland ATC.

"Yes, we are leaving flight level three-eight-zero now. We've had a small explosion," the F/O repeated.

"Roger, six-one-nine, you are clear to descend immediately to flight level eight-zero," confirmed the controller.

"Thank you," replied the F/O.

"Ask them for the nearest suitable airport," added the captain.

"Can you vector us to land at the nearest suitable airport?" the F/O repeated into the radio.

"Roger, six-one-nine. Do you wish to be vectored to land in Detroit?"

"Detroit?"

"Roger," the captain nodded.

"Roger that."

"Can-Air six-one-nine, descend and maintain eight-zero, turn right, heading of 300," directed the controller.

"Descend and maintain eight-zero, heading 300, Can-Air six-one-niner," the F/O acknowledged.

"Can-Air six-one-nine, please advise the number of souls, your fuel and if there are any dangerous goods on board for emergency services, please?"

"Roger. Umm, standby for that," the F/O replied.

"Standing by," answered the controller.

"He asked for the number of souls on board and for our fuel, Captain," the first officer repeated.

But the captain didn't respond. Suddenly, he was feeling a bit dizzy and confused.

"Captain?" Khurshid repeated.

"Something's wrong. I… I don't thin… You got… oxygen?" Ridley stammered, his head now spinning.

"Mine's not working right either, Captain," the first officer replied. The captain grabbed at the hose to his oxygen mask and found that it wasn't connected. His mind in a daze, it slowly dawned on him that Khurshid must have deliberately cut his oxygen hose.

"You bast..." Ridley said as he passed out.

Immediately, Khurshid grabbed the controls. His target was in sight.

"Can-Air six-one-nine, state your intentions," asked the anxious controller who'd been waiting on standby.

"WE'RE ON FIRE! WE'RE GOING DOWN!" Khurshid yelled into the radio.

"Repeat, please."

There was no immediate response. The only thing the controller heard was the sound of strained breathing as the wind noise started to increase.

The Terrain and Awareness Warning System Alarm sounded in the flight deck. Intent upon his rapidly approaching target, Khurshid ignored the alarm.

"Six-one-nine, state your intentions," repeated the controller.

"I RELY ON ALLAH!" Khurshid shouted in reply.

Moments later, Can-Air Cargo flight 619's blip disappeared from all radar screens.

William Anderson woke with a start. All was silent. He didn't know where he was. But he did know that he was in bed and something wasn't right. Instinctively, he reached across and, feeling nobody there, wondered, 'Where's Sydney?' It was unusual for her to rise before him.

Opening his eyes brought another surprise. Not only was his girlfriend not beside him, he hadn't even slept in their bed or in their home in Field, British Columbia. Instead, he'd slept in his childhood bed which was on his parents' farm back in southern Ontario.

Anderson Orchards was situated in Canada's deepest south on a hundred mile peninsula that jutted deep into America's heartland.

Only then did Will recall arriving at the farm on the preceding day. Taking in his surroundings, Will's eyes told him that he was in the same bed he'd slept in for the first nineteen years of his life. Yet something about it felt strangely unfamiliar and he didn't know why.

Will recalled the evening before and the lively conversation with his parents and two siblings, Kevin and Hana. They'd dined on a meal of baked whitefish, a family favourite. It had been caught in the local waters and his mom had stuffed it with wild rice, onions and garlic. Their dinner conversation took in many subjects as they had a lot of ground to cover since they last saw one another. His memory of the evening, combined with the sights his eyes now beheld, reminded him where he was and the knowledge helped put him back at ease.

He closed his eyes again hoping to sleep a little longer, but just as he did so, the same strange feeling returned. Despite what his eyes told him, something else was going on. And it, whatever it was, felt very wrong. He just couldn't put his finger on it.

'Perhaps Mom's done something different to my bedroom?' he pondered.

Reopening his eyes, he scanned the room, searching for the culprit of his unrest. The door was closed, the window was slightly open and curtains were drawn. These were all just as he'd left them when he'd turned in last night.

He took it all in. Everything about his room was as it had always been. The walls, floor and ceiling were as before. Perhaps they'd received a fresh coat of paint, but nothing more. The bed, covers and pillow were familiar. The closet, dresser, window, door and lights were all the same. Nothing was unusual or out of place.

'That's strange,' he thought. By all appearances, all was well. So, for now, he concluded that his uneasy feeling was wholly without basis.

'Perhaps I'm just overly excited about coming home,' he mused.

Again he closed his eyes and gradually he forced himself back to sleep.

~

For a while longer, Will slept in a dreamy state. Dreaming was not unusual for Will. Now he dreamt of clear blue skies filled with chirping birds. But the dream was disturbing. He tossed and turned between two worlds. Actually it was two earthbound places – British Columbia and Ontario.

When Will moved to British Columbia, he had initially found the mornings too quiet and it took him a long time to get used to the change. In Ontario, he'd grown up surrounded by sounds in the morning. They were rural sounds, sounds unique to the peninsula that didn't come from the usual causes known to urban dwellers such as the roar of traffic, screeching sirens, or the banging of garbage trucks making their rounds. Instead, sounds on the farm came mostly from nature and were caused by things like rolling waves, thunderstorms, or even birdsong.

Birdsongs were usually the most noticeable sound at dawn, just before many people got up. It was then, before the winds whipped up the waves or the sun's heat disturbed the skies, that the songs of birds ruled nature's airwaves. It was thought that the pleasant disposition of the farm-folk living on the peninsula was nurtured by the pleasing chirpings of the birds.

This was in complete contrast to the west. In the remote little mountain town where he had resettled, neither birds nor people were in over-abundance. There, the mornings were deadly silent, so quiet that the silence initially disturbed Will's sleep. Now he slept soundly in both places – or so he thought.

~

The silence jolted him awake again.

'Where am I?'

Open eyes answered, 'Ontario'.

'That's weird. Why does it feel more like British Columbia?' he wondered, still unsettled by the sensory battle being waged between his eyes and ears.

This morning's silence was such as he had, literally, 'never heard before' during springtime on the farm. Normally, only a seasoned local could sleep beyond dawn due to all the chirping that occurred during the annual bird migration. But Will still didn't realize that the silence was the cause of his anxiety.

The smell of frying bacon then awoke his olfactory senses. The familiar smell of breakfast gradually penetrated his subconscious, proclaiming that his father, Grant, was downstairs cooking. Will reopened his eyes and, in an instant, his nose and eyes overwhelmed his ears and ended, without any uncertainty, the sensory debate as to what was wrong.

'I'm in Ontario,' his mind cried out to him, 'and it shouldn't be quiet!'

Will jumped out of bed and ran to the window. For as far as his eyes could see, there were no birds. They were all gone. He had never seen this before.

Eyes, ears and nose now finally in full agreement and reporting back to his brain the same story, his lips broke the silence by mouthing his first words that morning, "Where are the birds?"

Looking out over the lake's horizon, he saw why the birds weren't chirping. Off in the distance on the American side, he saw an awful sight floating upwards. It was a most unusual looking cloud. For years, he had been used to seeing a lone white cloud of steam rising over there. He knew that that cloud rose out of Fermi, the American nuclear power generation plant.

But the cloud he saw this morning over Fermi wasn't white and it certainly wasn't normal. This morning's cloud was dark and it boiled up towards the heavens with a dreadful rage. Like the birds, he instinctively knew that he must flee away from it.

Rushing downstairs, then into the kitchen, Will found his family glued to the television set. The scene brought back chilling memories, life changing memories, of the last time he'd come upon a scene like this on the fateful morning of 9/11.

Sophie Anderson's eyes were red with tears.

"What's wrong, Mom?"

Nobody answered. His father, seated beside his mom on the arm of her chair, was shaking his head in disbelief and muttering to nobody in particular something about, "They've done it again".

"Who's done what?" asked Will.

"Shhhhhhh," came the reply from the kitchen. Will's sister Hana was trying to listen to the television from there.

Will focused on the TV. Listening to it, he heard the news anchor repeat the developing story about Can-Air Cargo flight 619 being deliberately crashed into nuclear power plant Fermi. Although the story was still in the making, it was speculated that the immensity of the damage had caused a core meltdown and, at that very moment, massive amounts of radioactive debris were spewing into the atmosphere. For the second time that morning, Will couldn't believe what he was hearing. Then he remembered seeing the angry black cloud and put it all together. This was for real!

The word 'deliberately' said it all. There had been another terrorist attack.

~

"Holy shit", he said.

Just then the family vehicle came speeding up the drive to make an abrupt stop right outside of the farmhouse. Out jumped Will's brother Kevin who came running up the walk to the kitchen door.

"There's a line-up at the station. I was lucky to have got the jump on them. The truck's full of fuel and I've filled some extra fuel cans just in case we have problems refilling later. We could nearly drive to Will's in BC if we have to. I say we should leave now before the roads are jammed with other evacuees."

As if on cue, Hana came out of the kitchen carrying a box full of food and supplies.

"You'll have to eat breakfast on the road, Will. It's ready for you in the kitchen and, while you're there, grab the other box of food."

'God, my siblings are quick thinkers in an emergency,' thought Will. After picking up his breakfast and the extra food, Will quickly returned to his bedroom for his backpack, which he used for his traveling luggage. Luckily, most of his gear was still packed.

In short order, the farmhouse was locked, the car packed and they were ready to leave. His father put the truck in gear and then shifted it back into park.

"The gun", he said.

"Don't bother with that now, Grant. We'll be fine", Sophie said confidently.

There was no time for debate. In an emergency, everyone knew to trust Sophie's instincts. With the roar of the engine, the Andersons were off. Like the birds before them, they fled eastward, into the wind, and away from the sight of the angry black plume of smoke.

~

CHAPTER II

As It Fitfully Blows

"Freedom and fear are at war."
— President George W. Bush, addressing the
American nation, September 20, 2001

" — and fear is winning."
— the Author

~

The Andersons sped toward an undetermined destination hoping to escape the fallout. They travelled along the secondary highway known as the Talbot Trail which had been named after the colonel who'd planned and constructed it in the last century. It was one of the first roads built through the region and known to many generations of the Anderson family. Their familiarity with the steadfast trail gave them some sense of comfort.

Nowadays, most people drive along the Talbot Trail totally unaware and unappreciative of its historical significance. The highway parallels the north shore of Lake Erie on the Canadian side, just as most of the old pathways follow some historic water route. It provides a land link from Amherstburg, at the extreme west end of the lake, to Fort Erie at the east end.

Until about two hundred years ago, it was easier to travel from place to place by water than by land. Most communities were founded along these waterways. Eventually, trails were built alongside the waterways in a network which crisscrossed over the land. The trails with the most traffic, like the Talbot Trail, were later paved into roads for fast moving motorized vehicles. Later, using massive earth moving equipment and modern methods to bridge over the old waterways and tunnel through mountains, super highways were built. Today, people can drive in their automobiles from point to point totally ignorant of the true nature of the countryside and waterways that surround them.

More than a generation has now passed since people have used the old trails which parallel the waterways. Yet many of those forgotten and neglected trails still exist to this very day. These trails are the sanctuaries of only a transient few, those who prefer to wander about in peace, out of sight, out of mind and 'off the grid'.

The Talbot Trail was not usually the fastest way to drive east. The four lane super highway 401, which lay a dozen or more miles off to the north, was normally much faster. But today was an abnormal day and the Andersons expected most others fleeing the fallout would, out of habit, choose the 401 and jam it up. Indeed this is what happened, but soon even the traffic on the Talbot Trail began to build and slow their progress.

The shocking news of Fermi's destruction had everyone stunned. Slowly, they drove along contemplating the day's news in silence. Occasionally, Grant Anderson switched on the radio and tuned into an American station to get the latest updates. Finding one, they heard the news commentator confirming that Can-Air Cargo flight 619, out of Toronto, Canada, had been deliberately crashed into nuclear power plant Fermi causing a core meltdown that released radioactive debris into the atmosphere.

Not all the facts were fully known, yet a biting new litany of words was born. Now, phrases such as 'their porous border' and 'the safe haven of terrorists' were being used to describe Canada. These cutting words rang harshly in the Andersons' ears. With constant repetition, all listeners became educated with a new terminology that heralded in the era of paranoia. The world was about to change, again.

The angriest proclamations came from a previously unknown American colonel named Kuhn who seemed to have no doubts where the blame should be placed: Canada.

"Once again, these attacks have come out of Canada", he bellowed over the airwaves. Nobody bothered to correct him. The fact that the 9/11 attacks had not come from Canada now seemed passé. Sure, in a knee-jerk reaction, Canada had been wrongly accused then, and again on a number of occasions since then, but this time there seemed to be no doubt in anyone's mind.

After a while, Grant switched off the radio so they could drive in peace. As if to find some additional sanctuary from all the angry rhetoric and finger pointing, Will's mind drifted off to BC and Sydney.

He loved it there, in the mountains. Ironically, he'd left Ontario and moved to the mountains because of 9/11. At the time, he'd planned on vacationing in Europe, but his flight had been cancelled due to the border backup issues and security concerns.

He had already booked time off work and, not wanting to risk crossing over any border, he decided to stay domestic and travel within Canada. He headed out west instead. His journey ended in the Rockies where he immediately felt at home. The surrounding mountains seemed to shield him from the literally terrified post 9/11 world. In the mountains, he found a different kind of world, one that was more in tune with his inner self.

In the mountains, one traded man-made risks for natural ones. There, one lived in an environment where one could still be eaten by wild animals, or become hopelessly lost in the vast back country, or buried alive by an avalanche.

Those were now his everyday realities. Oddly, those were exactly the sort of risks that he could live with. He wasn't terrified of nature's realities for he was naturally a good animal and instinctively knew how to survive.

It was the risks associated with living amongst other unpredictable people that made him uncomfortable. Unlike the creatures in the wild, he found some people to be beyond his understanding and trust. Consequently, he was drawn to less populated places such as he found in Field, BC.

So comfortable had he found it in Field that, within a week of arriving there, he had put a deposit on a nice quaint little place on the edge of the forest. It was located on a small piece of property that stretched down the mountain slopes to touch the outskirts of the pretty little town. A month later, he'd packed up all his worldly possessions and moved there.

A short while later, he convinced Sydney to come and join him. Once she did, she felt completely at home there too. Together, they built a new life in the west. They'd both found work as mountain

guides. That was ten years ago. The intervening time had been
a blur.

A bump in the road jolted him back to the present. The radio had
been turned on again. Looking around at the faces of his family, he
could see that the depressing news was wearing on them.

"I should call Sydney," he said to change the subject. "Is anyone
carrying their cell phone?" In the rush to leave, he'd left his on the
night stand beside his bed.

"Use mine," offered Hana, giving hers to him.

"Thanks."

He tried, but got a 'No Service' message.

"No service," he said, handing the phone back to his sister. "I'll
try again when we're nearer to London."

Behind them, black smoke could still be seen rising above the
lake waters. Six days out of seven, the prevailing winds came from
the west. On this day, the breeze came from the east and, unbeknownst to the Andersons, they were in no danger of the fallout.
The black cloud ascended upwards, occasionally eddying in the
higher atmosphere, but then drifted off to the northwest, back
into Michigan.

Occasionally, traffic passed the Andersons going in the opposite direction.

"Those people must be crazy!" Hana voiced what everyone else
was thinking.

Traffic slowed to a crawl and then came to a halt.

"Damn it! What now?" Kevin was not easily perturbed and his
words betrayed his inner anxiety.

They rounded a bend in the road, revealing bumper to bumper
traffic that stretched far ahead of them. As they gradually inched
their way forward, the cause of the traffic jam came into view.

A road barrier had been set up. Around it, they could see
uniformed soldiers. One by one, the soldiers spoke with the occupants of each vehicle that pulled up to stop beside them. After a
short discussion, most vehicles were turned back. That explained
the oncoming vehicles they had encountered.

"I guess they weren't crazy after all," Kevin said.

Only a few vehicles had been allowed to pass and it now
appeared to the Andersons that they too were likely to be
turned around.

Hana saw red. "What the hell are they doing? They can't do this!"

Taking her hand in his, Will spoke gently to calm and soothe her.

"Don't worry Hana, we've put quite a few miles between us and Fermi. We've got time to stop. They're not going to send us back into danger. Besides, nature calls." With that, he got out of the car and walked into the foliage of the roadside trees.

When Will returned, he heard his father whistling which told him that his dad was immersed in his own thoughts. His father was a serious and confident man. He was also a man of few words. To Will, he seemed to come from another time, a more noble time, like the Victorian era. His dad was a gentleman and he had a strong sense of duty. Will thought that he had inherited about half of his characteristics from his father; hopefully, the good half. His father could also be very obstinate. Under the circumstances, he wasn't whistling happily, he was whistling to release the stress. Everyone was on edge.

Occasional glances were cast back at the sky. Distance made the black cloud appear low in the sky, just touching the red horizon, but now it was more spread out.

'Red sky in the morning, sailors take warning,' thought Will.

~

It took the Andersons over an hour to reach the soldiers manning the barricade. It was a hastily constructed barrier of concrete blocks laid so as to funnel the traffic to the checkpoint. Finally, they pulled up to the armed guards. One soldier, uniformed a little differently than the others, was an officer who finished speaking with a soldier and then turned to face the Andersons.

"Good morning, folks. Captain Owens. Prince Rupert Regiment, 1st Battalion."

"Good morning, officer," Grant answered.

Captain Owens nodded in reply. "May I ask where you're heading?"

"Not really sure, Captain." Mr Anderson was always disarmingly honest. Sometimes it cost him, but most of the time, it put people at ease. His approach suited the captain.

"Maybe out to the Maritimes. Maybe out to the Rockies. We've got family in both places," Grant added.

Owens nodded again. "Where do you live, sir?"

"Anderson Orchards near Point Pelee." As an afterthought, Grant thumbed back towards Will in the rear seat of the cab. "Except for our youngest boy who lives out west."

"May I see your ID?" Owens asked Will.

Will passed him his BC driver's licence. Captain Owens glanced at it and passed it back.

"Is everyone else a resident of Essex County then?"

"We are," everyone but Will answered.

"Then only he is allowed to pass. The rest of you will have to turn around and go back home." And then as if to answer the unspoken question, he added, "Everyone is being told to return to their homes. There are no exceptions. Your son from BC can proceed."

Will looked at the barricade. Its very sturdiness betrayed its ultimate purpose and he had no doubt that the captain's words were final and could be backed by force, if necessary. Only a few soldiers visibly manned the barricade, but Will figured that the captain probably had more soldiers who could be quickly called upon. Looking around, he spied some standing amongst the bushes and trees just off the road.

The captain stepped away from the vehicle to give his soldiers the room to guide the Andersons' turnaround. At that moment, Hana thrust her face forward from the rear compartment of the vehicle.

"We're not doing that! Haven't you heard, officer? There's been a nuclear catastrophe back there!"

Upon hearing this outburst, Captain Owens stopped. For a moment, he stayed perfectly still with his back to them. Then, as though he'd taken a moment to make up his mind, he did a quick about-turn and re-approached the vehicle looking for his challenger. The captain's patience was at an end. He'd had all he could take that morning dealing with all the unruly 'civvies' and listening to all their whining. Orders were orders. He was a soldier trained for armed conflict against enemy hostiles and was in no mood for this civilian crap.

Looking into the vehicle for the mouthy culprit, his eyes fell upon Hana. Unyielding to him, Hana met his eyes with even greater fury.

She too was a fighter and her steadfastness checked his actions. He couldn't help but respect her. It was disarming.

His soldiers had become agitated by the commotion. One glance from the captain put them back at ease and then, as if ignoring Hana altogether, he looked to Mr Anderson.

"It's safe to return to your farm, sir. The fallout headed west. Even if the wind turns around now, it'll all settle far west of you."

Hana continued to glare at him. Trying to ignore her, he continued to explain. "I'm just following orders, sir. A state of emergency exists and Martial Law has just been declared in both Kent and Essex Counties. All residents from there are to return to their homes and stay in their community until the local emergency is over. We need to clear the roads of unessential traffic so that the emergency vehicles can get through to the people who need their help."

Looking straight at Hana, he added something which he hoped would calm and reassure her.

"You and your family will be safe, miss. You have my word on that."

Hana's eyes held his for an extra long moment. Slowly, they softened and finally she nodded her acceptance to his pledge. He knew that her look held him honour-bound to his words. And he intended to honour them.

Will broke the silence. "Then I'll go back too."

"No, Will. That won't be necessary."

"We should stay together, Mom."

"We'll be fine. I agree with the captain. We should all return to our homes and yours is in BC. Let's not make the situation any worse than it already is. Besides, it appears that we are fortunate that our home hasn't been affected. There will be others less fortunate than ourselves who will be in need of this officer's protection. Let's not debate this, Will. We've held up the line too long already and we shouldn't be tying up the captain from his duties."

Everyone marvelled at her clarity. She made sense. She was always remarkably composed when confronted with difficulties. The more uncertain things were, the more level-headed she became. Will hoped he'd inherited some of her qualities so that he too could endure hardship with similar strength. Fortunately, he'd never yet been put to the test.

She continued. "Give Sydney our love, dear. Once things return to normal, come back and see us again."

These words deeply impacted the captain. Experience had taught him that things don't always return to normal or go according to plan and that the only thing you can be certain of is the here and now. He never took anything for granted anymore. Afghanistan had cruelly taught him that lesson. There, he'd made the mistake of falling in love. Her coffin beat him home.

The Andersons could see the inner struggle taking place on the captain's kind face. For a moment, nobody spoke. Somehow they understood. Their silence was comforting.

The captain's eyes refocused on the Andersons. He was quick to size people up. Afghanistan taught him that too. He'd just returned from there and had hoped to be reunited with his own family soon.

It saddened him to think that those plans would undoubtedly change now. He had heard reports from higher up that this was going to be a Big Show. With Martial Law already being declared, he foresaw that the curtailment of all non-essential travel could potentially remain in effect for a very long time to come. Perhaps even become an accepted way of post-Fermi life. He'd seen it happen elsewhere. One more freedom lost to the endless War on Terrorism.

The unusually long delay caught the attention of the guards again. One resolved to approach the captain.

"Sir?"

The captain didn't seem to hear him.

The soldier repeated, "Sir, is everything ok?" This time he finished with a nudge.

This jolted the captain back. He'd made up his mind. He was a quick read and a good judge of character. Trusting his instincts had saved his life on more than a few occasions. The Andersons reminded him of his own family and he wanted to do something for them.

Above all, he wanted to please their feisty daughter, Hana. He would not forget her, or her eyes, or his pledge.

"I can give you a letter that will help your brother..., I mean your son", he checked himself, "to travel. With it, it will be easier for him to return later."

Sophie Anderson replied gratefully, "That's wonderful of you, Captain."

With a nod from Will, and an enquiring look from Hana, the deal was sealed.

~

CHAPTER III
God Keep Our Land

"The fourth is freedom from fear, which, translated
into world terms, means a world-wide reduc-
tion of armaments to such a point and in such
a thorough fashion that no nation will be in a
position to commit an act of physical aggression
against any neighbour — anywhere in the world."
— President Franklin Delano Roosevelt speech on
'The Four Freedoms', delivered January 6, 1941

~

The destruction of Fermi marked the beginning of a new era
— one that needed a leader. Before the crash, Colonel Kuhn had
been unknown to the general public. This terrible day catapulted
him into stardom. Out of the tragedy, destruction and mounting
chaos, a new American hero was born.

The statistics were grim and frightening. Fermi's destruction
caused the release of a massive amount of long-living radioactivity
into the environment on a scale estimated to be more than 1,000
times that of the atomic bomb dropped on Hiroshima. Where it
would settle was anyone's guess. Fear of the unknown quickly
turned to panic and people, rushing to leave the area, vacated their
properties. Those lurking on the fringes of society took full advantage of the situation. Villains and thugs had a heyday.

So did Colonel Kuhn. As chaos ensued, he was part of a
massive military exercise involving over 20,000 military personnel
at Camp Grayling, Michigan, situated along the western shore of
Lake Huron. The troops participating in the exercise came from the
National Guard, the Regular Army and Reserve Units from Indiana,

Illinois, Michigan and Ohio. Even troops from Canada had come to participate.

When the alert was sounded, most of the radioactive plume was drifting westward toward Chicago and the fertile soils of the American Midwest and would likely settle along the state lines between Michigan, Ohio and Illinois. This meant that the troops at Camp Grayling would be effectively cut off and isolated. At the same time, the unpredictability of the wonky winds, which threatened to send the plume northward onto the troops, had everybody alarmed. They could not afford to lose these troops as the situation developed.

Responding to the emergency, Colonel Kuhn made an immediate decision to evacuate all of the troops at Camp Grayling to safer ground. There were only two safe routes for the troops to take: flee north to the Upper Michigan Peninsula or drive into Canada.

What made Colonel Kuhn a singular hero was that, in the urgency of the moment, he made the decision to redeploy the troops into Canada without seeking authorization. He took full charge and accepted the consequences. He neither consulted the President nor forewarned the Canadian authorities. For that, Americans loved him and admired his daring. After all, such an emergency required a man of action, not a slow moving diplomat.

The speed of the deployment showed Kuhn to be exceptionally capable and he got full credit for the efficient way his marching orders were carried out. Within a half-hour, the troops were on the move. All the fuel and supplies were on hand. He'd anticipated everything. As efficient as his troops were, he was always a step ahead and out in front leading the huge column of troops across the border into Canada. Thousands of personal video cameras recorded the procession and news stations broadcasted the scene live to the world.

For those who had spent time in war-torn countries, the scene of the armoured column brought back some dreadful memories. Experience had taught them that nothing good ever came from such happenings. Yet for those who, through good fortune, had always lived in North America and had always known peace, the sight of the troops brought hope. Kuhn's quick thinking actions were credited with calming the panic and restoring order.

When asked later why he hadn't notified the President before deploying the troops into Canada, Kuhn replied with a question. "Would you have preferred me to chat with the President or save our army? Cuz I didn't have time to do both, ma'am."

Americans hailed him for his wise decision. Even though no fallout ever settled on Camp Grayling, it was believed that Kuhn's quick thinking manoeuvres had saved the troops.

~

Kuhn's redeployment was the first 'good news' story to come out of the disaster and he instantly became recognized as the best man on the ground capable of handling the growing crisis in Michigan. It was said that having Kuhn at the helm would ensure that law and order would be quickly restored to that wounded state and that the looters and lawbreakers would soon be apprehended and punished.

Within hours of the first news broadcast of the disaster, Colonel Kuhn's face and the story of his heroism was known to almost everyone across the globe. It was one of those few moments that happens from time to time and becomes forever embedded in humanity's collective memory.

Also forever embedded, especially within the memories of every living Canadian, would be the first words Kuhn said about Canada's role in the situation. Pointing and shaking his index finger directly into a TV camera, he bellowed, "WAKE UP AMERICA! Once again, Canada has been caught harbouring those who have attacked us. I say the friend of our enemies is our enemy. Therefore CANADIANS ARE OUR ENEMIES, NOT OUR FRIENDS! And what makes them our worst enemy is that THEY ARE ALREADY AT OUR GATES! "

Every Canadian who saw that broadcast felt that Kuhn was pointing his finger directly at them. He accused Canada of harbouring terrorists and being a safe haven from where they could launch their attacks. It was a recurring theme incorrectly regurgitated by other high ranking American politicians in the post 9/11 world. But this time the facts seemed clear and Kuhn took it to the next level. This time it was personal.

"I swear this to you. We're going to resolve, once and for all, the problems caused by our troublesome neighbour in our north," he promised.

He said 'in our' north, not 'to our' north, yet nobody took notice of the subtle difference. Under the circumstances, nobody would have suspected him of shrewdly crafting each and every statement he made. Had he only been called to explain himself then and there, perhaps the course of history would have changed. Maybe he would have lost some momentum and confidence. Yet that didn't happen. And his doctrine spread.

His message touched off a nerve that had lain dormant in the subconscious of his nation for generations. Because of the attack, America was spoiling for a fight. And, due to the horrendous nature of the attack, an enemy had to be identified. Blaming Canada provided the answer to those in need of a profound explanation. Suddenly, it all made perfect sense.

The media replayed Kuhn's tirade again and again in what seemed a continuous repetition throughout the remainder of that day. The crisis gave Kuhn's message complete credence. All of the politically incorrect statements he had made in the past, which had caused him to be sidelined within the army, were found, dusted off and replayed by the media. His extremist rants didn't sound so extreme anymore. Now they all rang true as prophetic warnings. And his message was pointed, straight as an arrow, at Canada.

"My fellow Americans, lift up your visors and clear your vision. Canadians are our enemies."

He seemed dead right. His simple and direct assessment won for him the complete confidence of the American people. Americans were in the mood for a straight talker and, with Kuhn, that's exactly what they got. The anti-Canadian movement was born and soon took on a life of its own.

Following Kuhn's lead and sensing the popular, albeit belligerent, mood of the nation, the media took over and continued to build a case on his words. Nobody cared that the same accusations about harbouring terrorists could have been said of any other nation, including America.

Once Americans, Canadians and other people all over the world heard those malicious accusations, the effect was immediate. Americans reacted by calling for swift retaliatory action against

Canada. Lacking any quick response to placate their anger, Americans bought Canadian flags and deliberately hoisted them upside down all across the US. This was the first of many anti-Canadian gestures to be made.

By midday, Canadians felt ashamed and trodden upon by the constant barrage of angry words. So fast, frequent and furious were the accusations coming from the States that most Canadians were stunned into silence. It was hopeless for the American voices outnumbered theirs ten to one. Quickly, they learned to filter out the angry accusatory words coming over the airwaves from across the border.

There was no time for words. Instead, Canadians busied themselves with the most urgent task at hand. As far as Canadians were concerned, there was no border during such an emergency and truckloads of supplies and emergency response teams were readied to go stateside to help Michigan deal with its crisis.

Many Canadians had mixed emotions and were torn as to how to respond. Canadians were mourning the tragedy as if it had happened to them. Many Canadians had American friends and families who had been affected. Lacking strong leadership at home, they too admired the boldness of Kuhn to act decisively. But Kuhn's accusations and finger pointing brought that sentiment to an abrupt end. He wasn't their hero. He was their foe.

America was on the warpath again. Canadians familiar with history knew this had happened in each generation since the US was formed and, for the fourth time in American history, Canada was being called the enemy.

Instead of dwelling on the theatrics, Canadians did not panic. They accepted the fact that the attack had come out of Canada and, for that, Canadians were prepared to shoulder some of the blame — even if the attack was the act of a single madman who was not in any way representative of them.

Many acts of kindness poured forth from Canadians, but in that hostile and confusing environment, the Canadian government was stymied on how to respond. In consequence, no official response defending Canada came from Ottawa on the first day. The vacuum from the Canadian government made Canada appear guilty by default. The denials the government issued a few days later seemed politically orchestrated. The diplomatic damage had already been done.

~

Upon hearing of the Fermi explosion and of the nuclear cloud blowing west, hundreds of thousands of Americans fled from the area. Instinct told them to go in the opposite direction so many fled eastwards into Canada where they were funnelled en masse to the border crossing points. The great number seeking refuge from the fallout caught the Canadian border guards 'off guard' and the flight of the panic-stricken crowd ground to a halt.

Since 9/11, the border guards had been well trained to be wary of any diversions. They were required to follow proper procedures and protocol under all circumstances. They were all aware of Fermi being destroyed and the whole affair reminded them of 9/11. But nothing could have prepared them for this onslaught of humanity.

Despite the protocol and training, seeing the fear in the eyes of the people trying to cross brought out the border guards' compassion and they reacted in true Canadian fashion. They opened the border and stood aside to allow the panicked Americans unimpeded access into Canada. Common sense and decency overruled protocol.

This decision got the border traffic moving again; however, other evacuees, upon hearing that the border was open, quickly flocked there hoping for an easy crossing to safety. Soon, their numbers choked the bridge over the border and again traffic slowed almost to a halt. At the same time, the troops being led by Kuhn arrived at the border. It had always been the custom of both nations to advise the other in advance of any cross-border troop movements. The US troops' unexpected arrival took the border guards by complete surprise and significantly compounded the border congestion.

The congestion was all distasteful to Colonel Kuhn whose rapid deployment into Canada was now being slowed. To him, it was another glaring example of Canadian incompetence. As far as he was concerned, he and his army should be the only valid exceptions to normal protocol and he demanded of the border guards that they clear all the civilians off the bridge so that his troops could pass first.

Breaking protocol themselves, Kuhn's force blocked the border to US evacuees to allow the troops swift crossing. Across the Ambassador Bridge at Windsor – Detroit as well as at the Sarnia and Sault Ste. Marie crossings, the troops flooded into Canada.

~

One hour after Kuhn led his troops into Canada on June 19th, the Canadian Government officially consented to the American incursion. Some saw the date as a bad omen for it was the anniversary date of the American declaration of war which led to the invasion of Canada, beginning the War of 1812.

It was around that same time that a detachment from the main American force came to Captain Owens' road block, the same barricade encountered by the Andersons earlier that day. Seeing the long line of cars ahead of them and following Kuhn's example, the commanding officer's motorcade, with sirens wailing, pulled over onto the shoulder of the road and forced their way to the front of the line. Obediently, the queued cars moved aside, making way for the truculent military vehicles.

At the barricade, both forces came face-to-face. It was an extremely awkward moment. The Canadian forces were combat ready, but unaware of the American troops being deployed into Canada. Being amongst American forces was not new to them. Yet, this time the Americans had the air and appearance of an aggressive force.

Major Douglas of the Michigan Patriot Defence Force, 2nd Battalion, brought the American column to an abrupt halt within feet of the barricade. He was in no mood to stop. His orders were to drive eastwards as quickly and far as possible. His American detachment had been at Camp Grayling and was comprised mostly of his Michigan PDF personnel and a smattering of guards and regular soldiers. Feeling inwardly inferior to the guards and regulars, Major Douglas had something to prove. They were the leading edge of the right flank of the main force.

Douglas' personal objective that day was to reach and secure the Peace Bridge, the bridge that spanned the border between Buffalo and Niagara Falls. That would put a nice feather in his cap. Just moments ago, he had been at the peak of happiness charging through foreign territory at the head of his troops. He didn't want anything barring his way to threaten his self-imposed objective.

Major Douglas looked down at the Canadian officer, whom he considered to be his subordinate, with obvious disdain. He was by nature a moody man and he was annoyed at being blocked by what appeared to him to be an inferior force.

"Lift the gate and be quick about it," he shouted down reproachfully at the captain.

The captain showed no immediate response except to raise his eyebrows. This opening didn't go unnoticed by his troops either who, seen only by the trained eye, came suddenly to full alert. Despite all appearances, the major's outburst annoyed the captain. Since his recent return from active service overseas, he'd already had about as much as he could stomach of power-tripping COs who didn't know one end of a rifle from the other.

Now the two annoyed officers faced off. The situation was extremely tense and sensed by all, including the civilians in their cars still waiting patiently in line. For a full minute, the two men stared at each other. Owens didn't like what he saw and, taking charge, he broke the silence.

"My orders are to..."

"I don't give a damn about your orders, Captain," interrupted the major. "Now lift that gate," he snarled, adding, "And be quick about it or I'll drive through it."

Owens held his breath and counted silently to ten. He had learned to do so to check emotions that often caused him to act in a way he would regret later. '...Nine. Ten.' All emotion had been checked. 'That was a threat', he noted. A subtle glance to his troops signalled to them to be prepared for anything. He looked back at the major.

"I wouldn't do that if I were you." Then, after a deliberately long interval, Owens casually added, "sir."

Meanwhile, the Canadian troops quickly, invisibly and soundlessly dispersed to their prepared defences. They blended into the landscape and surrounding forest. They had a job to do and they knew it well. They were battle hardened professionals and this was business as usual.

Captain Owens was fully prepared to face down the foreigner. He had complete confidence in his troops and he had his orders.

He was to not let any unauthorized people pass and, as far as he was concerned, the American troops were not authorized to be here. He smiled as he realized that he was really needed here at home.

Major Douglas was oblivious to his precarious situation. He knew the political game well and he was not going to tolerate being challenged by a subordinate officer, especially in front of his men. Seeing only a handful of foot soldiers opposing them, the major confidently decided to pull rank.

"Raise the gate, Captain. That's an order!" He punctuated his statement by glaring down at Owens.

His eyes were met by Owens' who glared back in open defiance and without fear. Major Douglas tried to hold Owens' stare, but couldn't and, in defeat, he turned away. This confirmed to Captain Owens that the major was a spineless coward just like other flabby faced desk officers he'd encountered. He had seen too many lives lost by the stupid acts of pretentious officers who'd never tasted battle. He felt sorry for the major's troops.

"Your orders don't mean anything here. Least not to me..., sir." Again there was a marked hesitation before the word 'sir'. "You are an American officer. But this is Canada. You have no business here." Owens' looked at the major's uniform. "What unit are you from, sir?"

"I repeat, I'm Major Douglas of the Michigan Patriot Defence Force, 2nd Battalion," he asserted boldly as though that was enough.

"You're acting outside of your realm, aren't you..., sir?"

"All of North America is within our realm. Including Mexico," the major declared.

"This conversation is over, Major," Owens concluded. As he looked off towards the following US column, he laid his eyes on a regular forces officer watching the bumbled proceedings of the major from the turret of his LAV. Seeing the officer germinated an idea.

"I'll only discuss this matter with a regular forces officer..., sir. Over there," Owens said, pointing. "I see there is one amongst you. Excuse me, there," Owens hailed his counterpart. "I'd like to speak with you, sir."

"What the f...," spouted the major.

Owens ignored the major's outburst and signalled to the other officer to come forward.

Captain Martin saw Owens wave to him and smiled. He too had been amused at the major's blundering.

"Me, sir?"

"Yes you, Captain. You're regular forces, aren't you?"

"I am, sir," he answered proudly, saluting smartly. "Captain Martin, 1st Battalion, 125th Infantry Regiment, sir." Martin's reply shifted the focus away from the major who continued to utter profanities.

"Good. May I have a few words with you, sir?"

Martin dismounted from the LAV, stopping momentarily to speak with the fuming major. What he had to say to the major couldn't be overheard, but it effectively shut him up. The major fixed his most ferocious stare upon Captain Owens, but Owens ignored him. The major didn't matter anymore.

Martin did an about face turn and marched up to Captain Owens, giving him a crisp military salute.

"Captain Martin, 1st Battalion, 125th Infantry Regiment, sir," he repeated.

Owens returned the salute and nodded. "Captain Owens. Prince Rupert Regiment, 1st Battalion."

Martin's eyebrows rose and his face broke into a smile. "Captain Owens of Panjwayi?"

"Same." Gesturing to the soldiers around him, most of whom were unseen, he added, "My soldiers were there with me covering my back." The gesture confirmed Martin's suspicions that they were, in fact, surrounded.

"Well done, sir. It's an honour to meet you." Martin turned toward his troops and shouted, "Captain Owens of Panjwayi and his men."

"Soldiers, sir."

"Excuse me?"

"I would prefer that you refer to them as soldiers, sir."

Martin looked confused so Owens clarified it for him.

"We have a few females in our ranks, Captain. They've earned their stripes every bit as much as the men."

Cheers coming from the American regulars interrupted their exchange. The regulars had all heard of Captain Owens' exploits. Only the major's defence force personnel remained silent for

Panjwayi meant nothing to them. Owens smiled in acknowledgement and then turned back to Martin.

"Looks like we've gotten ourselves into a little face-off, Captain. The major there is way out of line."

Martin nodded. He glanced around at the surrounding forest and the defensive features of the landscape. Martin knew that there were many more eyes on him than he could set his eyes on. Captain Owens had chosen the spot well.

Martin also knew that behind him sat an impatient and unpredictable major who lacked field experience. It was a dangerous combination that had impelled the major to recklessly drive their forces into the jaws of a well prepared trap. Yet there the major sat, all puffed up and full of himself, totally oblivious to the unseen dangers that surrounded them.

Martin made up his mind. He knew the capability of Owens and his soldiers. He knew that the major was outmatched. And he knew what he must do to extricate his men from the situation.

"He's an idiot," Martin confessed. "Captain, I apologize for the alarm that we have unwittingly caused you."

Owens nodded, looking down the long line of waiting cars. He knew the civilians were becoming impatient. For them, the crisis was real and they were becoming desperate. Things would soon come to a boiling point.

Martin continued. "It seems that our column has overrun both of our communication systems."

This made sense to Owens. He had often experienced the same problem overseas.

"May I suggest that we should get in touch with our respective HQs and let them sort this out?"

They were of the same mind.

"Agreed." That settled, Owens relaxed a bit. "Cigarette?" he asked, fishing out a pack of DeMauriers and offering one to the American officer.

"Thanks," Martin accepted. He wasn't a smoker, but at that moment, a cigarette symbolized a peace pipe and he didn't want to insult Owens by refusing the gesture.

Owens lit one, took a drag and handed it to Martin.

"I don't imagine your major would want one."

"You're right about that, Captain. I couldn't imagine him doing anything that would put his health and wellbeing at risk," Martin sneered. "He doesn't even allow his men to smoke. That doesn't stop them, of course. It's their way of tasting danger."

Owens realized that Martin wasn't a smoker, but had accepted his offer as a courtesy. He suspected that Martin also wanted to send a message to the major that he wasn't under his thumb.

The American officers were not cut of the same cloth. The major talked tough when surrounded by armour. But, unlike Martin, he wasn't the type to dismount and face an adversary on equal terms. Owens liked Martin and he detested Douglas.

"Well then, Captain, let's make those calls."

Together they went behind the Canadian lines, leaving the fuming major to stew about the likelihood of failing to achieve his grand objective.

Both Will's parting and the captain's display of kindness contributed to Hana's feelings and she had to struggle to hold back her tears. She didn't want Captain Owens to think she was weak. There was something about the captain that she was drawn to. He seemed so strong and sure of himself, yet also kind.

Will knew Hana better than anyone else in the world. He knew that Hana's tough exterior was only a façade, disguising her true sensitive nature. The impression she had on the captain hadn't gone unnoticed by Will either. It was comforting to think that the captain may be interested enough in Hana to check in on them occasionally. If something more should come of the day's events, he would be a good person to know, Will thought.

With his pack on his back and the captain's letter stowed within one of its many pockets, Will set off alone on foot. He continued eastwards paralleling the north shore of Lake Erie. At first he tried hitching a ride, but few vehicles got through the barricade and those that did drove by him showing no inclination to stop. Most of them were either too crammed with passengers with no room to spare or were simply in too much of a rush.

He decided to leave the main road opting instead for a more scenic one nearer to the lake. It was late afternoon when he approached a park, situated not far from the lakeshore, where he decided to spend the night. He hadn't slept out in the open under the stars for years and was excited to see the night sky again. The thought of gazing into outer space leaving all of earth's problems behind, was especially appealing to him right now.

He'd just found an open spot, where the tree-line didn't interfere with his unobstructed view of the night sky, when he was hailed.

"Ha-lu over there."

Will acknowledged his greeter with a wave.

"They're calling for rain overnight."

"Are they?" 'Oh great,' Will thought to himself, realizing that he was ill-prepared to overnight it there if it rained.

"I've got some extra room in my tent if you want to stay dry," the other fellow hollered, answering Will's concern.

"Sounds good to me," Will replied. He regretted having to abandon the idea of sleeping under the stars, but it had suddenly become dark and overcast. They were in for a storm. He picked up his backpack and headed over to the stranger.

"My name's Hacker. Barry Hacker. But I prefer Hacker cuz that's how I play hockey."

"I'm Will. Will Anderson," he answered, shaking Hacker's extended hand.

Hacker had a small two-man tent. It was tight, but adequate, and Will just managed to get himself situated and his pack stowed under the fly when the rain started falling in heavy drops. No doubt it would have been a wet and miserable night without Hacker coming to his rescue.

They talked about their individual experiences that day. Hacker had encountered the same barricade and got through it just as Will had. He'd been visiting friends in southwest Ontario and together they had all tried to flee from the nuclear fallout. Like Will's family, his friends had been turned around and only Hacker was allowed to continue to travel to his home.

Will told Hacker about his plans to head back out west to rejoin Sydney.

"Have you talked to her yet?" Hacker asked.

"No. I tried to, but couldn't get through. She must be having a conniption fit right now."

"You've got to call her, Will, and put her at ease."

"I know, but I haven't got a phone. In the rush to leave, I left mine behind."

"No problem. I have one," Hacker offered, handing it to Will.

"Thanks."

Will entered Sydney's number. She picked up after only one ring.

"Hello?" Will immediately sensed the strain in her voice.

"Hey, Syd."

"Will! Oh my god! Are you ok? Where are you calling from?"

"Firstly, I'm fine and I'm in a tent." He told her all that had happened over the course of the day. It had been one of those days when everything was so disjointed and confusing that it seemed as though it all happened over a much longer period.

"Right now it's raining cats and dogs and I'm in the tent of a newfound friend named Hacker," Will concluded.

"Ha-lu, Sydney," came Hacker's muffled voice through the receiver.

"Say 'hello' back," she answered.

Sydney knew much of what had happened from the news and had been anxiously waiting to hear from Will. Throughout the day, more horrifying reports were coming from out of the States and she'd begun to imagine the worst. The news was full of reports of rioting and vandalism and she could imagine Will being stupid enough to try to stop any wrongdoing he saw. She loved that characteristic about him, but the magnitude of the day's events scared her. Inwardly, she was worried about what desperate people were capable of doing, not to mention what might happen to Will if he had to confront such people. She'd tried to reach the Andersons countless times and finally got through to Kevin around 3pm. Kevin explained to her what had happened to them and, from him, Sydney learned that Will didn't have his cell phone. She was very relieved to hear Will's voice.

"Where are you camping, Will?"

"In a park west of Port Stanley. I'm so fortunate to have run into Hacker. He's prepared for everything."

"That's great. But seriously, Will, you've got to get back here soon and stay until things settle down. The Americans are out for revenge. They're calling it a Nuclear 9/11. It's all crazy and I'm really scared. They're saying that we Canadians have aided the terrorists with our lax immigration policies. They say we're unwilling and unable to secure our own borders. Will, you need to get far away from them. They are blaming Canada this time, not Iraq, not Afghanistan, not Yemen. They're calling for their troops to be deployed here to secure the situation. For sure, something big is going to happen. Be careful and get back here as fast as you can."

This news and the sound of concern in her voice sent chills down Will's spine.

"You know the Americans. Everything that happens to them is overblown," he replied to comfort her. Neither of them knew that American forces had already been deployed to Canada and lay only a few miles off to the north and west of him.

"I hope you're right, Will. Regardless, come home soon."

After Will hung up, Sydney's words began to sink in. He too had been shaken by the frightening rhetoric he'd heard on the radio. Even American senior politicians, not just the usual war-hawks, were now calling for action against Canada. Earlier, he'd been fleeing the fallout. Now he was fleeing something equally terrifying, the unknown response from America.

Hacker had a portable radio. He turned it on periodically to get updated on the situation. The broadcasting stations had coined the phase 'Crisis in North America.' Throughout the day, the media was busy uncovering all of America's greatest fears and suspicions about Canada. The message that a terrorist had entered the United States from its neighbour to the north was repeated again and again. It was said that either Canadians were stupid, because they were naively harbouring terrorists, or they were evil, because they were deliberately collaborating with them. Some theorized that Canada was purposely trying to destabilize America and knock it off its pedestal so that Canada could ascend to dominate the continent.

'Fool US once, shame on Canada! Fool US twice, shame on US!' placards read.

Compounding the complexity of the problem, the co-pilot's family had immigrated to Canada from the Middle East. This gave credence to the allegations that Canadian citizenship was too easily handed out. On top of this, a team of engineers from Canada's Nuclear Commission had just toured the Fermi Plant a few days before the crash. It was alleged that some of these engineers were assisting the co-pilot from the inside by sabotaging Fermi's safety systems to ensure its total destruction. The Canadian connection to terrorism was compelling and taking on a life of its own. The tone of each successive news report from the States became more and more aggressively anti-Canadian. Increasing numbers of likeminded individuals joined the chorus of those speaking out passionately about their personal experiences of the Canadian threat to American peace and security.

All fingers were pointing at Canada.

"The Canadian border is extremely porous to undesirable immigration. The Canadian government makes it easy for bogus refugees to enter Canada. The Canadian Treasury supports terrorists! The Canadian public service is rife with immigrants alleged to have connections with known terrorists." And on and on it went.

Not wanting to raise the ire of the Americans, Canada's media stuck to reporting the facts of the tragedy rather than responding to the rhetoric. Hearing the facts, many Canadians felt guilty about what had happened, just as they might have felt proud if a Jamaican-Canadian had won gold at the Olympics for the 100 metre dash. Will knew that Sydney thought such sentiments were silly. He could hear her saying, 'how could a lazy couch-potato feel at all connected to a highly trained athlete who was brought in from another country as a ringer?'

True as that was, most Canadians tended to think otherwise, feeling proud if their hometown baseball team won the World Series even though the team was loaded with American and Cuban players.

As these thoughts went through Will's head, the radio announced that the President was about to speak. For thirty seconds, the radio was silent and then they heard the voice of the President.

My fellow citizens:

I speak to you tonight from the Oval Office. Like you, I am stunned by today's horrific events. I abhor that such hate can exist and it makes me question mankind's purpose and meaning.

I am mindful of the massive array of force and retaliatory capability that you have bestowed upon me as your President. You have given me the power of a God. It is a tremendous responsibility to wield such power. With your authority, I hold the fate of the world in my hands. I can, if you want, call anyone and everyone into account. Should I annihilate a people out of revenge? Should I annihilate a religion? Or even a country? Should I stop there? I could do all these things. And in so doing, I could also assure myself of popularity and so surely win your support in the upcoming presidential election. It's the proverbial win-win proposition. I know this as a veteran politician. So what do I do? What would you have me do? Advance my career?

I have thought long and hard about this. I have been fully apprised of the gravity of the situation. The facts are grim. Today, we have suffered the most horrific attack in human history, an attack perpetrated by one lone suicide pilot who deliberately crashed his plane into the Fermi nuclear power plant. He did this because he hated us so much that he wanted to kill as many of us as possible. He did this because he wanted to create chaos and anarchy in America. He chose his target well. It is a target we created and presented to him. In doing so, he unleashed a whirlwind of death and destruction and martyred himself by becoming his first victim. The perpetrator is dead, vaporized instantly. Thousands, we do not even yet know how many, of innocent lives have been lost to the most despicable and appalling attack ever perpetrated against an innocent people. Hundreds of thousands have been made homeless and unemployed. Two cities have been destroyed and their surrounding hinterlands laid to waste. Like many of you, I too have lost loved ones. Among them was my close friend, the Governor of the great State of

Michigan, who, as fate would have it, was touring that same plant on this fateful day. Millions more will suffer in the days to come. We pray for them and console their families.

So how do we respond? Our emergency people are doing whatever they can. Volunteers are coming forward. People are opening their homes to those made homeless.

Is this enough? Or as a people must we also retaliate? We have always retaliated against someone, but the suicide pilot is dead. We have been hotwired to retaliate during a crisis. We retaliated after 9/11. That process has sent our troops all over the Middle East on a witch-hunt to seek and destroy all who might harm us. In fact, all throughout our history, we have always chosen the path of retaliation. Always, it has been "an eye for an eye" and "a tooth for a tooth". Some would even say it's been more like "eyes for an eye" and "teeth for a tooth". But our 9/11 retaliation is still going on and it didn't prevent today from happening. Perhaps it may have even caused it.

Perhaps the error in choosing retaliation is that, when we eliminate one enemy, we inevitably create two or more. Ultimately, we are caught up in a circle of ever escalating violence.

Perhaps our history and our awesome might have combined to bring us to a very dangerous precipice.

Perhaps we need to think before jumping.

Perhaps we need to act differently this time.

Perhaps it is time for us to foresee the finality of our warrior journey and see the present precipice for what it is. Armageddon.

Perhaps the time has come to decide to turn back and walk in a different direction on a different path.

I may be your President, but I am still only a man, not a God. As a man, I am afraid of God powers. I am also a hu-man. And God gave me a brain. He wanted me to think for myself. And in so doing, despite the advice I have been given, I must do what I think is right, to remain a good man. And so, in defining 'good', I asked myself a simple question, 'What would Jesus do?' Immediately, I had my answer and all became clear.

After giving everything all due consideration and fully understanding and accepting total responsibility as your President and Commander in Chief, I have resolved on taking the path of peace.

My fellow citizens, the time has come to bury the hatchet — to turn the other cheek. For only by doing so do we raise ourselves to a higher plane. We must not retaliate just because we can. That is the ultimate hallmark of civilization. Let us not only be a beacon of liberty to the world, but now let us also be a beacon of peace. Let us sheath the sword. This is the only way to secure eternal peace. And this is how I will direct our government to proceed.

Let our troops come home to their waiting families. But let us not stop there. Let us lead the world in nuclear disarmament, for these are the tools of mass destruction. Let us shut down and dismantle our nuclear power plants, so that never again will we expose ourselves and others to such a cataclysmic event.

Yes, we may need to lessen our wants. But our country abounds in the necessities; we can do without the luxuries. Let us lead by example. Let us heal the world.

This is how I will respond. May we promote peace on earth by being ourselves peaceful. May we promote friendship by being ourselves a friend to all.

So instead of smiting those who trespass against us with a deadly blow, let us forgive them for their sins by saying together, as one people, the Lord's Prayer:

Our Father, who art in heaven,
hallowed be thy name.
Thy kingdom come,
thy will be done,
on earth as it is in heaven.
Give us today our daily bread.
And forgive us our trespasses,
as we forgive those who trespass against us.
And lead us not into temptation,
but deliver us from evil.
For thine is the kingdom,
the power and the glory,
for ever and ever.

Amen.

Thank you. God bless you and God bless the United States of America.

~

Will and Hacker had simultaneously mouthed the prayer with the President. As they did so, they heard the murmur of prayer coming through the fabric of other tents hidden in the surrounding forest.

Without breaking the peaceful silence, Hacker shut off the radio. What a difference a day can make. A morning that had begun so violently had ended in peace. They slipped into their sleeping bags and listened to the rain beating upon their tent. The sound didn't seem to fit the moment. It sounded more like war drums being beaten to incite warriors into battle. That was the last thought on Will's mind as he fell asleep.

~

CHAPTER IV

Does That Star-
spangled Banner
Yet Wave?

The rain had stopped and morning had come. Will heard the
birds chirping, making everything seem normal again. The radio
was on low and barely audible.

Sitting up, Will pushed aside the tent's flap and peered out.
Hacker was bent over the fire pit, feeding more kindling and sticks
onto a smoky little fire.

"Morning."

"Coffee?" Hacker asked, not taking his eyes off the flame that he
was nursing into life.

"OK. You're sure running a full service outfit, Hacker."

"Don't get your hopes up. Coffee is all I have to offer."

Looking upwards, Will saw most of the clouds had dispersed
revealing a blue sky. The rays of the morning's sun shone through
the tree canopy and onto the tent. Will pulled on his clothes and
rolled head first out of the tent.

"If you hang your wet things over there on the line, the sun will
help dry them out," Hacker suggested.

He pointed at the clothesline strung between two trees in the
sunshine. There, Will saw that Hacker had hung some of his things
and already they were almost dry. Will went to gather some of his
own wet clothes to do the same.

Returning with an armload, Will saw Hacker look over at him and
smile approvingly. He felt lucky to have run into Hacker as it would
have been a very miserable night being caught out in the rain with
no shelter. To show his appreciation, he tried to make himself
useful. He saw that the fire would soon consume all the burnable
materials Hacker had stockpiled nearby, so he headed off into the
bush to gather more firewood. Once there, he took advantage of
the cover of brush and emptied his bladder. He soon returned to

the campsite carrying as much firewood as his arms would hold. He stacked the wood beside the fire so the fire's heat would help evaporate the rain's moisture out of it.

"Thanks." Hacker smiled genuinely, signifying he never took any assistance for granted.

Hacker was a likeable character and they had made an instant connection. His smile and open face made him seem personable even before his first word was spoken. His words only served to reinforce the first impression he gave. The circumstances that brought them together played a large part in their connection, but it was more than that — they seemed to relate to one another as though they'd known each other for a long time. If time permitted, Will had no doubt that the instant connection they had would only develop and they could end up becoming good friends.

It seemed to Will that Hacker and he were of the same age. Hacker's hair was darker as were his eyes and he stood an inch or two taller than Will. He looked more wiry than athletic, as he was a little on the thin side, but his slim, lanky body seemed fit enough. Will expected that, even when loaded down with their heavy backpacks, they'd be able to click off the mileage quite quickly.

Despite having to use rain-soaked materials, Hacker's fire was soon ablaze and the comforting smell of perking coffee filled the air. Will now recalled waking up and hearing the radio. Hacker had turned it off when Will had rolled out of the tent, but Will recalled sensing then that something had concerned Hacker. Perhaps Hacker's mind had wandered back to the radio too for he seemed to be full of thought. Will waited a few moments and then broke the silence.

"So what are your plans now?"

Hacker looked up, blinked his eyes, reached out and took Will's mug from his outstretched hands and filled it full of steaming coffee.

"Thanks." Will savoured his first sip while gazing into the mesmerizing flame. The coffee was strong and black, which was fine, but his preference was to add a little canned milk and unpasteurized honey to make it more soothing.

"There's some cream and brown sugar in the top zipper of my backpack over there," Hacker said as if reading Will's mind.

After helping himself, Will returned to the fire and asked again, "So where are you headed?"

"Me?" he asked as though surprised Will might even care to wonder.

"Is there anyone else here?" Will quipped.

Hacker smiled. "I'm going up north to my father's place."

"Where's that?"

"Peterborough. Ever been there?"

"Nope. Is that where you're from?"

"Used to be. Right now though, I'm in transition. I just graduated from the University of Toronto where I majored in English."

"You majored in English? That's useful. Lucky for me I learned it from my parents," Will joked.

Hacker smiled in response. "Me too. I admit my diploma is probably a ticket to nowhere unless I want to teach like my father."

"Teaching would be a rewarding career. Good pay and hours and lots of time off. What's your dad teach?"

"He's an Anthropology prof at Trent. At least that's what he was doing the last time I spoke with him. He's not what I'd describe as the most connected guy. Doesn't even own a cell phone and spends most of his time outdoors."

"How's that? Doesn't he have a classroom?'

"Yes, but he barely uses it. Textbooks either. He and his class spend most of their time outdoors. Often, students are drawn to his course because of his good reputation and because they think it's a bird course. They soon learn otherwise. They're tested on things like starting a fire without matches. If they can't, they fail. His course has the highest dropout rate at the University."

"My bet is you'd pass," Will said, pointing to the roaring campfire. "Your father sounds like my kind of prof. He sounds like a teacher I had back in high school. Best teacher I ever had. Taught us real life skills that few seem to care about anymore."

"That's true. The University only puts up with my dad's eccentricities because he's profitable for them. Even with the high percentage of dropouts, there's always a waiting list for his course. And his graduates adore him. They're known to go on in life and make something notable of themselves. They're also the most generous benefactors amongst all the alumni."

"Has it been long since you've seen your dad?"

"I haven't seen him since last Christmas. But we both have the summer off so we're going on a big canoe adventure together. For me, it will be a welcome change from the big city. For him, it's the way he keeps connected with his subject. My plans were to head up and meet him there in August. Yesterday's hit on Fermi simply brought those plans forward. What about you, Will?"

"Me? I'll probably return to my folks' farm. The evacuation cut short my time there, but after hearing the President's speech, it seems that my reasons for leaving have disappeared."

Hacker glanced at the radio. "You might want to think that over a bit longer."

Again, Will suspected Hacker had heard something worrisome on the radio that morning and was about to ask him about it when Hacker sidelined his thoughts with another question.

"Where were you heading, Will?'

"Home, which is in British Columbia."

Hacker whistled. "I've never been out west. My dream is to someday see the Rockies."

Will fingered through his backpack and pulled out a few photos of his place in Field and one of Sydney.

Hacker looked at them and grinned. "BEA-U-TI-FUL."

"Are you grinning at our place in the mountains or my girlfriend?"

"Both!" he exclaimed, handing Will back the photos of their home.

As Hacker continued to gaze at the photo of Sydney, Will playfully snatched it out of his hand and with a proud, knowing smile reprimanded him by saying, "Quit drooling, you pig!"

With pride of possession, Will carefully tucked the photos back into his pack. While doing so, he discovered some unexpected items in it – a picnic from Hana. She must have snuck them in there when he wasn't looking. 'My thoughtful sister!'

Will fished them out. She'd packed peanut butter, strawberry jam and some of her homemade bread. By toasting the bread, it would make a perfect breakfast. Typical of Hana, it was both a practical and effective meal to grab in their rapid departure.

Sydney and Hana shared the same ideas when it came to food. For them, every meal had to be real food. Something nutritionally balanced with a healthy mixture of carbs, protein and fat. Will could hear them both sermonizing, 'Fat doesn't make you fat. Laziness makes you fat. You simply need to burn what you eat.' It sounded so simple, but nowadays people were inundated with so many choices filled with empty calories, that it was harder.

'So what, then they can choose to get up off their backsides for their donuts, instead of idling in the lazy-lane,' they'd retort.

'That's true,' Will thought. It always seemed surreal to him to watch cars idle while waiting in the drive-through lane during smog alerts.

Will's growling stomach brought his focus back to Hana's bread which he sliced and laid on the grill to toast over the fire.

After breakfast, they rolled up and stuffed the tent, then packed up their belongings. Soon they were ready to leave. By 8am, they were walking eastward towards Port Stanley, the closest community to the east. From there, Will figured that he would have a decent chance of finding a ride back to the farm.

~

Will's thoughts were full of the wonderful possibilities the President's words had made feasible. Ideas and dreams raced through his head as they trudged on. He imagined the positive effect the United States' reaction would have on the rest of the world.

Unbeknownst to him, billions of people all over the world had prayed with the President that preceding night when he'd delivered what was being called a message of peace. People in different countries had woken to see the Stars and Stripes flying together in solidarity with their national flags. Not only did it fly from the world's Capital buildings, Old Glory flew from some of the most unexpected places. Places such as Havana, the north side of the Korean DMZ as well as in the Russian space station circling high above the earth. Some American flags had been hidden away for so long they were out of date and lacked the current number of stars to mark America's most recent expansions.

The flags flew as an expression of public condolence, but mostly in recognition of the President's speech. Earlier on the preceding day, the initial news of Fermi's destruction had shocked and heightened fear in the world. It was then that some flags were lowered to half mast. Markets closed knowing the emotional impact would be devastating. Everyone everywhere gasped and held their collective breath, waiting to see how America would respond. They expected a violent response, one that exceeded the reaction that followed 9/11 to account for the more horrifying attack that had just occurred. People across the world understood that America and the world stood at a dangerous crossroad. To everyone's surprise, America chose the path of peace and the world applauded its wisdom and unparalleled leadership. On the following morning, American flags blossomed like spring flowers heralding a new beginning all over the earth.

America held out its hand, not a hand full of dollar bills nor one holding a club. This time, for the first time ever it seemed, it was simply the hand of friendship. The entire world reached out and grabbed onto it.

Pins of unity, resembling corsages cut from flowers in bloom, emblazoned lapels with each nation's flag coupled with the Stars and Stripes. This sight promised great new possibilities for peace.

The President had spoken words that no previous President ever dared to say. Some reacted by christening him as 'their saviour', a saviour returning after some cataclysmic event, as foretold by the ancient prophesies. Denying any preordained destiny, the President replied almost humbly that he was only 'too human' and suggested they should look for their returning saviour elsewhere.

For the most part, his modest response only added to the admiration he was receiving. If an election for World Leader had been held that day, the President would have won it with ease. He had united the world in a common expression of grief and relief.

Americans travelling abroad noticed the difference immediately. They didn't have to pretend to be Canadians anymore, pinning Canada flags onto their backpacks, to receive better treatment. Americans were no longer ostracized. America was no longer alone.

The world's population expressed their sympathy and applause in many different ways. Those living in the most well-to-do nations sent material relief. Those in poorer nations, who had little or nothing of material value to give, gave in spirit by their prayers. Never before in recorded history had so many people come together united by a universal will to fulfill the President's wish for peace.

Peace had broken out. All battlefields were silent. Reports told of soldiers laying down their arms and leaving their positions unguarded to cross to the other side and meet their adversaries face-to-face. People opened their homes to their enemies and shared a peaceful meal with them. For a moment in time, the whole world believed it was possible to live in peace. Hope restored, the future seemed bright.

But all this had happened while America slept and by the time the sun's rays had circled the globe, America had woken up.

~

Walking eastwards, Will recalled what he'd forgotten to ask earlier.

"Was there anything interesting on the radio this morning?"

"More like alarming, I'd say. As you'd imagine, most of the discussion focused on dissecting the President's speech. Americans are totally divided into two camps. The most hostile reactions are making the headlines."

"What about the rest of the world?"

"There's not so much in the news about that. Many foreign high-ranking officials have expressed their condolences and American flags are flying at half-mast in many countries."

"Anything else?"

"Ya, the President has also appointed that Colonel ummm… what's his name?"

"Kuhn. Colonel Kuhn."

"Ya, Colonel Kuhn. He's been appointed as the interim Governor of Michigan, replacing the Governor who was killed yesterday."

"Isn't that unusual?"

"That's what some are wondering, but apparently it's only a temporary emergency measure. It's been done before. Colonel Kuhn is very popular right now so anybody questioning his appointment gets shouted down pretty quickly. It's said that, during wartime, the President has extraordinary powers and can basically do whatever he likes. Although I doubt he's a Kuhn supporter himself. More likely he was forced to make the appointment to pacify those who are the most hostile."

"Wartime? I thought peace was declared?

"Apparently not," Hacker replied. "So what are your plans now?" Will shook his bewildered head as he didn't know the answer.

~

Major Douglas wasn't happy that he had failed to reach his objective. The Peace Bridge was still in 'enemy' hands. He blamed two people: Captain Martin and that cocky Canadian captain, whatever his name was. He didn't remember names well.

For the moment, he would have to repress his anger. Soon though, he would get his revenge. It was just a matter of time. Colonel Kuhn had assured him of that.

'Maybe I should have noted his name…,' he pondered.

Events were finally turning around in his favour exactly as he'd hoped and planned. This time, he'd hitched his cart to the right man. He'd been held back too long, sidelined because he wasn't in the 'politically correct' group. He came from a different era, but things were going to be different now and it was about time.

As far as Douglas was concerned, having a black man as President was the final straw. He felt the President's gross incompetence was now obvious to anyone who cared about what America stood for. That speech was the final nail in his coffin.

In hindsight, Douglas now saw that everything happened for a reason. The political left had infiltrated the country to its highest level and failed miserably. Soon, everything would be restored and America would again be the uncontested ruler of the world. Big stick politics would return and he was well positioned to ride the new wave of popularity.

'My time has come,' he thought to himself, standing proudly, overlooking the parade grounds. As if to illustrate the point, he called out to a corporal marching by smartly with her platoon. She responded immediately.

"Platoonnn!……, HALT!" she ordered. The exact instant the 'T' was spoken, all feet came together, heels together and toes apart, bringing the column to an abrupt stop. After a few seconds she ordered, "Platoon, right TURN." With that, they turned to face the major. He liked the respect being shown to him.

"Platoonnn!… stand… at… ease!… Stand easy!" The platoon followed her sharp commands with utmost efficiency. With the final command, her platoon let loose their arms, but did not dare move a leg in case she might notice. She was a hard taskmaster and her platoon had come to respect her. They were the pride of the parade ground.

Having addressed her platoon, she spun clockwise, marched smartly up to the major, halted, and saluted.

"Yes, sir?"

He raised his empty coffee cup to her.

"I could use a refill, miss."

"Yes, sir," she answered sullenly. She too foresaw what lay ahead.

~

It took Will and Hacker almost three hours to reach Port Stanley. The Kettle River, dotted with leisure boats, guided them southwards into the pretty lakeside community. The dimensions of the boats grew in proportion to the deepening river which meandered down to the lake.

In the main harbour, there were about a half-dozen commercial fishing tugs tied up along the main dock. Port Stanley was an important commercial fishing base for the north shore fleet. Being relatively ice free all winter, commercial fishermen often brought their fishing tugs there from the western basin before it froze over. This way, they could extend the fishing season throughout most of the year.

A fishing tug was coming in toward the harbour. Although he couldn't see the name at that distance, Will knew the lines of the Ana Teresa well enough to suspect that it was her. His suspicions were soon confirmed as the name Ana Teresa came into view along with the friendly familiar face of Ernesto Fortuna, her pilot and captain, looking out through the windows.

Ernesto had been Will's classmate in grade school as well as his teammate in soccer. He'd taught Will the game just as his father had taught him. He'd quit high school to work on the boats. That too was something he'd learned from his dad. Soon, he gained a reputation for hard work and was sought by the best captains. He was rewarded by earning more money and, eventually, saved enough to buy his own boat and commercial fishing licence. He was now a full captain and, despite all the hardships incurred through years of hard labour and exposure to the most foul weather conditions on the lake, nothing seemed to impair his cheerfulness and welcoming spirit.

'It must be in the wine,' Will thought, knowing that Ernesto probably made his own wine too.

Will headed down to the pier to help Ernesto with the dock lines. A smile lit across Ernesto's face when he spotted him. Will caught the line as it was tossed and looped it securely to the pier. A moment later, Ernesto's face appeared again through the port hatch of the tug.

"Thanks, Anderson. Shouldn't you be out west somewhere?"

Grasping Ernesto's extended hand, Will realized that he'd seen many, many people shaking hands that day. Although he still didn't know why, it was a comforting sight.

"I was back visiting. What about you?" Will countered. "It's not your season to come east. I suspect we've both come to Port Stanley for the same reasons."

"You've got that right. And I've brought with me a whole boatload of trouble."

Just then a female came to the opening and held out her hand for assistance. Will helped her ashore. No thanks was offered, which did not surprise Will for he recognized seasickness when he saw it.

"My family and most of our relatives are with us," Ernesto explained. "Some don't have their sea legs yet and last night's storm was a wee bit too rough for some of them. I had my hands full, I tell ya."

As he said that, a dreadful reeking combination of fish and vomit emitted from the hold as testimony to his words. Ernesto grimaced as he caught a whiff. It reminded him of their epic voyage.

"Unfortunately, I didn't have any of my regular crew with me. They had their own families to worry about so I was short handed."

Will didn't recognize anyone else as he held out his hand to help the flow of pale green passengers feebly swaying themselves ashore.

"I trust Ana weathered it as well as her namesake?"

Just as Will spoke, Ana Teresa appeared, leaned over the side and vomited. Looking up, she half smiled.

"Not quite, Will." Then she turned to Ernesto as if in revenge. "I've got a list of things for you to do, Ernesto. First on the list is for you to scrub the fish stink out of this boat. If it's going to be our home, it better smell like home."

"Aye-aye, Captain." He grinned and winked at Will. "Only set foot ashore and I've already been demoted."

"Only you could look beautiful and barf at the same time," Will said to Ana, hoping to take the attention off poor Ernesto. Saying it, though, was simply acknowledging the truth. Ana was a dark haired, dark eyed, olive skinned beauty.

"Thanks, Will," she smiled back, pulling herself upright to fix her posture. "It's hard to keep oneself presentable at times like these," she apologized. "I need some cooperation," she concluded giving Ernesto a look that drove home her message.

With that, Will and Ernesto turned their attention to putting right the tug.

"We'll help," Will offered. "Eh, Hacker?"

Hacker looked up as if he hadn't been paying close attention for he didn't want Ernesto to be more embarrassed then he was already.

"What?"

"I said we'll help the captain clean up the tug," Will repeated.

"Ok, whatever," he agreed.

They put themselves to work, washing and scrubbing the vomit and years of fish stink out of the boat. By the time they were finished, the sun had risen to its high noon zenith and the stink had been overpowered by the smell of ammonia.

During the cleanup, Ernesto told them all about the voyage from Wheatley. They'd set course for Port Maitland, but the weather got rough as the easterly winds mounted and the tug crashed through the waves sending cascades of angry spray against the cabin's windows and over the vessel. By the time they reached the vicinity of Port Stanley, almost all aboard were seasick and complaining so Ernesto decided to put in to avoid a mutiny. Without the help of his regular crew, he had to manage the tug all by himself.

"Thanks, guys," Ernesto said gratefully. "The tug's never smelt so clean. Hopefully, it's up to Her Highness's high standards," he said half jokingly and half seriously. "By the way, if you don't have any better plans, you're more than welcome to come along with us. I sure could use some reliable hands to help take her to Maitland."

Ernesto could see by their reaction that they would consider the idea so he laid out his plans.

"It'll be about an eight hour voyage unless we have another mutiny and have to put in at Port Dover," he said with a wry smile. Actually, as they discovered later, the rough seas encountered on the first leg of the journey had in effect renewed Ernesto's family's respect for him. They'd been given a small taste of what he endured on a regular basis to provide them with a comfortable life. They couldn't even imagine what it must be like to weather a storm under freezing winter conditions.

Hacker's look said 'I'm in,' and he readily accepted. He seemed to be up for any adventure, especially one he knew his father would be keen to hear about later.

Thanking Ernesto for the offer, Will told him he was probably going to head back to his parents' orchard, but would consider the idea. In the meantime, Will and Hacker stowed their packs aboard the Ana Teresa and went ashore to explore the village.

Being from a lakeside community, Will sold Hacker on the idea of finding a restaurant where they could have a good feed of the local specialty, yellow perch.

"I'm not particularly fond of perch," Hacker said.

Regardless, after Will explained to him that he hadn't had the mildest and best-tasting yellow perch until he'd eaten it from Lake Erie, Hacker submitted and ordered the same as Will. Afterwards, he admitted that he'd enjoyed it immensely and, with full stomachs, they decided to give each other some space and go their own separate ways for the remainder of the afternoon.

Hacker headed for a tavern to meet the locals and get caught up on the day's news, whereas Will headed for the beach. Will had always been drawn to water. Swimming was so much a part of him that he couldn't even remember a time when he couldn't swim. His mother had told him that he swam before he walked and just after he learned how to stand on his head. Will didn't know if she was joking, but he could still stand on his head quite easily.

He removed his shoes when he reached the beach. He loved the feel of sand beneath his feet. At the water's edge, he stripped down to his underwear, then ran and dove into the clear cool blue waters. Underwater, he glided until his speed was almost spent and then broke through to the surface. He swam straight out into the lake a few hundred metres, stopped and turned to look back at the shoreline. Treading water, he was surprised to see quite a number of people had come down to the lake to enjoy the beach and the sun. 'Had yesterday's events, which rendered such a large area uninhabitable, made these people appreciate such simple things more?' Will wondered. 'One could only hope.'

Boys and girls played at the shore, splashing each other with water. At the other end of the age-scale, tender footed seniors tip-toed across the beach to the water's edge to seat themselves in their Canadian Tire collapsible lawn chairs.

After treading water for a while longer, Will swam back to shore and sat upon his piled up clothes. Feeling comfortable and refreshed, he relaxed and let the sun dry him off. It was a pleasant place to spend a beautiful sunny afternoon.

A funny thought hit Will. Perhaps it was because he knew that, at that very moment, countless lives had been turned upside down by yesterday's horrendous attack. Not only that, many lives had been lost. It did not seem fair that he was so little affected and could enjoy the luxury of bathing in sunshine while others suffered.

Troubled by those feelings, Will wondered, 'If I'm simply enjoying my surroundings, is that a sin? Why do I feel bothered about it?'

Then, Will realized what it was. In part, it was that he felt fortunate that the wind had blown in the opposite direction when Fermi was hit, for the prevailing winds normally blew from the west. It would have carried death and ruin toward his family and friends. He also felt fortunate to have met Hacker and to be able to spend time outside in the sunshine on such a glorious day.

'If these are sins, then I am indeed a sinner!' Will admitted to himself.

With many thoughts on his mind, sunshine warming his body and the soft sand taking shape comfortably in the contours of his back, Will nodded off in complete bliss.

~

Will dreamt. Birds were once again the main subject. His return from the west had given him a greater appreciation of birds and their songs. In his youth, while lying in bed, he'd come to know their unique voices so well by making a guessing game out of trying to identify which song belonged to which bird.

Often the first birdsong sung in the morning would come from the mourning doves. They would start with their "coo-ah, coo-coo-cooing". As if in response, the cheery robins would join in, singing "cheerily, cheer up, cheerio" which they'd repeat a few times before taking a needed breath. After that brief introduction, the stage was set for the other species of birds to join the ensemble.

The chickadees sang "chick-a-dee-dee-dee" and the cardinals chirped their "wheat-wheat-wheat-wheat-wheat-wheat-wheat-wheat-wheat." There were warblers, orioles, jays and rarer species too. So dense were their numbers that birdwatchers flocked to the area every spring and fall.

Of them all, Will's favourite bird was the common red-winged blackbird that sang "o-ka-reeeee, o-ka-reeeee." It wasn't his favourite because of its song nor for its appearance, which was fairly lacklustre when compared to the others. Instead, Will admired it for its bravery.

Will had seen a red-wing defend its territory from much larger birds and animals. Anything that dared to enter the red-winged blackbird's domain, including birds of prey, crows, seagulls, egrets and blue herons, was fair game. Will had heard that red-wings were known to attack squirrels and cats and dogs as well. He could believe this as he once had a red-wing swoop down from above and give his baseball cap a warning peck. Looking around at the time, he realized that he'd just run under a tree branch that held the bird's nest causing it to defend its territory.

'Talk about punching above your weight!' he dreamt.

He also liked the red-wing because it was a clean fighter and, therefore, a kind bird at heart. He'd never seen one go after a smaller animal.

Will hated bullies. He'd seen his older brother Kevin bullied enough in grade school. Kevin had been small for his age then and, because he was a kind and gentle boy, was an easy target for bullies.

There was a period when those mean boys had started to turn their unwanted attention on Will. More and more they roughed him up. Each time it got worse. That was when Kevin finally stood up to them. A couple of black eyes later and those bullies wisely decided to move onto easier targets. Kevin's days of being bullied were over when he defended Will. And because of Kevin's protection, Will's experience with bullies was short-lived and didn't leave any lasting scars. For Kevin though, it had been a prolonged and demeaning experience that shaped his life. Now Kevin stood a couple of inches over six feet and remained as kind, gentle and peaceful as ever.

Squawking seagulls woke Will up. A discarded carton of french fries had been discovered by the noisy flock, hence the source of their dispute. Will glanced at his wristwatch and realized it was time to find Hacker. After checking various places, Will found him seated at a table in a tavern cavorting with the locals. Hacker obviously made friends easily. Most of the group were young ladies who'd been drawn to his charming smile and his flattery.

Upon seeing Will enter the tavern, Hacker jumped up, grabbed a chair from another table and put it down beside him. He was obviously pleased to see his new friend. As Will sat down and joined them, he realized the feeling was mutual. He was not looking forward to parting ways with Hacker the following day.

As they sat with their new acquaintances, Will got trapped into a heated discussion with a beady-eyed man whose red face revealed that he'd had too much to drink. Listening to him constantly interrupt the main conversation, Will occasionally glanced at him. The windbag assumed he'd caught Will's interest and directed his discourse directly at Will, claiming the President was a wimp. He droned on and on until Will couldn't ignore him any longer. Enough was enough.

"It took a lot of courage for the President to put his whole political career on the line by offering peace."

Everybody at the table hushed. Their attention and their eyes focused on Will. He had definitely caught their interest. The red faced man had been the local bully since he was a kid. Nobody ever challenged him and having some outsider do so made things interesting for them. Knowing he was in the spotlight, the bully recognized this was a crucial moment to reassert his standing. As a regular at the tavern, the patrons knew him well. They knew what was coming and stayed quiet.

Will suspected he had crossed some invisible line. Too late, he started to regret calling this man out in front of his peers. Hoping someone would change the subject or at least do something to diffuse the situation, he waited expectantly.

As the man's leering red face turned purple, he shouted, "So you think running from a fight takes courage do ya, stranger?"

"I didn't say that. What I said was..."

"Our boys lost Afghanistan because of yellow bellies like you," interrupted the bellicose man. "I bet you never supported our troops. It's easy for you to sit here and...."

Will was rapidly losing interest in this pointless conversation. Everyone in the tavern knew where he stood regarding the President. That was enough. Will knew nothing could be gained by prolonging a conversation with this man. So he stopped listening and ignored him, turning to face Hacker and exposing his defenceless back to the angry man. He felt confident the drunk wasn't in any condition to enforce his views physically. Hopefully he wouldn't be stupid enough to make the first move.

Hacker looked at Will, smiled and rolled his eyes. Instantly, the man became invisible again. His moment had come and gone and his bluff had been called. No one noticed when he got up and moved to a separate table in a dark corner.

After dinner, Will got up and excused himself, explaining it was time to return to the Ana Teresa. Everyone said a cheery goodbye except for the invisible man who opted instead to glare at Will with vengeful eyes.

Hacker chose to stay a bit longer. Will figured he had managed to find better accommodations, as he'd noticed the coquettish behaviour of a pretty brunette who'd caught Hacker's interest.

"See you later then." With a smile and a wave, Will headed back to the pier.

~

That night, Will slept outside atop the foredeck of the Ana Teresa with the stars shining brilliantly above. Looking up, and not having anything other than the sky in view, gave him the feeling of floating in space. Feeling queasy, he lowered his sights to the shoreline, where tiny pin-lights shone out from the pretty little houses which dotted the shore. The seaward view was inky black, broken only by the occasional green and red flashes coming from lighthouses at the harbour entrance.

Will slept soundly through the night, lulled by the sound of the waves gently lapping against the hull of the tug.

In the morning, from his perch, Will watched the sunrise. Occasionally, a seagull crashed into the water, coming up with a fish for its breakfast. As the sun climbed higher in the sky, others began to stir within the vessel. A short while later, the smell of bacon frying and coffee brewing wafted up from the galley. To Will, it smelt like home.

Ana Teresa's face soon appeared through one of the open hatch windows. She smiled beautifully, appearing fully recovered.

"Coffee, Will?"

"Yes please, Ana."

Out of the hatch stretched one of her hands holding a steaming, full mug, a spoon and a couple of packets of cream and sugar. Next came a plate full of bacon and eggs, hot buttered toast with homemade peach jam and scalloped potatoes. The seagulls eyed Will jealously as he wolfed down his hearty meal.

After breakfast, Will headed back to the beach for a quick morning dip. 'What a great way to start the day', he thought. Refreshed and re-energized, he drip-dried on his way back to the tug.

By the time Will returned, Ernesto already had the engine running and was almost ready to cast off. It was nearing 9 o'clock, the scheduled time for departure. Will was surprised to see Hacker wasn't there. Hacker had assured Ernesto he would be at the pier in the morning. Having only known him for a day, Will was still confident he could be relied upon. Maybe he had a weakness for the opposite sex?

It looked as if Ernesto was going to be shorthanded again. Just as Will was about to fetch their belongings and toss them out onto the dock, they heard some hollering. Everyone looked up to see

Hacker running along the pier yelling to get their attention. As he got closer, his words became audible.

"WAIT FOR ME!"

He arrived out of breath, full of the morning's news and could hardly get the words out fast enough.

"Important news. There's been a terrible turn of events."

Bit by bit, Hacker told everyone what he'd heard. Despite the President's speech, there had been a huge political fight in Washington over the issue of Canada being a haven for terrorists.

"They are still accusing us of harbouring terrorists. It's said that not since the Civil War has there been such division over an issue. Elected government officials opposed to the President's peace policy are quitting their parties and declaring themselves Independents. Their main base of support is coming out of the Midwest where the fallout fell, but they also have large support coming from other states. They're seeking to form a new party and they're asking Colonel Kuhn to head it."

Hacker stopped to take a couple of needed breaths.

"I'm telling you, everything has changed. And it's more than just political rhetoric. They're demanding immediate action and they are going to get it with or without the consent of Washington or the other states."

He took a few more breaths.

"Life as we know it is not going to be the same. People are demanding that all nuclear power stations be shut down and both governments, Canadian and American, have agreed to do so immediately. There's to be no more wasting of energy. No leisure travel at all, not even in our own cars. And to ensure that there will not be another Fermi, all civilian air traffic has been grounded."

"For how long?" Ana asked.

"They didn't say. Probably until things settle down and return to normal," Hacker replied.

"That could take a long time," Ernesto predicted.

For a moment, nobody else spoke, letting all that had been said sink in.

Finally, Ernesto broke the silence.

"So we'll keep heading east as we had originally planned. If it means we sail all the way back to Portugal, so be it. The Ana Teresa could make the voyage if she had to."

Ana dreaded the thought of crossing the Atlantic in the belly of a rolling, smelly fish tug. She knew the clean smell of ammonia would soon be overpowered by the underlying odours from many years of fishing embedded deep within the pores of the concrete floor. She'd rather face the Americans.

Thinking ahead, Ernesto made a list and sent the others off to get great quantities of food, water, essential supplies and cash. Hacker and Will did the same.

Will was not sure whether to head back to his family or return home to Sydney in BC. Hacker settled the matter by offering Will his cell phone so he could call his parents. They had also heard the news. Once again, Will's mother convinced him to continue on his homeward journey.

"We'll be fine, Will." These were her eternal words. She was so solid. The family's rock. Will wondered if she'd ever mouthed the words 'I need some help.' He doubted it.

"Besides, Will, you'll be happy to hear that your bedroom has been put to good use."

"It has?"

"Yes, we've taken in a nice young couple from Michigan who just lost their home and aren't being allowed to return. They're from what's now being called the Exclusion Zone. They've lost almost everything and they're so grateful to have a place to stay. Their names are Dillan and Angela Gallagher. Angela's pregnant and Dillan's an eager helper on the farm."

"That's great, mom. I bet Hana is looking forward to having a baby around."

"She is. It'll help keep her mind off that handsome gentleman York."

"Who's he?"

"You know, Captain Owens. His Christian name is York. He's already shown up to see if all's well. We have no doubt he'll be back."

"I'm not surprised. I saw the effect Hana had on him."

"So, you can go back to BC with a clear conscience. We're fine."

Within minutes, the Ana Teresa cast off from the pier and Ernesto pointed her out into the lake and gunned her reliable Detroit diesel engine.

~

The voyage to Port Maitland was uneventful. It was a calm sunny day and nobody seemed to suffer from seasickness. A noisy flock of seagulls escorted them the whole way, eagerly waiting to grab any loose fish falling from the net the tug was dragging.

En route, Hacker and Will each took a turn at the wheel to give Ernesto time to take a short cat nap. Around lunchtime, they cut the speed for a short while to bring up a small load of smelt. Ana battered and fried them up and they washed them down with a mug of Ernesto's homemade wine.

Hacker enjoyed living the life of a fisherman. There was never a dull moment and it was easy to find something useful to do. He was a people person and, whenever he got a break, he was drawn to spend time with the others in the aft of the tug. Soon, laughter would be heard coming from the stern, as Hacker had a talent for lightening the atmosphere and he helped everyone forget about the mounting troubles ashore.

Will, on the other hand, preferred some solitude. So many thoughts had entered his mind and he needed time alone to work things out. He also found that the smell of diesel fumes in the aft, mixed with the ever lingering fish odour, did not agree with him. So instead of following Hacker, he preferred to climb up through the forward hatch to relax in the sun and fresh air on the top deck and think.

It was a hot summer day. Mid afternoon, Ernesto stopped the tug so those who wanted to cool off could dive into the calm lake and tread water for a while. Will took full advantage of the offer and dove directly off the top deck plunging deep into the water. From there he could look up and clearly see the others' legs hovering above him as they treaded water. The tug's hull cast a dark shadow that penetrated far down into the depths. Summer algae hadn't yet formed in this cool, deep part of the lake. The calm water's visibility was excellent so he could even see fish hovering around him as though they were suspended in space.

It was late afternoon when the Ana Teresa tied up to the pier in Port Maitland. Ernesto was pleased to have had Will and Hacker's help and offered them the opportunity to stay onboard indefinitely if they wished. If he chose to go further east, he'd have to take the Welland Canal to get to Lake Ontario and that would make it harder to turn back. He wasn't prepared to commit to doing that yet. Instead, he intended to remain docked for a week in order to think things over and decide their next move.

~

CHAPTER V

Thy Broad Domain

"We will make no distinction between the terrorists
who committed these acts and those
who harbour them."
— George W. Bush, Address to the
Nation, September 11, 2001

~

Will and Hacker decided to continue their journey on foot. They figured it would take about five days to walk to Toronto, which seemed to be where they should go. With Toronto being the main hub of Canada's transportation system, Will thought he could find an easier way to travel west from there. So they thanked the Fortunas for their hospitality and they all went their separate ways.

For two days, Will and Hacker headed north on a pathway that paralleled the edge of the Grand River. It was a picturesque trail, well known to natives who'd lived in the area for centuries. There, they found respite from all the craziness and gloomy news. Along the path, they often came upon others who, like themselves, were on a journey or were simply out enjoying some fresh air while on a riverside stroll. Occasionally, they saw paddlers in canoes coast by leisurely, heading downriver with the current. Seeing them put Hacker in mind of his upcoming canoe trip with his father.

"That'll be us in a couple of weeks."

"Us?"

"Yep. Me and my dad. You'd be more than welcome to join us, Will. It would be fun to have you along. I just know you'd get along great with my dad."

"Who knows, maybe if you're canoeing in my direction, I just might!" said Will, but he doubted if that would ever come to fruition. His mind was now set on going home, back to Sydney. Seeing the ease at which the canoeists coasted by, Will couldn't help but think, 'There are worse ways to travel 3,500 kilometres.' That thought put the task before him in perspective. Just a few days ago, he had covered the whole distance by jet and car in about eight hours. Travelling on foot would take over a hundred times that. His world had just got a whole bunch larger. 'How drastically things can change overnight,' he realized.

The next leg of the journey confirmed Will's thoughts about the downside of walking. They'd woken up early in the morning, hoping to get to their destination before the forecasted thunderstorms overtook them. That day they veered away from the peaceful riverside trail at Caledonia. From there, they bee-lined it directly to Hamilton along the gravelled edge of a major roadway. Along that road, they'd expected to encounter heavy traffic and hoped to hitch a ride. But fuel rationing, a ripple effect of shutting down the nuclear power stations, had already been enacted and had instantly put the brakes on any pleasure driving. Thus, there was very little traffic on the road. As if to accentuate the unexpected quiet, Will saw an even stranger sight – an empty donut shop.

"Look at that Tim's," he exclaimed, pointing ahead.

Hacker had seen it too.

"No kidding. That's a first." Not one single car idled in the drive-through. Peering inside, they could see the silhouettes of only two patrons. Both were seated at the same table and the single police car in the parking lot gave away who they were.

"Fewer cars will at least help improve the air quality," Hacker said, trying to look on the brighter side of things.

The same thought had occurred to Will. He wasn't disappointed to see people being less wasteful either.

Yet the transition of going from one extreme to another, shifting from wasteful extravagance to cutbacks and economizing in such a short time span, felt very disconcerting. The difference was that before it had been voluntary and self-inflicted whereas now it was being forced upon them.

'What a difference a few days makes,' Will thought.

~

Hacker held out his thumb as they walked along the road, but it was a waste of effort. They were passed by many emergency and law enforcement vehicles with their emergency lights left perpetually on and flashing. Looking off into the distance, Hacker and Will observed that there seemed to be lights flashing constantly. The sight reminded them of the incessant nature of the emergency and kept them on edge.

"I guess those are the so-called 'eternal lights' foretold in the Bible," Hacker quipped.

"I guess so."

The traffic's white noise had become so much a part of urban culture that, without it, the roadway now seemed foreign. Hacker and Will were able to hear the ominous sound of thunder farther off in the distance. Its rumble followed them and, as its volume rose, they knew it was only a matter of time before it would catch up and overtake them. Still under blue skies, they could see the distant storm front approaching and the heavy torrents of rain that fell from it. They picked up their pace knowing that, soon, the storm would be on their heels. A short while later, the sky around them darkened and a burst of cool turbulent air hit them. Again, they picked up their pace. As they approached the denser populated area, they began to encounter more people. Few returned their waves.

'Very un-Canadian,' Will thought.

The people had their reasons. The alarming allegations of Canada being infiltrated by terrorists had made many people suspicious of strangers. In consequence, Will and Hacker were under scrutiny and, strange as it may sound, they felt like foreigners.

"Is it my imagination or are people passing by staring at us?" Hacker asked.

"Nope, I think you're right. I feel it too, Hacker."

Walking on the trail, they had fit in and raised no suspicion. Yet here, along the roadway carrying their backpacks, they stood out.

"I imagine this is how it would have felt living under Soviet rule," Will surmised.

"Ya, under constant fear and showing no trust for your fellow man."

"I thought we won that war, Will."

"Me too."

Their feelings were soon validated when two police cruisers pulled up and stopped them. Both cruisers had their lights flashing.

Will and Hacker laid down their packs to lessen their discomfort and sat down on them to rest. This move irritated one of the officers who immediately jumped out of the car with his gun drawn.

"FREEZE!" he hollered.

"What the f....?"

"Take it easy, Hacker," Will interrupted him. "I hope you don't have any pot on you."

"Don't be silly. If I did, we would have smoked some last night!" Hacker quipped.

Three other officers calmly exited the cruisers. They were older than the first and seemed to have a lighter disposition. As the senior officer walked up to the gun wielding officer, he asked, "What do we have here, Rambo?" He put his hand on the other's forearm so that he had to lower his weapon. Will saw the other officers smile knowingly.

Hacker hadn't been the least bit intimidated by the gun and hoped to say something to continue to lighten the mood.

"Were we speeding, officers?"

Ignoring him, the senior officer revealed their purpose.

"We're responding to a call about a couple of dubious looking characters walking along this road carrying backpacks. You two fellas seem to fit the description. You've got some people nervous."

"No one has anything to fear from us," Will assured him.

"That may be so. But now that we're here, can we see some ID?"

Recognizing that they should take this seriously, without further discussion, Will and Hacker gave him their ID. He handed the ID to one of the junior officers who took it back to the cruiser.

"Have you been stopping and checking many people, officer?" Will asked, trying to ascertain the current level of emergency alert.

"You'd be surprised. Good thing for you fellas is that you don't match the profile."

"Profile?"

"Yes, but I never said that. But if you had any darker tan, we'd be doing this down at the station," he admitted.

After what seemed like an unusually long wait, the other officer came back from the cruiser.

"They're clean," he said to his senior officer.

"Here," he said, handing them back their ID. "We're going to have to go through your packs though. You picked a bad time to travel," he explained.

Soon all of Will and Hacker's belongings were spread out for police inspection. Nothing unusual was found, except for two knives which they both carried for their usefulness. The officer who'd pulled his gun seemed vindicated that 'weapons' had been found and set them aside. By his look, it seemed the knives were going to be confiscated and Will and Hacker were in trouble.

"Last time I used that knife was for decapitating and gutting...."

As Hacker spoke, Will saw Rambo's hand move back towards his holster. Will glared at Hacker with eyes that screamed, 'SHUT UP, YOU IDIOT!'

"...fish," he finished with an award winning smile.

Will braced himself, held his breath and felt adrenaline surge through his body in preparation for whatever might happen next. Hacker's words took everyone by surprise, but the other three officers smiled and their reaction took the edge off the situation. The senior officer stooped down to pick up the knives.

"That's a pretty nice blade," he said.

"German made," another officer added. "They're the best. Hold their edge the longest."

"Here, fellas. We wouldn't want to be without ours either," he acknowledged, handing the knives back to them. The officers were sportsmen too and fully appreciated the utilitarian value of knives.

"Where are you headed, fellas?" the senior officer asked.

"We're heading to Toronto, sir," Will answered. He explained their plans and showed him the letter from Captain Owens.

"Next time, you'll save yourself a lot of time and hassle if you show that letter first."

"Ya, that's your get out of jail free card, buddy," another officer piped in.

Suddenly, an ear-piercing roar from above drew their attention skywards. Coming overhead at barely treetop level was a large military plane descending on its final approach to the airfield nearby. Until then, Will and Hacker hadn't noticed the airfield or the large squadron of military aircraft parked there.

"Wow, look at all the planes!" Hacker exclaimed.

"I didn't know that our Air Force was that large," Will added.

"They're not ours, fellas. They belong to the Americans," said the senior officer. "They flew here from all over Michigan and other areas affected by the fallout. The airports at Windsor and London are already jammed full of them and can't take anymore. These are just the overflow."

"Impressive," Hacker voiced the obvious, "and scary too."

With a boom of thunder, lightening struck nearby and brought their attention back to the storm. The plane had just landed in time. Even it was no match for Mother Nature.

A cool wind whipped up, betraying the air's turbulence. Moments later, the sky opened up with a drenching downpour. The storm had overtaken them and they were caught out in the open. Alert to the natural danger which was around them, they forgot everything and ran about trying to gather up all of their belongings. Realizing the predicament they'd put them in, the officers lent Will and Hacker a hand.

"Throw your stuff in here," shouted one officer, who'd just opened up the trunk of his squad car. "Then get in! We'll drop you off downtown where there's shelter."

"Great! Thanks!"

Minutes later, Will and Hacker roared away under police escort. In the eyes of those watching, it appeared that the police had apprehended and arrested some wrongdoers. Will and Hacker didn't care what other people thought. It was pouring out and they'd finally got their ride.

~

At the police station in Hamilton, Will and Hacker were each given a transit letter to assist them as they travelled. It took them two days to walk to Toronto. The thunderstorm had removed the humidity from the air and watered the planted fields. They found a quiet off-road trail that paralleled Lake Ontario's waterfront. As they walked along it, passers-by took no particular notice of them. Everyone just seemed happy to be out enjoying a beautiful day.

Society had undergone a profound transformation in little over a week. Will and Hacker found the approach into Toronto to be unusually still. Motorized traffic, the primary disturber of urban peace, had been curtailed by the imposition of fuel rationing.

Overloaded streetcars and buses still passed by, but they were too infrequent to have much impact on the general prevailing calm in the streets. At first, it left Will with a more favourable impression than the claustrophobic atmosphere he'd felt on his previous trips to the city. Now the wide avenues were vacant of the perpetual traffic gridlock which had seemed to be a permanent part of the cityscape. Cyclists and pedestrians were able to spread themselves out onto the vacant streets.

Despite the forced economizing, the city was still lively and there was still plenty of hustle and bustle. Will and Hacker blended in with the general mêlée and travelled downtown until they reached the University of Toronto's main campus. Hacker was familiar with the campus and, through his connections there, secured them a room in student residence. They were both glad to get settled and have a shower.

It took only a few days for Hacker to reconnect with a number of his former classmates. Will found himself immersed in Hacker's world. One of Hacker's favourite places to go was Chinatown where he introduced Will to his friend, Ellen Lee. Ellen lived in a modest sized red brick house. In addition to herself, her parents, her grandmother and her three younger siblings, other members of their extended family occupied all the other nooks and crannies of their home.

"Let me take you on a tour of our property," Ellen said. "Our home and yard might be small, but it can fulfill most of our needs."

Their front yard was miniscule compared to what Will was used to and provided barely enough room for a small square of grass. A sidewalk divided their front yard and led up to a veranda on which there were a number of chairs. Ellen's grandmother was a permanent fixture on one of the rockers.

Leading him through the house and out the back door, Ellen turned around and pointed up the second floor where green plants were rising behind the windows.

"That's our greenhouse. Its purpose is to extend the growing season," she explained.

"Come," she said, taking him farther into the backyard. The yard was enclosed by an old fence and was almost entirely cultivated with a garden growing a tremendous variety of vegetables. Like many first generation immigrants, Ellen's parents had come from a country in turmoil and held on to their customs. To them, a garden was part of a self-sufficient way of living which helped ensure they could look after their own needs.

Will and Ellen took many walks together around her neighbourhood. Will's questions and comments soon made Ellen realize that the way of life she took for granted was admired by him and this caused Ellen to observe her neighbours with new respect and appreciation. Many had recently installed rain barrels at the bottom of their eavestroughs. Disregarding city bylaws, some were fencing in areas for chickens and rabbits in their small backyards. Children and adults lined the pier with fishing rods and worms, catching pails full of fish.

Will applauded them for their determination. To him, these people were the modern equivalent of Robin Hood and his men, hunting illegally in the King's forest. Without seeking permission from above for their fish or backyard chickens, they had continued with a way of life that could sustain them regardless of shortages or cutbacks.

At the same time, Will worried for them. Recent lay-offs, a growing scarcity on grocery store shelves, a shaken and weak government and fewer city lights at night, all conspired to create an atmosphere ripe for mischief. Should people become desperate, the neighbourhood might no longer be safe. Will wanted to leave the city and he voiced his concerns to Hacker. They could both see that the city was becoming more dangerous every day.

Early one evening, they heard 'pop-pop-pop' in the distance. Hacker asked, "What was that?"

"Gunfire," answered Will, who'd often heard the same sound during duck and pheasant hunting season.

Gangs were now roaming the city freely and, each successive night, the sound of gunfire drew closer as they solidified and expanded their turf. The police were too preoccupied by the growing chaos during the day and so surrendered the night. Neighbourhoods that fell to gang-rule were marked by flashing blue lights to alert the public that to enter was done at their own risk. Hacker and Will decided to leave the city.

~

Before leaving, Will and Hacker needed to gather supplies to continue their long journey. First, they went to the bank and withdrew as much cash from their savings as they felt comfortable carrying. Then, they went shopping for non-perishable food. Although available supplies were already dwindling, with the help of Ellen and her family, they got what they needed. Next, they headed to an outdoor store where Will ticked off a small camp stove, fuel, a water-filter pump and iodine pills, reusable water bottles, rain gear, and a tent.

Having acquired all the things they needed, all that remained was for Hacker to say goodbye to all his friends. As he did so, Will went to the city library where he found and copied maps and other pertinent information for their journey. He also visited the Royal Ontario Museum to review the exhibit devoted to the early pioneers, natives and the courier-de-bois fur trappers. He noted the methods and tools they employed to survive.

Seeing the exhibit and all the artefacts made Will realize just how ill-prepared he was to live outdoors for an extended period of time. He'd always thought of himself as an outdoors person, but he realized that his previous trips had always been brief, two weeks at most. He had often gone into the backcountry in the Rockies, but on those trips, he'd always packed in enough food to outlast the trip. Reviewing their plans, and taking a cue from the immigrants he'd seen at the pier, he headed back to the outdoor store and acquired a compact fishing rod, hooks, line and sinkers. Once he was on the move, if food ran low, he hoped to catch a meal. He recognized too that footwear would be an important necessity so he bought a durable pair of walking shoes that would last many miles.

By the time he'd finished, his backpack weighed over 70 lbs and he wasn't looking forward to carrying it on a long journey. Hacker had the same problem. They decided to obtain some bikes, knowing they could ride comfortably at four to five times the speed of walking. Although they had great difficulty finding bikes, Ellen came to their rescue and helped them procure a couple of decent used ones. As a bonus, she found them a couple of BOB trailers to pull behind the bikes and carry their heaviest gear. They bought the equipment with cash, no receipt and no tax. Thus, they became a part of a rapidly developing underground economy.

~

Before leaving Toronto, Will called Sydney as well as his parents. He made the calls on a land line as he'd seen many immigrants do. They'd become distrustful of the authorities and knew that cell phone conversations could be listened in on and a user's location easily triangulated. With all the hysteria and, especially after their own recent experience with the police, Will thought it was a wise idea to take this precaution as well.

They exchanged stories and useful information. Will was relieved to hear that things weren't too bad where they were. In contrast, Will told them how desperate things were becoming in Toronto. His dad wasn't surprised.

"We're closer to the land, Will. We won't starve," he said.

Sydney said the same, but her food source was different.

"The hunters and fishermen are keeping us well supplied with elk meat and cut-throat trout," she reported.

"But what about you, Syd?"

"Well, I'm no longer a vegetarian. It's either meat and fish or starve. I have dreams about eating a fresh salad, but the veggies we're getting here aren't worth the price they're asking for them. On the bright side, though, it's been a great year for wild strawberries and raspberries."

Having checked in with family and having said goodbye to their Toronto friends, Hacker and Will were now prepared for the next leg of their journey to Peterborough.

"We're off!" Hacker exclaimed as they started out. He was glad Will was joining him and looked forward to Will meeting his father, the professor.

They departed Toronto in early August riding eastward along the lakefront.

~

Meanwhile in Ottawa, politicians focused on the declining relations with the States and turned their backs on the rapidly declining economy as the private sector disappeared underground. Washington wasn't to be appeased and Canadians braced themselves. They knew that their fate was now in the hands of Washington.

The Prime Minister had been unable to exert any meaningful influence on the unfolding political situation. He tried to exude confidence in Ottawa while smoothing over relations with Washington. Being a veteran politician, he'd learned the art of doubletalk so, in addressing the public, he tried to sound both conciliatory to the Americans and bold to the Canadians. This approach failed miserably as the Americans soon distrusted anything the PM had to say. The leader of the opposition fared no better for any criticism he levelled at the PM was construed as being anti-American. Every Canadian politician was afraid to speak for fear they'd say the wrong thing and make the situation worse. A cartoonist for the Ottawa Citizen made the point by drawing a white flag flying on Parliament Hill's flagpole, symbolizing the ignoble defeat of the Canadian government.

~

Stateside, the presidential election was in full swing and Canada was the focal point. Politics there reached a fevered pitch. The President's chief rival was Governor Kuhn of Michigan, who'd officially declared his candidacy for the presidency as leader of the newly formed Continental Party.

"Your time is up, Mr President," he declared with great fanfare while standing on top of the Ambassador Bridge spanning the Detroit River.

Initially, Kuhn's support had come mainly from the Midwest, where the devastation caused by Fermi's fallout had been felt immediately and most severely. Hundreds of thousands had been made homeless there and they needed help from the only man they trusted – Kuhn. Midway through the campaign, when the economic impact of losing such a large tract of America's heartland was spreading all across the nation, Kuhn's popularity spread.

As Kuhn's campaign gained momentum, so too did the anti-Canada movement, upon which most of his Continental Party's 'ultimate solution' rested. His party's platform called for bringing Canada into the Union as the only way out of the growing economic crisis.

"It's time for Canada to join the rest of the Continent," Kuhn insisted. "Without Canada, it is impossible to guarantee America's peace, security and independence."

His tone and objectives resonated with the American public and the Party messages consistently painted Canadians as the enemy. Bowing to the popular concern about Canada, the President conceded that some of the American forces deployed to Canada should remain there until the situation was secured.

All the American rhetoric about Canada was a new experience for Canadians. Few alive recalled Canada being at the forefront of American politics and, having now achieved that dubious status, most Canadians longed for their former state of invisibility.

The official Canadian response was to welcome the American troops and the great numbers of Homeland Security officials who accompanied them.

"We've invited the Americans to help us secure the whole North American perimeter from outside terrorists," the PM assured Canadians. "It is for the mutual benefit of both countries."

Nobody dared to ask why Canadian troops were not similarly deployed to the States under this so-called environment of mutual exchange. This inconsistency betrayed what most people had come to believe, which was that the true battlefield lay in Canada itself.

As Kuhn declared, "Canada is where the terrorists are."

~

CHAPTER VI

The Twilight's
Last Gleaming

"I cannot imagine any condition which would cause a ship to founder. I cannot conceive of any vital disaster happening to this vessel. Modern ship building has gone beyond that."
— Captain Smith, Commander of Titanic
(Sunk by an iceberg April 15, 1912)

~

It took a couple of days for Will and Hacker to reach Peterborough. During the first half of their journey, their path was often crossed by others heading northwards, leaving the city and its hard times behind. Like Will and Hacker, most travelled either by bike or on foot. Those lucky enough to travel by car had connections in government who'd supplied them with extra gasoline ration cards and travel permits.

"Lucky aristocratic buggers," one man remarked with unabashed envy.

Most of those who crossed paths with Will and Hacker travelled in medium sized groups, small enough to be mobile and flexible, yet large enough to offer some protection.

"Safety in numbers," uttered Will to himself.

They were witnessing an act of self-preservation that had begun when some cavemen wanted what their neighbours had. Migration was simply the natural response of those seeking peace, economic stability and safety.

In the preceding years of peace and stability, Toronto had become home to most of Canada's immigrants. Many had moved there for jobs and an income that would give them a better life. As these jobs disappeared, so too did their reasons for staying. As people became more desperate and safety in the city became more questionable, people left.

All sorts of people were migrating, young, old, rich and poor. They shambled along, bewildered and overwhelmed by circumstances beyond their control. For most of them, their final destination was still unknown.

The manner of the young stood out in stark contrast to the depressing mood of their elders. Will was heartened to realize that, for the children, it was an exciting time, a fun holiday from school and a new adventure. There were children pulling small pieces of wheeled luggage or carrying tiny back packs along with whatever mattered most to them – their stuffed animals, dolls or some other prized possession. For their benefit, their parents tried to put on brave faces.

Will and Hacker encountered one young boy wearing army fatigues and carrying a small American toy soldier in his hands.

"That's a little ironic," said Will.

"I wonder how long it'll be before he discovers he's fancying the bad guys?" Hacker added.

~

Ahead, the recently shut-down colossus of the Pickering nuclear generating plant came into view. Given recent events, it now seemed to Will to be a monument to short-sighted stupidity, illustrating for future generations how his generation lived only for the moment. Touted, until Fermi's destruction, as a 'cheap, clean and safe' form of power generation, the availability of nuclear energy had encouraged everyone to live wastefully. An affordable failsafe container that would outlast its deadly by-product had not yet been invented and the decommissioning costs for the hundred plus plants now closed across the continent would be paid for years into the future.

"They should all be put in jail." Hacker spat out his words.

"I think they might be, if they live long enough," Will replied.

"Do you really think so?"

"Yes, I do. How long do you think people will be willing to pay for something and get nothing for it? They'll want to string up the culprits. Jail seems to be the easiest way out for them."

"It's hard to imagine what the final all-in cost of Fermi's destruction will be. I heard it'll be more than a 100 billion dollars."

"Ya, but that's just money. I think it may cost us our freedom and possibly our country," Will said. "Try to put a price on that."

An hour later, they rode by the Darlington nuclear generating plant. The shutdown of both plants had removed more than 6,600 megawatts of electricity from the power grid. That was about one-third of Ontario's electricity supply and enough to power a city of three and a half million people.

They were both uncomfortable as they rode by the plants and were relieved to turn north and leave the lakefront, with its nuclear monuments, behind.

~

Professor Hacker was outside tending to his garden when Will and Hacker rode onto his property, marking the end of this leg of their journey. An attractive young female stooped nearby tending to her own row. She wore loose fitting overalls, but her girlish figure was still evident.

"Looks like Dad found himself a keen student to help him with his gardening." Hacker winked at Will.

"That explains where you picked up your bad habits."

Hacker smiled back knowingly, taking what Will said as a compliment.

The professor and the girl looked up as they heard the squeaky gate to the yard creak open. The professor studied them thoughtfully for a long moment as if to size them up. Hacker had been away for some time and didn't look the part of a typical University student anymore. The professor finally nodded as though pleased with what he saw, whereas she beamed with delight.

"It's Barry, Professor. He's come back to us!" she exclaimed joyfully.

"Perhaps she's YOUR welcome home present, Hacker," Will whispered to him. The bewildered look on Hacker's face told Will that he didn't have a clue about who she was.

"Uhhh. Hello…" he fumbled for words.

The professor got up and came over to greet them. "Welcome home, Barry!" From that moment onwards, whenever they were in the presence of the professor, they called Hacker 'Barry'. While father and son embraced, the professor extended a soiled hand out to greet Will.

"Welcome to the Hacker Homestead, Will," he said. "Sarah and I were starting to wonder when you boys would show up, weren't we, Sarah?"

Sarah nodded sheepishly in agreement, but it was evident that Barry's coolness had set her back.

Will met the professor's hand and shook it. "Nice to meet you, Professor," he replied.

"You didn't have to worry about us, Dad. Nothing could have prevented Will and me from getting here. In fact, once you get to know Will better, I think you'll wish you had him as a student."

Barry then turned to Sarah, who now stood by shyly, sensing his curiosity. She clearly felt embarrassed that her initial reaction had not been met with equal enthusiasm. Now she waited, unsure of herself.

"So you're little Sarah? Not so little anymore, I see. Have I been away that long?"

She had changed beyond his recollection, become taller and turned into a fully developed woman. She was definitely not the tomboy he remembered. Peering into her eyes, he concluded, "Yes, it really is you in there."

"Hi Barry," she replied awkwardly.

Will recognized how uncomfortable the situation was for both of them.

"So you're the Sarah Barry has told me so much about," Will lied.

That comment suddenly clarified things in her mind. With fingers crossed, she stepped forward and boldly threw her arms around Barry and gave him a welcome kiss. Her boldness was rewarded, for Barry happily kissed her back.

The professor was delighted to see their bikes and Will got his first lesson in the professor's lexicon of words, giving a glimpse of how he saw the world.

"You've brought us some 'horses!'" he exclaimed.

"He means our bikes," Barry whispered to Will out of the side of his mouth.

"There's room over there in the stable, boys," the professor continued, pointing at the shed beyond the garden.

Opening the shed doors, they saw over a dozen bikes, of all shapes and sizes, hanging neatly side by side from their front tires. Will lifted his 'horse' onto a vacant hook, tire side touching the wall like all the others.

"They're badly needed by folks around here," said the professor. "The local bike shops have already sold off all their inventory. They say they'll be out of stock until next spring and they're offering good money for used bikes. It's so typical of people. They don't know what they need until they need it. By then, it's often too late."

"Quit lecturing us, Dad. We get it."

"And you say that it took you only two days to ride from Toronto, eh? Good show, boys!"

"Bikes are hard to get in the city too," Will replied. "It was only through Barry's friend Ellen that we were able to round these ones up. We've broken them in nicely, although now I'm a little saddle sore." Will was getting into the professor's horse theme.

"You've built up quite a stockpile of bikes here, Dad. Are you preparing for Y2K again?" Barry asked a little mockingly.

Barry had forewarned Will about his father's numerous eccentricities. He'd told Will how his father had gone to extraordinary efforts to prepare for Y2K, marking the turn of the last century. At that time, some predicted there could be widespread computer failure due to computers not being able to read any dates beyond December 31, 1999. In preparation, the professor had taken their home completely off the grid. Now they drew their water directly from the Otonabee River, purified it through an ozone treatment system and then heated it in a solar furnace. High efficiency wood burners kept the interior of their home toasty warm. He obtained all the wood from his own large tract of forest. And within his forest lived small game and the occasional deer. He caught fish from the river. Produce from his organic garden was stored down in the cellar which was maintained at a constant cool temperature. Oil lamps and candles lit the home's interior and what little electricity they needed was supplied by batteries kept charged by their windmill and solar collectors.

Barry previously considered his father a pessimist as he was constantly preparing for some cataclysmic disaster. Yet, after witnessing the goings-on in Toronto, he was starting to think that his father had been wise to think as he did.

Barry had hinted to Will that somewhere outdoors on their property was a secret stash of gold. For more than twenty years, his father had directed a sizable part of his earnings towards acquiring real silver and gold bullion. Barry knew his father well enough to know that he would never risk storing the bullion in some bank's safety deposit box and figured that it must be buried somewhere nearby. With the recent price of gold soaring beyond $3,000 dollars an ounce, Professor Hacker must be a millionaire, Will thought.

"I see they're solid and they've got decent multi-purpose tires," the professor continued, ignoring Barry's Y2K remark.

"They're sturdy and simple, no unnecessary gearing or parts that will wear and break. They'll be easy to maintain. Yes sir-ree, just the occasional drop of oil is all they'll need. Good choice, boys!"

~

From the moment they arrived, the professor took Will under his wing. Barry didn't mind that his father had immediately captivated Will's attention as Sarah was now the object of his. Since their reunion, they'd become inseparable and were often out on their own.

Consequently, Will was often left to spend time with the professor and he learned to treasure each and every moment. The professor's simple ways immediately endeared him to Will. Yet as simple as he seemed, Will discovered he had great depth and was particularly gifted with a remarkable sense of intuition that kept him one step ahead of the times.

"Will," he'd said one day, "remember this above all else. It is as it has always been and will forever continue to be."

At first, Will considered those to be the words of an eccentric man who talked in riddles. But as he came to know the professor better, he realized his mind worked differently than others for it wasn't constrained by linear measurement of time. To the professor, the past, present and future blurred together into one continuous, repeating storyline. In the days that followed, Will learned to understand the timeless wisdom of the professor's words and how living in accord with them made life much easier and predictable. But at that moment, he merely smiled in reply.

~

Will was torn between continuing on his journey back to Sydney in BC or returning to the farm. His heart urged him west, but his brain told him Sydney was safer than his family. He postponed his decision by staying on with the Hackers for awhile longer to see how events unfolded.

The professor did not let the deteriorating political and economic climate cancel his plans to go on the canoe adventure with Barry. For him, the news made it all more worthwhile. He'd made his life pretty much invulnerable to the events that were now shaking up so many lives so, for him, it was business as usual.

Barry reminded Will that he was welcome to come on the trip. Will realized that a canoe trip would give him a good chance to clear his head and escape the grim political and economic realities of the moment. Once he agreed to join them, they needed a fourth person and Barry happily invited Sarah along.

By the end of the week, they were prepared. They descended downriver in two canoes, the professor and Will in one and Sarah and Barry in the other. The current was hardly evident as the 44 locks and 160 dams built along the 386 kilometre long Trent-Severn Waterway had levelled out most of its former turbulence.

~

CHAPTER VII

Our Home And Native Land!

*"It is every man's obligation to put back into the world
at least the equivalent of what he takes out of it."*
— Albert Einstein

~

It took two days of easy paddling to reach the Hiawatha First
Nation Reserve on Rice Lake. Will was surprised to discover
that such a place actually existed. To him, *The Song of Hiawatha*
by Longfellow existed only as a poem that his mother had often
recited to him in his childhood.

The magic of the name Hiawatha held Will spellbound as they
landed their canoes on the shore. Surely this was sacred ground.
Arriving by way of canoe made it feel as though they'd gone
through a time warp and Will was surprised to see that the young
man who came down to greet them wasn't dressed in buckskin. It
was only his facial features and reddish complexion which told of
the past.

'Could this be a descendent of Hiawatha?' Will wondered.

"Hello, Professor," he greeted them. A number of others
descended to the waterfront to lend a hand unloading the canoes
and soon they were all settled at their campsite.

The professor was well known and liked by the people of
Hiawatha. He'd spent a considerable amount of time living
amongst them. At first, they had put up with him, but he was
considered an outsider, another academic who wanted to study
and document them and their ways. Soon they recognized that he
was different from others who had come before him. He wasn't

there to sermonize or lecture to them and he definitely hadn't come for the money. In fact, he wanted to become more like them. Other scholars joked about him, contending that today's natives had lost any connection to their roots, but the professor believed that traces of their noble culture could still be found. It was that natural spirit that the professor sought to know and understand.

He had spent a year living with them, accepting them exactly as he found them. In time, he saw how they communicated with their eyes and their expressions, making it unnecessary to verbalize to communicate. He saw their natural spirit shine through in their children who, being seldom punished by their elders, developed a distaste for authority. If he had any impact on their lives at all, it was that his sensitivity for them helped to rekindle their own appreciation of the old ways. Gradually, they came to accept him too and, eventually, he became a trusted friend.

The professor had brought some gifts which he gave to the chief. It was she who would decide how they would be distributed. The least expensive gift was homemade strawberry jam which the professor had made from berries picked from his own garden. They appreciated the effort and care which had gone into its production and this gift of time was the most treasured.

That evening, a reception was held in the large community wigwam. In honour of the professor, the people of Hiawatha wore their traditional native dress. To their amusement and in keeping with the spirit of the evening, the professor came dressed in fur trapper's garb.

Over the course of the evening, Will became acquainted with a few Hiawathans and soon felt comfortable enough to ask them about something that had been troubling him ever since they'd arrived.

"Why is your community called Hiawatha?"

It was the chief's daughter Tuwa, seated next to Will, who answered.

"The elders chose the name Hiawatha to honour what his memory represents to our people."

"And what does he represent?"

"Peace. Our people believe that Hiawatha was a follower of the Great Peacemaker. What he learned from the Great Peacemaker he put into practice. He brought the ancient tribes together to form the Five Nations of the Iroquois Confederacy."

"So you are Iroquois?"

"No, we are Ojibway. Our tribe was part of a larger Band known as the Mississaugas of Rice Lake."

"I don't understand. Then why name your community after Hiawatha, an Iroquois and historic enemy?"

"As were your people, Will," she reminded him. "But now we are friends."

Her comment set Will back and he blushed. Tuwa smiled and continued.

"You see, we are all the children of our Great Earth Mother. The Iroquois are our brothers. The professor is our brother. You and your warrior ancestors are family too, William Anderson," she smiled. "Through Her, we are united. By naming our community after Hiawatha, we honour what his story represents which is peace and balance."

She slid off her headband and put it in Will's hands.

"This design is made in the image of Hiawatha's Belt."

Will looked closely at her headband in his hands. There were white symbols of a tree with two squares on each side. All of the symbols were connected together by a white line which, when worn, completely encircled her head.

Will was just about to ask what the symbols meant when a glance from Barry told him that he'd asked enough. Beforehand, Barry had forewarned Will not to be too talkative.

"It's not their way," he'd warned.

Recalling that advice, Will quickly concluded his inquiry with a "thank you" and handed the headband back to her.

"May I bother you with just one more question?" Will saw Barry roll his eyes.

"Yes. I don't mind."

"Why is it called Rice Lake?"

"At one time, wild rice grew abundantly in these waters. When the canal was built, the higher water levels destroyed the rice beds." Then, she added with a friendly smile, "I'd be happy to tell you the meaning of my headband later if you'd like. I could tell that you were wondering about the design."

"Yes, I would like that very much. Thank you, Tuwa."

"Ahem," Barry interrupted. Tuwa's mother, the chief, was about to say grace, a traditional Native prayer, before the meal was served.

We return thanks to our mother, the Earth,
which sustains us.
We return thanks to the rivers and streams,
which supply us with water.
We return thanks to all herbs,
which furnish medicines for the cure of our diseases.
We return thanks to the moon and the stars,
which has given us light when the sun is gone.
We return thanks to the sun,
that has looked upon the earth with a beneficent eye.
We return thanks to our friends,
who give us strength and fellowship.
Lastly, we return thanks to the Great Spirit,
in whom is embodied all goodness,
and who directs all things for the good of her children.

~

In keeping with the theme of the evening, they were served an authentic native meal that included venison steaks, partridge, wild rice and cranberries, and the professor's favourite, dandelion and bass stir fry. Wild blueberries were served for dessert along with lichen tea.

When the peace pipe was passed around after dinner, its symbolic meaning bonded everyone together.

"Peace be with you," said Tuwa to Will as she passed the pipe to him.

Once the celebration concluded, Tuwa took Will aside to explain the meaning of her head band.

"The colour purple represents the sky," Tuwa said. "The colour white represents purity and positive mental energy such as good thoughts, forgiveness and understanding. The four open white squares and tree symbolize the Five Nations of the Iroquois Confederacy. The tree is for the Onondaga Nation which was the capital of the League and keeper of the fire. The Nations' symbols are all connected by a white band that has no beginning and no end, representing all time now and forever. The band does not cross through the centre of the squares or tree, meaning that each Nation is supported and unified by a common bond and that each respects the others as separate in their own identities and domain. The open centre also signifies the idea of a fort protected on all sides, but with open hearts and minds within."

The symbolism amazed Will in its timeliness and its current relevance.

~

The following morning, they waved goodbye to their new friends and paddled away. Making good time, they stopped briefly to see the Serpent Mounds. These ancient mounds were situated at the tip of a peninsula called Roche's Point and each appeared to be a wavy five foot high mound of dirt. The longest one stretched about two football fields in length.

"What are they?" asked Will.

"Burial mounds." Barry answered. He was happy to show his father that he had learned a thing or two from him as well.

"That's right, Barry. What else do you know about them?"

"That they were built by an ancient tribe which inhabited this area about eighteen hundred years before the Ojibway."

"Excellent," the professor answered.

The explanation made Will wonder, 'Who will be around to call this land their home eighteen hundred years from now?'

Their voyage downstream ended in Trenton where they found the Canadian Forces Base. Something significant was in the works.

Not even during the height of the war in Afghanistan had there been so much activity at the base. Yet nothing official about the goings-on within the base had been in the news.

The foursome went their separate ways at Trenton and each of them overheard bits and pieces from the whisperings of the locals.

"They're building up their forces over there."

"Biggest build-up I've ever seen. And I've lived here for 75 years."

"No, they're not Air Force."

"Mostly ground forces."

"There's at least five thousand of them."

"Ten thousand."

"All a bunch of buggers if you ask me."

"It's their training."

"Power-tripping whores."

"Special forces."

"Rude. Not like either the Air Force personnel or regular soldiers, who are polite and respectful."

"They're being trained by the Yanks to be jerks."

"They come in here and treat me and my patrons like we're suspected terrorists."

"To them, you're guilty until proven innocent."

"Call themselves Canadian Perimeter Services."

"The customs people never used to behave this way."

"Changed their style."

"Special agents."

"Arrogant."

"Inland Control agents."

"Trained to spy on us all."

"They carry side arms, pistols."

"They make me feel as though I'm their enemy."

"Their job is to make enemies."

"Well I sure don't like them, so I guess we are enemies."

~

That evening, the four of them reconvened, talked about all the things that they'd heard and pieced it all together.

"Aren't Perimeter Services agents really only glorified Customs agents, dad?"

"Not exactly, Barry. They oversee customs, but that is only part of it. Customs used to focus mostly on tax collection, but Perimeter Services is a new agency created after 9/11 to address heightened national security concerns. In truth, it was created in response to the US government criticizing Canada for not doing enough to secure the North American frontier."

"The people in town make them sound like the Gestapo. There's real fear in some of their eyes," Sarah piped in.

"If it's all about border security, then why do we need an Inland Control Agency too?" Will asked. "Borders are on the periphery, not in the interior. And why are they expanding that service so much?" he added.

"Good questions, Will. So what do you think is really going on?"

Will thought it over for a moment. All of the Canadian ports of entry had been 'secured' and were now closed to civilian aircraft and foreign vessels.

"I think they're going to fish out those among us who they consider to be threats to national security."

"Right. Whose national security, Will?"

"The United States."

"Exactly. And at what cost?"

"Our freedom?"

To that, no answer was given, nor required.

~

As they paddled upstream back to Peterborough, Will was able to reflect upon the preparations they had seen in Trenton. He realized that they could soon be living in a police state. It all depended upon the outcome of the American election, but it seemed as though the anti-Canadian Kuhn was about to win a landslide victory.

These thoughts did not depress Will. He was too pragmatic. At the same time he was thinking these thoughts, the tranquil environment of the river removed him from the escalating conflict and helped put everything in perspective.

~

A few days after their return to the Hacker residence, the school year began and the professor went back to his classroom at the University. He planned to introduce his new students to the field of Canadian anthropology and indigenous studies by skipping textbook lessons and instead heading outdoors to live off the land as the original Canadians had done. In this way, he thought he could instil in his students a deeper, more personal understanding and appreciation of the subject.

He asked Will and Barry to join him as his assistants. Their recent trip had qualified them for the task and, as it promised to be another worthwhile experience, they both gladly accepted.

"I'd be happy to help, Professor," Will responded enthusiastically.

"Good. Then it's settled. I'll see to it that you're paid in real money, Will."

"That won't be necessary, I'm more than happy to help. Besides, you've done so much for me that I'm already in your debt. Helping out will enable me to balance our accounts and it will help me to hone my survival skills."

But the professor wouldn't have it.

"I decline your terms, Will. I won't have it any other way. I'll hire somebody else if you won't take payment. Besides, you pull your own weight, plus some, around our place."

They were at an impasse. Later, Will spoke to Barry about it. Barry offered Will a fresh perspective.

"Will, you have to understand my father's predicament. This is his job for which he gets paid. To him, it's a separate matter altogether from you being our guest. Besides, he's right. You do pull more than your weight around here. Cripes, you make me look like the freeloader."

Will accepted the professor's terms. The draw of the adventure and the risk of being left out countered his normal obstinacy about such matters.

Accepting the job delayed his departure for the west, but he justified the delay, thinking that a little more time with the professor would make him better prepared for his trip. Also, staying in the region kept him not too distant from his parents. He was still uneasy about them as they were situated in the area of greatest unrest and uncertainty.

It was late in September when they paddled away from campus with their canoes heavily laden with gear, food and tents. The most optimistic of the bunch thought of the three week excursion as a much-needed diversion from all the depressing news. A day or two into the voyage, rather than worrying about politics, they were soon worrying about how to adapt to a wilderness environment. Gaining control over their own situation brought immediate relief from the stress caused from worrying about the unknown. Gradually, the students began to understand and appreciate how their experience with the professor could provide them with another calling they'd never considered – living self-sufficiently.

The urgency of the times brought out the best of the professor. He had always lived for uncertain times, without which he considered life to be rather dull.

"It is required of a man to share the action and perils of his time to truly experience and appreciate living," he'd often said. Will believed he was quoting somebody he'd read. He meant to ask him sometime, but forgot.

The professor was on a mission, shifted into overdrive by the times, to instil in his students the basic knowledge and life skills that they would require when nobody else was there to depend on. He spoke of total and absolute system failure including no jobs, no social assistance and no medical care. It would have been more appropriate to call this course 'How to Survive Any Catastrophe 301'.

After a few days, the professor took away the tents. The choices for the group were to sleep under an overturned canoe or the stars or build a shelter. Next, he took away their matches. He replaced these with pieces of flint so the group learned how to make fire as the cavemen did. He led them north, deeper into the woods, took away their compasses and GPS devices and challenged them to find their way back to camp. Then he took from them their paper maps. They recalled the river lay to their south and so learned to navigate during the day by knowing that the sun rose in the east, set in the west and was due south at high noon. By night, they were guided by locating the North Star. The professor had taught them that civilization is always found downstream so once they found the river, it was easy.

"Therefore, safety is found upstream," he explained. It was all counterintuitive.

As their food supplies dwindled, the professor taught them how to recognize edible plants and to hunt and fish. To hunt successfully, they learned how to blend in with their environment and noiselessly stalk the prey. He taught them how to communicate noiselessly and work as a hunting team by signalling each other with their hands and imitating the sounds of animals.

"Shhhh." Professor Hacker would hiss. "Walk soundlessly like a Native wearing moccasins. Yes, that's better."

Along each step of the journey, a few students quit. They'd signed up to learn from textbooks rather than through personal experience. The remaining self-titled 'Trent Tribe' began to work as a food-seeking, shelter-building unit. They began to laugh and joke about whatever hardship the professor was conjuring up for them next.

"No paddles, sir? No problem! There's plenty of wood around to make another one."

"No bullets for the gun? Then we'll build a snare!"

Near the end of the three weeks, the tribe could see how proud the professor had become of them.

"We are restoring the balance," he would say.

In the end, less than half of the original class remained, but those who stayed had endured and surmounted every obstacle he threw in their way and knew they'd passed the highest test of all — the test of independent life.

~

During the three weeks, the group often visited a First Nations reserve. There, they learned about the native belief that reciprocity is the natural way of living with the Earth Mother.

"We too should live by reciprocity," the elders would say. "Giving is the natural way of the Earth and keeps things in balance. The Earth gives us so many things. The sun gives us warmth. The land gives us food. The lakes give us fish and water. To be in balance with nature, we too must give. If we only take, then we live out of balance with the Earth. We deplete the Earth and it will stop giving."

Their outdoor living experience made this outlook more sensible to the tribe and they were always relieved when those who didn't contribute to the tribe left. The tribe members learned that they were a micro-community, an example of how larger communities could live respecting the land, the earth and each other.

The elders looked at the post-Fermi world philosophically. Their prophesies foretold of some cataclysm that would signal the coming of the final days.

"We are living in Time of Death, the Time of Depletion."

"I wonder if this is to be the end of mankind's story, Will?"
Barry asked.

That question made Will think of Detroit, which lay only sixty kilometres northwest from where he grew up. Upon Detroit's founding in 1701, La Mothe Cadillac wrote to the King of France:

"This country, so temperate, so fertile, and so beautiful that it may justly be called the earthly paradise of North America, deserves all the care of the King to keep it up..."

"Deserves all the care.... to keep it up..." Will mumbled.

"What's that?" Barry wondered.

"Oh, nothing. Just talking to myself," Will answered, thinking how these words had fallen upon deaf ears. Detroit was no longer an earthly paradise. It had been depleted and knocked off balance so much that one could now barely see the earth under its decrepit pavement.

"They paved paradise and put in a parking lot," Barry sang aloud the song Will been unconsciously whistling. Detroit's many smokestacks belched smoke endlessly into its smog filled skies. Its pure water had been poisoned and cancer rates had skyrocketed. Fish now caught in the river had grown large tumours.

"Yes! And for what purpose?"

"Jobs." Barry answered.

"Where are they now? China? India? It has self-destructed. Depleted by greedy people who lived as though there was no tomorrow."

The elders seemed to know what was coming.

"The Time of Restoration is at hand," they'd said.

"When?" Will asked.

"When the tribes unite."

"What tribes?"

To this, the elders did not reply. Perhaps it was because they didn't know the answer. Or perhaps it was because they were afraid of the answer.

Will took it all in. At times, he felt more confused and then at other times, when he was amongst the trees in the wilderness, it all seemed to make sense. This was another reason he preferred the wilderness where he found freedom, a unique Canadian style of freedom, that only space can provide.

Under the encouraging guidance of the professor, the Trent Tribe flourished. Even though Will wasn't a student, he was conscious that the professor was evaluating him as well. Will felt frustrated. As much as he wanted to measure up to the professor's expectations, he didn't know by what standard he was being measured. He couldn't understand what quality the professor saw in him that had caught his mentoring interest. There were some in the tribe who were much better students than Will and there were those who were better at surviving in the wilderness and living self-sufficiently. Since Will couldn't figure out what it was that had caught the professor's interest, he decided to simply act like himself.

At the end of the three weeks, they all paddled back to the University's campus. With newfound pride and no fear in their disposition, they arrived with an esprit de corps and a confidence that they could take care of themselves. They parted ways, pledging to maintain the camaraderie of the Trent Tribe and meet again whenever future challenges should dictate.

~

Canadians still welcomed the incoming American refugees but, despite their extraordinary efforts, the numbers quickly overwhelmed regional relief efforts. Insufficient resources made it necessary to impose rationing, giving priority to women and children first. A small and angry faction of men weren't willing to queue for assistance and, thinking themselves justified, they helped themselves to whatever they needed. To them, it was simple justice in compensation for their losses. It became a daily occurrence for shops to be looted and homes to be robbed at gunpoint.

Business owners were dismayed. One day, they'd be in business and the next day, an angry mob of refugees would descend upon them in broad daylight, kick in their door and rob them of everything of value.

What made it worse was that the police and army were often present while the looting occurred. Even though Martial Law had been declared, it was only being enforced on Canadians and the officers did nothing to stop the American gangs. It was all part of Ottawa's appeasement policy.

Realizing that their government would not protect them, property owners took the defence of their properties into their own hands. Soon kicking in somebody's door could result in an open exchange of gunfire as property owners asserted their right of self-defence. Hindered this way, the looters then turned to their own government for support. The timing was perfect for Kuhn's campaign.

"How are the refugees to be compensated fairly for their losses?" was a key question the media put to the presidential candidates. Fairly is such a plastic word, therefore perfect for the lexicon of politicians.

"That's simple," assured Kuhn boldly. "I will make Canadians pay reparations to us. I promise to restore America's lost farmland, acre for acre," he pledged.

He didn't describe the details of his plan, but it was clear that his solution somehow involved Canadian farmland. His promises significantly improved his ratings in the polls, which meant everything in the golden days of unfettered democracy.

"I promise to restore America's food security and restock the grocery shelves," he declared, emboldened by his growing popularity and building upon the same theme.

"Frankly, there's no easy solution," the President countered. "Only one madman, acting alone, is responsible for orchestrating and carrying out the attack on Fermi. And that madman is now in God's hands and beyond the reach of us mortals. Canada is not to blame."

This was not what the public wanted to hear.

"The public treasury will fairly compensate Americans who have suffered losses," he offered.

"How?" demanded the media.

"We'll either have to reduce military expenditures or increase taxes," he answered.

"America's broke!" scoffed Kuhn at the President's suggestion to offer paper dollars from the already depleted public treasury.

The idea of receiving compensation in the form of the falling American dollar held no appeal to the public and Kuhn's offer of something more tangible and lasting seemed a much better deal.

~

Recalling the situation in Trenton had made Will fearful of the government.

"They're being trained to watch us all" and "To them, you're guilty until proven innocent" were unforgettable statements which echoed in his head.

"Whose side is Ottawa on?" asked Sarah.

"The side of serving and protecting America!" said Barry, concluding that the very institutions he'd thought were there to 'serve and protect' Canadians were instead being transformed into an instrument of their torment.

Without much knowledge as to the government's technological ability to spy on its citizens, Will's vivid imagination started to play a game of sorts. He presumed the government's dependence on technology could be its Achilles' heel and he set out to become completely low tech. This way, he hoped to disappear from the proverbial radar screen. This strategy was already within easy reach since he had recently been living without most modern conveniences and off the grid. Nonetheless, he had still been using his bank and Visa cards which could easily give away his whereabouts so he completely withdrew all his savings, paid off his Visa bill, then chopped the cards up into little tiny pieces and threw them away. Doing so brought an immediate sense of freedom.

He voiced his concerns, by land line, with Sydney. She was not at all surprised. She too had witnessed some disturbing happenings out west.

"Will, there was a man who lived nearby who was taken into custody for saying the wrong thing on the phone," she cautioned him. "Everyone believes that his conversation was being listened in on and taken the wrong way. He paid taxes, didn't have any police record and was born and educated in Canada. One evening, three RCMP constables came knocking at his door and took him away. Nobody has heard or seen anything of him since and some American refugees have now moved into his home."

The man Sydney described seemed as squeaky clean as he and Sydney. Yet that didn't stop the law from moving in on him. Sydney's story made it clear that all were vulnerable to government eavesdropping and Will resolved to minimize their contact, fearing that the same thing could happen to her. This suited Sydney, as she was also a realist, with heartfelt regret. But they both realized that they would have to be cautious about how they communicated with each other.

"We can e-mail each other through an anonymous hotmail account from a public internet café," Will suggested.

Taking it to the next level, they gave each other their secret Hotmail addresses through clues so that they wouldn't have to say them out loud on the phone. Luckily, they knew things about each other that nobody else would know.

"What's my favourite bird, Sydney?"

"That's too easy, Will. Anyone who knows you knows the answer to that question!"

"Ok, then where did we first kiss?"

"How can I ever forget? It's perfect. And nobody would ever believe it!"

"Exactly."

"Are you capitalizing the first letters only?"

"Yes."

"Perfect. Then I've got it. It's ten letters right?"

"Exactly."

"Ok, I'll email you and then you'll have mine as well. Love you, Will."

"Love you too, Syd."

~

A thick blanket of frost now covered the landscape every morning. The sight reminded Will that it was time to move on and continue on his journey back to Sydney. It was going to be difficult for him to say farewell to Barry and the professor for many reasons. His time with them had marked him for life. By providing him shelter from the external world, they had given him time to think and collect his thoughts.

Barry had become more than a best friend to Will. He was like a brother and the professor was like a father figure. The professor's calm outlook helped Will to make sense of all the babble. If the knowledge Will had gained in Toronto had been a step towards his personal enlightenment, his time with the professor was a giant leap. Yet when he was alone, Will still felt somewhat incomplete and remained anxious about leaving behind such a solid character during these volatile times.

The professor, Barry, Sarah and Will had just finished a splendid meal and were sitting around the dining table when, out of the blue, Will decided to make his departure plans known.

"I plan to leave tomorrow," he announced after their meal, "and I want to thank each one of you for everything you've done for me. You made me feel like a member of your family and I look forward to seeing you all again." Then, turning to the professor, he added, "You've helped me sort out a lot of things, Professor, things that seemed so complex and out of control. Now things make sense and I think I can manage on my own," he reemphasized to the professor, "but I'm going to miss your guidance."

"I expected you would be leaving us tomorrow, Will. I too have noticed the frosty mornings. Tonight's meal was a special send-off. That's why I wanted Sarah to be here as well. This way, you part from the same company you found when you arrived. And the birthday cake Sarah baked represents a new beginning for you."

Will had noticed the cake with a candle stuck in it and wondered whose birthday it was. He never guessed it was to be his own. The professor got up and walked over to the book shelf which took up most of one wall in the living room. After a few moments of reflection, he seemed to come to a decision and took a particular book off the library shelf.

"Woo-ugh," he blew a thick layer of dust off it, then walked back to the dining table and laid it down before Will.

"A parting gift, Will," he said. "Should Kuhn win the presidency, as I expect he will, I think you will find this little souvenir to be a valuable companion."

"Thank you," said Will not understanding its significance. He had perused many of the professor's books during his stay, but he hadn't noticed this one.

Will picked it up and examined it. It was not an ordinary book. The leather book cover lacked any writing except for the signature:

Above the illegible signature was a coat of arms that contained the image of a badger and a fleur-de-lis. The book appeared to be very old. Will looked up questioningly at the professor.

"Open it, Will."

As he did, Will discovered that he was holding the personal diary of Sir Isaac Brock, the Hero of Upper Canada, under whose leadership the ill-supported Canadians had rallied and turned the tables on the American invaders in 1812. Will knew his history and he knew Brock's deeds had fortified the Canadian public's morale when they had almost lost hope in that seemingly unequal contest. It was the perfect parting gift because it was such a parallel to the present troubled times. The mere thought of Brock's exploits made Will feel hopeful. He could only imagine how much more he would be inspired by reading Brock's account in his own words.

"It's not unlike our times. But I…" Words failed him.

"It's the same storyline, Will."

"But I can't accept this. It's a treasure."

"All right. Then let's call it a loan. You're only borrowing it. Is that better?"

Will smiled gratefully in response.

"Yes, it is a treasure, Will, and you must treat it as such. Not only because it's old, but also because of its secrets. Secrets that will help you manage during these trying times."

"I believe its secrets will reveal themselves to you," the professor continued, "when the time is right. But be careful with it," he warned. "Even though most readers would fail to grasp its message, some would. And those who would may be enemies – so keep its existence a secret."

"I will," Will promised. With that explanation, he felt as though he held onto the most important book in the world.

"Thank you. Professor…?"

"Yes, Will?"

"May I ask how you got this?"

"In June, I was doing some research in the University library and found it in an unmarked box in the archives. It must have been placed there by accident, possibly from some earlier move, and become forgotten or lost. It could easily have been discarded. Knowing it wouldn't be missed, I took it home and, reading it, I discovered its value."

"How do you think the University got it?"

"That's a harder question to answer. Brock's final wish was for a token of remembrance to be given to his sister, Elizabeth, after his death. After reviewing the historical records, I believe the token she received was his diary. I believe she later passed the diary to Brock's niece, Harriet. Harriet married a Captain Robert Pengelley who was appointed agent for the Brock estate in Canada, including 3,000 acres near Peterborough. After the Pengelleys died, their own diaries and other materials were donated to Trent University. There is no official record that Brock's diary was part of that donation. I can only surmise that it was either mistaken for something of no value or the University somehow just lost track of it. Regardless, here it is."

"Why are you giving it to me?"

"Because I think you'll identify well with Brock and his life. You possess a strong mind, you're courageous and you have a natural ability to relate to others. I've seen how you make friends by earning the trust and respect of people. You have a talent for bringing different people together. Brock's characteristics were exactly what Canada needed in 1812. You will come across many people in your travels and I think that those characteristics you share with Brock will serve you well. I believe that his diary may inspire you as the current political situation unfolds. This is why it's the perfect parting gift to you. May it help to guide you on your path."

~

Exhausted, Will slipped beneath the covers of his bed that night. In doing so, he picked up Brock's diary one more time. Opening it to a page bookmarked by the professor, the words on the page jumped out at him.

> *Is he equal to fill the situation? Has he discretion, and is he distinguished by a strong mind and undaunted courage, as these are qualities that can alone be serviceable at such a crisis?*

He read on.

...the task imposed on you, on the present occasion, is arduous; this task, however, I hope and trust, laying aside every consideration but that of the public good, you will perform with that firmness, discretion, and promptitude, which a regard to yourselves, your families, your country, and your king, call for at your hands.

Will felt as if Brock was speaking directly to him, personally charging him with that arduous task. He was determined to rise to the challenge.

~

CHAPTER VIII

Terre De Nos Aïeux

"Make the strangers welcome in this Land, let them
keep their languages and customs, for weak and
fragile is the realm which is based on a single language or on a single set of customs."
— Excerpt from Saint Stephen's admoni-
tions to his son Prince Emeric, 1034

~

Will rode into North Bay on November 2nd. Once there, he realized how close he was to the Province of Québec. He had always
been fascinated by the French language and he felt drawn to go
to Québec to experience the culture there. Although he had fully
intended to go directly home to Sydney, he spontaneously decided
to turn east. He had a faint sense that if he immersed himself in a
place where he couldn't understand the language, he would find
refuge from all the madness of human affairs that kept intruding
upon his life. It would give him solitude and time to think.

Perhaps he was also subconsciously under the influence of the
words he'd read in Brock's diary that morning.

> *...It was my decided intention to ask for leave to go
> to England this fall, but I have now relinquished the
> thought. Several untoward circumstances combine
> to oppose my wishes. The spirit of insubordination
> lately manifested by the French Canadian
> population of this colony naturally called for
> precautionary measures, and our worthy chief is*

induced, in consequence, to retain in this country those on whom he can best confide… fate decrees that the best portion of my life is to be wasted in inaction in the Canadas…

The first obstacle blocking Will's path into Québec was the mighty Ottawa River. At its bank, he turned downstream and continued on to Rapides-des-Joachims where he came upon a bridge crossing over the river.

Winter was gaining on him as he rode his bike into Québec. His progress diminished in proportion to the daylight hours as the days grew shorter and shorter. During the day, he tried to put as many miles behind him as he could and then, at dusk, he tried to find a suitable place, preferably beneath the cover of trees, to set up his tent. There, he would shiver through the night, looking forward to the following day when the spinning of his legs would again circulate his blood and generate some warmth in his body.

Eat-ride, eat-ride, eat-sleep and repeat was his daily fare. Quite often, he slept in graveyards amongst quiet and incurious neighbours. Slowly but surely, the numbing cold forced him to acknowledge that he needed to find better lodging for the winter than his tent. Even the first Canadians had to settle down in their wigwams and log cabins in wintertime. Like those earlier generations, this became his primary objective.

~

…the American government is determined to involve the two countries in a war; they have already given us legitimate cause, but, if wise, we will studiously avoid doing that for which they shew so great an anxiety. Their finances, you will perceive, are very low, and they dare not propose direct taxes.

Most Canadians hoped and prayed that the President would be re-elected, but instead, America elected Kuhn as the forty-fifth

President of the United States. Desperate times had dictated drastic change at the top.

Kuhn's 'triple hammer' platform had been built upon three allegations. The first was that Canadian security measures were so inadequate that reliable American forces must be sent there to secure the porous border. Secondly, he alleged that Canada was already a haven for terrorists planning to attack America, so a primary goal of the American forces would be to seek, find and secure every potential terrorist being harboured in Canada. Thirdly, he declared that Canada must accept responsibility for the destruction of Fermi and pay for the loss of life and property resulting from it. America would extract reparations from Canada to compensate the fallout victims for their losses.

In effect, Kuhn had promised that Canada was to come under the complete control of America. Suddenly, America's future seemed brighter as Kuhn's *Canadian Solution* answered all of their economic and security problems.

The Dow Jones had a momentary heyday. Canada had surplus farmland, fresh water, raw materials and energy resources for everyone. It was the land of plenty. Without concern for the human side of the equation, Wall Street coldly calculated the cost-benefit ratio of the Canadian takeover. In those terms, it was a windfall for the US as Canada possessed all the natural resources and assets America needed. The American stock market found its legs and rebounded dramatically in the aftermath of Kuhn's victory. Having full access to Canada's resources would free America from the need for foreign resources, including oil. In consequence, other markets around the world plummeted.

If anything positive thing could be said about President-elect Kuhn's platform from the Canadian perspective, it was that Canadians themselves became more aware of and began to better appreciate what they had. Unfortunately, America had already staked its claim. It was too late. The final chapter of America's Manifest Destiny doctrine was about to be written.

~

*Sir George Prevost was pursuing a suicidal course,
as to wait for the enemy till he shall have prepared
his forces and passed your frontiers, to plunder
your towns and occupy your country, is a very
recent expedient recognized by no government, and
practised by no people of ancient or modern times.*

As a last ditch attempt to calm the American rhetoric and
to demonstrate the Canadian resolve for change, the Minority
Government of Canada was quickly brought down by a non-confi-
dence vote. Although the ousted Prime Minister, with an aptitude
for working harmoniously with the Americans, was probably the
best person for the job, the perceived need for drastic change in
Ottawa sent him packing.

Newly elected Canadian Prime Minister Gage did his utmost to
appease and pacify the Americans by assuring them of Canada's
friendship and his government's resolve and commitment to
cooperate with the American forces. Much to-do was made by the
Canadian press about Gage's trip to Washington to meet, befriend
and congratulate President Kuhn in person; however, an embarrassed Gage returned to Ottawa without having met any senior
American government official, including the new president.

Not only did Gage receive the cold-shoulder treatment in
Washington, but upon his return to Ottawa, the American ambassador publicly presented to him a long list of grievances, including
a demand that Canada officially apologize for its lax immigration
policies and publicly acknowledge that those policies directly led
to the Fermi disaster. It was obvious that the demand was to be the
legal footing upon which Kuhn's reparation plan was to be built.
Gage acquiesced, hoping that by doing so it would be enough to
satisfy the insatiable Kuhn.

"PM signs Canada's dead warrant!" proclaimed the
Canadian press.

Two days later, an angry mob descended upon Parliament and
the Prime Minister's Ottawa residence. Protests were staged all
across the country and polls showed near unanimous outrage at
what Gage had done. To protect himself, the new PM slipped out
of the country. His departure left Canada without a leader.

In response, Kuhn decreed that he and his administration would assume the responsibilities of the PM's office until peace in Canada was restored after which another free democratic election, under the careful watch of the President, would be conducted.

Parliamentary Members accepted that it was only a matter of time before they too would be forced to succumb to Washington's demands. In protest, most publicly resigned and returned to their home ridings. In doing so, they gave up their salaries and gold-plated pensions. It was the boldest act of defiance most living Canadians had ever witnessed coming from Ottawa.

~

The Canadian private sector reacted to the American agenda by preparing for the worst. Knowing they could not depend on their own government anymore, fewer and fewer remitted their interim tax instalments, knowing full well that collecting taxes had become one of their government's least concerns. Having its funding foundation pulled out from under it, like a bunch of dominos that had nothing left to lean on, the Canadian public sector came apart at the seams.

~

Will awoke shivering. It was still dark and unusually calm and quiet. He pressed the light button on his watch. It was 9:10 am and he'd overslept.

Sitting up, his head hit the roof of the sagging tent and the impact caused a mini avalanche. Suddenly, it was brighter.

'It must have snowed overnight,' he thought.

Winter had caught and overtaken him. Unzipping the tent's fly, he peered out into a winter wonderland. Everything was so peaceful and silent. The boughs of the pine trees were bowed under the heavy weight of their snowy loads. The sun glowed through a light haze that blanketed the sky. Out of habit, he reached for his waterbottle. It was frozen solid.

Feeling a new sense of urgency, he quickly packed up his things, unburied his bike and BOB trailer and then began pushing them, with great difficulty, along the same road he'd been travelling on the previous day. He had no idea of what lay ahead of him. He only knew that he couldn't stay put there or he'd freeze to death. And so he simply kept moving.

After a couple of hours of slogging over a snow covered road, a lone 4X4 pick-up truck, sporting a snow shovel on its nose, passed by.

The driver slowed and came to a stop. After a few moments, the driver backed up and came to stop right beside Will. The elderly man behind the wheel rolled down his window. The features on his ruddy face were deeply creased and his watery eyes were slightly bloodshot.

"*Bonjour, monsieur. Vous voulez un lift quelque part?*" ["Would you like a ride somewhere?"]

"No, Mar-cee." Will hadn't a clue of what he said, but deep within his memory banks, he was able to retrieve some semblance of his grade school French.

It seemed that the driver was about to drive off when the woman seated next to him jabbed him in the ribs to get his attention. Will waited as they exchanged a few words after which she leaned over to get a better look at him. She had a kind face and sparkling blue eyes. Will surmised that she had probably been a beautiful woman in her younger days. She must have liked what she saw too for, a moment later, she instructed, "Get in, m'sieur," with a slight Québécois accent.

"Oh. No…thank…you…ma'am," Will stammered. He knew he looked and sounded like an idiot.

'Why was I speaking slowly,' he wondered. 'Her English was fine.'

"Where are you going?" she asked, not satisfied with his response.

"I don't know, ma'am. East," he answered honestly.

"You have to be going somewhere. And if it's east, your journey will soon end for this is a dead-end road." She glanced down at his frozen water bottle. "*Mon Dieu!* You can't stay outdoors on a day like this." After a moment's hesitation, she came to a resolution. "Get in. You must come with us or you'll freeze to death."

Will was in no position to argue. He knew she was right. So he swallowed his pride and loaded his bike and trailer onto the bed of their truck along with the rest of his gear and then got into their cab.

Within minutes, the heat inside the cab hit him like a ton of bricks. Soon, he was soaking wet as the frozen moisture trapped in his clothing melted. Bit by bit, he stripped off a layer of sweat-soaked clothing until he was down to his last base layer. Feeling faint, he cracked his window slightly for a breath of fresh air.

It was only then that he noticed the couple had stopped talking and were watching him with concern in their eyes. Will spoke first.

"Mar-cee... poor...la...ride," he stammered. "Jeuh...may-pell... Will. William Anderson," he said, pointing at himself.

She smiled at his clumsy effort.

"Pleasure to meet you, William. I am Madame La Forêt and our overly suspicious driver here is my husband, Robert. He suspects that you are in trouble. Perhaps a criminal on the run or perhaps even a terrorist trying to evade the Americans?"

Before Will could answer, she continued.

"Well you don't look like either to me. So tell us, William, what were you doing walking along the road with your bike on a day like this?"

Will realized that anything he had to tell about his journey was probably less than M'sieur La Forêt had imagined. So Will freely explained who he was, where he was from and how he came to be there that snowy day.

After hearing what he had to say, Madame La Forêt spoke with her husband in French. Occasionally, they glanced back at him through the rear view mirror. Madame La Forêt did most of the talking. Whatever it was they were saying, it was obvious they were not in full agreement as their conversation rose and fell repeatedly for what seemed an uncomfortably long period of time. Monsieur La Forêt seemed to need a lot of convincing, but eventually Madame La Forêt won and turned back to face Will again.

"William, you must come and stay with us."

"Mar-cee," Will replied as he realized he had no other option.

Together, the three of them drove into town and picked up some groceries and supplies. In return for their assistance, Will offered them money, but on the verge of being offended, they flatly refused.

Will stood his ground.

"I can find somewhere else to stay here in town. I'm sure somebody here will gladly accept my money." Then, looking straight into the eyes of Madame La Forêt, he added, "I'm not going accept charity, ma'am."

She returned his look and then smiled.

"You'll be better off with us, William," she cautioned. Taking some dollars from his hand, she added, "Let's just call this gas money. Merci, William. But no more. Once we get back to our place, there'll be plenty for you to do to earn your keep. Our home is just a small cabin in the woods. It's no Taj Mahal."

"Compared to my tent, anything will feel like the Taj Mahal, madame! Merci," said Will, smiling proudly at her. Having listened to them carefully, he'd now learned how to pronounce 'merci' correctly.

~

The La Forêts' log cabin was situated in the middle of an open meadow where the sun's rays would find it in every season of the year, particularly in winter when the light and warmth was needed most. The meadow was fronted on three sides by a large forest. The cleared side faced the south and afforded a fine view down to the lake and the road which paralleled its shore.

Behind the cabin was a small shed which had a fenced area beside it, denoting a small garden which lay buried beneath the white covering of snow. A trampled snow-covered trail led off into a dense pine forest out of which rose jagged granite cliffs.

Facing the lake and the sunny side of the cabin was a porch upon which two benches stood beneath windows situated on either side of the main entrance. Upon one sat a healthy looking man of about Will's age, dozing in the warmth of the sun. His complexion was darker than Will's and he wore his straight chestnut brown hair tied back in a tight ponytail. As Will walked up to the cabin, the man lifted his face, revealing his piercing blue eyes. Will did not need to be told that he was the son of Madame La Forêt.

Madame La Forêt's son showed no inclination to recognize their arrival, his cool reception betraying his reservation toward strangers. A mutt lying at his feet showed more interest in their approach by cocking his head and raising an ear. His wagging tail betrayed that he was friendly.

"Bonjour, Yves," Madame La Forêt began. *"Nous avons amené quelqu'un ici avec nous et je voudrais que tu fasses sa connaissance. Yves, voici William Anderson. William va rester avec nous pendant un certain temps. Ça va être une bonne occasion pour toi d'améliorer ton anglais."* ["We've brought somebody home with us whom I'd like you to meet. Yves, this is William Anderson. William will be staying with us for a while. It'll be a good opportunity for you to improve your English."]

After addressing her son, she then turned to Will. "William, this is our son Yves." Will nodded and extended his right hand out in greeting.

Half-heartedly, Yves shook his hand.

"Allô," Yves grunted.

Madame La Forêt gave Yves a disappointed look and then opened the front door which led into the cabin.

"Come, Will, I'll show you around."

Entering the cabin, they came into the main room which took up most of the space. Immediately to the right of the door were a number of open faced cupboards and hooks for storing boots and outdoor clothing. Across the room stood a long table around which five chairs were situated along with a bench which had been built into the far wall. The entire left side was used for sleeping. Two bedrooms had been framed at floor level, equally dividing that side of the cabin, above which was an open loft that stretched across the entire span. A ladder, situated midway between the two bedroom doors, led from the planked main floor up to the loft.

"You'll sleep in the loft, William," said Madame La Forêt.

Suspended above the open area was a drying rack full of clothes which had been loaded on the lower level and then hoisted aloft by means of a rope tied off near the ladder.

On the wall opposite to the entrance was the wood burner used for heating the entire cabin. It was lit and two kettles rested on top of it. Will followed Madame La Forêt into the kitchen where pots were hanging down from hooks screwed into the round roof beams. At the far end of the kitchen was another door that led outdoors to the outhouse.

"Bienvenue chez les La Forêts, William."

~

Yves was very uncomfortable with Will staying in the cabin and Will knew it. To Yves, Will was a stranger who'd imposed himself and his English ways upon their family. Yves put up with Will being there out of respect for his mother, but he found it annoying when his parents spoke with Will in English. Whenever this happened, he would leave the cabin. Monsieur La Forêt would then look at Will and shrug his shoulders as if to ask 'what can I do?'

Madame La Forêt sensed that, under the surface, Will and Yves were very much alike and she suspected that, in the right environment, they could become friends. Whenever Yves stormed out of the cabin, she would urge Will to go outdoors and help Yves with whatever work he was giving his attention to. Although Will felt uncomfortable around Yves, he wanted to show his gratitude and so he did as she asked.

At first, this strategy only added to Yves' irritation and, feeling bitter about Will's intrusion, Yves would simply return indoors and leave Will to work outside alone. This was fine as far as Will was concerned but didn't sit well with Yves either, as he did not like Will labouring outdoors in the fresh air and sunshine for their benefit. Yves wanted to be working outdoors too and so, eventually, he became resigned to Will's presence.

Slowly they began to accept each other. As they grew more accustomed to each other's abilities, they began to coordinate their work for better efficiency. Working together replaced the need for idle conversation. Finding themselves to be an efficient team and working in an environment they both related to, they bridged their linguistic differences and soon began to realize how alike they really were. They both had a love of the land, the forest, the water and the animals. These things they shared together were real and bonded them together more than words ever could. When they didn't talk, they had complete communion with one another. Their initial preconceptions were gradually broken into petty pieces.

It was only when Will broke the silence and spoke in English that Yves was jolted back to his old prejudices, but week by week, as Will acquired more French, this occurred less and less frequently.

Often, Will would see Madame La Forêt peeking out at them through the curtained windows as if to reassure herself that they weren't fighting. Will imagined that seeing them working together harmoniously made her happy. He would chop wood while Yves carried armloads of logs over to the cabin and stack them neatly. Yves would pump water up from the well while Will held onto the bucket. They also enjoyed fishing together, but it was when they went hunting that they found the full measure of their coordinated teamwork.

Will had honed his hunting skills during his time with the Hackers whereas Yves had a military background, serving as a sniper with *le Régiment Nordique* in Afghanistan. As a sniper, Yves was a crack shot with a rifle, but favoured hunting with a bow. To hunt with a bow and not cause an animal undue pain, one had to have perfect aim. Under Yves' tutoring, Will became a proficient shot with the silent bow.

On December 25th, they all celebrated a comfortable Christmas meal indoors as a family. As a clear demonstration of how their united effort benefited everyone, Yves and Will had provided wild venison, fish and partridge to grace the table.

~

At night, up in the loft, under the flickering light of a candle, or sometimes from oil lamps casting their soft light about the interior from the room below, Will found time to relax and to read Brock's diary. Although he presumed that the professor had overstated its meaning, he welcomed having something interesting to read. From the moment he opened its cover, he couldn't put it down. The similarities between Brock's times and his own grabbed his attention and drew him into Brock's world. The recurring subject matter of troubled relations between Canada and the United States made the diary still relevant. As the professor had said, 'the story of man is one continuous circle.'

The diary became Will's porthole between the past and the present. History was replaying an old theme. The Canadians were currently outnumbered ten to one, but that had also been the case in 1812. Realizing that gave Will confidence that there was a way to counter America's seemingly overwhelming might. It restored his hope for the future.

Brock's diary anchored Will and helped him speak about current events with a insightful, objective view. Those who met Will that winter met a man full of confidence and old world wisdom and, since the Québécois were so very connected with their own past, many were drawn to him for that simple reason. He soon earned a reputation amongst them for being an honest Englishman.

That winter, news of Anderson's sincerity spread far and wide throughout rural Québec. Like Brock before him, they were glad to have Will among them and he felt honoured to have earned their trust and respect. He also felt the irony of the change in just two months from being a mistrusted stranger to now living amongst friends.

'In Québec of all places,' he thought.

~

It may appear surprising that men, petted as they have been and indulged in every thing they could desire, should wish for a change. But so it is — and I am apt to think that were Englishmen placed in the same situation, they would shew even more impatience to escape from French rule.

Once again, Brock's timeless words helped Will to put things in their right perspective.

~

One day, while they were working outside together, Will did something that annoyed Yves. "*Non, c'est pas comme ça qu'on fait ça. Anderson, t'es vraiment stupide!*" ["No, that's not how it's done. Anderson, you are truly stupid!"] Yves grabbed away the object of concern, punctuating his annoyance with a final insult.

"*Maudits Anglais!* " ["Damn English!"]

"Mais je ne suis pas Anglais. Je suis Canadien." ["But, I'm not English. I'm Canadian."]

"Tu es vraiment con, Anderson. Ce que tu dis n'a aucun sens. Si tu n'es pas anglais, ben moi je suppose que j'suis pas français?" ["You're truly an imbecile, Anderson. If you're not English, then I suppose I'm not French?"]

"Tu n'es pas aussi intelligent que tu le crois. Mon nom, c'est Anderson...et Anderson, c'est un nom Scandinave mon ami. Je suis de descendance scandinave et non anglaise." ["You're not as intelligent as you think. My name is Anderson... and it's a Scandinavian name my friend. I'm a descendant of Scandinavians, not the English."]

"Mais tu parles anglais. C'est tout ce qui compte!" ["But you speak English. That's all that matters."]

"Je parle français maintenant, mon ami, au cas où t'avais pas remarqué." ["I'm speaking French right now, my friend, in case you hadn't noticed."]

The fact that Yves hadn't noticed that they were conversing fluently in French was a testament to how much Will's language skills had improved.

"C'est vrai, mon ami," Yves conceded. Perplexed, he furrowed his brows in thought.

Will continued, giving Yves something more to think about.

"Par conséquent, je suis une personne de descendance scandinave qui vit au Canada et qui parle anglais et français. Avec un nom comme 'La Forêt', tu es une personne de descendance française qui vit au Canada et qui aussi parle anglais et français." ["By coincidence, I am a descendant of Scandinavians, but I live in Canada and speak English and French. With a name like La Forêt, you're a French descendant who lives in Canada and who also speaks English and French."]

"Je suis Québécois."

Suddenly, it all made sense to Will. Americans aren't English, but they speak English. Mexicans aren't Spaniards, but they speak Spanish. Same with Canadians who are neither English nor French. They simply speak English and French and often other languages.

Yves was a proud Québécois, but he wasn't any more French than Will was English. Any Frenchman in France or Englishman in England would have told them that.

'They should be proud! And they should not forget their story,' Will thought. *'Je me souviens.'*

Then another thought crossed Will's mind, but he didn't discuss it with Yves. 'Yves is a Québécois. But is he also a loyal Canadian? Could one be both? And if it came down to another contest between Canada and the United States, would Yves be a Québécois-Canadien and stand together with all Canadians, or would he turn his back on us? Would he truly remember?'

~

CHAPTER IX

Then Conquer We Must

"The acquisition of Canada this year, as far as the neighborhood of Quebec, will be a mere matter of marching, and will give us experience for the attack on Halifax the next..."
— Thomas Jefferson in a letter to Colonel William Duane, August 4, 1812

~

"That the whole continent of North America and all of its adjacent islands must at last fall under the control of the United States is a conviction absolutely ingrained in our people."
— Henry Adams, 1869

~

It was Inauguration Day for President Kuhn. That evening, a crowd of friends and family were invited to the La Forêts' cabin to listen to Kuhn's inauguration speech on the radio. They had radios in their own homes, but they came to hear Anderson's interpretation. In preparation, Will had gone through Brock's Diary in search of some inspiration.

The president's address is sufficiently hostile, and if I thought that he would be supported to the extent of his wishes, I should consider war to be inevitable.

...it only awaited a favourable moment to invade the Canadas, which were supposed ripe for revolt and would therefore fall an easy conquest...

...Are the inhabitants of Canada prepared to become willing subjects, or rather slaves, to the despot who rules... with a rod of iron? If not, arise in a body, exert your energies, co-operate cordially with the king's regular forces to repel the invader, and do not give cause to your children, when groaning under the oppression of a foreign master, to reproach you with having so easily parted with the richest inheritance of this earth...

We are engaged in an awful and eventful contest. By unanimity and dispatch in our councils, and by vigour in our operations, we may teach the enemy this lesson, that a country defended by free men enthusiastically devoted to the cause of their king and constitution, can never be conquered!

By speech time, everyone had a beer in their hands and the cabin was so full of people that their combined body heat warmed the interior. Despite the freezing temperatures outside, windows had to be opened to release the trapped heat and let in some fresh air.

"*Taisez-vous tout l'monde!*" ["Shush everybody!"], barked Yves as the President was about to speak.

Good evening.

My fellow Americans, a year ago today, we believed we were secure from international terrorism. Over a decade had passed since 9/11 and nothing else had happened.

Then, while our troops fought valiantly on foreign battle-fields, we experienced here at home the most horrific attack in human history.

Following that attack, the former President called for laying down our arms and capitulating to our enemies. I could not believe my ears when he said 'Let us sheath the sword.'

The attack and his lack of response shook America right to its roots and divided it into two camps. Once again, we were on the verge of Civil War.

Who does he represent, I wondered? Surely not the American people I know! For Americans I know don't sheath their swords! Instead they sharpen their swords, lower their visors and conquer their enemies!

That was when I realized that America was not being lead by a suitable president. America needs a president willing and able to face any challenge, no matter how horrific, with great resolve. A president who would establish, once and for all, America's rightful place in the world. A president not chained to the old party politics.

Then, out of the ashes and destruction of Fermi arose the Continental Party of America and they chose me as their leader. I couldn't join the old parties because they led America down the wrong path, encouraging economic expansion abroad so our troops had to be sent overseas to defend those interests. That reckless path made enemies abroad and ultimately exposed our economy, our way of life, to attack. Inevitably, that policy led to 9/11 and Fermi. The old parties led us astray.

There were those who said that Americans would never elect a president running under the banner of a new party. Today, we are vindicated and my victory is your victory.

Tomorrow, as your President, I will lead America down a different path, a path that will lead to bringing all of our overseas interests and troops back to North America where they belong. A path which calls us to bring the whole continent of North America under our control.

Securing North America is our ultimate destiny and always has been. During the latter part of the 20th Century, America lost sight of that goal. Fermi horrifically demonstrated the cost of that mistake and proved without a doubt that the real war is in North America, and that includes Canada.

Our path was not unknown to our predecessors. Once we were 13 states and now we are 50. Historically, whenever we became overcrowded and our wants couldn't be provided at home, we solved that problem through expansion across North America where we could guarantee our security. This will be our path once more.

Today, you have elected me as your leader. Together, we embody the true spirit of America. This spirit will get us back on track, back on the road to greater heights.

The Continental Party of America reflects the rebirth of America, reborn to become greater than ever before so that nobody will be able to threaten or challenge us ever again.

We will fight a winnable war. It's winnable because, this time, we will not depend upon our allies who desert us on the battlefield. This time we cannot lose. As Thomas Jefferson said: 'It is a mere matter of marching.'

And we will not stop there. Due to Fermi's destruction, we have lost irreplaceable land, precious resources and critical energy generation capacity. Canada is responsible for this and they will pay for our losses with their land and resources. This I promise you.

With Canada, will come a brighter future. Our greatest vulnerability is that we do not have sufficient domestic energy and natural resources to maintain our envied standard of living. We been held hostage too long because of our dependence on others for their resources.

The Continental Party of America does not ask you to humble yourselves by lowering your standard of living. In fact, with the untapped resources that will soon be available to us, we will raise America's standard of living to new heights! And we will also guarantee that, once again, Americans will live in peace and security under the banner of *American Liberty* which includes civil, political, and religious liberty. Those three pillars have historically given guidance to our councils and energy to our conduct. Those liberties conducted us safely and triumphantly through the stormy periods of the past and have raised us to an elevated rank among the nations of the world. To those liberties, we will add freedom from terrorism.

The Continental Party of America has promised to free you from terror. Not only will we deliver on that promise, we will do so without asking Americans to lessen their wants as the former President did when he told you our country 'abounds in the necessities' and that 'we can do without the luxuries'.

We will do so by taking another path, a path that will not compromise America's security and a path that will free us from foreign oil, bring freshwater to the arid southern states and replace the farmland lost in the Midwest.

My fellow Americans, this is the Final War of American Independence and our victory will ensure our rightful place in the world.

To be independent from the Old World, we must have the ability to isolate ourselves from them in any shape or form – for now and forever.

Winning the Final War of Independence requires that we must be independent of their unreliable armies, independent of their envious anti-America mindset, independent of their slave produced goods and services and independent of their filthy oil, energy and natural resources.

Complete independence requires that we sever our umbilical cord with the Old World. Then, if they want to access our market, it will be on our terms.

To achieve this, we must first completely seal off the North American perimeter with reliable forces and then we must only source our oil, energy and natural resources from North America.

So, effective tonight, we are declaring our complete independence from the Old World and, in doing so, we will realize the ultimate dream of our forefathers.

Finally, I say this to our Canadian neighbours, our fellow North Americans. Now is the moment. You are either with us or against us. Do not doubt for one moment our resolve to prevail. Tomorrow and the days to come will be days of action on a scale never before seen on the North American continent. We will not rest until those who are America's enemies are vanquished from the continent – when our complete economic independence and freedom from terror has been won.

Thank you. Good night. And God bless America.

~

Yves turned off the radio. Maurice Lachance spoke first.
"*Que le Canada aille se faire foutre! Laissez les Américains faire ce qu'ils ont à faire. On devrait même les aider. Eux ils vont nous récompenser pour être leurs alliés...eux vont nous donner notre juste liberté. Je suis d'accord avec le Président. Il est grand temps que les Québécois se libèrent des chaînons de leurs oppresseurs. Vive le Québec libre!*" ["I say to hell with Canada! Let the Americans have their way. In fact, we should help them. The Americans will reward us for being their allies and grant us our rightful liberty from the English. I agree with the President. Now is

the time for Québeckers to throw off the chains of our oppressors. Vive le Québec libre!"]

A few others nodded their heads in agreement. Maurice was well known for his extreme separatist views and his reaction was predictable. Still, for many in the room, his words seemed unduly harsh and didn't mesh with their own life experiences. Many had friends and family living in other provinces outside of Québec who would say, just as convincingly, that the federal government favoured French-speaking people. No other province had sent more Prime Ministers to Ottawa than Québec. That was an undeniable fact.

Will could hardly believe his ears. From reading Brock's diary, he'd discovered that Brock had worried about Québec's loyalty too. Brock's worst fear was that those who called for an independent Lower Canada would succeed. Brock feared that the French people in Canada might be persuaded to join the Americans and Napoleon's France in an alliance to attack Canada. The separatists in that day promised, like Maurice, that by doing so, they would win their independence. Brock knew that, with a hostile province in his rear and the American forces in his front, he couldn't possibly hold onto Upper Canada. His success depended on Québec remaining loyal. As Will saw it, it was the same old theme, only different players.

It took a few moments for the murmuring to die down.

"Qu'en penses-tu Will?" asked Madame La Forêt. ["So what do you think, Will?"]

For a moment, Will remained silent in order to compose his thoughts. With emotions running high, he knew that he had to choose his words carefully.

Everyone gathered around him felt his intensity and knew that what he was about to say came straight from his heart. It was what they'd come to expect from Anderson.

"Comme l'a dit le Général Isaac Brock, je pense que, sans le Québec, le Canada n'est rien du tout." ["In the words of General Isaac Brock, I think that, without Québec, there is no Canada."]

Maurice beamed with delight. To his surprise, it seemed that Will agreed with him. Everyone was taken aback by Will's words and commotion filled the room. Will raised his arm to ask for silence and, as the others became quiet, he continued.

"*Je vous le répète: sans le Québec, il n'y a pas de Canada. Et savez-vous quoi: je suis sûr que plusieurs d'entre nous ne seraient pas capables de se retourner contre le Canada. Qui d'entre nous peut affirmer avoir été offusqué par un Canadien? En plus, aucun pays au monde n'a connu une telle prospérité et une croissance aussi rapide que le nôtre! Mais je sais bien aussi que ce n'est pas uniquement la prospérité économique qui vous fera rester dans le Canada. Autant je crois que sans le Québec, le Canada n'existe pas...et bien que le contraire est aussi vrai : sans le Canada, le Québec n'est rien non plus! Et ça, je suis sûr que vous le savez autant que moi!* "* ["As I said, without Québec, there is no Canada. But I also believe that there are not many here who would turn against Canada. Who among us can truly say that they have been injured by the Canadian people? Where else in the world can be found a growth in wealth and prosperity as rapid as this country has had? But it is not for economic reasons alone that I believe you'll stay with Canada. Just as I believe that, without Québec, there is no Canada, I equally believe that, without Canada, there is no Québec. And I believe you know this too."]

"*Donc je vous le dis vive un Québec et un Canada unis!*" ["So I say long live Québec and Canada united!"]

In a couple of weeks, many more Québeckers heard Anderson's words. In their hearts and minds, they knew he had spoken the simple truth. They also knew that the Americans didn't give a damn about Québec's culture or their language. Only in a sovereign united Canada would future Québeckers be free to travel throughout all of Canada and find communities, products, services and schools devoted to their language and traditions.

...unless the inhabitants give an active and efficient aid, it will be utterly impossible for the very limited number of the military, who are likely to be employed, to preserve the province.

~

Within days, Operation Crimson Red was launched. American troops charged into Canada in full force and took over all of the foreign entry points. In only one week, they had achieved all of their primary military goals and secured the North American perimeter.

By more than doubling its geographic area of control, border security manpower was stretched beyond its limits. Personnel were soon working an inordinate amount of overtime and the unions threatened work stoppages if something wasn't done immediately to alleviate the situation.

In response to the union demands, Washington declared the Canadian-American border open and transferred the freed up manpower out to the periphery.

Parliament having been dissolved, the CBC was now the only remaining 'official' voice of Canada. In compliance with Washington's request, the CBC issued a bulletin that all Canadian soldiers were to immediately report to the nearest Continental Army HQ. There, the Canadians were ordered to exchange their uniforms for those of the newly constituted Continental Army and swear allegiance to the Continental Party and its leader, President Kuhn.

Overwhelmed by America's superior numbers and weaponry, most Canadian soldiers reluctantly laid down their arms, formed up and did as they were told. But a significant percentage of soldiers disobeyed the order, instead choosing not to surrender dishonourably. These rebel soldiers headed north and disappeared into the vast Canadian wilderness, taking their arms and munitions with them. In response, roving check-points were established along roads to prevent the unauthorized movement of people.

~

With the perimeter secured by the Armed Forces, Operation Crimson Red moved into Phase Two.

Phase Two was the mission of the Inland Control Agency which notified those whom Washington had identified to be potential security risks that they must report immediately to their local Inland Control office. Those not doing so within 48 hours were considered fugitives from the law. It was a very broad sweep meant to purge the whole continent of any potential domestic terrorists.

Under the new Fugitive Persons Law, those who reported were finger printed, then fitted with a GPS ankle band and told to remain in their communities until they were instructed to move elsewhere.

The CBC announced that anyone caught harbouring fugitives would also be breaking the law and would be severely dealt with by the authorities. Rewards were placed on the heads of fugitives, whether brought in dead or alive. In this way, Canadians were encouraged to spy on their neighbours and trust between people plummeted.

Captain Owens was one of the rebel Canadian soldiers who headed north rather than enlisting with the Continental Army. Choosing otherwise would have dishonoured his dead fiancé's life and memory. Adrira had been a Canadian Red Cross volunteer working with her 'sisters' in Afghanistan, when she was killed by a road side bomb. Adrira's mother, Cantara, and younger brother, Salim, now lived in Canada, but because Cantara had been born in Afghanistan, they were considered to be potential security risks. Not having turned themselves in, they were now fugitives from the law. Owens had tried to speak to the Inland Control Agency on their behalf, but was unsuccessful.

That was the final straw for Owens. His honour demanded that he quit and head north, but first he had to see to it that Cantara and Salim were safe. He would see to that by hiding them at his parents' house.

~

A dreadful crash is not far off— I hope your friends have withheld their confidence in their public stocks. There have been many failures at New York, and the merchants there are in a state of great confusion and dismay.

Reading that, Will was glad he'd freed himself from the market and withdrawn all his cash. He too had begun to horde some silver.

~

The harsh days of winter passed slowly. The euphoric days that followed the election caused the financial markets to rebound, but only temporarily. The full potential of Canada's resources was locked away in the frozen tundra until some unknown time in the future when more advanced technology would aid their extraction. For the present though, it soon became clear that there was no short-term solution to America's energy and resource problems.

The contamination of the Midwest farmland resulted in widespread food shortages which became acute in the winter and caused food prices to skyrocket. With more than 100 nuclear power plants shut down, energy prices soared too. All of this combined to cause the inflation rate to increase beyond twenty percent, a rate that hadn't been seen in America for thirty years.

The Fresh Water and Food Security Bill was passed in Washington. The bill detailed the losses incurred as a result of the nuclear fallout and called for reparations from Canada through the expropriation of Canadian properties owned in the States and farmland in Canada.

Under the new law, any Canadian properties in the States left vacant for more than six months were considered abandoned and forfeited. The fact that Canadians weren't allowed travel permits didn't matter. Most of these properties had already been re-occupied by the victims of Fermi who, by squatters' rights, claimed possession for themselves.

Within Canada, farmland was expropriated under a lottery system that transferred title to a Midwest farmer who was a victim of Fermi. Because there were no jobs available, Canadian farmers who lost their land by lottery had no option but to offer their services to their new American landlords. Many did so in exchange for basic lodging and sustenance.

Also, commercial fishermen were forced to surrender half their catch, through means of the regulated quota system, in reparation for contaminating America's fish stocks. When the news broke, the Ana Teresa was iced in at her home port. Ernesto Fortuna made up his mind that, once the ice broke free on the lake, he would be in no rush to set his nets for the next season. Ana Teresa was going to get a well deserved rest.

Feeling snubbed by America and critical of its occupation of Canada, the rest of the world was giving America what it wanted from them – nothing. America had isolated herself.

~

CHAPTER X

From The Terror
Of Flight

*...the Americans are busily employed in drilling
their militia, and openly declare their intention of
entering this province the instant war is determined
upon; they will be encouraged to adopt this step from
the very defenceless state of our frontiers...*

~

Pierre Gauthier worried about the future of his farm. His family had farmed their land for 200 years and, having only one daughter and no sons, he had feared that title to the land would someday be transferred to another name. He never imagined he would see that day come so abruptly.

"Relis-la moi, Renée." ["Read it to me again, Renée."] For the third time, his daughter translated the registered letter they'd received earlier that day from the Farmers' Reparation Lottery. According to the form letter, an American farmer named Victor Gates had legally obtained title to their land. The letter also indicated that Mr Gates' son, Mr Bryce Gates, would be visiting the farm within the next 10 days to claim it and handle the transition.

"Mais c'est pas possible!" ["How can this be?"] Pierre asked. His worries gave way to tears as he looked down at his trembling hands. In one hand, he held a cheque from the Receiver General of Canada and in the other, an eviction notice. Both bore his name.

"Ça y est, Pa." ["It's over, Dad."]

"Mais c'est du vol." ["But this is theft."] The value of good farmland had soared after Fermi, but the Gauthiers were being paid only the pre-Fermi valuation of their land.

"Oui, Pa, mais du vol légal." ["Yes, Dad, but it's legalized theft."]

"On doit aller en appel!" ["Then we must appeal!"]
"Non, Pa. On peut pas. Ça dit que le jugement est irrévocable. C'est fini, Pa!" ["No, Dad. We can't. The notice says that this judgement is final and cannot be appealed. It's over, Dad."]

~

A week later, Bryce Gates arrived to claim the Gauthier farm on behalf of his ailing father. The Gates were not farmers. Despite it being the intention of the Farmers' Reparation Lottery to transfer Canadian farms to American farmers, few American farmers had given their names to the Lottery. To ensure that America would be fairly compensated for its lost farmland 'acre for acre', the American government had opened up the lottery to any American who'd been displaced by the fallout.

Consequently, most of the American lottery winners had little or no experience in farming, so it was common for a new owner to offer the evicted farmer the option of remaining on the farm as a tenant farmer. This was precisely what his father had asked Bryce to do.

Without knocking, Bryce swept into the Gauthiers' farmhouse to see Pierre Gauthier sitting on his easy chair smoking a pipe.

"Name's Gates. Bryce Gates. And you're in my chair."

Pierre Gauthier looked up at the intruder with raised eyebrows, but made no effort to move.

Bryce continued. "I've come to claim our farm. You have twenty-four hours to clear out. Anything remaining after that is ours."

"Je ne comprends pas, m'sieur."

"And another thing, no more speaking French on this farm, ya hear?"

Mr Gauthier stared back at him. Still he made no effort to move.

"What, are you stupid?" Bryce growled.

"He's not stupid. He doesn't understand you," Renée answered as she entered the room from the kitchen. "He only speaks French."

"Well, that's his problem. You tell him what I said. You've got twenty-four hours." Then looking at his watch he added, "Make that twenty-three."

~

The next day, Bryce's mood had improved. As soon as he woke up, he called home and spoke with his father who was alarmed to hear that Bryce had ordered the Gauthiers off the farm.

"Are you nuts? You don't know anything about farming. You'll run it into the ground. I need that farm to earn money. Our government pension is worthless."

Bryce had not thought about that. He searched his mind for an excuse and, finally, one came.

"But they're French," he retorted.

"What the hell does that mean? Of course they're French. You're in Québec, you moron. Everyone in Québec speaks French."

"Not everyone. His daughter speaks English," Bryce countered, feeling momentarily superior.

"I don't give a damn. They can speak whatever the hell they want. But the last thing we want is for them to leave the farm. We need them. Your job is to keep them there. UNDERSTAND? CAN YOU DO THAT, SON?"

"Yes, Father," Bryce mumbled.

Bryce was a moody guy and had learned, out of necessity, how to manufacture some excuse to help explain away his previous bad behaviour. His moods allowed him to do so without feeling the least bit foolish or inconsistent. He decided to rectify the situation by making it seem that he had decided to change his mind and to generously offer the Gauthiers the opportunity to stay on.

Leaving the guestroom he'd assigned to himself, he went downstairs and was annoyed to see that the Gauthiers had already eaten breakfast without him and hadn't left anything for him. In his parents' home, he had been accustomed to having all the cooking and household work done by his mother. He was still a spoiled forty-five year old boy.

He found Renée in a bedroom, packing up their belongings.

"What are you doing?"

Renée glanced up at him without replying and continued with her work.

"I asked what are you doing?"

"Packing to leave our.... the farm," she corrected herself. "Or don't you recall your grand entrance last night? 'Name's Gates. Bryce Gates. I've come to claim our farm. You have twenty-four hours to clear out. Anything remaining after that is ours'," she mimicked him. "You're such an asshole."

Bryce took her verbatim quote of him as a compliment. He'd made an impression on her. He had already sized up them too. He didn't like the father. Didn't know why. Didn't matter. Too French probably. Therefore untrustworthy. Renée was French too, but in a sexy foreign way. That type of Frenchness was ok.

He smiled at her.

"You misunderstood what I meant. I said twenty-four hours, but I didn't mean from last night. I meant from whenever I officially told you that you must leave. It's called giving notice. Landlords often give tenants notice before they're evicted. You'd know what I meant if you spoke English more better."

"It's just better," Renée replied.

"What are you talking about?"

"You said 'more better.' It's just 'better'. You don't put 'more' in front of 'better.'"

"Whatever," he sneered. "Besides, that's just the British way of saying it. I speak American English. And this is part of America now, so get used to it."

"So you're saying we can stay now?"

"I never said you couldn't."

"And that's it?"

"That's it. Except that means you're my tenants."

"You mean we're your father's tenants," she corrected him.

"Whatever. Either way, I'm still your boss."

"My father's my boss."

"Well I'm his boss, so it's the same thing."

Renée hated him already.

"You pay your rent by taking care of the farm. And me," he added dropping his eyes over her body.

She stared at him. So that was it, she thought. He'd put his all his chips on the table and was going to bargain with her. She was to be part of the stakes.

"What do you mean by that?" she asked. She spoke before he could answer: "No, wait."

She left the room for a moment and returned in the company of her father. This irritated Bryce as he'd intended to make a private deal with her.

"You were about to say something?"

"Was I?"

"Yes, you were. You were saying that we could stay on as tenant farmers. I'm wondering what you meant by saying I was to look after your needs? I'd like my father to hear what you have to say."

"But he doesn't speak English."

"I'll translate."

'You bitch,' he thought to himself. His eyes darted back and forth in search of something to inspire his reply. They came to rest on the mug of coffee Mr Gauthier held in his hands. It made him recall how he'd been excluded from breakfast.

"By looking after me, I meant you're to cook my meals. All three. Breakfast, lunch and supper," he demanded triumphantly.

"Fine," she answered. "Anything else?"

"And you must do my dirty laundry too," he smirked.

Renée translated for her father what had been said. Bryce watched and listened. Had he understood French, he would have discovered that they intended to accept his terms, but only until they could figure out alternative arrangements. Then they would leave him high and dry. Bryce mistakenly thought by their expressions that they were not going to agree to everything.

Renée turned back to face him.

"I'll cook, but I'm not doing your dirty laundry," she bargained. She already had him all figured out. "And you must do all the dishes including the pots and pans," she added.

He was happily surprised. That was a better deal than he'd expected them to agree to. No doubt, he would be constantly left behind in the kitchen scouring out deliberately burnt pots and pans and washing an inordinate quantity of cups, glasses, bowls, dishes and cutlery. Like him, she had bargained for a better deal. And she had done so in front of her dad. She had brains, he conceded, realizing that could be dangerous. He nodded his acceptance, knowing he'd get even with her in the future.

~

Within the cozy confines of the La Forêts' cabin, the night-time glow of the wood-burner stove lit up faces of the occupants. Lacking a television, they often played cards to pass the time. It had become a nightly ritual for Will to lie up in his loft reading Brock's diary. It was a ritual which put his mind in a sort of trance. In this state, he would nod off, lost to his time, dreaming vivid dreams about another.

Most mornings, fresh snow lay so deep around the cabin so that only the windows and the roof, itself heavily laden with snow, could be seen from the outside. Heat being released from the windows often meant that they were less buried than the entrance doors.

After a large snowfall, Yves and Will had to dig their way out to escape the cabin. To avoid opening the main entrance and causing an avalanche of snow to cascade into the cabin, they had to slide open and exit through a window, sinking down deep into powder snow on the outside. With shovels in hand, they dug a deep trench around to the kitchen door. After that, they still had to dig to the outhouse and cut a path to the shed where the firewood was kept. This covered the necessities. By this time, breakfast would be waiting for them, after which they would head back out to clear away the snow from the front door and then cut a path to the truck and its plow.

These wintry days spent working together completed the bonding of their friendship. They were still different, but they respected each other's differences.

'Vive la différence, vive le Canada libre,' Yves thought to himself.

~

The reparations forced from the Canadians did not stop the continued decline of the American economy. With people struggling to fulfill their most basic needs, the luxury-based economy fell like a bunch of dominos. Retail sales plummeted causing massive layoffs. Production ground to a halt. Plants closed. More banks closed and the markets dropped to all time lows. The American dollar collapsed. This cheapened American-made goods internationally but, due to the international boycott, nobody was buying.

Conversely, the prices of natural resources soared. A barrel of crude oil reached over $200US and an ounce of gold bullion soared above $5,000. Officially, the Canadian and US dollars were 'at par', but, in the Canadian underground economy, one Canadian dollar now bought two US dollars.

To save the US dollar from total collapse, Washington decreed that exchanging dollars at anything but the official rate was prohibited and that no more Canadian dollars would be printed.

Before Fermi, a par dollar had been touted by Ottawa as being particularly beneficial for Canadians whose jobs depended completely on the Americans. Now Canadians saw it differently. Current events had clearly demonstrated that Canadian natural resources were desperately needed by the Americans. Indeed, those resources were the envy of the world and could be easily marketed anywhere.

~

America's general mistrust of everything foreign led to a declaration that English was the sole official language of North America. It was thought that English-speaking Canadians, representing the vast majority of the country's population, would rejoice at the ruling. Ever since Prime Minister Trudeau had mandated that elementary school students must learn French, most students outside of Québec and New Brunswick had done so begrudgingly and half-heartedly. Because of this, the Americans assumed that Canadians were deeply divided along language lines and that this linguistic division could be exploited to drive a wedge between English and French Canadians.

The plan backfired. The American occupation brought Canadians together, making the old language divide now seem petty and superficial. When Washington cut the funding for French classes and schools, Canadian students all across the nation rebelled demanding that French instruction be brought back. The more it was suppressed, the more speaking French became chic. It was common for university students to be tattooed with a Maple Leaf with the words 'Je suis Canadien!' written beneath.

The language revolt spread from campuses into communities across the nation where Canadians of all ages and ethnicity made considerable effort to insert some French into their daily conversations. 'Bonjour', 'bienvenue' and 'merci' were commonly heard even at the most staunchly British club houses. Even the Monarchist League of Canada added stories onto their bilingual webpage about the historic loyalty of the French Canadians, standing united with the rest of Canada against the previous American invasions.

Rather than admit that their plan had backfired, President Kuhn's administration tightened the screws. Washington decreed that speaking French in public was prohibited. Offenders were jailed if they were caught speaking French in public places. Immediately, widespread violence broke out in Québec amongst those who only spoke French and had no other choice.

Soon, the Québécois learned to stay together in groups and to swarm around any victim and the apprehending officers if an arrest was being made. If the prisoner was released, the officers were set free, but if the officers persisted, they were overwhelmed by the swarming gang, disarmed and beaten. Photos of all such officers were posted online and on public posters along with the words: *oeil pour oeil, dent pour dent!* [an eye for an eye, a tooth for a tooth!] The Washington press called it barbaric, but the world press called it 'justice à la Canadienne'.

~

Everyone was confused. Those who had been friends were now mortal enemies. Yet the Andersons had the good fortune to have made loyal friends of their American guests. Dillan and Angela Gallagher simply ignored all the hate-filled rhetoric and genuinely appreciated each day as they found it. Having lost their home and all their belongings, they didn't take anything for granted anymore. They knew that the winds could as easily have sent the fallout east to land on the Andersons' property. Had that happened, they honestly couldn't say whether they would have opened their own home to foreign strangers. But the Andersons had and this cut across all the politics. The Gallaghers would never turn on them.

Having voluntarily taken in American victims of Fermi, the Anderson farm was exempt from the Lottery. In addition, the American authorities tended to leave the Andersons alone, assuming that the Gallaghers would turn them in if anything suspicious was going on.

Dillan learned quickly from Kevin and Mr Anderson about how to prepare the farm for the approaching growing season. Dillan was an avid fisherman and gentle Kevin, out of necessity, had started to hunt. This way, the young men ensured that everyone had a healthy supply of protein in their diets. Mrs Anderson was a creative cook and she included the orchard's apples, peaches and pears in many of the meals she prepared. There weren't many homes that could boast such a plentiful variety of wholesome food on their dining tables.

Angela's baby was due any day now and nobody, except perhaps Angela herself, awaited its arrival more than Hana. Hana was Angela's self-appointed doula and Angela wouldn't have had it any other way. Seldom was Hana out of Angela's earshot and Angela barely needed to lift a finger. Only when Captain York Owens snuck back for a visit did Hana leave Angela's side and, even then, it would be just for a short while.

When York showed up, it was always without warning. Although he was now a fugitive, his understanding of the security forces' ways made it easy for him to travel unimpeded.

He always showed up carrying some staples for Mrs Anderson's kitchen, such as sugar, salt and butter, which were now hard to find at the market. In addition to this, he always brought a picnic which was solely for Hana and himself. Together, they would stroll through the orchard down to the lake where he would spread out a blanket and lay out their picnic. It was always full of delectable items and put her in mind of the time before the war. Although the conflict was only in its second year, peacetime in Canada seemed like a lifetime ago.

After sharing their picnic, they would sit together, with their arms intertwined and their legs dangling out over the edge of the cliff. There, they would chat away the afternoon, listening to the lapping of the waves against the shore, feeling the sun's warmth and watching the wind turbine propellers slowly turn in the distance.

~

CHAPTER XI

Where The Foe's Haughty Host In Dread Silence Reposes

... expecting a descent from the American army, the Canadians have, for ten days past, been removing their families and effects from the river into the interior. These men are generally those who have "seen service" in various parts of the world.

~

A flood of political outcasts and dispossessed continued to leave the larger urban centres to escape the violence. Those dependent upon government assistance couldn't leave since that would automatically make them ineligible to collect. Ration cards were needed to buy goods at the public markets and fingerprinting became mandatory for any Canadian adult to obtain a ration card. On the other hand, if one had friends in the underground, almost anything could still be obtained. All one needed was gold, silver or something of value to trade.

~

The solitude of the wilderness cabin isolated Will and the La Forêts from the exodus and the takeover. Will was in good spirits and cheerful as winter was drawing to a close and the days were getting longer. Sunup was almost equal to sundown heralding the approaching equinox. As always, Will eagerly anticipated the coming days of spring when the warming sun and south wind would melt away the snow and awaken the life lying dormant beneath it. The snow was darker now and more heavily packed too, having become solid and icy, so that it was now difficult to walk without slipping. Slowly, buried rocks, bushes and tree stumps appeared, making themselves known to Will for the first time. In contrast to the disappearing snow, icicles formed and grew down from the roof's edges which added a new view from the cabin's windows.

The tranquility of the cabin came to an abrupt end when a young boy carrying a backpack came walking up the driveway. At the time, everyone else was in town except Will. He was seated outside on the porch enjoying the sun when he noticed the boy approaching. Upon seeing Will, the boy checked his stride and hesitated for a moment. It was obvious Will had surprised him.

"*Bonjour*", Will called out to him.

"*Excusez-moi, monsieur… je suis bien chez les La Forêts?*"
["Excuse me, mister… is this the La Forêts' place?"]

"*Oui. Mais ils sont allés en ville. Ils devraient revenir bientôt.*"
["Yes. But everyone is in town. They should be back soon."]

The boy's face relaxed somewhat. He'd found the right place, but it was obvious he didn't trust strangers.

"*Venez vous asseoir*" said Will, welcoming him to have a seat. "*Vous pouvez les attendre.*" [You can wait here for their return."]

The boy nodded yet didn't move towards the porch. Instead, he tottered under the weight of his pack. Seeing this, Will jumped up and ran over to help, lifting the straps from the boy's shoulders. Relieved of his pack, the boy gave Will a grateful smile and they walked up to the cabin together.

"Je m'appelle William," he said, offering his hand.

The boy extended his own small hand and shook Will's.

"Renée", he replied while falling with exhaustion onto the porch bench. Will knew the boy was in need of some nourishment so he went inside and gathered some water, cheese and bread.

"Merci", the boy said. Will figured the boy must be a relative of the La Forêts for he had both Yves and Madame La Forêt's strikingly blue eyes, but before he could ask about that, their truck pulled into the driveway.

For a moment, the La Forêts didn't exit their vehicle. Instead, they stayed put, with their eyes fixed on the boy as though they didn't know him. Seeing this, the boy reached up and removed the large fur hat from his head and, glancing sideways at Will, gave him a big beautiful smile and shook her hair loose.

Instantly, Madame called out, "Renée! C'est Renée!" The car doors flew open and the others came running up the path to welcome her.

Renée brought sad and disturbing news. She had made the long trip alone. Fear and desperation had kept her moving. She'd fled her family farm fearing Bryce's cruel revenge after she'd gotten the better of him for accosting and manhandling her. Bryce had cleverly waited for Monsieur Gauthier to leave for church before making his unwanted advances. Renée had woken to find herself pinned beneath his weight.

"Get off me!" she'd screamed, but undeterred, he shamelessly reached down under the covers with his hand. Momentarily unbraced, she was able to roll him over sideways and topple him down onto the floor. He fell hard with a thud.

"You bitch!" he'd yelled, drawing his switchblade. "I'll have you whether you want it or not."

In an instant, she launched herself out of bed and ran out of the bedroom. Bryce followed in hot pursuit. Panicking, she flung herself down the stairways. Stumbling and recovering, she ran frantically to get away. She could feel that he was right behind her and narrowing the gap. As she flew into the kitchen, he caught hold of her hair and threw her violently onto the floor. Immediately, he was on top of her, holding his knife in front of her face.

"It's either this or me. This will hurt a lot more," he grinned wickedly.

"Get off me," she screamed.

"Wrong answer," he sneered as he'd reached behind with his knife.

With her arms stretched out over her head, she touched a dustpan. Her fingers worked around its handle until she grasped it and then, with all her might, she swung it around into his head with a stunning CRACK!

The impact dazed him and she knew that she must either kill him now with his own knife before he regained his senses, or run for her life. Foolishly, she ran. In a daze, she reached the door, grabbed the keys to his car and raced out of the farmhouse.

She barely got the car started when he stumbled out of the farmhouse screaming.

"You're dead, you bitch!"

She hesitated as the thought of killing him with the car crossed her mind. She could either drive into him and rid the farm of their tormentor or reverse out of the driveway and leave him be. Bryce must have been able read her intentions for he too hesitated, his eyes pleading for her to spare his life. Making a quick decision, she put the car in reverse and backed out.

"COWARD! " he chastised her, knowing full well her chance had passed. "I'm still going to kill you. That's a promise."

These were the last words she heard him say as she drove north towards her Aunt Cécile's cabin. Roadblocks en route foiled her attempt to drive there. Approaching the first barricade, she turned about and ditched Bryce's rental in a woodlot. The rest of her journey was on foot after dark with barking dogs marking her progress. By the time she arrived at the La Forêts', she was another name on a growing list of fugitives wanted by the Inland Control Agency.

~

Renée feared for her father's safety and her story made Will fear for his own family and farm.

Yves was livid. "They took your farm and the bastard tried to rape you? He threatened to kill you?"

"My poor dear," Madame La Forêt said sadly, patting her hand tenderly. A tear trickled down from Monsieur La Forêt's eye as he gazed thoughtfully out the window. He was a man of few words and the tear betrayed his soft heart.

"Let's go get that bastard, Anderson," Yves said.

"I'm in," Will nodded.

"Papa, we'll need the truck."

Before he could answer came Renée's response.

"No. It's foolish. The roads south are all guarded so I can't travel with you by truck."

"Then stay. Anderson and I will go. I'll bring you his head on a platter if you want proof." Nobody knew for sure if Yves was joking or serious. He looked serious.

"No," Renée repeated. "I need to be there. This is my battle."
For a moment, nobody spoke. Yves came up with
another suggestion.

"Then we can walk or bike there. If Anderson can do it,
anyone can."

"Do you realize I just walked 400 kilometres too?" Renée
reminded him. "Once I regain my strength and with better preparation, I'll be able to make it there and back again."

Nobody would deny she needed some R&R. She'd arrived all
skin and bones. It was a testament to her determination that she'd
got there at all when so many people more prepared than she
had failed.

Will's mind turned to the prospect of doing an 800 kilometre
journey. He reflected on his own recent canoeing voyage with
the Hackers. He also recalled envying the canoeists he'd seen
floating down the Grand River with ease as he'd trudged along on
foot. This sparked an idea in his head. The cabin's upriver location
offered them the same opportunity. From this higher ground, they
too could float easily downstream with the river currents. Taking the
Ottawa downriver would get them to the St. Lawrence and downriver from there was Montréal. It was a route free of road blocks.

"I have another idea," Will offered. "I see outside that you have
a canoe."

~

*Today I received a letter from Colonel J.A. Vesey
wherein he stated, I wish I had a daughter old enough
for you, as I would give her to you with pleasure.
You should be married, particularly as fate seems to
detain you so long in Canada— but pray do not
marry there.*

~

The sound of constant dripping could be heard everywhere. The snow's disappearance revealed a new landscape. Around the cabin stretched a meadow framed on one side by the lake and on the other, a forest. Soon, the life giving sun would rouse the wildflowers and the most colourful days of the meadow would return. The log cabin stood solid in the midst of it all. It had become the centre of Will's world. Most others would think of his situation as living on the fringe.

'If it is the fringe,' Will thought, 'perhaps it's a fringe that defines society's limits.'

Will was content with these simple surroundings where he had everything he needed. From the moment he'd arrived, he'd been cut off from his other life and was aware only of the present moment.

It had only been two weeks since Renée's arrival. In that time, the peace of the cabin had been broken as her problems had become theirs. Renée reminded Will of Sydney and Hana combined into one person and that made fighting her battle feel personal to him.

No more did Will have the whole upper loft to himself. Instead, blankets had been draped from the support beams to separate his bed from hers. As he lay in bed, Will looked around as if to memorize his surroundings so they would not be forgotten in the days ahead. Out of the loft skylight, he saw the moon and stars sparkling in the sky overhead. He knew those would always be his anchor and his constant companion wherever his journeys took him.

Staring skyward, he wondered, 'is Sydney is gazing skyward at this moment too or are her eyes earthbound and limited to her immediate surroundings?' He hoped she was looking skyward too for, without any other means to communicate, a common sight would somehow connect them.

'Look up, Sydney,' he whispered to her.

~

Renée was helping Will to improve his French. They both desired companionship and it helped to keep her mind from worrying about her father. Very quickly, Renée realized that Will was not the best class student so she put aside the pen and paper and conversed with him naturally instead. In this way, he progressed rapidly and they became close friends. Speaking French well would help to eliminate some unnecessary harassment on their journey as the native population would be more than willing to assist *les évadés*.

Will still found time to read by candlelight at night. Brock's diary had infected his whole being so that he would unknowingly mouth the words while reading them, as if they were his own.

"*Qu'est-ce que tu as dit, William?*" ["What did you say, William?"]

"*Pardon?*"

"*Je croyais que tu avais parlé, non?*" ["I heard you say something, no?"]

"*Je pense pas, non.*" ["I don't think so."]

"*Excuse, je suis en train de lire quelquechose.*" ["Oh, I'm reading something. Sorry."]

"*Ce 'quelquechose' a-t-il un titre par hasard?*" ["Does that something have a title?"]

So despite the professor's warnings, Will told Renée about the diary. She was intrigued.

"*Lis-en un bout pour moi, William, veux-tu?*" ["Read some to me, William."]

"*Ok...où est-ce que j'en étais?...ah oui...*" ["Ahhhh sure...Now where was I? Oh ya..."]

> *By what new principle are they to be prevented from defending their property?*

"*Il a raison, William. Alors quand est-ce qu'on part?*" ["He's right, William. So when do we leave?"]

"*Demain.*" ["Tomorrow."]

~

They outfitted two canoes for the journey on the Ottawa River to Montréal. Being the most experienced white-water canoeist, Yves paddled solo in one while Renée and Will paddled together in the other. Like a true voyageur, Yves paddled a birch bark canoe which had been built by their neighbours. Renée and Will paddled a more practical, but less charming, fibreglass canoe.

Yves led the way so that Renée and Will could follow his line through the trickier parts. Always, they stayed well clear of the shoreline where toppled trees still clinging onto the shore with their roots, could easily capsize them. The river, swollen by the spring's melt, propelled them swiftly towards their objective.

The Ottawa joined the St. Lawrence just above Montréal and was the busiest leg of their journey. They marvelled at the mighty freighters as they passed by, with their bubbled noses pushing huge volumes of water into swelling waves as they ploughed their way upriver against the flow.

In just over a week, they came to rest on the south side of the St. Lawrence opposite Montréal and they left their canoes there with some of Renée's friends so they could continue to the Gauthier farm by land. Since they did not have travel permits, two vehicles were required to shuttle them for the remainder of their journey. Shuttling had become a common way of dealing with the road blocks by moving from home to home, friend to friend and gradually leapfrogging into the next district. The leading vehicle acted as a scout for mobile checkpoints on the road. If a checkpoint was spotted, the leading scout called back to alert the other vehicle to turn around before being spotted. The following vehicle would then return to where they began and wait until the next day to proceed. Using this shuttle system, it took them five days to reach the Gauthier farm.

Bryce's car was in the driveway signifying he was there. The plan was for Yves and Will to simply go up to the door pretending to be friends calling upon Renée. Meanwhile, Renée and their shuttle driver would remain in the vehicle and out of sight. Yves and Will intended to entrap Bryce somehow in a lie and then get him to confess his failed attempt at raping Renée. In this way, they hoped to win back the farm for Renée and her father.

It was a crude plan with many holes for they hadn't even thought about what they would ultimately say to the authorities about how they'd got to the farm without the proper travel permits. Those details seemed secondary and they put their hopes on being judged leniently for doing what any honourable person would do – seek revenge on Bryce for what he'd done to Renée.

~

"Knock again, Anderson," Yves said impatiently.

For the third time, Will rapped loudly on the door. They could tell someone was home because the first knock had caused some stirring within.

"Maybe go around to the back door," Will suggested. "Perhaps he's outside in the backyard and can't hear me. I'll stay here and keep knocking."

Just as Yves started to move, someone's shadow moved across the window blinds. Whoever it was, that person was now peeking out at them.

"Hello," Will hollered and waved.

There was no reply.

"I said hello to you there peeking through the blinds," he repeated.

"Who the hell are you? And what do you want?"

"My name's Will. Will Anderson. And this is my friend Yves. We're here to see Renée. I'm her friend and Yves is her cousin."

"Renée's not here."

"When will she be back?'

"How should I know?"

"She lives here."

"Not anymore she doesn't."

"Can we speak with Pierre then?"

"No."

"Why not?"

"Because he's not here either. Now beat it!"

Yves glanced at Will. This was unexpected since Pierre seldom left the farm on weekdays, especially in the spring.

"*Il y a quelque chose de bizarre,*" ["Something's fishy,"] he whispered to Will.

"Who am I speaking with?" Will demanded.

"Name's Bryce Gates and this is my farm. The people you're looking for don't live here anymore. This farm's mine by rights. Now get off my land or I'll call the Inland Police."

"Can you tell me where Mr Gauthier has gone?"

"TO HELL FOR ALL I CARE!" Bryce screamed in reply, coming to the door and carrying a shotgun.

"This is private property and I said leave!" he ordered, levelling the gun at Will. As Will backed away from the door, Bryce started to move toward him. Suddenly the gun went off into the air as Yves tackled Bryce from behind and landed on top of him. Will reached down to retrieve the dropped gun.

"We're all going back inside for a little talk!" he ordered, pointing the gun back at their assailant.

Renée and the shuttle driver came in to join them.

"Where's my father, you son-of-a-bitch," Renée demanded.

"Like I told him," Bryce said, looking at Will, "he's gone."

"Where?"

"How should I know?"

"LIAR!" she shouted. "Maybe you better jog his memory, Yves."

"*Avec plaisir.*" He bowed slightly and then smashed his fist into Bryce's face.

The impact caused Bryce to fly backwards and, with a thud, he landed on the floor, rolling around in pain with his hands covering his face.

"Get up," Yves ordered. Bryce hesitated. "Or I'll help you get up."

Bryce crawled back to his chair. Still holding his hands to his injured face, he looked to Will and saw an indication of sympathy. Will had no stomach for torture and was glad to hear a car come speeding up the laneway diverting everyone's attention from the interrogation. Moments later, Renée's neighbour ran into the kitchen.

"*Renée, ma pauvre!*" she wailed. "*Il a tué ton père. On pensait qu'il t'avait tuée aussi!*" ["He killed your father. We thought he killed you too!"]

It was all a blur for Renée as the neighbour explained that there were no witnesses to the crime. The investigating officers had accepted Bryce's story that Pierre had sought revenge after his farm was wrongfully expropriated. They determined that Bryce had acted lawfully out of self-defence.

Renée's mind whirred and she thought she was going to black-out. Seeing her sway, Will held onto her. She knew her father was a peaceful man and would neither start nor willingly participate in a fight. Bryce must have provoked him or simply killed him in cold blood. As her eyes began to refocus, the smirk on Bryce's face told her the truth. She had refused Bryce's advances and he had killed her father in revenge.

"YOU BASTARD!" she screamed, lunging at him with her fists.

He had expected that and, throwing her aside, he drew his knife.

"You all saw that!" he yelled. "That bitch attacked me first. I've got a right to defend myself!"

Frantically she got up and ran from the farmhouse. He followed her with the others trailing behind. As Bryce reached out to grab her, she spun out of the way at just the right moment. Instead of catching hold of her, his momentum drove him straight past her. Seeing him on her left, she turned right and ran recklessly towards the open barn doors.

"HELP ME, WILL!" she implored with her eyes full of terror. A moment later, she reached the barn and disappeared from view. Bryce entered right behind her and Will realized that he couldn't catch Bryce before Bryce caught her. A second later, he heard a sickening 'thump' and a whimper. He assumed the worst. She'd been caught.

Will ran through the barn doors into the darkness. As his eyes adjusted, he saw the back of Bryce hunched over Renée and still holding the knife in his hand. Then Yves arrived.

"*NON!*" he shrieked.

In a flash, Will and Yves were on either side of Bryce, grabbing his arms to stop him from doing more damage. In horror and then relief, they saw that Bryce had already been stopped by a pitchfork held by Renée. Bryce's fury had carried him full force onto the pitchfork and it was protruding through the back of his jacket. Renée held onto the other end, which was anchored solidly into the ground.

Bryce was impaled, but still alive. Will was so relieved to see Renée unharmed that he let his arm drop and the knife fell from Bryce's weakening grasp.

"Help me," Bryce whispered. "Have mercy."

But Renée would hear nothing of it. Justice rested in her hands alone.

"The pitchfork was for what you tried to do to me," Renée said to him with a hollow voice. As she spoke, she nudged the pitchfork handle to drive home the point. Then, with a swift motion, she picked up the fallen knife and slashed open his throat. Blood cascaded out of his severed jugular vein onto the dirt.

"And *that's* for what you did to my father."

"*C'est juste,*" said Renée's neighbour, confirming the justice of his sentence.

~

It was two weeks since they'd returned to the cabin and Will was anxious to return to his parents' farm to see how they were. He planned to leave the cabin during the night as he didn't want to involve anyone else in his plans. Will owed the La Forêts so much that he didn't want to add to their problems. When the moon and stars shone brightly and everyone else slept, he silently slipped out and blended into the shadows. Something nearby caught his eye.

"*Qui est là?*" ["Who's there?"]

"*C'est nous,*" answered Renée.

"*Qui ça nous?*" ["Who's us?"]

She and Yves came forward. "*Nous,*" she repeated. "*Sorti pour une promenade nocturne Will?*" ["Out for a midnight stroll, Will?"]

"*Je…*" he began.

"*On le sait*", Yves interrupted, "*tu nous quittes. On te connaît trop bien cher ami. On comprend pourquoi tu gardais ça secret. Mais on ne peut pas te laisser partir sans que tu dises bonjour à mes parents. En plus, ma mère t'a préparé de la nourriture pour la route*". ["We know… you're leaving us. We know you too well, my friend. We understand why you didn't tell us, but we can't let you leave without saying a proper goodbye to my folks. Besides, my mom's prepared some food for you to take along on your journey."]

"*Il y a autre chose, Will,*" ["There's one more thing, Will,"] added Renée.

"*Quoi, Renée?*" ["What's that, Renée?"]

"*Je viens avec toi,*" ["I'm coming with you,"] she announced.

"*Tu peux pas… c'est trop dangereux.*" ["You can't. It's too dangerous."]

"*Ce sera pire pour les autres et pour moi si je reste ici. Combien de temps avant que quelqu'un rapporte que Bryce est disparu? Ensuite, ils vont partir à ma recherche…et tôt ou tard, ils vont aboutir ici. Donc je dois quitter…je vais me sentir mieux avec toi."* ["It's more dangerous for me and the others if I stay here. How long do you think it will be before somebody reports Bryce missing? And then they'll be searching for me. Sooner or later, they'll come here. So I've got to leave too and I'll be safer if I'm with you."]

Will realized that she'd spoken the simple truth and there was no point in arguing. He nodded his assent and together they walked back to the cabin.

Shortly after breakfast, with hugs, kisses and tears, they said their goodbyes. Monsieur La Forêt gave Will two cans of his pure maple syrup as gifts to the Hackers and Will's parents. Yves drove them to the western boundary of Rapides-des-Joachims and from there, Renée and Will, laden with food, outdoor gear, BOB trailers and two bikes, set out on a remote secondary road which led southwest.

~

CHAPTER XII

May Stalwart
Sons And Gentle
Maidens Rise

*"My home is a tent, floor is of grass, grub varies at
times, my book is nature, each day but a page, my
music the breeze through the pines."*
— Author unknown

~

Bumping their way along quiet roads at about 20 kph, they took
three days to reach Peterborough. They biked directly to the professor's and saw that his home had become a beehive of activity.
Among the large gathering of students there, Will soon saw Sarah.

"Will!" she beamed with delight, giving him a hug.

Sarah led them to the basement cellar where they were surrounded by cupboards full of canned and jarred goods, root crops
and cases of beer and wine.

"Please stand over here," Sarah instructed them as she stepped
forward and reached into a cupboard. Will expected her to retrieve
some prized item, but she knocked on the back wall instead. A
section of the wall moved and opened like a door on hinges.

Sarah stood aside and gestured for to them to walk through
the doorway into a secret room. Barry and Professor Hacker
were inside, wearing gowns. They were in the process of carefully
pouring molten metal into a mold. Barry looked up from his work
and grinned.

"Hello, Barry," said Will.

"We were beginning to wonder what became of you," he answered.

"Can you take over from me here, Sarah?" Professor Hacker asked. As she did, they all warmly shook hands in greeting. The professor pulled a silver coin out of his pocket and handed it to Will.

"We've gone into the minting business, Will."

Will examined the coin. It was the same size as a quarter. On one side was the image of the Maple Leaf within a shield and the words *Canada* and *25 Cents* inscribed on the top and words *Maple Leaf Forever* on the bottom. Will gathered it was made of real silver.

"I imagine it's worth more than twenty-five cents, Professor."

"A lot more."

As he flipped the coin over, he saw the profile of a man's face with the words *Surgite!, Major-General Sir Isaac Brock* and *1812* inscribed along the edge.

Will nodded. The image of Brock on the coin made perfect sense.

"What does surgite mean?" he asked.

"To rise," Renée answered.

The professor smiled at her as she came forward. As Will was about to make introductions, the professor spoke first, asking, "And this beauty must be Sydney?"

Renée and Will exchanged smiles.

"Actually, no. Although she is beautiful and smart, she's not Sydney. Sydney's still back in BC. Professor, Barry, I'd like you to meet Renée," he introduced her. "She's a good friend of mine and the niece of the Québec family I stayed with last winter."

"Pleasure to meet you, Renée."

"Do we have a Latin scholar in our midst?" the professor asked her.

"No. I speak French and English," she replied. "The word surgite is a common root word of both languages. It's one of those common words I taught you, Will."

'Of course,' Will thought. Surgite. It was almost exactly the same as the English word 'surge'. To surge, meaning to well up. To heave. And to rise.

"*C'est vrai, Renée. Je suis désolé.* I am indeed a disappointing student. You taught me better."

"So what do you think about our coins?" Barry asked.

"They're beautiful Barry, but, if they're real silver, I'd say you've undervalued them."

"No doubt," the professor piped in. "The face value may say 25 cents but they are 92.5% per cent pure silver so they're about thirty times more valuable than the old steel quarters."

"We're also minting silver dimes," Sarah added. "Each one of those is really worth about three dollars today."

Will was puzzled. "But why?"

"Why are we minting coins that don't denote their true value, or why are we turning our precious metal into coinage?" the professor asked.

"Both."

"Well to answer the second, we're minting them because paper dollars are almost useless, Will," explained the professor. "Paper dollars are only backed by the government and that doesn't mean much to most people anymore. Since the beginning of the occupation, people have turned to owning precious metal coins, but it's difficult to exchange gold for everyday goods. On top of that, the US government has made it illegal to be in possession of gold or silver coinage."

This gave Will a lot to think about, but before he asked another question for greater clarification, the professor continued his lecture.

"Like gold, these silver coins will hold their value, yet their lesser worth makes them far more practical for most people to use day to day. People can hide them and sleep soundly knowing that they'll still be able to buy the same thing a year or two down the road. Or two hundred years from now for that matter," he winked at Will.

Noting that, Will recalled what Brock had written on the subject of currency.

We are on the eve of substituting paper for bullion. I am aware of the Canadian prejudice against such a circulating medium...

"People want stability and for that they need a stable currency," the professor continued. "And we're going to give it to them. Because their denoted value is different from their true value, we will fly under the radar of the currency police," he concluded.

"But isn't it really just a drop in the bucket?"

"Think of it more as sowing seeds, Will. We're not the only ones who have precious metal that can be melted down into coins. Seeing these coins may spur on others to do the same."

"And Brock's image?"

"Just giving events a little psychological nudge. His face may jog a few memories. Give us hope", the professor added with a smile.

"You've come at the perfect time, Will," Barry added. "We need someone to help deliver some coins into the Toronto market. Are you headed that way?"

No answer was necessary. Everyone knew where Will was heading, and why.

~

They had to be quite inventive in figuring out how Will could covertly transport the coins. The frames of his bike and BOB trailer were cut, so that rolls of coins could be stuffed into the hollow tubes, and then welded back together. Re-welded, it appeared as though Will was riding a normal bike, unless someone tried to lift it. He also carried a pouch full of ten cent coins that could be discarded if necessary. In all, the face value of the coins he carried was only about three hundred dollars. But, the true value of the silver 'Brocks' was over ten thousand paper dollars and climbing steadily each day.

Despite her disappointment and objections, Will convinced Renée that she should stay at the Hackers' where nobody would expect to find her. The plan was for Will to go alone and deliver the coins to Ellen in Toronto. If successful, the route would become a steady stream using the professor's Trent Tribe students as carriers. By summer, this little trickle of coinage would add up to more than a million paper dollars worth of Brocks being delivered into the Toronto marketplace.

Within a week, Will was en route. He found getting into Toronto was more difficult than when he had left it. Over the winter, a barricade had been erected around the city, running down the centre of Lawrence Avenue on the north, Bayview Avenue and Jarvis Street to the lake on the east and Jane Street and Spadina to the lake on the west. The barricade was constructed of two parallel wire fences separated by about 10 metres, both topped with coiled barbed wire. Along the entire length of the *no man's land* between the fences, laser-beam sensors and raised guard posts were placed at regular intervals.

The sight of it all was shocking and reminded him of photos he'd seen of the perimeter fences built around the Nazis' concentration camps. Like those, the Toronto fence was constructed to keep people in, not out. Recognizing the high percentage of ethnic people in Toronto, the Inland Control Agency had constructed the fence to contain a large number of people deemed as potential security risks. Once the fence was completed, the Agency had started moving inwards from block to block, evaluating residents for their risk to security. The same thing was happening in Halifax, Montréal, Calgary and Vancouver.

As Will approached the North gate of the barricade, he could see a long line of people waiting to be let out on the other side. Curious, Will stood silently by the gate and watched the process. Those trying to exit the city were fully searched and questioned by the guards. A few people were handcuffed and taken away. It was obvious that this made others in the line more nervous and some changed their minds and left the line. The guards were suspicious of those who did so and, along with their police dogs, immediately rounded them up for detailed questioning. Seeing the treatment those on the inside were receiving made Will extremely apprehensive about entering. He recalled how people in Trenton had talked about the Inland Enforcers presuming guilt first and expecting people to prove their innocence.

'Everything is backwards now,' he thought. 'Maybe I shouldn't risk it.'

With that concern in his head, he was just about to turn around and leave when one of the guards finally noticed him.

"Are you waiting to enter?" he asked.

"Yes," Will answered honestly.

"Fine then. Why are you coming into the city?" asked the guard.

"I'm on my way home."

"Can I see proof that you live here?"

"I didn't say I live in Toronto. It's just a temporary stop on the way home. I'm planning to stay with friends who live here."

Will showed the guard his ID, Captain Owens' letter and the transit letter from the Hamilton police station. The guard seemed satisfied and Will had the impression all was well until the guard added, "I'll need to look in your backpack."

This request sent a jolt through Will's body. Absentmindedly, he had totally forgotten about the pouch of dimes stowed in his backpack.

'I should have dropped them when I had the chance,' he thought. Now he was forced to empty the contents of his pack in front of the guard, including the illegal coins.

"What's in the bag?"

"Rolled coins." There was no point in lying.

Nonchalantly, Will glanced over his shoulder trying to figure out where to run should he need to make a quick escape. All the other guards were still focused on the long line of people queuing up trying to leave. Yet nothing in his view offered any chance of escape.

With baited breath, Will watched as the guard carelessly unrolled the paper wrapper holding a line of dimes. As he did so, the roll of dimes broke apart and they fell onto the ground.

"Whoops. Sorry about that." The guard handed the roll of paper and the few remaining coins to Will.

"Pick up your dimes. I'll give you a three day NEXUS pass and you can proceed. The NEXUS pass will let you leave through the fast line," he said, pointing to the booth without a line. "But you must leave the city before the pass expires. Otherwise you'll be stuck in that line. Understood?"

"Yes." With a sigh of relief, Will entered the city.

If Toronto had looked gloomy last summer, it looked absolutely depressing now. The presence of the Inland Enforcers had prompted some people to vacate their homes and apartments and move inward further into the city. As quickly as the dwellings were abandoned, they were claimed either by American refugees or by those who simply wanted to improve their lot in life. Toronto had once been a clean city, but now garbage was strewn everywhere, blowing into yards, trapped by fences and accumulated in piles, for nobody seemed to care.

Within the city, only the well-connected travelled by car. Special passes were required to travel on buses and trams. The subway system had become too dangerous for most people to use. Therefore, most residents travelled like Will, by foot or bike. This shrunk their world down to small communities, beyond which the residents would seldom venture, unless armed. Most satellite communities could provide for most essentials of daily living including security. Those that couldn't were readily brought under the control of another.

On Will's trip into the inner city, he was forced to bypass one of the more prominent communities, Rosedale, around which security gates had been erected and guards posted. The unlucky residences on the undefended outer side of the gates suffered from constant raids by gangs of thieves and most of these homes had been vacated by their owners and reoccupied by thugs or their friends. The contrast was now extreme.

Few people moved across neighbourhood lines and those who did were either fleeing or linked with a gang looking to cause trouble. Those fleeing usually carried their most valuable possessions and were easy targets for thieves. Sensing this, Will made it a point to keep moving. As he biked closer to the centre of the city, the streets became noticeably more crowded. He noticed that the people appeared to be more desperate. Line ups of hungry, gaunt-looking people snaked along the sidewalks waiting their turn to be fed by charity soup kitchens.

~

Will found his way to Ellen's and knocked at her door. As he did so, he heard the shuffle of little feet. When all became silent, somebody behind the door asked, "Who's there?" Whoever it was had a timid, shy voice.

Will was sure those inside were anxious about having an unexpected Caucasian visitor.

"Hello. Sorry to bother you. My name is Will Anderson. I'm a friend of Ellen's. Is she home?"

"Please wait."

Just when he thought he'd been forgotten, Will realized he was being scrutinized through the door's peephole.

"Will!" Ellen exclaimed.

"Hi, Ellen."

The door swung open and, glancing quickly left and right to be sure nobody else was watching, Ellen grabbed his hands and pulled him in. Inside, she gave him a welcome hug and a kiss.

"It's so good to see you, Will."

"I didn't mean to cause a commotion, Ellen," he apologized.

"It's ok." Then she raised her voice, speaking in Mandarin. "It's ok to come out."

One by one, others appeared and Will found himself in the midst of about a dozen of Ellen's friends and relatives. They all seemed as curious about him as he was about them.

"Were you having a party?" he asked Ellen.

"No, we're running a hotel, silly," she joked.

Their home had become a safe place for their extended family and friends who had come together for greater protection. The Inland Control Agents considered the Chinese to be 'safe', but they feared the other inner city dwellers who preyed upon others as they became more and more desperate.

"I've brought something from Professor Hacker that I think your father will be interested to see," Will said. "Can we go somewhere private?"

Ellen led him and her parents into a bedroom where he removed his pouch and showed them the coins. They didn't know the meaning behind Brock's image on the coins, but the fact Will had wanted to show them made her parents think they must have some value. Ellen's father said a few words to her and she turned to Will.

"My father wants to know if they're made of silver?" she asked.

"Yes," answered Will.

Taking a single coin from the roll, Will did exactly what he'd seen done in some old western movies and bit it to confirm its content. With that, Mr Lee smiled to confirm his understanding. Silver and gold is an international language.

~

The banks of the river Detroit are the Eden of Upper Canada, in so far as regards the production of fruit. Apples, pears, plums, peaches, grapes, and nectarines, attain the highest degree of perfection, and exceed in size, beauty, and flavour, those raised in any other part of the province. Cider abounds at the table of the meanest peasant, and there is scarcely a farm that has not a fruitful orchard attached to it. This fineness of the fruit is one consequence of the amelioration of climate, which takes place in the vicinity of the Detroit River and Lake St. Clair. The seasons there are much milder and more serene than they are a few hundred miles below, and the weather is likewise drier and less variable. Comparatively little snow falls during the winter, although the cold is often sufficiently intense to freeze over the Detroit River so strongly, that persons, horses, and even loaded sleighs, cross it with ease and safety. In summer, the country presents a forest of blossoms, which exhale the most delicious odours; a cloud seldom obscures the sky; while the lakes and rivers, which extend in every direction, communicate a reviving freshness to the air, and moderate the warmth of a dazzling sun; and the clearness and elasticity of the atmosphere render it equally healthy and exhilarating.

Two days later and with his three day pass in hand, Will left the city behind. Heading southwest, he rode into spring. The flatlands unfolded in front of him. Ahead, clouds in the sky marked the warmer waters of the lake. Mile by mile, the landscape became greener and, once again, he woke to birdsong.

'I'm getting close to home,' he thought.

Something seemed different too. The sky was clearer and the air more pure then he ever remembered, revealing the potent fragrance of spring. Perhaps with fewer pollutants coming out of the smokestacks and tailpipes, the natural environment had finally been given a chance to return to its former glory. If that trend continued, he could picture himself and Sydney owning a small farm here someday.

'The Time of Restoration is at hand,' the elders had said. Maybe this was what they foresaw, he hoped with optimism.

His bike looked like Frankenstein since it had been sawn apart and welded back together again, but it was a lot lighter after he unloaded its contents in Toronto. He rode the final leg of his journey with confidence knowing that he was free of any contraband. He came upon roving checkpoints daily but, after showing his transit letters, he was always allowed to proceed. Compared to Toronto, life in the country felt peaceful as people were more independent in supplying their own needs and so not in a state of desperation. As Will rode up the driveway to his parents' farm, he could see Hana's face in the kitchen window.

'She's probably in the middle of making supper,' he thought.

She looked up, saw him, looked harder as if to make sure and then smiled and hollered. "Will! Will, is that you?"

"You better set another place at the table, sis, cuz I'm home!"

"Great! I just set another place for York and now you're here too!"

A short time later, Will had exchanged hugs and kisses with the whole Anderson clan, even his dad. His dad wasn't by nature a demonstrative man and their hug reminded Will that these were uncertain times.

Dillan and Angela Gallagher were carrying their newborn baby as they came downstairs to meet Will. The sight of Dillan gave him quite a shock.

"Now you know why we didn't miss you that much, big brother," Hana quipped.

A glance sideways at the hall mirror and then back to Dillan confirmed that Dillan could be his twin.

"Dad, is there something you want to admit?" he joked, nudging his father gently in the ribs.

"I had nothing to do with it," he laughed.

Dillan was perhaps a shade heavier, with lighter hair and more freckles, but from a distance, it was hard to tell them apart. Dillan had been caught off-guard as well even though he knew of their likeness beforehand. He'd already caused much confusion in town.

"Good thing you have different names," said Angela.

"And different accents," added Hana. "Although I must say you're sounding more and more Canadian these days, Dillan."

"You think we're aboot there, eh?" Dillan said, mocking their accents.

It was only then that Will noticed that his brother Kevin was not there.

"Where's Kevin?" He could see from his mother's face that his question had raised an underlying concern.

"He's been arrested," his dad answered flatly.

"Arrested? What for?"

"Hunting," Hana piped in.

"Hunting? Arrested for hunting?"

"That's right, son. Hunting," his dad confirmed.

"He's accused of killing our neighbour's deer," Hana added.

"The Reids wouldn't do that. Was it their pet?" Will asked confused. Nothing seemed to add up.

"No, it was a wild deer. And the Reids don't live there anymore," Hana replied.

"That doesn't make any sense. There must be more to it."

For a moment, nobody spoke. It was Dillan who broke the silence.

"They're trying to be polite in our presence, Will," Dillan said, eyeing Angela. "They don't know how to tell you what happened without offending us. The Reids' property was expropriated and given to some victims of Fermi. I don't mind speaking the truth. Angela and I owe your folks so much."

"It's wrong and we're embarrassed by the behaviour of these new neighbours. They've caused nothing but trouble since they arrived. Kevin shot the deer, but he only wounded it so he followed it onto their property where his second shot killed it. The neighbours have witnesses who saw Kevin carrying the deer from their property so they're saying he stole the deer from them. It's their word against his and he's in jail waiting for a hearing."

"Why don't you just give them the damn deer?" Will suggested.

"Kevin tried, but they wouldn't take it," said Hana. "They want him."

"Where has he been taken?"

"He's still being held locally, but we've heard he's going to be moved to the Chatham or Windsor jail shortly."

This was the most disturbing news Will had heard to date. Kevin was a big gentle guy who would hurt no one. Kevin being in jail symbolized the extent to which things had changed.

Suddenly, the war had come home. Now it was personal. Peace and justice were over.

~

CHAPTER XIII

We Stand

Heaven will look favourably on the manly exertions which the loyal and virtuous inhabitants of this happy land are prepared to make...

...dispel any apprehension which you may have imbibed of the possibility of England forsaking you;

Our gracious prince, who so gloriously upholds the dignity of the empire, already appreciates your merit, and it will be your first care to establish, by the course of your actions, the just claim of the country to the protection of his royal highness.

Although perfectly aware of the number of improper characters who have obtained extensive possessions, and whose principles diffuse a spirit of insubordination very adverse to all military institutions, I am however well assured that a large majority would prove faithful.

~

Will put down the diary. As relevant as Brock's writings had seemed until then, he doubted the modern Monarchy would ever come to support Canadians as they had in Brock's day. In this respect, he thought, times had certainly changed.

Regardless of the lack of support Will expected from the Monarchy, or anyone else for that matter, once again he was called to act on behalf of another who'd suffered grave injustice under the occupation. Only this time it was for his brother. The war had finally come home to roost at the Andersons. In consequence, he prepared to do as Brock had advised, to act in defiance of the occupation forces.

~

Will knew that it would be easier for him to assist Kevin if he did so before Kevin was transferred to the Windsor jail. Due to its close proximity to the States, there was a higher level of security at the Windsor facility. Because of this, many Canadians were sent there to await their Inland Control hearings and serve out their time. Fortunately, the Windsor jail was full, delaying Kevin's transfer.

Kevin's case was considered to be quite minor, but it had become bogged down because a weapon was involved. Despite the fact that the gun had been used against a deer and not a person, it still complicated matters. The normal sentence for those found guilty of his offence was about two weeks, but already he'd spent more than that behind bars. With the current backlog of cases to be tried, it was going to be a long time before his case would be heard.

Will visited Kevin in the jail and found him to be extremely depressed.

"I can't stay in here indefinitely, Will. Not knowing what's going to happen to me is the hardest part of all," he confessed. He didn't elaborate, but Kevin's sad eyes told Will all he needed to know. Kevin had lost weight and Will could see that his spirit was starting to fade.

"They treat us worse than the real criminals, you know. Get me out of here, Will."

"I will."

"Promise?"

"I promise. Just hang in there, Kevin." Will needed time to think and, recognizing this, he explained to Kevin that he wouldn't be seeing him for awhile. But he swore to make good on his promise.

"Just promise me this, Kevin."

"What's that?"

"That you'll hang in there, even if it's for a few weeks."

"A few more weeks? I don't know if I can, Will, honestly."

"Two more then. Tops.

"Promise?"

"Ok. I promise."

"Good."

~

Will spent most of the next few days sitting quietly out of sight, watching the daily routine at the jail. At times, when he felt most frustrated about how to gain Kevin's release, he could barely restrain himself from rushing into the jail with guns blazing. But he knew such rash behaviour would likely backfire and go badly for Kevin.

Instead, he cautiously watched from a safe distance where he wouldn't arouse any suspicion. He studied the habits of the jailers and watched for anything that might provide him with a way to free his brother. He paid particular attention to those coming to and going from the jail. The only regular visitors arrived in an Inland Control vehicle every Monday and Friday. A man in a suit and two bodyguards always travelled together in the vehicle. Often, they left with a prisoner in handcuffs being transferred to another facility. Each time he saw them, it was always the same man in the suit, but seldom was he accompanied by the same guards.

On the following Monday, as the Inland Control vehicle was en route to the jail, the guards noticed a pretty girl riding in the opposite direction, carrying groceries on her bike. Her rare smile and wave lifted their spirits. The man in the suit, agent Daniel O'Connor, was a very suspicious and cautious person making him wary of anything that captured the guards' interest.

Every Monday and Friday after that, rain or shine, she passed them on her bike. As they approached the jail in the third week, they came upon the scene of an accident. They saw a bike crumpled beneath the tires of a car and, in the ditch ahead, O'Connor saw the pretty girl lying face down. The driver of the car appeared frantic and stood beside her, shouting, "I didn't see her! I didn't see her!"

"Stop!" O'Connor ordered his driver. He and a guard jumped out and ran over to the scene.

Immediately upon their arrival, the frantic man pulled a club from under his jacket and smacked it with a thud onto the head of the guard, knocking him unconscious. A split second later, O'Connor was looking into the barrel of the man's pistol as he ordered O'Connor back to the vehicle. O'Connor had no other option but to obey.

When they returned to the vehicle, O'Connor saw that the other guard had also been knocked unconscious and was being stripped of his uniform by a second man.

"Get in!"

"Where are we going?"

"To the jail."

The unconscious guards, blind folded, bound and gagged, had been dragged off the road and tied tightly to a tree. The whole incident took less than five minutes. O'Connor and his captors sped towards the jail.

By the time they arrived at the jailhouse, O'Connor had been told of the part he was expected to play in their plan. His presence would enable them to enter the jail without raising suspicion. If successful, they promised him that he would live. Otherwise, they guaranteed he would die. O'Connor recognized that most of the inmates had committed very minor offences and he certainly wasn't prepared to sacrifice his life for them.

They arrived at the jailhouse on O'Connor's usual schedule and nobody at the jail noticed anything suspicious. Captain Owens, who was comfortable in uniform, especially looked the part. He took out a pack of DeMauriers and lit one.

Will entered with O'Connor and a jailer escorted them down the hall to a room without windows. Inside, there were two seats, facing each other on opposite sides of a table, and a side table with a coffee butler and cups on it. Will and the jailer remained standing.

Will knew there was only one other jail guard in the building. This last guard soon came into the room escorting a prisoner. As he left, the remaining jailer turned to Will.

"You can leave the room too," he advised Will.

"Right," responded Will, not knowing the protocol. "Mind if I take a cup of coffee with me?"

"Go ahead," replied the jailer.

Helping himself, Will stumbled intentionally and dropped his hot coffee all over the guard's pants.

"SHIT!" exclaimed the jailer, reaching down to his scalding legs.

As he did so, Will drew his pistol and walloped him over the head with its butt-end. As the jailer fell unconscious to the floor, Will pointed his gun at O'Connor.

"No funny business," Will cautioned him.

"Sweet!" the prisoner exclaimed and then furrowed his eyebrows as he attempted to figure out what was going on. Finally, he understood and he smiled broadly.

"Thanks. Name's Lefty. Who are you?"

"That doesn't matter right now." Will tossed Lefty a bag.

"Bind, gag and blindfold him."

"Gladly," he smiled.

Without warning, in walked the other jailer.

"What's causing all the racket?" he demanded, looking from one person to another. He saw Will's gun, trained on O'Connor, and then he saw the guard lying unconscious on the floor.

"HELP!" he yelled at the top of his lungs as he turned and ran.

"Guard him!" Will barked at Lefty and took off in pursuit. The jailer had nearly made it out the front door when Captain Owens came through the entrance. Seeing his way blocked, the jailer abruptly stopped. Will, however, couldn't stop and ran right into him so that they both tumbled head over heels onto the floor. When they came to rest, the jailer was pinned beneath Will. Looking up, Will saw Owens was smiling down at him.

"Nice tackle, Anderson."

Before Will could answer, two shots rang out from the room where he'd left Lefty to guard O'Connor. Instinctively, Owens drew his weapon and crouched beside the front counter where he could see who was coming down the hallway.

"Drop your weapon and get your hands up where I can see them!" Owens ordered. Lefty obeyed and walked towards them.

"Justice served," he said simply. Seeing Owens drawing a bead on him, he added, "He went for the jailer's gun but, unfortunately for him, I got it first. Shot the jail keeper by mistake too. Guess my aim's not so good," he admitted, smiling.

Owens lowered his gun, reached down and disarmed the man Will had pinned. Then, he and Lefty walked cautiously down the hall and went into the interrogation room. A moment later, they came back out.

"They're dead," Owens confirmed.

The prisoner pinned beneath Will started to squirm. Will held on with a firm grip, forcing the jailer to give up and look him squarely in the eye. He seemed to recognize Will.

"I know who you are," he hissed.

Suddenly, Will recognized him too. In his grip was the very man he'd had a run-in with last summer in Port Stanley, the man who'd accused him of being yellow and unpatriotic. Here was the same bully who got his jollies by hurting others.

"Hey, you're hurting me," he protested to Will.

Will realized he'd been gripping the man tighter and tighter. As he loosened his grip slightly, the jailer looked scornfully at him. He would have never done the same.

"Come for what's left of your brother Kevin, have ya?" he croaked. "Took real good care of him, I can assure you o' that. Like to get me hands on your sister too. What's her name? Oh ya, the lovely Hana."

Will could easily have killed him with his bare hands at that moment and York Owens would have been glad to watch it. This man was obviously cruel. The only thing that stopped Will was the thought that, if anyone should have the satisfaction of getting even with the jailer, it should be Kevin.

"Keys!" Will demanded, getting back to the business at hand.

"Don't know," the jailer smirked.

"Liar!" came a female voice from behind the counter. Will couldn't believe he'd forgotten about the front desk clerk. She must have hidden herself when they'd arrived.

"I'll get you the keys, Will. Let's get Kevin and the others out of this hellhole."

~

All Kevin saw when they entered his cell was another uniformed person to escort him down to the interrogation room as they did every Monday. It was a break in the mundane life behind bars and from the dreadful guard whom everyone called Willard. The man was a sadist and used any excuse to make their lives living hell.

As they walked by the front desk clerk, Kevin noticed that Kelly was smiling cheerfully, which was odd as that rarely happened anymore. Kelly Renwick had been in a grade between Kevin and Will in elementary school and Will had played soccer with her younger brother Eric. Her smile caused Kevin to wonder what was different. That's when he noticed that the guard was smiling at him too. With great relief, he realized the smile was unmistakably his brother's.

"Working for the enemy, Will?"

"Just temporarily."

"Took longer than I expected."

"I'm sorry."

"I knew you'd keep your promise. It was the only thing that kept me going."

"Let's get you out of here."

With Kelly's aid, the two other prisoners, Valerie and Dale, were freed. With Willard as their hostage, the small troupe numbered seven. With the jailers' weapons, all of them were armed. Will had their escape plan all worked out. Kevin, Will and Valerie immediately left together in O'Connor's vehicle while Owens and Lefty donned the jailers' uniforms and stayed behind with Kelly. Their job was to keep up normal appearances at the jailhouse until closing time, after which they too would make their escape. Kelly was an unexpected asset as she fully cooperated with their efforts to delay the discovery of the breakout by helping to keep the jail running normally until the day's end. Dale and Willard remained behind too.

Willard was a man without friends. His given name was Roy, but everyone called him Willard for having 'ratted' on so many of his fellow Canadians. By becoming an informant, he had improved his lot in life for the Americans rewarded him well, but the Americans also saw him as untrustworthy and only kept him around because he made their jobs easier. They made their true feelings known by calling him Willard just as the Canadians did. Willard found himself ostracized by both sides.

Meanwhile, Will and company drove north of town where Hana was waiting for them in her pick-up truck. From there, Hana led the way acting as a scout in the same manner Will had learned in Québec. This proved to be a wise precaution for it wasn't five minutes before Hana notified the others that she'd come upon a roving checkpoint. It was easy for the others following to detour around the checkpoint because there were numerous other roads to choose from. They simply routed themselves around the checkpoint to rendezvous with Hana a few concessions on the other side. It took them only twenty minutes to reach their destination.

They came to a small creek within a Conservation Area. Will had planned for the creek to be their escape route, leading them to a larger waterway and, ultimately, safety. Will had taken the idea from Brock's diary which was full of little charts and drawings showing the multitude of waterways he'd used in his day. He had hidden three canoes in the brush along with all the essential gear they'd need during the first leg of their journey. He explained his plans to Kevin and Valerie.

"You're joking, Will. We're going to canoe out of here?" Kevin asked incredulously.

"Exactly. I'm all ears if you have a better idea, Kevin."

"That just seems too easy and a little crazy."

"That's exactly the point, Kevin. Let's hope it's so crazy that they won't even consider it and we'll sneak away right under their noses."

"But by canoe?"

"I love it!" Valerie exclaimed. "I haven't been canoeing in ages. Worst case scenario is that we're recaptured. At least we'll be able to say we had fun. Let's do it."

Having settled that, Hana hugged Kevin goodbye. Then she and Will returned back to the jail to retrieve the others. The jail was now closed for the day. After thanking Kelly for her help, they drove off, with Hana again leading as scout.

By the time they arrived back at the Conservation Area, Valerie and Kevin were long gone. Hana said goodbye to Will with mixed emotions. They were close siblings and parting ways was always difficult. But as much as she was going to miss him, she knew that with distance came safety and so she urged him to get away quickly. With both of her siblings leaving her now, she felt that her family was being completely ripped apart by the occupation and she sorely wanted to join them. Tears overcame her as she shook with emotion. But she knew she still had an important part to play in carrying out their successful escape. She and York were to ditch O'Connor's car and cover their tracks.

Travelling by canoe was becoming typical for Will and he felt completely at home. For the others, it was a novel adventure.

Although Dale and Lefty had lived in the area all their lives, they had never seen it from the water. The new perspective made it seem as though they'd already travelled far away from home. Feeling that way put them at ease.

Will paddled with Dale in one canoe and Lefty with Willard in the other. Will knew Brock had no patience for mutineers. After receiving a report that some men were planning to imprison the officers of Fort George in Niagara and then flee to the enemy, Brock had rushed to the scene, and pinned the ringleader with his sabre. This quick action nipped the threat of deserting over to the invaders in the bud. Brock had written in his diary,

> *...and those who were dastardly enough to join the invaders of their native or adopted country, were quickly taught to repent of their baseness and treason.*

"Lefty, Willard's now in your charge," Will told him. "Kevin's too nice and forgiving. Can you make sure he causes no trouble?"

"With pleasure," Lefty promised.

In a complete reversal of fortune, Willard was now Lefty's prisoner and Lefty made sure Willard knew it. Anything Willard did to annoy Lefty was quickly answered with a swift jab from the butt-end of Lefty's paddle.

Their mode of travel left Will's mind free to think about the future, in hopes of staying one step ahead of their enemies. He presumed that, by noon the next day, news of their escape would be out and the troops would be scouring the countryside in search of them. He imagined they would be described as armed and dangerous criminals for they'd left three people bound and gagged and two dead. It was critical to get away unnoticed and put as many miles as possible between themselves and the jail.

~

Out of sight, they paddled on the creek under the cover of its weedy, reed fringed banks and an overhead canopy of trees. Until nightfall, they were in no rush and so they paddled casually, enjoying their peaceful surroundings. Will couldn't imagine how

Kevin must be feeling, having just been released from the confines of captivity into wide open space. The peace of the slow moving creek was broken by the constant croaking of bullfrogs and the sudden splashes of carps' tails. Here, their main enemies were the numerous mosquitoes that attacked them in the shade during the later part of day.

It was dusk when the creek fed into the Thames River. There, they came upon Kevin and Valerie hidden with their canoe amongst the thick jungle of reeds that bordered the shore. They were so well-hidden that Will would have paddled by them had he not known where to expect to find them. Soon, they were all hidden amongst the reeds where they waited for curfew to begin. After curfew, most people would be indoors so they could continue unnoticed upstream under the cover of darkness. Time passed slowly as they tried to catch a few winks of sleep.

"It's time," Will nudged Kevin, who had switched canoes so they could paddle together. His words were quietly passed along to the others and they paddled single file out of the reeds, leaving enough space between each canoe to allow for some to escape if one was spotted. They took every precaution to avoid being seen or heard for they knew that they would be treated severely if caught out after curfew. Fortunately, clouds hid the moon, preventing its light from shining on them and very little light was emitted from the homes along the sparsely populated river.

They had wrapped the shafts of their paddles with cloth so that they wouldn't be heard rubbing the edge of the canoes. The canoes were dark coloured and anything shiny, such as the metal rim gunnels and screw heads, had been painted over. They themselves were dressed in dark clothing and their faces blackened. These preparations helped keep them hidden, but would also give away their intentions, if caught.

As dawn approached, the spiral steeple of their refuge came into view. The steeple towered above the surrounding flatland which, in Brock's day, had been swamp. The swamp waters had been pumped away long ago, exposing some of the richest farmland found anywhere. With a long growing season, the land yielded a wide variety of produce.

Will had chosen this particular church for its history. St. Peter's Parish on the Thames, or La Paroisse de St. Pierre sur la Tranche, as it was formerly known, began as a log cabin. It was first dedicated in 1802 when thirty-six French and Indian families came together to formed the first congregation. There had been no roads leading to the church in Brock's time and the surrounding swamps made it practically impossible to access it by land until a road was built years later. Most early parishioners reached the church by the Thames which, in springtime, was known to flood over onto its banks. A berm was built later along the edge of the Thames to hold back the floods. That night, the berm also served to keep Will's party hidden and out of sight from the road which ran parallel to the river.

Brock had written of St. Peter's Parish in his journal. It was the first parish Brock would encounter travelling upriver on the Thames. When Will found out that it still existed, and continued to provide services to its parishioners, he knew he'd found the perfect hideout for their escape.

Just like the first congregation, they arrived at St. Peter's by boat via the Thames. As they pulled their canoes ashore and mounted the berm, they couldn't help but admire the solid church. No longer was it made of logs. Sturdy red bricks, which had been floated downstream by barge from Chatham, replaced the logs when it was rebuilt by parishioners over the ashes of the earlier structure which had been totally consumed by fire in 1895.

West of the church was a cemetery holding the graves of some of the original parishioners as well as American soldiers who'd succumbed to wounds inflicted at the Battle of Moraviantown in 1813.

Beside the church was a house and there on the stairway stood Father Monahan.

"Hello, Will. I trust you made it here without any mishaps?"

"We did, Father, thank you."

Advancing one by one, Will's party met Father Monahan as they each walked to the church's entrance which faced the river. Will had many misgivings about bringing the escapees here for it could expose the Father and his parishioners to great risk and hardship. Father Monahan sensed Will's concern.

"All will be fine, Will. Hide your canoes beneath the church and then come join us in our residence. Sister Verda's got breakfast ready and we mustn't keep her waiting. Unfortunately," he apologized to the others, "the rest of you will have to remain hidden for awhile."

Everyone nodded in understanding.

In a short while, Will was seated in the dining room which fronted Sister Verda's kitchen from which great quantities of food and beverage poured forth in a seemingly endless supply. Sister Verda proclaimed herself to be the 'chief cook and bottle washer' and she staked claim to the kitchen as her own turf. Anyone, including the Father, who felt the need to venture into her kitchen did so at the risk of having their 'backsides tanned.' Sister Verda was a good cook and the generous concoctions she doled out were fully appreciated by all who hungered, including herself, for she had nourished her own girth to grand proportions.

Sister Verda's name spoke of her other talent for she had a green thumb and kept a beautiful garden. Her garden grew many things, but it was her grapevines that received her particular interest and care. She was known for many products made from her concord grapes including jelly, juice and wine. To justify her production of the wine, she explained that 'If the good Lord dost will it that a few batches of grape juice should ferment, then surely He wishes that thou may'st drink it.'

Will took an immediate interest in Sister Verda's eccentricities and she seemed to like his company as well. Knowing that he would be leaving them soon, she made an exception to her rule, allowing him occasionally into her kitchen.

There, Will noted that Sister Verda had a soft spot for the Monarchy. Special teacups and plates commemorating coronations, anniversaries and other notable Royal moments filled her special display case.

"Don't you think the Monarchy is passé?" Will asked, examining the intricate artwork painted on a teacup and matching plate.

"No, I don't."

"Well, what do they do for us?"

"Nothing. They let us be."

"Then, what's the point?"

"The point, William, is that the Queen will be there when we need Her to be. Canada is her domain just like this kitchen is mine. Her Majesty won't abandon us if we don't abandon Her."

"I read something to that effect recently," Will recalled. "I guess I've just never thought about the Monarchy that way."

"And we can thank our lucky stars we haven't had to."

"Looks like we could use her help now though."

"Amen to that."

~

Mrs Anderson arrived at the jailhouse to visit Kevin. She found it abuzz with uniformed officers who'd answered the call after the breakout was discovered. When Kelly Renwick had failed to come over for breakfast the following morning as usual, her father had gone looking for her. His search had ended at the jailhouse where he discovered the front entranceway locked after opening hours. Concerned, he called the police who broke in to find Kelly bound and gagged. Agent O'Connor and a jailer were found dead.

Kelly told how Lefty had overpowered the jailer and Agent O'Connor. He had been helped by two other men posing as Inland Control Officers.

"Together, they gained control of the jail and freed themselves along with the other prisoners," she stated.

The escapees had also left behind a note which read:

We have escaped our unlawful imprisonment. We allege that we have been held on unreasonable grounds. We have been denied our right to due process and to prove our case before an impartial court of law. Our imprisonment has gone beyond any reasonable period of time for what were, and this fact isn't in dispute, non-violent acts. Being imprisoned for an exceptionally long period of time, we have invoked our Habeas Corpus rights and liberated ourselves. We regret the deaths of those who stood between us and our rightful freedom.

*May no person who believes in freedom and liberty
stand in our way or come searching for us. We are
proud Canadians, strong and free, and someday so shall
Canada be!*

Lefty MacIntosh

Dale DeLaurier

Valerie Hillman

Kevin Anderson

~

Word of their escape spread quickly. Finally, Canadians had
evidence of ordinary people who'd stood up and, in effect,
shouted: 'Enough! This is not right! We shall be free!' Reports from
all over the country came from people claiming to have met either
the rebellious rogue Lefty MacIntosh or one of the others. The
breakout and the mounting popularity of the escapees made their
recapture essential for the situation called into question America's
ability to rule the Canadians. American authorities mounted a
nationwide hunt for the escapees, but the Inland Control Agency
got no help from patriotic Canadians who openly supported the
escapees and spoke of them with great pride.

Meanwhile, Will left Kevin and the others at the parish. Now
they were in the good hands of Father Monahan and Sister Verda.
Alone again, he boldly biked upstream on top of the berm in broad
daylight as though he had nothing to fear.

~

CHAPTER XIV
The True North Strong And Free

The parishioners did not suspect that anything unusual was going on at St. Peter's Parish. During the turbulent times of the past year, the parish had become a refuge for many in need. Father Monahan had a far-reaching reputation as a kind and welcoming host to all, whether 'believers' or not.

To make sure nobody took any particular notice of the escapees, they hid in the church basement, individually waiting for their turn to be called upon to leave the basement and integrate themselves with the parishioners. One by one, each staged their official arrival. As their faces were well-known, they all took care to alter their appearance in order to avoid easy recognition. Upon their official arrival, like all the parishioners, each was assigned various duties to perform in exchange for their food, shelter and clothing.

The first to meet the parishioners was Kevin, calling himself Brother Mark. Father Monahan introduced Brother Mark as his new assistant, brought in to manage the parish's ballooning community. Brother Mark's clean shaven head added years onto Kevin's youthful visage which had been previously topped with wild unkempt hair.

A few days later, Valerie was called up. She masqueraded her appearance for the occasion by tying her hair up in a tight bun and sporting horn-rimmed glasses. She was introduced to the parishioners as Maria and assigned to help Sister Verda in her kitchen. Nobody would have guessed that Maria was actually the attractive and stylish female escapee whose face was so well-known to the public.

Next was Lefty, renamed Roger, which was actually his real, but long forgotten, Christian name. Being a farm boy, he fit in easily as a 'jack of all trades' who could make himself useful wherever help was needed most.

Finally, Dale was called up and introduced as Daniel. He brought with him construction skills that Father Monahan immediately put to good use.

~

Everyone in the parish was in transit including Father Monahan. There had been many Fathers called to the parish before him and each one had left his imprint by making some improvement. Father Monahan's work of building a barn and a chicken coop mirrored the work of Father Parent who'd done the same in the late 1900s. Once again, the sounds of a working farm dominated the parish which housed not only a dozen labourers but two horses, three jersey cows, six pigs and six hundred chickens. Any eggs that the parish didn't need for themselves were taken to the farmers' markets in Chatham and Tilbury each Wednesday and Saturday.

Underground, beneath the main floor of the church and in the basement of his house, Father Monahan was making his most lasting mark. There, in what was little more than a crawlspace, Father Monahan gave Daniel the task of constructing a hideout and some escape routes.

Brother Mark was under the religious tutorship of Father Monahan so whenever he was absent from chores, everyone assumed that he was engrossed in holy work. During most of those absences, he was actually in the church's basement helping Daniel construct their hideout. Ample foundation stone leftover from the original barn had been stockpiled and stored beneath the church. This stone would avoid drawing attention to their renovations as it was the same age, shape and material of that used for the church and blended in perfectly.

The first room was a cell for Willard. There, he was left alone to repent for his sins beneath the church. Willard grudgingly gave his labour towards constructing what was, in essence, his own dungeon. His hideout was located right under the main entrance and had only one door, leading back into the main basement, and no escape exit.

Another space was blocked in at the head of the church under the chancel. There, an escape hatch was installed into the floor leading from the basement directly into the hollow altar table.

Crawling up into the altar, one person, with arms wrapped around bent knees, could hide there.

The third hideout was the smallest. A wall was put up beneath the east end of the study into the main part of the basement. Once it was all completed, to anyone standing in the middle of the main basement, the newly constructed walls appeared no different from the old, yet between them was now a hiding place. Within it, one could either exit into the main basement through an invisible locked door or escape up through a small hatch into the study.

~

Not only had the highly publicized escape and the hunt for the escapees struck a collective nerve among Canadians, it was as though a nationwide call to arms had been sounded. All across the land, people whispered about the need for an organized insurgency to resist the American occupation. Throughout that spring, Canadians formed a whole host of uncoordinated armed bands and began the work of misleading, foiling and harassing the occupying forces however, whenever and wherever possible.

Seeing the birth of a real resistance, Will conceived of using the letter 'X' as a unifying symbol to represent 'Expulsion' of the occupying forces from Canada. Through Father Monahan and Hana, he conveyed this idea to Captain Owens who Will knew remained closely connected with a large force of the disbanded army veterans. Being a student of history, Will knew that the BBC had restored hope to the dispirited people of occupied Europe during the Second World War with the use of the symbol 'V' for Victory. In the same way, he hoped the 'X' would become a modern symbol to rally together all the small factions into one substantial coordinated effort.

In no time, his optimism was realized when one morning the people in downtown Toronto woke to see a huge X banner hanging from the top of the CN Tower. A troop detachment was sent to take down the banner, but by the time they got it down, there was another huge X banner draped from another high-rise building. This game of cat and mouse went on for weeks and kept a good number of troops occupied. Finally, the troops gave up and let the banners fly freely in open defiance.

That summer, Xs were seen all across occupied Canada and the symbol began to electrify and unite the Canadian people. Owens soon found himself coordinating a disciplined underground army of Canadian partisans and, for the first time, the occupying troops were thrown on the defensive.

It took Will three days to reach the outskirts of London where the flatlands gave way to pleasant rolling countryside. Now the trees were in full foliage again and helped to keep him hidden, but there were places where the houses fronting the river interrupted his path and he found himself zigzagging in order to avoid people.

After London, there was a larger network of trails and he gave thanks to the planners whose foresight conserved them. Where the river split, he took the north Thames Valley trail to St. Mary's and, from there, walked along the Avon Trail which led to Stratford and his destination, Waterloo.

Once again alone with nature, Will rediscovered an easier state of being as he thought more about the bright side of things. Considering what he enjoyed and needed, rather than what he wanted, gave him a lot of personal comfort. For Will, this was a feeling that could be shared with another likeminded person, like Sydney, in silence. He recognized too that there were many people who were very discontented and, to him, it seemed that their discontent often sprang from a lack of thankfulness for what they had. He felt, as his mother had always said, that everyone had something to be thankful for. Thinking this way, he made a mental note to take time to be thankful for something, no matter how small, each and every day.

He was nearing the southern limits of the forest. Six days after leaving the parish, his trip ended in Waterloo where the waters of the Conestoga and Grand Rivers converged. As he entered the community, he lost count of the number of X symbols he saw scrawled and painted everywhere in defiance of the occupation.

He made his way to the home of York Owens' parents.

"Come in, Will," they welcomed him.

They were expecting him and were anxiously awaiting news of their son. Will brought them up to date. They were not surprised to discover how he had helped Will plan and execute the escape. They were obviously proud of their son. Knowing that their house would be a safe haven, York had previously brought a couple of other innocent, but persecuted, individuals to stay with his parents. The Owens had gladly taken in Salim and his mother, Cantara. Despite being cooped up indoors, Cantara remained cheerful by helping with the cooking and keeping the house.

"He likes her cooking better than mine," Mrs Owens complained jokingly about Cantara at dinner that night.

"So do you, if the truth be known."

"Well I must admit, Cantara can cook wonderfully tasty dishes. Fortunately, they don't go straight to my waistline."

Will noted that both she and Mr Owens appeared in good health and their photos showed that they had been much heavier in the not too distant past. Compared to the others, Salim appeared gaunt. Dark circles surrounded his dull eyes. Meeting Will and hearing of his plans to head north brought him hope.

"Can I please come with you?" he pleaded.

"No," Will answered him flatly. Will knew he travelled best alone and he recognized that Salim's Middle Eastern appearance would make their journey too risky.

"Excuse me," Salim said, leaving the table abruptly.

"He's gone off to read again," his mother explained. "Nowadays, it's his only form of escape."

"We've got to get that boy some more books," piped in Mr Owens. "He's read and reread all the books we have a number of times. He particularly loves ones like Tom Sawyer and Huck Finn. Says that he would like to live life as an adventure as they did."

That night, those comments of Mr Owens stuck in Will's head, disrupting his sleep. As he lay there, the moonlight illuminated a photo on the dresser of Salim with his elder sister, Adrira. She was dressed in her Red Cross uniform sporting a maple leaf on her lapel. To Will, it appeared that she looked straight out of the photo at him.

'She was probably wearing that same uniform when she was killed', he thought. Her arms were draped, like a protective shield, around Salim's small frame.

All night, Will lay awake thinking about Salim, weighing the pros and cons of his decision. It seemed to him that, just as Kevin had been unjustly imprisoned, so had Salim. York had told Will that Adrira's father had been killed fighting in Afghanistan leaving behind a pregnant Cantara. Widowed in a land where a pregnant woman without a man was worthless, she had no choice but to flee. She had immigrated to Canada when Adrira was just a young girl.

Cantara gave birth to Salim in Canada so he was Canadian by birthright. Adrira took it upon herself to help her mother at home and to raise Salim. She was strict and kept him out of trouble.

With the current paranoia surrounding foreigners, Cantara and Salim were trapped indoors because of their own skin colour. How strange it seemed to Will that their appearance, which made them appear more native to North America than he, would deem them to be more foreign. It suddenly occurred to him that if he thought Salim looked like a Native, perhaps others would too.

~

Will awoke to see Salim peeking out at some neighbourhood boys playing road hockey on the street. Salim knew which ones had the most talent, who was most likely to over-dramatize an injury and he knew who, under different circumstances, would have been his friends. Will's heart went out to Salim and he made up his mind.

"Morning," Will said.

"Morning, Mr Anderson."

"You can call me Will."

"Yes, sir."

"Will."

"Will, sir."

Will smiled thinking that Adrira had left her mark.

"I figure we should be on a first name basis if we're going to be travelling together. That is, if you still want to come with me, Salim."

Salim looked up as though he was hearing things.

"Pardon, sir?"

"I asked if you still want to come along," Will repeated. "So do you?"

"Really? You mean it?"

"Yes, I really do."

"Yes!" Salim exclaimed with his face suddenly coming alive.

"Then, if it's ok with your mom, you can come. We leave tonight."

"YES SIR, Will!"

For the remainder of the day, Will tried to make up for the sleep he'd missed the previous night. Having made the right decision, his conscience let him sleep peacefully. When Will woke again later, he could have sworn that Adrira's face in the photo was now smiling down at him.

"It could be dangerous," he mouthed to her. Regardless, she still smiled.

Cantara was thankful beyond measure. "May God protect you, my son. And may God protect you too, William Anderson."

At dusk and just before curfew, Mr Owens dropped them off at the Grand River Valley Trail where he wished them luck. They disappeared into the forest, heading northeast toward Peterborough, taking every precaution to avoid people. Most Canadians were now actively opposing the occupation and would have been happy to help them evade the authorities, but there were still some who would have turned them in for an extra food ration card. Knowing this, they moved only at night, fuelling themselves with smoked sausage, bread and cheese and filtering their water from the plentiful rivers and streams. Each day, they bedded down before dawn, hidden deep in a thicket, using a tarp as a lean-to in case it rained.

As soon as they arrived at the professor's, all activity stopped. The Hackers were prepared for Will's return and they were ready to celebrate with plenty of good food, drink, music and company. Many came that night to congratulate Will on demonstrating that the Americans could be bested. His actions had encouraged many others to join the growing resistance.

Will found the attention to be undeserved and embarrassing. In his mind, he'd done what anyone would do for a family member. As he tried to explain this and showed his honest modesty, their admiration for him grew. His exploits had spoken loudest of all and had helped to restore a sense of pride and confidence in being a Canadian.

~

CHAPTER XV

Protégera Nos Foyers Et Nos Droits

From that night onwards, Will began to keep a diary just as Brock, his mentor, had done.

Tonight I saw the first indication that a united partisan effort has been born. News of our exploits preceded my arrival in Peterborough and I found it overwhelming to be welcomed back as a returning hero. We'd bested the invaders and it was a needed ray of sunshine in what had been, until now, all gloomy news.

Our success in freeing the prisoners has energized more people to resist and I am the unworthy recipient for much of the credit for it. It seems to others that, as we have been the first to turn the tables on the Americans and continue to evade their efforts, we are the inspiration and natural leaders of the resistance. What has made me heroic on our side of the border has made me villainous on the other.

In truth, I lead nothing directly and I am no hero. Perhaps, if one could say I've provided others with an example to follow, in that way alone I lead. Most important is that the resistance has been founded. Its existence gives us hope, a way to release our pent up energy and to act out our private thoughts. It has unified us.

— W. Anderson

~

The search for the escapees escalated as though everything depended upon their recapture. The lack of success brought on more callous actions which, in turn, spurred on further resistance. For most of the regular troops amongst the American occupying forces, their heart wasn't into this sort of war. It was becoming too political and many of them privately sided with the political beliefs espoused by the resistance. For them, it was Mr Kuhn's War.

And so, President Kuhn's orders were carried out most faithfully by the Inland Control Agency. The Agency's method was to invade homes, neighbourhood by neighbourhood, in search of men and arms, but what they found, for the most part, were women, children and the elderly. It was disconcerting for them to realize that, all across the nation, most Canadian men had disappeared. The troops were ordered to go north to root out those hiding, but they soon discovered that Canada was far too large for any foreign army to control. Their defences were thinned and they were easy targets for the well-trained and well-hidden Canadians. Time and time again, the occupiers were overwhelmed in countless little hit and run battles.

Stateside, the call for more troops went out and the draft was reinstituted. A flood of draft-dodgers crossed the open border to seek asylum in Canada amongst their friends and relatives. Hunted down by the law, they declared themselves to be Canadian citizens and, therefore, exempt from the American draft. But Washington wasn't buying their defence, declaring them all to be traitors and sentencing them to death by firing squad.

Canadians too were called upon to fill the ranks of Washington's new combined Continental Army. Many Canadians enlisted, but most of those were actually partisans loyal to Canada who sought to do their part against the occupation by working from the inside.

By the beginning of July, the Continental Army had been forced to retreat from the Canadian north. Encouraged by the success of the resistance and realizing that the occupying forces weren't so invincible, more and more Canadians rose up to join in the harassment of the occupiers.

By the end of July, most of the occupation forces were bottled up within their garrisons and could not move safely in Canada unless shielded by their armoured vehicles and travelling in convoy to and from their barricaded compounds. Most of Canada, lying more than one hundred miles from the American border, was unoccupied and free. Still, a half million American troops were stationed along the Canadian side of the border. The war was far from over.

~

"Help!" shouted Willard. Kevin, in kindness, had allowed Willard out to join the others doing outdoor farm work. There seemed no risk that Willard would expose their secret to the parishioners for his own secret was more deplorable; he had assisted the invaders. But when Willard saw a convoy of American soldiers in armoured cars approaching, it was the chance he'd been waiting for.

"Help!" he shouted again, waving his arms frantically as he ran across the field towards them.

He was just about to yell a third time when Lefty tackled him hard from behind, pitching him face down on the ground. Lefty landed hard on top of him intending to deliberately knock the wind out of him.

"Bastard," Lefty cursed him, pressing down on the back of his head so that his mouth was buried in the soil. He hated Willard and had argued with Kevin about letting him out. Now he could do something about it. He pushed down harder on Willard's skull.

The convoy, now alert to the commotion ahead, had come to a stop nearby and had their guns trained on the both of them.

"What's going on there?" an officer shouted at them.

"Nothing, sir," Lefty answered, but beneath him, Willard's persistent struggling told another story.

"Get off that man. And put your arms in the air," ordered the officer.

"Yes, sir!" Lefty replied, putting all the force he could on Willard's scrawny neck. With one final thrust, he was rewarded with a *snap*. Beneath him, he felt Willard's struggling body jerk in one final contraction and then go limp. Feeling satisfied, Lefty stood up, raised his hands and smiled. Willard lay still on the ground.

"What's going on there?" demanded the officer again.

"Nothing sir. Just a personal quarrel. This man slept with my girl."

"He did, did he? What's wrong with him?"

"I think he's dead, sir."

"Shit," the officer replied, thinking that this would require formal investigation with a lot of paperwork.

"Cuff him, Sergeant," he ordered his subordinate, "and let's find out what really happened here."

Lefty was handcuffed and guarded while Captain Martin and his squad of soldiers had all the other parishioners rounded up and questioned. They soon realized that the girlfriend wasn't anywhere to be found.

"Maybe she's with Brother Mark," someone volunteered.

"Who's Brother Mark?" asked the captain.

A few minutes later, someone ran back from the study.

"Brother Mark's disappeared too, sir, and no one can find Daniel either."

While Captain Martin questioned the others about the incident, the soldier guarding Lefty called to him, "Captain, I think you should take a look here, sir."

"What's that, Private?"

"It's just the prisoner, Captain. He sort of looks like that Lefty, sir."

"Who?"

"Lefty, sir. You know. One of the four escapees we're all looking for."

Captain Martin came over for a closer look at the prisoner.

"Do you think so, soldier?"

"Sure do, sir. I'd put a wager on it."

"Save your money, Private. If you're right, you're in for a big reward. There's a million dollars on his head."

Soon they had retrieved copies of the photos of the escapees that had been so widely circulated. Martin looked back and forth between the photo and the prisoner. There was no doubt there was a strong resemblance.

"Sergeant!"

"Sir?"

"Have that man's beard shaved off, Sergeant. We need to have a better look at his face."

"Yes, sir!"

A short while later, Lefty was beardless and it was obvious they'd caught the notorious outlaw.

"Good work, Private. And congratulations, you're a rich man," Captain Martin said to the bright private who been first to notice the resemblance.

"Just doing my duty, Captain."

The other parishioners were still in the dark about what was really going on. They had bought 'Roger's' story that he had quarrelled with the loner, Willard. They knew that the two of them had been at each other's throats and had seen Roger rough Willard up many times before. Quite innocently, they'd fully cooperated with the investigation. Had they known the truth, that was the last thing they would have done.

"And when he arrived, he was clean shaven," one parishioner described Roger. "That was a few weeks ago."

Piece by piece, the whole story started to come together. Others unwittingly confirmed that Roger and the other three had arrived at the parish shortly after the news of their escape became public. At the time, their arrivals had seemed spaced apart, but in retrospect, it now appeared that they all arrived at about the same time.

"I saw Daniel and Maria head out in the canoe a short while ago," someone divulged.

The two were soon discovered a short ways downstream hiding amongst the reeds.

"We're going to have to search the grounds, Father," Captain Martin apologized.

The Father nodded. He knew he had no choice and a squad of soldiers was ordered to search through the house and the church. For a while, all seemed to be going smoothly until a group of soldiers came running out of the house. Hot on their heels was Sister Verda, wielding a broom over her head and yelling, "I warned thee, STAY OUT OF MY KITCHEN!"

Once they were out, she returned indoors to her kitchen, slamming the door shut behind her.

"They don't make them like her anymore," admitted the Father.

"Thank goodness for that!" replied the captain. "Or else you Canucks would be celebrating Victory Day in DC by Christmas!"

By early afternoon, everyone had been questioned and the whole parish had been dusted for fingerprints. It was now apparent to all the parishioners that Roger and the others were the infamous escapees.

Only Brother Mark remained missing. To everyone's surprise, he came walking out of the church.

"There's Brother Mark!" exclaimed a parishioner.

"I thought you'd checked the church," said the surprised captain.

"We did, sir," replied an equally surprised private.

Dressed in his formal robes, Brother Mark walked serenely up to Martin.

"I believe I'm the person you're looking for, Captain."

~

Father Monahan convened an assembly of the parishioners to explain what was going on in their normally pastoral community.

"You mean they're the escapees?" asked a parishioner.

"They are," answered the Father.

"Living here with us?"

"Yes."

"Even Brother Mark?"

"Yes. Even Brother Mark. He's Kevin, William Anderson's brother."

Nobody needed to be told who Anderson was or which ones were Lefty and Valerie.

"They're famous," a female parishioner stated.

"Heroes," said another. "I'm going to get my camera and ask for their autographs."

While others lined up to get their photos with the foursome, Sister Verda came out of her kitchen carrying a special little snack she'd made for each of the prisoners. One by one, she stooped to give each of them their treat and say a few words of encouragement. As she did so, the guards stood aside, knowing not to interfere with her.

When she finished, she pulled out the cross she wore tied around her neck on a simple leather strap. Holding it in her hands towards the sky, she defiantly faced the armed guards and began to sing.

"God save our gracious Queen,
Long live our noble Queen...,"

One by one, all the parishioners joined in. Video cameras recorded it all and the images were soon sent out digitally to the whole world.

By day's end, a crowd of angry protestors from the nearby communities of Tilbury and Chatham totally surrounded the parish.

"SANC-TU-ARY! SANC-TU-ARY!" they shouted.

~

Father Monahan and Captain Martin sat facing each other across the table. The process of extricating the escapees from the sanctuary of the parish had become bogged down with legal technicalities. Up to this point, the US had maintained that they had not invaded Canada, but had instead secured its porous borders from being infiltrated by international terrorists at the invitation of the former Prime Minister. In addition, Washington maintained that the abdication of the Federal Government in Ottawa was sufficient evidence to prove that Canada had consented to handing over federal control to Washington. In effect, Washington claimed, Canada had voluntarily joined the North American Union.

The resistance movement flew in the face of all these claims, but Washington maintained that the resistance was only made up of a small minority of Canadians who were being funded by international terrorism.

The question turned to what was the residency status of the escapees? Were the escapees now citizens of a united North American continent, as Washington contended, or were they still Canadians? If North Americans, were they subject to American laws? In this scenario, as the Canadians claimed, they'd undoubtedly been held in prison awaiting their trials too long and they'd been denied their rights under the 6th Amendment to a speedy and public trial. In addition to this, their forced removal from the church's sanctuary would be a violation of their 1st Amendment rights.

On the other hand, if the escapees were regarded as Canadians, it would be an admission that Canada was still a sovereign nation and, in this case, the Americans were outside of their jurisdiction and it was a matter to be decided by the Canadian courts.

The other scenario that Washington didn't want to publicly consider was that America and Canada were indeed at war and they were escaped prisoners of war.

Each argument brought greater complications and complexity to the debate and prolonged any official decisions. On the ground at the parish, however, the situation demanded immediate action as more and more protestors continued to arrive. Matters were very quickly escalating beyond control and the situation had become a powder-keg of emotion. Should it blow, it would cause huge negative repercussions on both sides.

Captain Martin knew the situation was very delicate and required tact. If he mishandled it, he'd be the scapegoat. Regardless of the politics, Martin was a man of action and he knew that it was still within his power to avoid unnecessary bloodshed.

"We've got Lefty. And the fingerprints of the other three have been found all over the parish," he repeated the facts to Father Monahan.

Father Monahan looked at the captain without any guilt. He knew that the canoes had been discovered and dusted for fingerprints. No doubt the tools that had been used to build the hiding spaces had also been dusted. If so, it was probably just a matter of time before the Americans connected the dots that would lead them to find the secret hideouts.

"So?"

"So, they're criminals."

"According to some. According to others, they're victims. If you allege them to be criminals, show me their victims." The Father added, "We both know, Captain, there's no such thing as a victimless crime."

The captain did know it. Being black, he knew better than most about unjust victimless laws. Who had Rosa Parks hurt when she bravely took her seat on that fateful bus? Yet she'd broken a law. Martin looked out the window. Out there in the darkness, he could see a network of torches and camp fires lit by the local people who had set up a vigil. There was no doubt they intended to see this thing through.

"They've murdered people," Martin asserted.

"This is war and they had no choice but to kill the enemy who tried to bar their escape."

"Hmmm." Martin knew he'd have done the same if the roles had been reversed. He actually admired the escapees for their actions. The Father could sense the captain's inner turmoil and surmised that he simply wanted an honourable way out of the mess.

"Captain, we are not lawyers. So let's speak freely," the Father offered.

Those words got the captain's full attention. Martin had already heard enough legal doubletalk and it had given him a headache.

"You already have Lefty. Take him and leave the parish now while you still can. I'll ensure your safe departure. As far as the others are concerned, I give you my word they will not leave the parish until the matter is settled by a higher authority."

Both men had different ideas as to who that higher authority might ultimately be, but it provided a compromise to the delicate situation. The captain knew that he had nothing to lose by accepting. He trusted the Father.

"Now, Captain, you must promise me something."

"Father?"

"Promise me that Lefty gets a fair hearing. You know what I mean."

"I promise, Father," Martin nodded in agreement. "This is truly a strange war," he added. "Here we are, two so-called enemies. Each of us should be trying to trick the other. We would be heroes if we succeeded. And yet I have no inclination to do that to you. I truly respect you, trust you and, in fact, I like you. And I believe you feel the same way about me."

"I do, my son," answered the Father truthfully. "Now let's get this thing over with before somebody else gets hurt."

A short while later, with the Father standing up in the lead vehicle for everyone to see, the American convoy departed with Lefty as their prisoner. Soon afterward, the pacified crowd dispersed.

~

President Kuhn was livid just as Colonel Douglas had expected. Still, he knew that he had to be the first to inform the President what had transpired.

"He did what, Colonel?"

"He gave his word that…"

"His word doesn't matter one iota. THIS IS WAR, DAMN IT! The whole world will be laughing at us if we can't beat a friggin' parish. I'll give them something to laugh at. We don't make deals with terrorists!"

"Technically they're not terrorists, Mr President."

"To hell with the lawyers and their mumbo-jumbo. As far as I'm concerned, they have no jurisdiction in the matter. If I say they're terrorists, then they're terrorists. Now you listen to me very carefully, Colonel. I want that man Lefty executed. And make it public. We've got to send a message to those insurgent bastards. I don't care how you do it, just do it. If you still don't think he's a terrorist, then give him the honour of a firing squad!"

~

Citizens of other countries sympathized with the Canadians, seeing that they were the clear underdogs in a grossly unequal contest. For many, Canada had been there during times of need and now they demanded that their governments openly condemn the American occupation. The whole notion that the Canadians had willingly invited the occupation to help ensure North America's security was being hotly questioned by the United Nations. Americans themselves were openly debating the matter and riots had become commonplace on college and university campuses.

Britain's Parliament had previously deemed it prudent to temporarily accept Washington's rationale for bringing Canada into the North American Union. Upon hearing of the escapees' plight and the suspension of the Canadian Parliament, the Queen decided to assert her rightful authority as Canada's Monarch and official Head of State. The British Prime Minister had cautioned Her to wait since much was at stake for Britain with its heavy reliance on its American ties, but, entering the mêlée of words, the Queen spoke on television and made her views known.

Tonight I speak to you as your Queen and I dedicate
myself anew to the people and the nation I am proud
to serve.

I wish to convey this message to everyone within the Commonwealth Realm, both in these Isles and overseas.

I have said before, and I repeat today, that Canada is a country that has been blessed beyond most countries in the world. It is a country worth working for and, if called to do so, worth fighting for. Let me reassure you that I am not just a fair weather friend to the Realm beyond these Isles and I am glad to represent Canada at this sensitive time. I hope my words of support may call to mind our many years of shared experience and raise new hopes for the future.

Over the course of this past year, we have been trying to arrive at an honourable solution pertaining to the question of the legitimacy of the American occupation of the territory of Canada, a land and a people who now vigorously contend to still rest within my Realm.

To date, we have been unable find a peaceful solution to the divergence of views between ourselves and the United States of America.

The United States has, until only recently, maintained that the legitimacy of their occupation is founded upon the general consent of my Canadian people. On this, we have had insufficient evidence to the contrary. Until now.

Over the course of the last few weeks, we have seen my Canadian people rise up in defence of their fellow citizens whom they believe have been unjustly treated by the courts of the United States of America. One such man is slated for execution.

This uprising, which has erupted all across Canada and has swelled to include a vast number of my Canadian people, cannot be disregarded by this Monarchy. The multitude of messages that I have personally received, beseeching my support, clearly refutes the claim of the

United States of America that my Canadian people have consented to the occupation.

We have seen throughout Britain, the Commonwealth and around the world, an overwhelming expression of support for the plight of my Canadian people. It has now become clear to all that the occupation has been forced upon them.

In response, the United States of America has declared their right to remain in Canada, if only to ensure their own security and extract their due reparations, but it is the view of this Monarchy that the status of Canada remains still unresolved.

As such, this Monarchy cannot, without dishonouring its own deeply held principles, accept the claims of the United States of America.

As a result, we are called to challenge those claims which have led a nation, in selfish pursuit of their own interests, to disregard the sovereignty and independence of another nation.

Such disregard has caused a peaceful people to take up arms in their own defence. We cannot deny the irony that much of the current conflict has occurred within a region renowned for providing sanctuary for fugitive Negro Americans fleeing unjust imprisonment during the dark days of slavery. Places such as North Buxton, in the Province of Ontario, Canada, mark the spirit of people such as Sir Thomas Fowell Buxton, the great leader of the British anti-slavery movement in the 1820s, and known in the language of the time as 'the friend of the Negro'. We hearken back to the spirit of those times. In this regard, I wish it to be known that your Queen is the friend of the smallest minority, which is comprised of each and every person individually, who seeks to remain under the protection of the Crown. With fortitude and resolve, I answer the call of this, my foremost, duty.

My family's association with this country over many generations allows me to see and to appreciate Canada from the viewpoint of history. One of the strongest and most valued assets of the Crown is the stability and continuity it can bring from the past into the present. For the second time in my lifetime, I must proclaim the everlasting message: might is not right.

I assure you that I do not desire to abandon Canada who, during our time of need against an equally formidable and determined foe in World War II, faithfully and voluntarily rendered these Isles their mortal assistance. In the timeless words of Queen Elizabeth I, 'I do not so much rejoice that God hath made me to be a Queen, as to be a Queen over so thankful a people.'

You have inherited a country uniquely worth preserving. I call on all Canadians to cherish this inheritance and protect it with all your strength. I call on my people all across the Commonwealth to make the Canadian cause their own. As free individuals, living within a Realm that seeks first and foremost to safeguard that original principle that dates back to the Magna Carta, I ask you all to stand united with your Monarch in this moment of trial and tribulation.

To my loyal Canadians, be assured that we will remain resolutely set on restoring your rightful sovereignty and committed to whatever service or sacrifice may be required of us and then, with God's help, we shall triumph. May God bless us and keep us all. Good night.

CHAPTER XVI

Their Blood Has Washed Out Their Foul Footsteps' Pollution

Were the Americans of one mind, the opposition I could make would be unavailing; but I am not without hope that their divisions may be the saving of this province.

The US regiments of the line desert over to us frequently, as the men are tired of the service...

~

"You ok, sir?"

Captain Martin heard his name and felt the hand that shook him, but his head was too full of conflicting thoughts to respond. The whole world seemed united against them. Who would have thought that the Queen of England was also the Queen of Canada? She had spoken of North Buxton and her words had drawn him there. Now he stood looking at a letter, mesmerized by its import.

Since being stationed in Chatham, he'd become aware of the area's history as a place of refuge for blacks fleeing from their masters during earlier times. The name North Buxton, a tiny community just south of Chatham, had sounded oddly familiar when he heard it for the first time, but he didn't know why. Until the Queen had spoken of it, its existence had been intentionally kept a secret from the troops. The difficulty he had found trying to arrange a visit to North Buxton had only heightened his curiosity. What he found when he arrived was a place dedicated to preserving black history. Here was where the Underground Railroad, the organized system of escape that led fugitive slaves to their freedom in Canada, ended.

Melanie, the museum's curator was more than delighted to show Captain Martin and the other troops around the museum and through the original one room schoolhouse. Due to austerity measures, her wages had been eliminated, but she carried on as before, volunteering her time to keep up the buildings and their history alive. Before the hostilities, most of the museum's visitors had come from the States, but those visitors were non-existent now. Captain Martin was the first black American to have set foot in the museum for almost a year and he had brought a number of other black Americans along with him.

Melanie was beside herself with excitement to educate them about their shared heritage. Martin removed his cap as he entered the museum. It was more than an automatic military reflex. He felt compelled to do so as though he had entered a sacred place.

"The Buxton Settlement was founded in 1849," Melanie began. She knew the routine well. "Reverend King purchased 4300 acres of land in Canada for the fugitive American slaves to settle on. As our Queen has said, Buxton got its name from the British emancipator, Sir Thomas F. Buxton. Under King's direction, the settlement prospered and by 1864 the community contained about 1000 persons and had a saw and grist-mill, a brickyard and other small industries."

"1864? That was during the Civil War, ma'am," Martin interrupted.

"That's correct. Very good, Captain!" Then Melanie blushed, realizing who she was speaking with. She was more accustomed to touring school age children or casual tourists who weren't as versed on military history as the captain undoubtedly was.

"Interesting."

"In fact, seventy Buxton settlers enlisted and served in President Lincoln's Union Army during what you call the American Civil War. I personally think of it as the Civil Rights War," she ventured. "And in the Civil Rights War, Canada played a vital part."

They stood together thinking about the past. All around the room hung photos of those who had pioneered their way to freedom.

"Check this out, sir," a private exclaimed, pointing out some shackles on display.

"Those were used for transporting slaves from Africa, Private," Melanie explained.

"Geez, ma'am…" The shackles spoke volumes. Nothing more needed to be said.

Martin looked at them and then back to Melanie. The shackles reminded him of the Canadian escapees he had cuffed in the cemetery at the parish. The thought sent a chill down his spine. He felt ashamed for what he'd done.

"You're black like us, ma'am. If you don't mind me ask'n, where are your roots?"

"Africa, America, now here. My family fled to Canada in the 1850s as fugitive slaves. Under the Fugitive Slaves Act, my family was hunted down right to the Canadian border. Here in North Buxton, they were welcomed and protected. I'm one of the last descendants still here in Buxton. Nobody kept any records from before, but my skin tells me my original roots are from Africa and my Granddaddy told me we came here from the States."

"Where'd all the others go?"

She smiled with obvious pride. "Mostly, they went back to the States. But they returned there as free people with their heads held high. Ex-slaves who came here believing they were lesser folk got an education for the first time here. They bought their own land and farmed it. Little by little, they saved up some money. Some moved to the cities and then, after the war, a number of them returned to the United States. Some started newspapers, others became involved in politics. Some became State Representatives. Others stayed in the Union Army and climbed the ranks," she said, looking at his captain's bars.

Melanie's eyes shifted to his name tag – Martin. She furrowed her eyebrows in thought and then lifted her gaze up to his face. Something had just occurred to her.

"Martin. Your first name doesn't happen to be Jerome, Captain? Jerome Martin?"

"That's right, ma'am."

She gasped sucking in air.

"But how would you know that?"

It took her a moment to regain her composure.

"Is Jerome a common name in your family?" she finally asked.

"Sure is, ma'am. I'm the fourth Jerome Martin, five generations removed from the first Jerome Martin. At least the first Jerome Martin we know of. He's where our family tree begins. I guess that's because he was the first one who learned how to write. He was my great-great-great-Granddaddy and was the first black officer in the Union Army, ma'am," he added proudly.

"I figured that," she whispered.

"Ma'am?"

"Come with me. I have something to show you."

Martin followed Melanie who stopped by a letter encased in an old frame hanging on the wall. A small photo had been inserted over the bottom corner of the letter. Looking closer, he realized it was a photo of his great-great-great-Granddaddy, the first Jerome Martin.

"How di... you git...," he stammered.

"Just read the letter, Captain. It will explain everything."

~

"You ok, sir?" the private repeated. This time Martin snapped out of it. Seeing the letter before him, he read it again.

My good Reverend King and dear friends of Buxton, I have been of late so much upon the move, that I had no occasion of writing to you before this date. God has blessed our cause for the war has been decided in our favour. We have carried the glorious Union flag of freedom through countless battles and now it flies over Charleston. Here I am stationed for some time and find myself called to raise up the spirit of my people, who've known only servitude. I foresee the day when we will all be treated as equals in America, as we were in Buxton, Canada, where I savoured the sweet nectar of personal liberty for the very first time. For this, I will forever credit you all for providing a safe sanctuary for me, raising my spirits and inspiring me to fight for the same treatment in my own dear country. Eternally grateful. Jerome Martin − South Carolina 1865.

For the first time in a very long time, Captain Martin broke down and cried. Seeing his distress, his men assisted him to a seat. They had all felt a personal reawakening and mixed emotions during their tour through the museum, but they had never seen their captain like this before.

"You ok, Captain?" one asked.

Breathing in deeply, he replied, "Now I am. Thanks."

Seeing their looks of concern and hearing their distressed murmuring, he pulled himself back together. Glancing back at the letter and the photo, he knew what he was called to do. He looked around and smiled with renewed confidence.

"That's my great-great-great-Granddaddy there," he said, pointing at the photo. "He came here to escape from slavery. Canada, Canadians, protected him and taught him that he was equal to anyone. He returned to the States as a confident free man and helped make things better for folks like us."

As he spoke, all was becoming crystal clear to him and the words flowed so naturally that he didn't even need to think about what he was saying. His men were awed by his clarity as he explained their history here and how it related to the current conflict and their role in it.

After his explanation, he asked, "What the hell are we doing here, fellas? That man there," he said, pointing again at the photo, "would be ashamed of me. Until now, I haven't earned his name. Now I will."

"Sir?"

"I'm declaring my tour of duty over. I didn't sign up for this. This is Mr Kuhn's War, not mine. Not any of yours either, brothers. I, for one, will not dishonour our roots. I've got no quarrel with the Canadians. Neither do you. They paid us a good turn and now it's time to say 'thanks' by letting them be."

For a moment, nobody spoke. They understood what he was saying, but they were still hesitant.

"You can't, sir, that's desertion. They'll string you up."

"They can try to, Private... just like they tried to string him up," he said, staring at the photo. "Better people than me have died for freedom. At least this way, I would die for the right cause. Giving freedom, not taking it away. This is a bad war and I choose to have no part of it. They can try to stop me if they want." Then, to emphasize what Buxton had taught, he added, "To hell with Kuhn and his Confederates. I'm going home."

The others couldn't help but be emboldened. They too had been inspired to a greater cause.

"I'm with you, sir," said the soldier who'd pointed out the shackles earlier. Holding them in his hands had forever unsettled him.

"Thanks, Private."

"Me too, sir."

It was unanimous. Even Smithers, the only white one of the bunch, joined in because, as he said, "America invented freedom. Can't let you brothers take all the credit for keeping it."

One by one, they began to lay down their arms. Martin stopped them.

"Keep your guns, fellas. We still have the right to bear arms. Besides, we've got one last job to do."

"Sir?"

~

We wish and hope for peace, but it is nevertheless our duty to be prepared for war.

The verdict in Lefty's case was guilty. The State's prosecution had asked for death by lethal injection, but in an act of clemency, the American judge sentenced him to death by firing squad. The diplomatic difference was that he was treated like an enemy combatant as the Canadians considered him to be. This recognition made the War for North America official.

Will was still in Peterborough when he got word of Lefty's fate. In response, he and the resistance readied themselves for open combat. Until then, the resistance had been sporadic and reactive and very few lives had been lost. Now he planned for an all out national effort to drive out the invaders. He knew the casualty numbers would be enormous, but it was a price the resistance was prepared to pay.

The occupying forces were concentrated in the populated areas. With ninety per cent of Canada's population living within 100 miles of the American border, most of Canada's sparsely inhabited north was still in Canadian hands. Although fewer in number, these were some of the toughest and most independent Canadians. Their isolation and the harsh climate had made them so.

To prepare themselves, Will and other members of the resistance gathered in secret training camps in the north. There, they spent their days training and preparing for real battles they knew must soon come. Their numbers were augmented by ex-servicemen, draft-dodgers and voluntary Commonwealth expeditionary forces.

The Americans had superior technology, but in the northland, one couldn't depend upon outside reinforcements or re-supplies so technology counted for less than simple survival skills.

> Our preparations are only rarely interrupted by an occasional drone flying over our heads. We ignore them since shooting them down would give away our positions. Instead, we learn how to hide from them as they drone on, looking for the proverbial needle in a haystack.

> We are an army of snipers. As such, we are trained to hide and kill when the time is right. Our purpose and general strategy is to descend from the north en masse and strike fear in the hearts of the enemy. We will do this by rendering the roads unsafe to their convoys and immobilizing them. We will storm their depots and hit other key targets. We are trained in hit & run tactics and, whenever possible, will avoid any conflict where we do not have a decisive advantage. We will also publicize our cause to the American media. This war will ultimately be won in the hearts of the American people.

> I write this as an afterthought. We recognize that our tactics will frustrate the Americans and, due to their difficulty in confronting us, we fear that our attacks could lead our enemies to take their revenge against innocent non-combatants, women and children. We will employ a more

effective and surprising counter tactic — showing kindness to our prisoners.

— W. Anderson

~

President Kuhn couldn't believe his ears.

"What do you mean he's missing?"

"I mean he's disappeared. Lefty's disappeared, sir."

"He can't have just disappeared. He was under guard, dammit!"

"That's the other thing, sir. It's not just Lefty who's gone. It's the…"

"Don't let me hear you use that name again. Nice nicknames like that make people feel sorry for him. Makes him human. WE NEED TO BE FIGHTING MONSTERS, NOT GENTLEMEN!" He too had read the newspaper. Some were now calling it the 'Gentlemen's War.'

"His surname is MacIntosh! Use it!"

The story just didn't make any sense to the colonel and he knew that the President would be livid. To avoid the embarrassment of another breakout, they'd taken every security precaution. They'd upped the armed security to the point that, short of a small army storming the courthouse and freeing him, there's no way he could have been broken out.

"What do the guards have to say about it?"

"Nothing, sir."

"What do you mean nothing?"

"That's just it, sir. They're absent from duty."

"AWOL?"

"According to the reports, sir. As far as we can tell, they simply left Lefty unguarded. Our security cameras show that they put the keys within Lefty's reach, sorry…. MacIntosh….while he was asleep. And then they just left. When MacIntosh woke up, he saw the keys and let himself out. Nobody was there to stop him. From the video footage, he appeared as surprised as anyone."

"Bring me those guards," sneered the President.

"That may be a problem, sir."

"What the hell...?" The anxiety on the colonel's face told Kuhn of yet a larger problem. "So let's have it all, Colonel."

"It's the black troops, sir."

"Come on, Colonel, out with it!"

"They're all leaving Canada, sir. They're coming home."

"They're deserting?"

"Not according to them, sir. They say they've been misled. Bottom line is they won't fight Canadians, sir. Anyways, I figure we're better off without them. They're too unreliable."

"The whole damned Army is becoming unreliable. Too many gays and blacks. It's only the Inland Control forces I can count on anymore. Do they have any support from us whites?"

"Some, sir. And it's spreading rapidly throughout the ranks. Seems a fair number of whites don't want this war either, sir."

"SHIT! THEY CAN'T QUIT. THAT'S TREASON! YOU MUST STOP THIS! AND THAT'S AN ORDER."

"Yes, sir, Mr President."

~

Just as Father Monahan expected, Captain Martin had kept his word. After freeing Lefty from captivity, Martin and his followers started their long march home. Some resolved to go peacefully and laid down their arms. Seeing this, some farsighted Canadians, who foresaw the trouble brewing out of this turn of events, readily snatched them up. They removed their tracking plates and put them into hiding for an uncertain future.

Due to the respectful way he'd treated his subordinates and his general good nature, Martin was deservedly well-liked and his reputation gave him respect and influence amongst the troops. Before long, most blacks had joined the lengthening column. They were homeward bound and only a larger, more determined army could stand in their way.

Word that it was the blacks alone who were deserting was spread deliberately throughout the ranks to try to create a racial division. Headlines reported: BLACK TROOPS DESERT IN CANADA! Yet the truth was there were thousands of non-black American soldiers deserting too. Many of the deserters had Canadian friends and relatives and the departure of the blacks was just the trigger they needed to go home. They'd questioned the justification of the occupation from the very start, but couldn't say so out of fear of being portrayed as being unpatriotic. The remainder of those who joined in the march did so because they were just plain tired of fighting 'Mister Kuhn's War.'

The patriotic troops staying behind showed their hostility by lining the route home and jeering their comrades' departure. But the departing troops left behind only a skeleton army that was incapable of stopping the haemorrhage. So those remaining watched with their guns ready.

"Traitors!" one spat.

Vigilantly aware of the tensions surrounding them, Captain Martin led the column. Mile by mile, the column grew in length as more soldiers squeezed through the line to join the homeward march. At the same time 100,000 Canadian soldiers, who had been forcibly drafted into the Continental Army, deserted and disappeared along with their weapons. It was an unstoppable tidal wave.

Canadian civilians showed up in droves in support of the departing troops. Many had retrieved their American flags which, until then, had been hidden out of sight. Seeing this support, the homeward marching troops started singing Lincoln's Union Army song, *Mine Eyes Have Seen the Glory.*

The lines were drawn and both sides were armed.

In an ironic twist that only the passage of time could allow, the troops remaining in Canada were being referred to as the Union Forces. But unlike their predecessors of the American Civil War, the modern Union Forces had nothing to do with liberating the slaves. This Union fought for one continent to be ruled only by one elite group of citizenry.

~

Captains Owens and Martin marched together over the Ambassador Bridge straddling the Detroit River connecting Windsor, Ontario and Detroit, Michigan. Wearing his Canadian fatigues for the first time in many months, Owens had joined Martin's troops on their homeward march. He noticed that his fatigues fit more loosely now that he'd lost weight. 'It must be due

to all the walking and cycling,' he thought. The thought pleased him
for he believed that flabbiness did not become a soldier.

He and Martin had become friends. Much had happened since
they first met a year ago and they both respected each other
even more for the experiences they had shared. Together, they
led the troops out of Canada. Owens had never seen such a
sight. Marching smartly nine abreast, a column equal to nearly a
thousand legions stretched seven miles behind them. They'd heard
rumours that an attempt had been made to block their return to the
US on the American side of the border. They ignored the threat
since their own numbers, plus the number of family and friends
who had gathered to welcome them at the border, made such an
attempt seem foolhardy. Already their unarmed families had easily
pushed aside the temporary barriers at the border, proving that
the border guards had been intimidated by the massive numbers
descending upon them.

All eyes were on the mass of humanity on the bridge causing it
to sway under their weight. Nobody noticed the Canadian steam-
ship *Comet* pushing its way upriver against the current. Aboard it,
Captain MacGregor had his hands full. Only moments ago, he'd
heard the dreaded call, 'man overboard.' Immediately upon hearing
it, the whole crew had been galvanized into action. No sooner had
they organized their rescue response when someone onboard
shouted "FIRE!"

Instantly, everyone dropped the thought of rescuing the person
who'd fallen overboard to refocus their attention on the much
greater danger, the fire. They knew what fire meant to a ship full of
munitions and explosives and would have gladly traded places with
the one who'd fallen overboard.

Captain MacGregor too knew the perilous situation they were
in as he radioed the Coast Guard for immediate assistance. The
fire spread quickly and, within minutes, it became obvious that
it was beyond the crew's control. With grave feelings, Captain
MacGregor gave the order to abandon ship. Throughout the ship,
the constant clanging of the ship's bell could be heard. The crew
all knew what to do. The nature of their cargo had necessitated
the practise of this drill. But now, the imminent danger sped up
the process. True to tradition, Captain MacGregor was the last to
abandon ship, but before doing so, he radioed the Coast Guard to

inform them that they were carrying explosives and had to abandon their ship.

He ended his final transmission, saying in a clear sober voice, "You must evacuate the Windsor and Detroit shorelines. A significant explosion is imminent. God save us. Over."

Leaving the bridge for the last time, Captain MacGregor noticed something strange. The freighter appeared to be altering its course and resetting its speed slightly from the autopilot setting.

'Too late to worry about an electronic glitch,' he thought as he went over the side and down into the last lifeboat.

The column halted atop the bridge to watch the approach of the burning freighter. It wasn't until the freighter floated to a complete stop directly beneath the bridge that a few started to panic and, as though on cue, everyone began pushing and shoving their way to get down off the bridge. What had been, only moments before, a display of military pomp and splendour, dissolved into chaos.

Captains Martin and Owens had just stepped foot on American soil and marched through the lines of waiting families to the live news cameras when shouts and screams were heard coming from behind. Immediately, they turned their attention back to the bridge and were stunned to see the whole bridge appearing to rise and momentarily float upwards and then it suddenly disintegrated. Instinctively, they both dropped flat down onto the pavement and, a split second later, the noise of the blast and its shock wave tore past them.

Owens raised his head to survey the damage. His eyes searched for Martin, but there was no sign of him and, under the circumstances, this likely meant only one thing. Martin was dead.

Alive and friendless in enemy territory, surrounded by death and destruction, Owens realized he must somehow quickly blend in with the environment. Looking around, he laid his eyes on a dead man in a corporal's uniform who appeared to be of similar build to himself. The corporal's head had been severed clean off from the blast, leaving the rest of his body and his uniform remarkably intact. Seeing this as his only option, he dragged the corporal's body behind some rubble, switched uniforms and took his ID. The few others nearby who were still alive were too stunned or injured to notice.

In respect for the deceased man and for what he was about to do, he had a moment of silence. Then he drew his knife and cut off the man's hands. He detested the act, but it was what he had to do to survive. He put the hands in a bag and stuffed them into his pack. Later, he would have copies of the corporal's fingerprints made into textured latex fingertips that could be worn over his own.

Without hands or head, Owens was sure that the poor soul's body couldn't be positively identified later. Instead, those who found the body would think they'd found Captain Owens since it now wore his uniform and carried his ID. As of that moment, Owens was officially dead.

CHAPTER XVII
The Havoc Of War

President Kuhn was in a jovial mood. It was his birthday and he wasn't going to let the news from Detroit, or the Vice-President's sombre mood, bring him down.

"We still don't even know how many casualties there are, Mr President."

"That's a damn shame."

"Yes it is, Mr President." He didn't know if the President meant it was a damn shame that so many had been killed or injured by the blast and the bridge's collapse or that it was a damn shame because they did not yet know the numbers. He had the uncomfortable feeling that it was actually the latter.

"It's a hard lesson to learn," the President continued, "but it's a valuable lesson all the same. The public needs to be reminded what's at stake. Looking on the bright side, which is how I prefer to view things," he smiled at the VP, "they'll now believe what I've been telling them."

"What's that, sir?" The VP had lost track of all that had been said recently.

"They'll believe that the Canadians are set on ruining us. First, they brainwash our troops into abandoning the battlefield, then they blow them to smithereens so that it looks like we did it."

"The Canadians did it deliberately? That thought never occurred to me, Mr President." In fact, no such allegations had yet been made.

"Don't be so naive. That's exactly what happened. They knew we couldn't allow the deserting troops to return."

"Couldn't we? Then why would they...." he stopped himself, realizing that it was just one more contradiction. What was the point in arguing with somebody who was always right? And if you thought otherwise, you were branded an unpatriotic traitor.

Realizing that he had said more than he'd intended, the President hastily added, "Irregardless, that's not the point. As you said, no allegations have been made, so the whole matter is purely academic and I don't have time for it." Kuhn smiled. He knew he was a master at confounding the VP's thought processes.

All the VP heard was 'irregardless'. He was an educated man and, to him, it made the President sound stupid. All he could do was smile at him.

"You mark my words, Ernie, the Canadians will jump at any chance to divide us so that they can slaughter us in cold blood. A divided house cannot stand. So do I have your support?"

"Yes, Mr President," he forced himself to say. Yet something was troubling him.

"That was an awful spectacle for people to watch on TV, Mr President. The cameras seemed to have been everywhere. It was as though they had been forewarned and were there expecting something to happen. And they caught every angle in horrifying detail. It should have been censored. My kids are still having nightmares about it."

"Hollywood couldn't have done it any better! Plus we Americans don't believe in censorship."

The President sounded as if he'd been paid a personal compliment. The thought that the President sounded proud scared the VP. Come to think about it, a lot of things about the President were scaring him.

Seeing the surprise on the VP's face, Kuhn added, "Ah Ernie, they'll get over it. Don't sweat it. Kids are tougher than that. Besides they see that sort of stuff on TV all the time. Look on the bright side, man. At least now they'll hate Canadians."

"Actually my kids fear Canadians now."

"That's basically the same thing."

"They ask me why they hate us so much? They ask me what's going to stop them from coming here and getting us next? The darn thing is, I don't have an answer for them. And they know it."

~

Once again, Canadians were publicly blamed for the disaster. The freighter's explosion had resulted in a massive amount of death and destruction. Within a mile radius of the explosion, the surrounding shorelines of the cities of Windsor and Detroit had been completely obliterated. Ten of thousands, who were crossing over the bridge at the time, were killed instantly and many thousands more, who were waiting to welcome the soldiers home, died from the debris falling from the sky. Over and over, America watched it all happen on TV. The live feed going blank in the maelstrom told all.

As far as anyone knew, both Captains Owens and Martin had been killed in the blast. Captain MacGregor, who'd miraculously survived along with most of his crew, made it known how, in the final moments before he'd left the bridge, the ship appeared to be steered as though by remote control. Remarkably, nobody seemed to question how or why a Canadian freighter would be carrying such a massive quantity of explosives. Conspiracy experts theorized that it was the Canadian insurgents who'd masterminded and carried out the whole attack.

The blast had damaged the GM Renaissance Centre, Detroit's iconic riverfront building that symbolized America's rebirth, to such an extent that it had to be taken down. America retaliated in kind on a grander scale by demolishing what it considered to be Canada's most revered icon, Toronto's 1815 foot tall CN Tower. Much ado was made of the double meaning of 1815, for it was since that year in history that the two countries had been officially at peace. The CN Tower's implosion emphasized the fact that peace had ended.

All the recent happenings in the south have only served to drive more Canadians north and into our ranks. Our camps are becoming overcrowded, which is a concern mainly due to the need to keep our locations secret.

To make space, we have deployed our first wave of freedom fighters to confront the invaders. Their mission is simple and nothing on a grand scale. They carry out lone wolf-style attacks to wreak havoc amongst the occupying forces. Their goal is to make the occupation seem futile and never-ending. In a long drawn out contest, we feel this is ultimately their Achilles Heel.

Already, we have received news that the freedom fighters' raids are being carried out with great zeal and energy. Risking their lives, they go forward courageously into every action. The successful accounts of these raids give us hope.

We realize now, more than ever before, that we have a couple of key factors in our favour. First is that we love our land more than they, and so we are more willing to fight and die for it. Second, the public reports of our insurgencies work in our favour for public recognition buoys up our efforts and demoralizes them. So often are we in the news that the occupying forces have become convinced that they are surrounded by a wily enemy. If only they knew the truth.

The media calls me the ring-leader of the insurgency. To them, I stand in the way of a united continent. Perhaps by the accident of my acquaintances and due to the circumstances that surround me, that is true, for I constantly seem to find myself in the middle of events and my circle has by now become quite large and influential.

But they are wrong in assuming that I masterminded the freighter's explosion. In doing so, they portrayed me as someone so evil and sick that I would stoop so low as to sacrifice my own friends just to strike at them. They've concocted a story that sounds so factually plausible that,

*had I not known the truth, they might have even fooled
me. But I know the truth and so do those around me.
Consequently, their story discredits them and points the
finger back at Washington.*

*I am beginning to suspect that it is we who are dealing
with a conspiring enemy and not the other way around. The
question is why?*

— W. Anderson

~

Fortunately for Will and his so-called gang of outlaws,
Washington's portrayal of them as bloodthirsty fanatics didn't mesh
with the firsthand reports being sent home by the US troops on the
frontlines. Instead, they referred to the Canadian freedom fighters
as a hard-fighting and a determined foe who gave humane treatment to any captured prisoners. It was not the story Washington
wanted told, but even they couldn't suppress it.

Canadians showed their enemies mercy, a concept that, until
then, had almost been lost in modern warfare. Reading in Brock's
diary about the more civilized ways of the past, Will had appealed
to his compatriots to act the same way. Any captured American
soldier who had been conscripted, therefore raising doubt as
to their personal support of the occupation, would be released
on parole. Their release was secured solely by them giving their
word not to harm another person. It was a gentlemen's agreement
based on their personal honour. The gesture had immediate and
far reaching effects and dramatically changed the direction the war
was heading. For the first time in a long time, the idea of swearing
on one's honour meant something. In effect, the policy disarmed a
great number of soldiers who, although they remained in uniform
and continued to carry a weapon, felt compelled to honour
their word.

The resistance soon found that freeing their captives did more
good than harm. When the captives were released and rejoined

their combat units, they often did so only in body and not in spirit. In subsequent actions, knowing how they would be treated, these troops were more apt to lay down their arms when the fighting got dangerous. Often this caused the collapse of their line and the others had no choice but to join them or die. Doing so, they were all rewarded with a few days rest with the resistance, enjoyed a few good meals, a few beers and then were sent packing. In exchange, the resistance kept the captives' arms and equipment.

Gradually the Canadian tactics, and therefore their struggle, began to be appreciated in America. Mothers cried upon hearing that their sons or daughters had gone missing, then rejoiced when they later found out they had been captured and treated well by the Canadians.

One released soldier phoned his parents, telling them, "We had a couple of beers with the Canucks and joked about old times, mom. You would have laughed too, dad. Despite everything, this one Canuck is still a diehard Sabres fan. He can't wait until the hostilities are over and the NHL starts up again."

That night, that mother prayed for all the other parents, including the Canadians, and for their children to come home safely from the conflict. These stories led to widespread sympathy and support south of the border. The American public branded the Canadian freedom fighters as chivalrous. In a country where the rulers were oppressing the people, that term was a badge of honour.

Brock's diary had inspired Will with confidence. The timeless-ness of the diary's message bridged the two hundred years and, for Will, history had come alive. Starting to write a daily journal himself had been only the first step. Now his choice of words, the way he phased his sentences and his style of writing bespoke of earlier times. Others noticed that Anderson was becoming more and more engrossed in his daily reading of the diary and writing of his journal, birthing the myth that Brock's spirit was being somehow channelled through him, and that he could, despite all odds, somehow guide the Canadians to victory.

Will had inadvertently become the de facto leader for the Canadians. The comparisons and parallels to Brock humbled and embarrassed him for, deep within, he still knew the truth. Yet the myth served their cause. All their exploits, whether or not he was even connected to them, were credited to him and thought to be inspired by the spirit of Brock. Thus, Will's reputation grew and further disheartened the enemy.

~

...a great deal might be done, in conjunction with the militia, in a country intersected in every direction by rivers, deep ravines, and lined, at intervals on both sides the road, by thick woods.

... destroy all the roads of communication in our front, leaving open the water route only, and these woody positions will be shortly occupied by the Indians of this neighbourhood and a corps of volunteer voyageur Canadians.

Water proved to be a formidable ally for the Canadians. To an extent never before seen in warfare, the occupation troops had to contend with a country that was saturated with water. Time and again, they found themselves literally bogged down and ill prepared to combat this obstacle.

Almost 9% of Canada, an area equal to the size of France and Germany combined, is water. It is a land interlaced with an extensive network of waterways that includes not only the Great Lakes and mighty rivers but also countless minor streams, creeks, ponds and marshes. Each one of these is a natural obstacle to continuous land movement for the waterways criss-cross the whole country. Furthermore, water delineates forty percent of Canada's boundary with the US. Using this to their advantage, the insurgents found that they could move almost everywhere, including into America, by water as their predecessors had done in the days before roads and super highways were built. This was a throwback to Brock's day when the natives and early Europeans travelled by water. Along the waterways, early Canadians canoed, fished and trapped their way right to British Columbia and the Pacific and Arctic Oceans.

"The waterways are our domain," Will told the insurgents. "On the water, we will be safer from the Americans. They are equipped for land and air warfare, but do not and cannot possess the quantity of watercraft needed to gain ascendancy over our vast inland waterways. From these waterways, we will target bridges and, by destroying them, we will immobilize and isolate our enemy on tiny islands."

With these instructions, bridges were blown up faster than they could be rebuilt by the American Army Corps of Engineers. The tactic worked as planned by splitting apart the ground forces and bringing land transport to an abrupt halt.

Much of the Americans' abandoned weaponry had been seized by the insurgents and they quickly conveyed them by water to where they could be put to best use. Hollowed out logs floated undetected past the enemy, carrying within them war materiel as well as a coded GPS tracking device so they could be retrieved downstream later.

The very immensity of the country was another unbeatable ally of the Canadians. Occupying Canada required many garrisons and the American troops became too thinly dispersed. One by one, these isolated garrisons were overwhelmed or simply starved out when their supply lines were disrupted. Seeing their materiel deficiencies, the American forces pulled back to a handful of perimeter forts within the Canadian major urban centres and these became the official entry and exit ports. The retreat left only five percent of the country occupied.

The other ninety-five percent of the land was again Canadian domain, won back by the insurgents. It was the domain that possessed the harshest climate and terrain in the country and where Will and the insurgents became hardened.

A protracted resistance upon this frontier will be sure to embarrass the enemy's plans materially. They will not come prepared to meet it, and their troops, or volunteer corps, without scarcely any discipline, so far at least as control is in question, will soon tire under disappointment. The difficulty which they will experience in providing provisions will involve them in expenses, under which their government will soon become impatient.

~

People around the world sympathized with the Canadians. Despite their governments not wanting to confront the American Forces militarily, private individuals, covertly supported by their governments, supplied them with the means to do so.

The French islands of St. Pierre and Miquelon, with about 6,000 inhabitants, are located just 25 kilometres off the south coast of Newfoundland. It was through these islands that arms and munitions were channelled into an underground pipeline that eventually flowed into Canadian hands. From these islands, fishermen carried war materiel in packages disguised as crab pots and ventured to rendezvous on the common fishing grounds with fishermen out of Newfoundland. Occasionally, an American naval ship would intervene, but not before the wary fishermen would drop their contraband to the bottom. When the coast was clear, these same crab fishermen would return later and retrieve the pots and their lethal catch.

The signing of the Treaty of Hans Island had settled the land claim dispute by making the island half Danish and half Canadian. Until the signing, the States had been Canada's sole neighbour. After the occupation of Canada, Washington had declared Hans Island to be America's alone and had established a military base there. The Danes, in order to assert their Arctic sovereignty, then established their own military base on their half of the Island. With the pull back, Americans vacated such outposts. Late that summer, Canada's Inuit began to routinely visit the Danish base. There, they obtained from the Danes all the guns and ammunition they needed. Most of this weaponry found its way into the insurgents' hands.

True to her word, the Queen sent her grandson, Prince Arthur, to represent Her in Ottawa along with her royal yacht, the HMS Britannica. Docked there, it was a floating symbol of the Queen's assertion that Canada remained within the realm of the Crown.

~

CHAPTER XVIII
The Home Of
The Brave

Curious things happened in America later that summer. Students at a number of prominent American college and university campuses began to protest the war. The protests should have been anticipated because more students than ever before were enrolled in French language programs. French had become symbolic of the resistance for the language distinguished Canadians from the invaders. For the American students however, studying French was a passive way for them to express their antiwar sentiments and acknowledge Canada's right to sovereignty. Consequently, French teachers were in high demand and many of them were fond of Canada. The meeting of likeminded teachers and students combined to make the campuses ripe for large antiwar protests. This time, it was not possible for Kuhn's administration to put a racial spin on the situation for the protestors came from every demographic.

~

Will recalled what the former President had said on the fateful day of the nuclear plant strike: 'Yes, we may need to lessen our wants. But our country abounds in the necessities; we can do without the luxuries. Let us lead by example. Let us heal the world.'

This had not been the course of the Kuhn administration. They maintained the shutdown of nuclear plants partly because the fearful public demanded it, but mostly because of their secret Canadian agenda. Their response was to replace the lost energy generation capability with Canadian resources so that all their wants, and more, could be produced.

Thus oil, the lifeblood of the US economy, became an even more vital commodity. Even before the war, Canada had been America's number one supplier of oil. The war and Washington's policy of economically isolating the continent from foreigners had left America totally dependent on Canadian oil. Understanding that most of Canada's oil to the States flowed down through pipelines from Alberta's tar-sands and that the length and remoteness of the pipeline made it indefensible, Will contacted Sydney to have her organize hit and run raids all along the pipeline. This was just one more piece of a grander strategy to encourage America to conclude that Canada was just too costly to hold. It was a strategy inspired by Brock who'd written a thought inspired by a naval historian named James.

Every thing in the United States was to be settled by a calculation of profit and loss.

By autumn, the Canadian treasury was wholly bankrupt, broken under the burden of reparation claims being paid by it. This had a domino effect Stateside where their economic hopes had been pinned on the reparations being paid. Now both economies teetered on the verge of complete and utter collapse.

Will called for a campaign to focus on making the process of extracting reparations too costly believing, as Brock had written, that the Americans would not support a prolonged war in which the costs outweigh the benefits. Thus, disrupting their food, raw materials and energy supplies became the primary goals of the resistance.

First, they targeted the lottery farmers by sabotaging the processing and packaging plants that received their produce. Attacking them during the peak harvest ensured their ill-gotten produce was left to spoil outside under the hot rays of the late summer sun.

To counter this new threat, some lottery farmers tried to transport their raw produce directly across the border into the States. Their efforts were in vain for they were often stalled at the edge of a waterway for lack of a bridge and were easy pickings for snipers. Soon the roadsides were littered with burnt out field trucks that had attempted to run the gauntlet. Later, attempts were made to convoy the field trucks using armoured cars as escorts, but most of these failed to get through before the produce spoiled and the cost was prohibitively high.

~

The energy crisis became acute. Gas at the pump soared beyond seven dollars a gallon and electricity costs escalated past fifty cents per kilowatt hour.

To counter this, Washington rushed to get alternate modes of power generation into production. A large component of this strategy involved the production of energy through wind turbines. Much infrastructure was already in place before the War. In 2010, massive wind turbine projects had been built on the farmlands of southern Ontario. In addition to these, plans had been drawn to install turbines in the Great Lakes. These plans had been so unpopular at the time that politicians had been forced to shelve them in order to appease the stirred up electorate. The concerns at the time related to the effect they'd have on migrating birds, fish stocks, navigation, the drinking water supply and, ultimately, their safe dismantling.

Such concerns were niceties to be debated about during good times, but those things didn't matter to a regime being starved of energy and so, with the Canadian politicians conveniently out of the way, Washington dusted off those plans to install a massive wind farm on the Canadian side of Lake Erie.

On a small scale, this still wasn't enough to satiate America's energy thirst. If it was proved that a reliable supply of energy could be produced this way at an acceptable cost, soon the whole Canadian shoreline would be littered with thousands of wind turbines.

~

How can I expect my men to go where I am afraid to lead them...?

Will closed the diary. Like Brock, he knew the time had come for him to act once again. It was time for him to leave the security of the north and head south.

~

Will tossed a few nickels to the captain of the barge as he exited.

"Thanks, mate," the captain smiled. It was a genuine smile as the real nickel coins would later be used to buy a loaf of good bread for his family. Paper money was almost useless these days in Canada. The historical Canadian distrust of the paper currency had resurfaced with a vengeance. Those trading their paper for goods or services were either Americans or Canadians dependent upon American handouts. Both paid dearly.

Yves and Will had travelled downstream on the Thames. Aboard a barge, they had disguised themselves and worked as hired deckhands. They disembarked in Chatham and from there made their way down to the north shore of Lake Erie where they had arranged a rendezvous with captain Ernesto and a small party of insurgents. Together, they were going to mount a nuisance raid on a newly constructed wind farm hoping to convince the Americans to abandon their plans.

Will briefed the party on their objective. Each had been trained for the enterprise and all were excited to put their expertise into action. It was no small undertaking. To better appreciate the obstacle they faced, Will asked them to visualize the immensity of a modern wind turbine set upon a huge foundation, embedded into the limestone bottom of the lake, with its blades whirling around up to the height of a forty story building. The objective they faced was a hundred of those turbines. With each turbine powering two thousand American homes and businesses, including war-making factories, their disruption would be consequential.

～

Ernesto was back on the lake again, but not to fish. Instead, the Ana Teresa was the taxi of the raiding party. Aboard Her, Will and the others pressed onwards to the target. It was clear and the moon was shining low in the sky. Ahead of them, the water shimmered with its reflection.

Will was still awake at 2am listening to the low rumbling growl of the diesel engine. Anyone onshore would be familiar with the sound and assume that they were out fishing. Commercial fishing was still permitted and, due to food storages, for the first time in two generations, it was again being encouraged. Although half the catch was confiscated by the food reparation scheme, an increase in quota offset the reparation tax to provide just enough incentive to keep them fishing.

"There they are," said Ernesto. Turning to his mate, he nodded back towards the stern where five two-man zodiacs were waiting to be launched. "Tell them they've got ten minutes to go," he added.

Alongside Ernesto, Will squinted in order to better see the small flickering red lights that had just come into view. The lights were atop the wind turbines and meant to warn low flying planes of their sky-high presence. At first, he saw only a handful of lights, but with the passing of each second, more appeared out of the dark. Within minutes, a hundred flickering lights filled the entire span of the wheelhouse window. Each light identified a target that helped feed the American war machine. Their presence, being visible from the Canadian north shore, made them even more meaningful. Their decommissioning, even if only for a short while, would serve a dual purpose.

"Thanks again, Ernesto," Will said as he left the wheelhouse.

"Light up the sky, Anderson," Ernesto answered with a smile.

In the stern of the vessel, the others waited by their zodiacs. Each zodiac was equipped with oars and a small 15 hp motor. A moment later, Ernesto cut the throttle and they coasted to a stop amidst the turbines.

"Now," Ernesto called from the wheelhouse.

"Let's go, Yves," Will said and together they pulled their zodiac over the Ana Teresa's side and, with a splash, they dropped it into the water. Will hopped in and held it steady for Yves who stepped into the stern to man the motor. Both aboard, they pushed themselves clear of the Ana Teresa and, immediately, Yves pulled the cord to start the small motor and they headed for the first turbine. One by one, each zodiac team followed suit and, within thirty minutes, each team was in place. Once the last zodiac team was launched, Ernesto throttled up the tug and was gone with his job done.

Each team had been assigned a block of twenty turbines to put out of action.

"You get first honours, Anderson," said Yves.

Will nodded and picked up his bow. They had practised this exercise a lot and he was confident of their success. A light wind was blowing, which was vital to make their method work. Will took aim at the revolving blades, focusing on the one rising in the seven o'clock position.

'One, two, three,' he counted to himself and then let fly the arrow. The arrowhead was a grappling hook and it carried a light line. It flew up over the top of the rising prop.

"Nice shot," beamed Yves.

Having snagged the prop, the light line immediately started to wind, gradually pulling a heavier line at the end of which they had tied a small explosive charge meant to blow a chunk off one of the three props, near the spinner, when it detonated. Damaged in this way, the meticulously crafted prop would snap off later under a heavy wind load and that imbalance would cause the other two to a stop. Yves and Will took alternate turns at shooting their arrows. Neither missed a shot.

"Ten each, Anderson. That makes us aces!"

Having put the final charge in place, they motored elsewhere within the wind farm to offer the other teams assistance where it was needed. To their delight, all seemed to have had similar success and, within two hours, still under the cover of darkness, they all headed to shore. The charges were set to explode simultaneously just before dawn. They planned to watch from the safety of the shore and then make their escape over the beach and into the marshes.

~

"Wake up sir. Looks like we've got company," reported the Continental Army soldier on guard duty.

Will flashed his small flashlight back towards the others, signalling them to cut their engines and lift them as they came to shore. Not far from their landing, a platoon of about thirty soldiers readied for their arrival.

"Wait until we see what they're up to," the captain cautioned his platoon. He had learned not to spring a trap prematurely as the wily Canadians were adept at executing a quick retreat. As if to foil his plan, the Canadians didn't advance blindly towards their positions, but instead sat themselves down on the beach and looked back at the lake.

"What do you figure they're up to, sir?"

The captain wasn't sure. "Maybe they're waiting for more friends," he theorized. He feared that would put them on more equal footing in terms of numbers and the thought caused him to question waiting. Perhaps it would be better to engage them immediately, he thought.

"Open fire on my word," he whispered. His order was passed from soldier to soldier. Just as he was about to signal, the first explosion went off. Instantly, all eyes were drawn seaward where, like a lit box of firecrackers, all the explosions started going off. The distance made it so the flashes of light from the explosions were out of sync with the concussion sound.

"Shit!" said the captain, suddenly realizing what was happening. Everything now depended upon apprehending the perpetrators.

Cheers of 'hip-hip-hurray' were heard coming from the Canadians.

"They're blowing up the windmills, sir."

"No kidding. Get the flares, Sergeant," he ordered.

"Yes, sir."

~

"Three cheers for us," said Bruce. He was a small athletic looking man who had acquired the pyrotechnical skills to build the charges.

After cheering the success of their work, everybody fell into thoughtful silence. It was not true to their inner nature to destroy anything even if it was an act of self-preservation. As they sat on the shore looking out into the lake, they had mixed emotions.

"What a waste," somebody voiced what the others were thinking.

But there was no time to contemplate their act. Dawn approached and visibility was not a good thing.

"Time to go," said Will.

They got up to leave. They'd already removed the small outboard motors from their zodiacs and, thus lightened, each two person team swiftly carried their zodiac over the beach to the marsh on the other side. Once there, one person stayed with the zodiac while the other returned to retrieve the engine. It was then, while they were split into two small parties, that the Continental platoon struck.

From ahead to their right, Will heard some voices and then all hell broke loose.

"Flares!" somebody shouted.

"Get down!" Will yelled.

Floating high in the sky above their heads, the flares lit up everything as bright as day. Instinctively, they all dropped to the ground. Those who were lucky dropped into a shadowed depression and could lie perfectly still praying that they wouldn't be seen. Those not so lucky were caught out in the open and machine guns and rifles fired towards them. After what felt like an eternity, the flare burned itself out and landed, fizzling, in the marsh. In complete contrast, it was blacker than ever.

"RUN!" Will commanded. Forgetting the zodiacs, they raced towards the marsh hoping that their feet would carry them away from harm. Doing so, some blindly bumped into others.

"Watch it!" somebody grumbled.

"Shhhh!" somebody else replied.

Again, night became day as another flare shot up into the sky. Again, everyone dropped. Another flare. With two in the sky, and their lights coming from different angles, there were no shadows on the beach. Almost everyone was an easy target. Cracks were heard coming out of the muzzles of rifles. They were being picked off one by one.

As the darkness came again, those who could ran again for the marshes, stumbling.

"Shit!" somebody cursed. They were where water would normally be; instead, dry reeds crackled underfoot. It'd been an unusually hot and dry summer and the marsh waters had, unfortunately, receded. Once again, more flares lit up the earth.

"Take cover!" shouted Will.

At last they'd found some ground cover to hide in amongst the dry reeds, depriving the shooters of their easy targets. This silenced the gunfire. Suddenly, there was another source of light. 'Searchlights?' Will wondered. But then it was dark again.

"I smell fuel," said somebody.

"Flame-throwers!" somebody shouted as a flame shot towards them. Instantly, the dry reeds and the methane gas created by the rotting compost exploded in a fiery inferno. Will found the heat unbearable and, desperate, he ran for his life. Even when his legs became bogged down, he kept pushing, not realizing that he'd found water. It was then that he felt a sharp crack on his skull. Dazed, he stopped and then fell forward. As he lost consciousness, the last thought on his mind was, 'I'm sinking into my own grave'.

~

CHAPTER XIX
The Gleam Of The Morning's First Beam

In his mind's eye, Will saw himself floating above his own body. Looking at his hand, he saw its silhouette surrounded by a blurry blue border defining its shape. Continuing to rise, he ascended until he could look down upon the whole scene. From above, he saw a funnel-shaped landform jutting out from the mainland into the lake waters and gradually tapering down to a point. Will recognized this as Point Pelee and it was completely on fire.

'That blaze must have consumed my body,' he thought. 'That explains why I'm seeing what I am.'

He rose up towards the heavens until he was able to look down upon the whole earth, diminished to a small orb amongst other orbs, all hurtling through space. It was clear which orb was earth for a smoky trail from the blaze followed in its wake.

His eyes were drawn to an immense orb that burned with blinding intensity. He knew it was the sun and he realized that both he and the earth were headed straight for it. Gradually, the sun's light filled his whole field of vision until he was blinded to all else.

'Into the light,' he thought. 'I must surely be dead.'

The thought brought his mind back to his body.

'Maybe I'm not dead.'

Then he recalled that something had hit him on the head. His head started to throb. Regaining his senses, Will realized the guns were silent and the flames were out. He could smell the pungent odour of the smouldering marsh. Then he heard the sound of a girl's voice singing a familiar sound, "O-ka-reeeee, o-ka-reeeee".

Will recognized the call of a red-winged blackbird. With his senses alert, he realized he must still be alive. By some miracle of luck, he found himself on the only piece of floating cattail bog that had been spared by the fire. He opened his eyes and the sun momentarily blinded him.

'Into the light,' he recalled thinking.

He shifted his eyes and saw his bird. It had perched on a nearby cattail. It saw him too.

"Are you my protector?" Will asked the bird.

As if in response, a shadow passed overhead and the little bird took flight. It was chasing away a turkey vulture. Or was it an American eagle? Will wasn't sure. Whatever it was, Will saw the larger bird pecked by the red-wing in mid-flight, causing the larger bird to release something from its clutched talons and flee. In Will's state of mind, the whole experience took on some deeper meaning.

'Who would have thought it possible that a bird weighing not much more than one ounce could make a bird weighing over 10 pounds release its prize and retreat? Could this be a sign? A sign from Brock?' he wondered. 'Perhaps it's a sign of hope for those, like us, who must face a bigger and stronger opponent in what would appear to be a similar unequal struggle?'

Will's head pounded from his wound. The throbbing had awoken him and was now keeping him conscious.

'I must get out of here,' he concluded, realizing that the smoke that helped camouflage his position wouldn't last much longer. He tried to get up by propping himself on his elbow and then swinging around to a seated position. In his effort to stand, his head spun, blackness filled his vision and he fainted.

"O-ka-reeeee, o-ka-reeeee," he heard his protector call out.

"O-ka-reeeee, o-ka-reeeee," called another.

'That sounded slightly different,' he thought. Then he realized it was the girl's voice that he had heard earlier. She was singing to the bird, his protector. Will squinted in the direction from which her voice came. A short way off, a girl in the bow of a canoe was heading straight for him. She was pointing at him. As she approached, her features became clearer and he could see that she was a native girl. As the effort caused his head to throb and caused him to see stars again, he laid his head back down to rest.

"O-ka-reeeee, o-ka-reeeee," she sang.

When Will lifted his head again, he knew she definitely saw him. Deliverance, he thought.

He didn't remember passing out again, but when he awoke, he found himself lying in the bottom of a canoe being paddled somewhere. Putting his hand to his throbbing head, he touched a cloth bandage that his rescuers must have wrapped around it. It felt moist and when he looked at his fingers he saw blood on them.

"Don't remove it or it will start bleeding again. You've lost a lot of blood. He should drink," Gavin said as he handed the girl a bottle. She laid aside her paddle, reached over and trickled a little water into Will's mouth.

"You're so covered with mud and soot, you blended in with the bog and we almost paddled right past you," Gavin explained. "The only thing that caught our attention was the motion of you lifting your head."

"The bird caught my attention," the young girl corrected him. "Does it hurt?" she asked Will.

"Yes," he answered honestly. He tried to smile, but it looked more like a grimace.

"You'll be ok," she reassured him.

"Where are we going?"

"Back home. My mom will know how to take care of you."

"Is she a doctor?"

"No," she answered. "But she probably could be if she had some schooling. Besides you shouldn't go to a doctor. They're being watched closely by the Americans to ensure they're not treating members of the resistance. After yesterday's raid, you can bet you'd be caught."

"Shhhhh, Ava. Let him rest."

With her sun-bronzed skin and braided dark hair held in place with coloured beads, Ava wore her native heritage proudly.

"Do you like birds?" Will asked, recalling what she'd said.

"I love birds. Mama says my brother Gavin and I have the spirits of birds. Gavin's is the hawk. Mine's the red-winged blackbird," she answered proudly.

"With a name like Ava, you've been well named," said Will.

"That red-wing led me to you," she added.

"I know," said Will, remembering the red-wing who had perched over him, protecting him. He also recalled how Ava and the red-wing had seemed to be communicating with each another. In his still dazed mental state, the idea didn't seem at all strange.

"Ava. Let him rest," her brother cautioned again. "You're exhausting him."

~

Will fell in and out of consciousness during much of the journey and he did not recall much of it. The next time he awoke, he was being driven somewhere in their vehicle. With Ava watching him, just as the bird had done, he drifted off peacefully.

Will was jolted awake again when they turned off the road and began slowly bumping their way up a washboard gravel driveway. Finally, they stopped in front of a house trailer. He closed his eyes as Gavin and Ava went into the trailer. He could hear a number of other voices respond to theirs and then felt pain as he was lifted gently out of the truck, carried into the tight confines of the trailer and placed onto a small mattress. Upon seeing Will regain consciousness, Ava smiled and left his bedside. A moment later, she returned in the company of an older woman.

"This is my mom, Yvonne."

"Hello, I'm Will Anderson."

"Yes, we know. That was quite the show you all put on last night."

"Do you know what happened to the others?"

"We'll talk about that later. First you must rest and not think too much." He could tell by her tone that it had not ended well.

Ava settled herself at the foot of the bed as Yvonne drew the curtains together and sat by his side. She put the back of her hand gently on his forehead to check his temperature.

"You have a fever," she confirmed. His skin was clammy and his bed sheets were becoming wet with his perspiration. His reflection in a bedside mirror showed him that his head wound had been re-bandaged while he slept.

"Is it bad?" he asked.

"Yes. All head wounds are dangerous. You've suffered a contusion to your frontal lobe. But you'll survive. Once the period of swelling has past, in about a week, we'll know better what the effect will be."

"What happened?"

Knowing that the severity of a head wound can be determined by one's memories, Yvonne answered his query with a question of her own. It followed a clinical path.

"Maybe you can tell me what you recall, Will, and then I'll fill in the blanks," she recommended.

Will responded by telling her about the raid and its purpose, about getting to the shore and being ambushed by the soldiers camped there. Recalling these things restored her hope that his head wound was superficial.

"The last thing I remember was running from the fire," he concluded.

Taking over from there, Yvonne continued.

"I suspect you were knocked out by a flat fragment of metal. Maybe from shrapnel or a ricocheting bullet. You must have a thick skull because it never penetrated it," she smiled. "As it turned out, it probably saved your life. Still, you've suffered a concussion and you've lost a lot of blood, which is why you're losing consciousness whenever you exert yourself. With head wounds, it's important for you to try to remain awake and for us to keep a close eye on you. Fortunately for you, Ava's been doing a good job at that."

"Thank you, Ava," Will smiled.

Ava smiled back. For once her incessant attention was appreciated.

"We had to re-open your head wound to clean it out properly, then stitch it up," Yvonne continued. "Your wound had a lot of muck in it from the marsh. Lucky for you, you landed on a pile of floating cattails. It seems that you live a charmed life, Will."

Will spent the next day resting in the trailer. During his convalescence, Ava was a permanent fixture at his side. Her family had contacted Hana and Will was pleased when she came to visit him. She was so relieved to find Will still alive, albeit bedridden.

"We all thought you were dead," she sobbed.

Ernesto had told Hana all about the raid and she had assumed that he'd been killed along with all the others.

"I'm sorry to hear about your friend Yves," she told him, confirming what he already suspected.

As happy as Hana had been to hear that Will lived against all odds, it had also restored her hope that maybe, just maybe, her York had miraculously escaped death too. It was with great reluctance that Hana left Will, recognizing that he needed his rest for the following day's journey.

The next morning, the trailer was hitched to the truck for the journey back home. Natives were allowed a freedom of movement denied other Canadians. Will sat up front with the family wearing their clothes and a hat to cover his head wound. With glasses, darkened hair and the redness of his skin from the fire authenticating his native heritage, they passed through the checkpoints without any trouble. The cranberries they'd collected in the marsh for their Thanksgiving dinner were enough explanation for their travels.

Their home was on Walpole Island, a Native reserve on the Canadian shore of Lake St. Clair. There, he was nursed back to health by Yvonne and watched over carefully by Ava. During the first week of his recovery, the swelling had put enough pressure on his brain to arouse great concern to all his caregivers. At one point, Yvonne thought they would need the assistance of a medical doctor. But before one could be found, Will began to steadily improve on his own.

"You are indeed charmed," she professed again.

Soon, Will was physically well enough to depart, but the time wasn't right. He needed time to think and the peace he found with Ava and her family provided the perfect setting.

~

The raid had achieved its objective and the expansion of the wind farm project was shelved. Washington concluded that all Canadian sources of energy were too costly to extract or too vulnerable to sabotage. America was faced with no alternative but to conserve and, for the first time in its history, wasting scarce energy became a crime.

Washington was in desperate need of any sign that the war had turned in their favour so they could convince the public that the unpopular war was coming to a conclusion. The raid was headline news and the faces of all of the raiders, including Will's, were soon well-known. The Americans claimed that all the raiders were dead and so nobody was looking for Will.

"We've ripped the heart out of the rebellion!" Kuhn claimed triumphantly.

As the raiders' deaths were being publicly celebrated in Washington, they were being mourned in Canada by both Canadian civilians and American troops. Canadians mourned the loss of their heroes whereas Americans paid homage to noble adversaries. In an unusual display of wartime kindness and sympathy, both sides put aside the conflict, laid down their weapons and momentarily gathered together in public to pay tribute to the fallen. It was the largest funeral procession in Canadian history.

President Kuhn bristled when he saw the television coverage of the American honour guard presenting their arms and firing off a final salute. Even the Vice-President attended the funeral to pay his respects despite Kuhn warning him not to do so. The Vice-President felt he had nothing to fear from Canadians. Since Detroit had been hit, he had come to suspect there was more to the President's motives than seeking reparations. Those suspicions were leading him to believe that the cause of the Canadian insurgents was legitimate.

Prince Arthur also attended the funeral. Symbolic of his position representing the Head of State, he sat at the front of the Canadian officialdom who had flocked to the funeral to affirm their importance during this time of undeclared truce. Will disparaged their audacity for he did not recognize most of them as he watched the proceedings on TV. Chills ran down his spine as he saw his own photograph mounted upon a simple wooden casket. The Canadian delegation was situated in the pews on the left side of the church, the American delegation on the right side. Traditionally, the right hand yields the sword, the left the shield and thus the seating arrangements represented the actual relationship between the two countries.

The families of all who had perished on Point Pelee attended the funeral. He saw Renée and Monsieur and Madame La Forêt in attendance and he regretted he couldn't be there to comfort them. In their minds, they'd lost two loved ones. He knew he must see them again soon so they would know the truth.

Much was said about those who had perished defending their country, but it was the words of the Prince that most affected the hearts of the millions who watched on both sides of the border. He spoke of their exploits recalling 'the tradition and spirit of *Anglo Freedom*', a sense of freedom which coursed through the veins of the British, Americans and Canadians alike.

"Canada is your sibling nation", he reminded America. "Both nations are the legitimate offspring of a common mother, Great Britain. This contest is but one more test on an eight hundred year journey that started with the Magna Carta. Throughout that journey, there have been occasions when it was necessary for free people to rise up against their oppressors. This spirit spawned America." To this, cheers came from the American side. "Today it maintains Canada." The Canadian side then erupted with applause. "History will tell of this time as one more of many occasions when the ideals of Anglo Freedom demonstrated to the whole world that it is possible to keep absolute power in check. That might does not make right. That, with right on their side, even a few hearty souls can stand up against the many. Today, we honour such individuals."

~

CHAPTER XX
With Glowing Hearts We See Thee Rise

President Kuhn was right about one thing. The loss of so many key people had ripped the heart out of the Canadian resistance. News became reality and, hearing that they'd lost their leaders, most Canadians gave up hope of winning the war. Those who sought the limelight to represent Canada to the States after the dangerous work was done were less inspiring leaders. Their leadership was based on words, not deeds, and they failed to inspire the confidence of the Canadian people. Soon, the occupation was once again resentfully accepted.

A few pockets of resistance soldiered on, but these were smaller factions that had splintered off to fight their own local battles. Cut off from any coordinated effort, one by one they were easily dominated and crushed by the numerically superior and more powerful Americans. The end of hostilities seemed at hand. Such expectations lifted the spirits of the occupation forces. Bridges were rebuilt and supplies could come through to refortify the needs of the troops. Plans were made to regroup during the winter to deliver the fragmented Canadian resistance a final coup de grace in the spring.

That fall, American agents used their methods to further widen the timeless divisions amongst Canadians. They knew their business well, encouraging such differences that cause most human conflict throughout the world, like culture, religion, language, power and money. They found fertile fields in the minds of Canada's diverse population.

Seeing that the Canadian cause was on the edge of defeat, Will made up his mind to leave the security of Ava and her family and to return north. There, he hoped to persuade the remaining resistance factions to reunite. He thanked Ava and her family for having saved his life and re-entered the battle-torn world.

~

Despite the good news from the frontlines, the treasuries of America were depleted. At the same time, the underground economy in Canada flourished. Minted coins made of copper, nickel, silver and gold had, drop by drop, trickled real currency into the Black Market. Like an iron injection into the blood stream, it refortified an ailing body and stabilized the market. Paper currency had fallen to new lows.

Consequently, more and more people rushed to buy gold and silver before their paper currency lost all its value. Soon private minters, like the professor, sprung up everywhere to meet the demand. In response, for the second time in a century, Washington outlawed the possession of gold bullion. This caused an ounce of gold to skyrocket above $7,000 and drove the exchange of gold underground. People needed a real currency and wouldn't be denied so they became unlawful and disrespectful of overzealous authority. Just like the War on Drugs, the War on Gold was an unwinnable war and, because of it, a whole new bunch of lawbreakers were born. Like the insurgents and drug lords, the gold dealers armed themselves. It was a war within a war which required more policing, allowing the state to gain even more power over the citizenry.

Such policies also caused the birth of a resistance force Stateside where those against the continuous encroachment of Washington into their private lives started thinking of the freedom-seeking Canadians as their most stalwart allies.

~

Will found it easy to make his way to Peterborough with everyone thinking he was dead. Nobody made the connection between him and the face they had seen so often in the media. Instead, he was just a familiar face to everyone he encountered and he was able to pass easily through each community. He'd become adept at avoiding checkpoints by waiting near the county-lines until after dark. Then he would slip into the next jurisdiction and blend in with the local population on the following day.

When he reached Peterborough, he was horrified to come upon the smouldering ruins of the professor's cabin. With his adrenaline surging, he raced next door looking for Sarah.

"One minute," Sarah called as Will hammered on her door for the second time. A moment later, he saw her face peek though the door's curtain. The door clicked open and she stood there looking as white as a ghost.

"Will?"

In his haste to find out what had happened to the professor's cabin, he'd totally forgotten how his sudden reappearance would shake her up.

"Will?" she repeated. She stared at him, wide eyed in disbelief.

"Yes Sarah, it's me. I'm alive. Just another lie in the media. I'll tell you all about it later. First, tell me, what happened next door?"

"Come in. They could be watching."

Once inside, Sarah's stoic demeanour transformed to one of heartfelt grief as her pent-up suffering was finally released.

"They found out about the professor minting coinage and raided his place," she sobbed.

"How?"

"We're not sure. I think they got a tip from a disgruntled student."

"I can probably guess who it was too," Will said, recalling one student in particular who'd quit the professor's outdoor experience program with much fanfare after only a few days of reality in the forest. He had threatened to report the professor's unorthodox teaching methods to the University's president. Everyone had laughed at him then, but Will had seen the depth of his vengeance when he had made his threat.

"What about the professor? Barry?" he asked, fearing the answer.

"The professor's been taken into custody. Barry's escaped and gone into hiding."

"Do you know where he is?"

"Yes. With Tuwa's tribe," Sarah answered.

Once again, Sarah and Will found themselves paddling to Hiawatha. This time, it was in search of Barry. When they landed on the riverfront of Hiawatha, Sarah went off into the village alone to notify the tribe of their arrival. Her announcement that Will was alive and waiting with their canoe at the riverside brought out the whole tribe. They formed a semicircle around him and, as they did so, he could hear a low murmuring amongst them. Many of them were not certain that his apparition was in a solid physical state. Their scepticism was soon settled.

"Ouch!" Will exclaimed as he turned to face his tormentor. There, looking not the least bit apologetic for her assault, was a frail elderly woman with a witch-like visage. In her hands, she held the walking stick she'd just poked into the small of his back. His reaction seemed to satisfy a question that had been troubling her.

"Now, now, grandma, let him be," Tuwa said, coming to Will's rescue. She turned to him with outstretched arms. "Welcome back, Will. I hear you've come back from the Spirit World," she winked at him.

"Have I now? Then that would explain a lot," he retorted, rubbing his lower back while warily taking in the superstitious crowd that surrounded him.

"Did you miss me?" she joked. Yet Will sensed that her query was not totally in jest.

"Like a brother misses his sister," he sidestepped her question. Getting straight to the point, he said, "We've come for Barry, Tuwa. Is he here?"

Will noticed the worried look on Tuwa's face.

"Barry is here isn't he, Tuwa?"

"No. He was. But he left with Renée only a few days ago. They didn't say where they where they were going, but I suspect Renée is taking him back to her relative's cabin in Québec. A troubled Spirit has taken command of him, Will," she forewarned him. "We will talk more of this later. First, we must celebrate your exploits and your rebirth!"

~

That evening, they were fêted in the great lodge where Will told them all about what had happened on the ill-fated raid and his recovery at Walpole Island.

"There is more," Tuwa's grandmother commented after Will had finished. She correctly assumed that he had only told them the conscious part of the story. She was wondering about the other part. So he continued.

"While I was unconscious," he said, "I dreamt that I hovered above my body as though my mind and body had become separated. Then I was woken by the voice of a young native girl, Ava, who was mimicking the call of a red-winged black bird, singing 'O-ka-reeeee, o-ka-reeeee.'"

It was this part of his story that most keenly held their interest. For the second time that day, Will heard a murmuring amongst them.

"How was she able to find you when all the search parties failed?" one asked.

"I don't know," he answered frankly. Then Will smiled recalling what Ava had said to explain how she'd found him. He hesitated to say anything about it as he didn't feel perfectly comfortable recounting the more bizarre parts of the story.

The grandmother nudged Tuwa impatiently.

"Go on, Will," Tuwa encouraged. "There's more to it than you may understand. Tell us so that my grandma may be able to explain the deeper meaning. She has a gift for interpreting such things."

"Well it's really nothing, Tuwa," he said looking at her grandmother who now sat staring into the fire. "It's just what Ava told me about how she'd found me. But you've got to realize, she's just a young girl with an overactive imagination." By the look on Tuwa's grandmother's face, he saw that she wasn't yet satisfied.

"Children have an innocence that allows them access to the Spirit World. An innocence adults have closed their minds to," explained Tuwa's grandmother without taking her eyes off the fire.

With that encouragement, Will continued.

"After hearing 'O-ka-reeeee, o-ka-reeeee; I opened my eyes to see a little red-winged blackbird. I made eye contact with it. I sensed we had made a connection. Like it knew I was hurt and that I needed its protection."

"Protection from who?" asked somebody.

"From the Americans," speculated another.

"Actually, no. It wasn't from the Americans. It was from the vultures," Will answered.

"Vultures? Then you must have been dead....or barely alive."

"Did you see yourself outlined in blue light? That's what people see when death surrounds them," stated another.

"Shhhh!" came the grandmother's response. "Let him tell his story." And then she began a low mesmerizing chant.

Will felt himself falling into a trance. He imagined himself back in the burnt marsh. Yes, his body was surrounded in blue light. In his trance, he occasionally mumbled a few words while his body acted out his story. His eyes stared down at his own hands. Suddenly, those hands intertwined to form the image of the red-wing flapping its wings and driving away the vulture. Will then embodied the vulture by standing up with outstretched soaring arms.

"Her sister, the red-wing, led Ava to me. That's how Ava found me," he said. Then he became still.

The others continued to observe him in silence. Few words had been used to convey his story, yet by the movement of his body, his limbs and by his facial expressions, he had told them everything in a style best suited to their ancient customs.

Will didn't know how long it took him to come out of his trance. He became aware of his own heartbeat, beating as though to the rhythm of a drum. Gradually, the drumbeats became external and he became aware of his surroundings. When he finally opened his eyes, it was dark out and the fire had died down. Someone was beating on a drum. He could see by the expressions on their faces that his story held them mesmerized, especially the elderly who recalled hearing similar stories told around the fire pit in their youth.

Being fully conscious now, he felt foolish realizing he didn't remember many details of the evening. He wondered if his memory loss was due to his head wound.

"I had a head wound and things were foggy," he explained.

"Did you dream up Ava?" asked Tuwa's grandmother who was now seated next to him and holding his hand.

"No. Ava was real. She found me," Will whispered.

"And did she not say that she'd been led to you by the bird?"

"She did."

"What do you think this all means, Grandma?" asked Tuwa.

The old woman took his other hand and looked him directly in the eyes.

"You have found yourself a strong protector, William Anderson. And it has given you a message."

"It has?"

"Yes. It has shown you that it's possible for something small and seemingly weak to drive away something large and powerful. This message will determine the future course of your life. From now on, you will be known to the people of Hiawatha as 'O-ka-reeeee', for that was the name given to you by your protector. The red-wing blackbird embodies the spirit of active defence. You must follow its path. You must attack those who have invaded our land, even against all odds – just as the red-wing does."

"But I have tried and we have lost."

"You haven't lost until the red-wing spirit abandons you. Is it not true that the red-wing weighs only one one-hundredth of the weight of the vulture? Yet it attacks again and again when the vultures intrude upon its territory! It never quits!"

"*Jamais capituler!*" he repeated the last words Yves had said to him.

"William Anderson, you too must never quit. You are meant to follow the ways of the red-wing and drive out the vultures."

"Your destiny is to drive the vulture back to its own nest," agreed one of the elders.

"The little red-wing's message is clear and its spirit has found you, O-ka-reeeee," concluded Tuwa.

Jamais Capituler!

From then on, Will was treated differently by the Hiawathans. Most truly believed he'd died in the swamp and had been sent back with an important message from the Spirit World. Under their influence, Will too began to believe that he had lived to fulfill a greater purpose. Will's closer friends noticed a change in him too. Some of them attributed the change to the grievous head wound he'd incurred. Still others believed the rumour that Anderson had become so deeply immersed in Brock's diary that he had become confused and taken on Brock's personality traits. A few looked upon him with wary eyes, wondering whether he was an imposter.

Regardless of the cause, nobody, including Will himself, could deny that a certain third presence seemed to surround him like a shield. It was as though nothing could harm him.

"You have a strong protection, my son," the chief had said.

"Your dreams aren't normal, Will," Tuwa said to him. "They mean things."

"And then you travelled all the way back here right out in the open. It's like you're untouchable," added Sarah. Her own personal experience had shown her how vulnerable to the enemy others were.

"You can't stop a Spirit from fulfilling its mission, its destiny," clarified one of the elders.

"It may be true what they say about you, Anderson. Perhaps Brock's spirit has found your body," someone hypothesized.

"Or Tecumseh's," said another.

"I highly doubt it. Why me? Why now?" Will argued.

"Why not you? And why not now? Now is the perfect time. What better reason would there be for a determined spirit to rise?" the chief countered.

It was pointless to argue. They had made up their minds.

'I am alive and well.'

Sydney stared at the private hotmail message she'd just received from Will. She had heard all the news reports about the raid. She'd talked openly and honestly with Mr and Mrs Anderson and, together, they mourned his death. She'd watched his funeral on TV. Anyone who had listened in on their conversations would conclude that he was truly dead, for she believed it to be so. At first she doubted the authenticity of the message, so convinced was she that he had been killed. But the message was typical Will, abrupt and right to the point. He ended his message with the assertion that 'Tuwa will call.'

'So now what? And who's Tuwa?' she wondered. The next day, she received a call that answered all her questions.

"Hello?"

"Hello. This is Tuwa."

"Tuwa?"

"Yes. Am I speaking with Sydney?"

"You are."

"Did you get our message?"

"Yes. But how do I know this isn't a sick prank?"

"He says you'll understand by imagining the letters 'A' and 'C'. I hope that tells you what you need to know now because I haven't a clue what it means."

Sydney knew immediately that Will must have told Tuwa to use their agreed code letters. 'A' meant 'All's good' and 'C' meant 'I'm in good company'.

"It does. Thank you, Tuwa."

"I have to get off the line now."

"I'm relieved to hear from you, Tuwa. I would like to tell you something."

"What's that, Sydney?"

"That I heard from Hana's boyfriend. He's been promoted to corporal in the Continental Army."

~

Together Will, Tuwa and Sarah went on what became a wild goose chase in search of Hacker. They knew he had gone northeast with Renée so they headed first to the La Forêts' cabin.

"T'es en vie!" ["You're alive!"] Renée cried, throwing her arms around Will.

"Ça a l'air que oui !" ["So it would seem,"] he replied, returning her hug. *"Est-ce que Hacker est avec toi?"* ["Is Hacker here with you?"]

"Tu le manques de peu..." ["You just missed him,"] she confirmed. *"Ils sont partis en canoë il y a environ une semaine."* ["They left by canoe about a week ago."]

"Qui ça 'ils'?" ["They?"]

"Yes, they," she said switching to English as a courtesy to the others. "He went with a native man who came here looking for you. His name was Tadita. Barry told him you'd been killed, but that he was a colleague of yours who was carrying on your work. That seemed to satisfy him. A few days later they left by canoe. For our safety, they wouldn't say where they were going."

"How did he seem to you, Renée?"

"Physically, he's fine. Mentally, he's not well, William. His father's in prison and he thinks you're dead. He blames himself for not being with you at Point Pelee and for what happened at his father's place."

"What happened there?"

"He was just getting home when he came upon the Inland Control Agents about to raid it. Instead of doing anything to warn his father, he ran. Now he hates himself. Will, I'm afraid of what he's capable of doing. In his mind, he's got nothing to lose."

"What about me?" Sarah piped in.

Renée looked sadly at Sarah. She knew there was no easy way to respond. Knowing how much Sarah had loved and idolized the professor, Barry couldn't face her. It was Will who answered.

"I expect he knows he's wanted by the Inland Control Agents and is staying away from you for your own protection."

"I guess so," Sarah accepted sadly.

After spending a night at the cabin, Renée and Will headed south in pursuit of Hacker while Tuwa and Sarah headed back toward Peterborough. Reluctant as Sarah was to give up the chase, she accepted that Hacker's present mental state would make him feel ashamed in her presence. All of them hoped he would snap out of his depression once he found out that Will was alive.

After a few more weeks of searching, they eventually found Hacker hiding amongst the Kichesipirini Tribe on l'Isle-aux-Alumettes, an island on the Ottawa River upriver from the capital.

"So you're alive," he said flatly to Will. "Why am I not surprised?" That was not quite the reaction they were hoping for.

"I'm not hiding," Hacker told them. "I'm seeking something."

"And what's that?" asked Renée.

"The solution," he answered. Despite their best efforts, he would not tell them more.

Like Will, Hacker had changed. His father's capture and the destruction of their home had been too much for him to bear. Over the following week, seldom did they see a glimmer of his former carefree nature.

Being Anderson's self-proclaimed replacement, Hacker had won instant respect from the Kichesipirini Tribe. The Tribe had been in long-term negotiations with Ottawa to gain full recognition of their land claims and to address their grievances for the harm caused to them and their land by the nearby Chalk River nuclear plant. Many Tribe members were ill with cancer and other diseases due to being exposed to radiation from the plant.

"Our victory will be yours," Hacker had promised the chief. Will's sudden reappearance put all their reverence and his plans in jeopardy. At the end of the week, Hacker pulled Will aside so they could talk privately.

"Will, I would like you to leave me alone for awhile. I've got a lot on my mind that I need to sort out for myself," he stated, knowing that solitude was Will's way too. But Will wondered why Hacker had become so aloof and he couldn't understand why Hacker had ostracized himself from Sarah.

"What's up, Hacker?" Will asked.

"What do you mean?"

"Well, for one thing, you haven't asked about Sarah since we got here."

"So?"

"So? She's your girlfriend."

"Not anymore."

"But you love her."

"Exactly. And that's why I must stay away from her."

"You're about as clear as mud, Hacker."

Perhaps all Hacker needed was some time and space to mull things over. Perhaps his divorcing himself from the others, particularly Sarah, was just an act of self-preservation. Eventually, Will decided to agree to Hacker's request and leave him alone. Winter approached and there were other things Will had to attend to. The resistance had all but collapsed. It was time to head north again.

Only much later did Will reflect upon this time as being a very crucial turning-point. In hindsight, he wrote,

> I should have paid closer attention to Hacker and tried to mollify his inner anxiety, but I too was being swept away with the times and felt pulled in too many different directions. Instead, I decided to let him be, hoping that the old Hacker would return once time healed his wounds. I now know that this was a mistake.
>
> — W. Anderson

~

CHAPTER XXI

We Stand On
Guard for Thee

*The lures to desertion continually thrown out by
the Americans, and the facility with which it can
be accomplished, exacting a more than ordinary
precaution on the part of officers, insensibly produce
mistrust between them and the men, prejudicial to
the service.*

~

Will's surprising return north reunited the resistance and reopened the divide between the Americans. Not only had most black Americans given up on the war, all Americans as well as Kuhn's administration were now split down the middle on the issue. The war in Canada had brought America to the brink of civil war.

"IMPOSSIBLE!" Kuhn shouted at the reporters who'd asked him to comment on the rumours that Anderson was alive and rebuilding the resistance. "That story's verging on journalistic terrorism," he threatened, shaking an angry finger at the cameras.

Since 2010, when WikiLeaks had been publicly charged by Washington for releasing sensitive diplomatic cables, the definition of journalistic terrorism had gradually got wider and wider. In the second year of the war, Kuhn's administration defined journalistic terrorism to include any public press release that harmed the image of Washington or helped its enemies. A story reporting that Anderson was still alive committed both crimes. That was just one more thing the Vice-President and Kuhn were at odds about.

"We can't allow him to be alive, Ernie," Kuhn advised the Vice-President in the Oval Office.

"I'm not sure if I follow you, Mr President. Allow?"

"YES, ALLOW!" The President fumed.

"But they've quoted credible witnesses, sir. And our sources concur. They're just reporting the truth, sir."

"So? Even if he's alive, reporting that fact shouldn't be allowed. That's careless destructive reporting," Kuhn declared.

"How so, Mr President?"

"Because stories like that hurt America, and therefore freedom," Kuhn clarified.

"Freedom?"

"Yes freedom, Ernie. American stands for freedom – remember?"

"Those ideals are known to me, sir."

"Good! And don't you forget!"

"Never, sir."

"The foremost duty of the American press is to report our side of the story, Ernie. If their reports hurt America, then that's journalistic terrorism, dammit!"

"And freedom of the press means…?"

"Don't be so naïve, Ernie. All reporters are biased. They're human just like the rest of us. In times of war, Ernie, you're either on our side or the enemy's. There's no middle ground. In wartime, freedom of the press simply means you're free to choose to side with America or go to hell! Just because you have a press badge doesn't give you any special status. Loose lips sink ships, Ernie! Remember that saying? The ultimate meaning of freedom is the freedom of choice. And the choice is to be on our side or shut up!"

~

The Christmas celebrations held in Washington were meant to mark the end of the year and to reflect America's commitment to bringing a successful conclusion to the conflict over Canada in the following year. President Kuhn wanted the celebration program to show the fractured American public that most Canadians actually supported the idea of a North American union. He also knew many Canadians would be watching the televised event. The whole evening was going better than even Kuhn had hoped. His plan seemed to be working. Christmas was a natural time for people to unite in common understanding. Nearing the end of the program, the MC took to the stage.

"Mr President. Ladies and Gentlemen," the MC said. "It gives me much pleasure to welcome to the stage the Canadian All Girls Choir. They've come to Washington from every part of that vast country, representing the true spirit of Canada and bringing with them a message of hope. Their youthful spirit joins with ours in a common cause. We pray for victory this year against those few remaining insurgents who stand in the way of peace. Without further ado, please join me in welcoming them to sing tonight's final Christmas hymn: 'Let there be Peace on Earth.'"

It took a number of minutes for the thunderous standing ovation to die down. With TV cameras rolling, the choir walked proudly out to centre stage and bowed to the audience. President Kuhn smiled. He knew better than most how to create public opinion through an orchestrated event.

Trying not to disturb the tranquility of the moment, reporters whispered into their microphones.

"The girls' uniforms were designed by Louis Garneau of Montréal."

"To show their support for North American unity, along with the red and white colours which are, of course, the traditional colours of Canada, American stars adorn their blue and white ties."

The choir mistress nodded to the audience and then spun around with outstretched arms to face her girls. The organist started with the overture and the girls' voices followed, filling the auditorium with beautiful sound.

"Each word of the hymn is enunciated perfectly by their clear Canadian accented voices," reported one journalist.

Suddenly, an uncomfortable feeling came over some members of the audience. When the girls sang the repeating chorus of "and let it begin with me" it sounded like they were singing 'with thee', not 'with me'. To those who heard it, it sounded accusatory and seemed directed at everybody in the audience, including the millions who were watching at home on TV.

Nobody was one hundred percent sure of what they were hearing. Yet the girls enunciated their words so well that, by the end of the hymn, most in the audience understood their message. Before the curtains fell, the defiant girls removed their star-spangled neckties as if freeing themselves from a hangman's noose. By that gesture, those in the audience still unsure as to the song's true meaning were quickly brought up to speed.

For what seemed an inordinate amount of time, the audience sat still in silent reflection. Then came a few boos from some outraged audience members. That response brought forth a rebuttal and suddenly, great applause erupted from the hands of many audience members as they rose to their feet. The applause was not to indicate that they agreed with the words, but instead was to acknowledge the daring spirit of the girls to come to Washington to deliver a message. It was freedom of speech the way it was intended to be in America. And their message was clear. Canada was indeed united – against the occupation.

President Kuhn was not available for comment. Before the curtains had dropped, he'd slipped out the back.

~

CHAPTER XXII

Mon Pays Ce N'est Pas Un Pays, C'est L'hiver

Experience has taught me that no regular regiment, however high its claim to discipline, can occupy the frontier posts of Canada without suffering materially in its numbers.

~

General Douglas was on a three coast tour to rally the troops. The esprit de corps had plummeted over the winter so with great fanfare he had flown to the Yukon to start his tour. He and his entourage found themselves in a land of total darkness because, at this time of year, the sun never rose in the north country. Each day, they got ready to leave only to find that, with snow covering their route or extreme cold crippling their vehicles, they'd have to delay their departure until the following day.

"Get moving!" came their orders from Washington. "This has become embarrassing."

One paper had nicknamed the tour the 'Gong Show On Snow'. Another headline billed it as 'Lost In Canada's Space'.

Finally, the weather broke and, humbled by harsh reality, they began their journey. First they limped their way southwest towards the Pacific Coast, zigzagging overland to Vancouver. Civilians didn't come out to cheer them en route. Their own troops, who were too spread out to be numerous in any one community, grudgingly came out to parade for their superiors. By the time the tour arrived at its scheduled destination and settled into heated enclosures to review the troops, the parade soldiers were half-frozen. The General was proud of himself for braving the cold for fifteen minutes while inspecting the troops. Their chattering teeth annoyed him.

When the tour finally got to Vancouver, they all boarded a train and headed eastward on the Northern Express which had to chug its way up to the Continental Divide high in the Canadian Rockies. Once they reached the summit of the Divide, the trip would be mostly downhill all the way down to the Atlantic over 3,000 miles away.

The rhythmic sound of clickety-clack marked off another section of track in their seemingly endless journey. Clickety-clack. They had been travelling for three weeks and they had only covered a small fraction of the total distance. Clickety-clack.

'How could we ever hope to hold such a vast territory?' General Douglas wondered. 'Especially when it's populated with such hostile people?'

It was a journey that was meant to bolster the morale of the troops and instill greater confidence in their leaders, but with every clickety-clack, the General started to feel vulnerable surrounded, as they were, by the vastness of this northland. Clickety-clack. The high valley they were in was surrounded by peaks which seemed to swallow them whole. Clickety-clack. It was dark in the valley because the winter sun was still hidden behind the towering mountains to their south. Only the whiteness of the snow gave off some reflected light.

'Maybe it's only the darkness that is affecting me,' he thought. Clickety-clack.

During peacetime, the Canadian Army had been employed to shell the slopes that overhung Rogers Pass and the steep valley to the east to trigger controlled release of the accumulated snowfall. Those duties now fell onto the American troops who considered them to be a waste of manpower and ammunition and a low priority on their growing list of problems. So the snow accumulated on the steep slopes.

Clickety-clack. Clickety-clack. The tempo of each clickety-clack became faster as the track began to level out slightly.

'Soon we will start the long descent and get back on schedule', General Douglas hoped.

"Corporal, bring me another whisky," he slurred to his attendant. His aide brought him another drink and, within moments, he'd drained it too.

"Another," he ordered, "and make it a double."

Clickety-clack. Across the valley from the train, Sydney nodded her head. Small puffs of smoke appeared in the snow on the other side answering her order. The carefully laid explosives she and her gang had planted on the wind-loaded slopes were doing their job. The explosions came from a line of charges strung along the ridge situated between two monstrous peaks. They had been laid during the fall and had become deeply covered beneath a heavily wind-loaded cornice. They heard a series of muffled Ka-booms! as the sound travelled to them from across the valley. The dullness of the explosion confirmed the deepness of the snow. For a moment, nothing appeared to happen and then they saw a crack form along the whole length of the cornice as the lower part began to shear away. Down the slopes rushed a massive avalanche toward the valley floor and the train carrying Douglas.

The noise of the exploding charges was also heard inside the train.

"AVALANCHE!" somebody shouted.

The passengers looked through their windows at the mountain of snow that plummeted towards them. For most, it was the last sight they ever saw.

"General, get down under this table!" the attendant ordered.

The general dove under the table and, a moment later, the corporal landed on top of him, shielding the general with his own body.

"I'll see to it you're promoted, Corporal."

The corporal ignored the comment.

"Put this in your mouth as I do. It'll help you breathe if we're covered with snow. Do it now while you can and brace yourself."

The general followed the corporal's example. Together, they braced themselves for the impact as the roar of the avalanche became louder and louder.

~

...a respectable force might be trained and rendered exceedingly useful on any exigency, were the least encouragement given to the spirit which at present pervades a certain class to volunteer their services.

"I'm freezing," said Matthew Bates, a British mercenary soldier who'd joined the insurgents.

"Good. Welcome to Canada, my friend." Will smiled as he tossed him a heavier blanket. "Be thankful for it."

"Are you serious, Anderson?"

"Very. The cold is our ally, just like you are, Bates. You can imagine how cold it would be if you were travelling under these conditions in metal boxes like the Americans. Here we're dug in and sheltered from the wind. It's comparatively cozy and I wouldn't trade places."

Outside their hideout, the freezing wind howled to a higher pitch as if to emphasize the point. Things would be far worse for the Yanks. Their expensive equipment and clothing had met its match in the Canadian winter. That winter was proving to be a particularly cold one and, in consequence, the morale of the occupation forces had fallen to a low point.

'These Canucks are tough,' Bates thought. The thought echoed the stories he had heard from his grandfather who had fought alongside the Canadians during the Second World War. His grandfather had told him how the Canadians had come to aid the British Isles during their darkest hour.

"The Canadians have always been there for us, Matthew. We knew we could rely on the Canadians from the beginning to the end."

Bates had taken those stories to heart and he felt duty-bound to act in support of Canada now that it was their turn to need help. He knew his grandfather would be proud. A number of other Brits felt the same way and had found their way into the ranks. So had Aussies, Kiwis and other mercenaries who had come from all corners of the Commonwealth.

"Ya, these conditions favour us, Bates. The worse the weather, the better for us. Provided that we are as tough as the terrain we claim to be sovereign over. I think of living under these hard conditions as a test. It will toughen us up and make us appreciate what we've lost," Will added.

Will thought back to the previous year. Then, he'd privately had his doubts about whether they could meet the challenge of pushing back their enemies. Once again, he'd been encouraged by reading Brock's diary for Brock had had the same concerns during his day. At that time, Britain had its hands full fighting Napoleon in Europe and could only spare a skeleton force from the regular army to help protect Canada. It was then that the United States invaded thinking it was the right time to attack a vulnerable under-defended British North America. If the Canadians hadn't rallied against the invaders, it would have been a cake walk as Thomas Jefferson had predicted. Yet Brock's inspiring leadership brought the Canadians together and pushed the invaders back. As far as Will was concerned, the War of 1812 was when Canada first showed itself as a true nation, although that only became official many years later in 1867.

Still, Will wondered if Canadians today would be equal to the task. These doubts resurfaced whenever those around him complained about their lot. Some envied the American troops who lived in relative comfort, but that was happening less and less as they all learned again how to endure the land they'd inherited. The land was as beautiful as it was unforgiving.

Only the hardy, who give it due respect are worthy of it.

Maybe we don't deserve to have so much . . .

confided Will to his diary.

"If we can make it through this winter, we can endure anything," Bates stated, rubbing his big mitts together as though he'd been reading Will's mind.

Will nodded to acknowledge the comment. Through the winter, he had come to know his 'kids' individually. They'd become like family to him. Despite that familiarity, he made a point to refer to them by their last names. He also encouraged them to salute one another in greeting. This was not only to encourage discipline, but also to show mutual respect. Will employed such military traditions to remind them that they were legitimate combatants and not simply the 'unlawful radicals' the Washington press kept calling them.

"Any regrets, Bates?" Will asked.

"None, sir. Absolutely none."

His sentiments weren't uncommon. Only the few who were the toughest had come north to join their ranks. Their strength boded well for the future.

~

General Douglas awoke in the dark. He remembered the panicked shout of 'Avalanche!' as a wall of snow smashed into the train and through the windows knocking the train off the tracks and rolling it over again and again.

"He's waking up," he heard someone say. Slowly, his eyes adjusted to the low light. The drugs he'd been given to render him unconscious were just now beginning to wear off.

"You ok, sir?"

That voice seemed familiar, comforting. Then he recalled why.

"You saved my life, Corporal," he said, opening his eyes. Looking around him, he added, "or we died and we've both gone to hell."

"Actually you're sort of right on both counts. We're being held captive in a cave, sir."

The corporal filled the general in on what had happened. Their train had been completely derailed, rolling until it came to rest beside the trees bordering the tracks. The train had been completely covered by the avalanche. Snow had blasted through the windows and packed the interior. The table they dove under had formed a small pocket in which they had been able to survive until they were uncovered. Unfortunately, the Canadians who unburied them, upon seeing the general's uniform, decided to hold them captive.

"We're prisoners, sir."

"Prisoners? Whose prisoners?"

The corporal didn't feel the need to answer the obvious.

"What's your name, Corporal?"

"O'Neil. Patrick O'Neil, sir."

"And you said that we were the only two of a dozen survivors, O'Neil?"

"Luck of the Irish, sir," he said with a smile.

~

"HURRAY FOR ANDERSON!" they heard the guards cheer.

"Why all the cheering?" General Douglas asked them a little while afterward. They didn't respond to his query, but he could see by their smiling faces they'd received good news. Later that day, the guards gave him a copy of the latest edition of the New York Times.

'ANDERSON LIVES!' exclaimed the headline on the front page. Beneath it was Anderson's blurred photo which had been taken by a surveillance camera.

"Tell us something we don't know," mumbled the general to O'Neil.

The story not only confirmed that Anderson was alive, it told how he'd reorganized the Canadian resistance into a unified force that was striking fear again into the hearts of the occupation forces. Anderson seemed untouchable and he seemed to be everywhere at the same time. The article claimed that Anderson was involved with planning the avalanche that had swept over the train.

The general scanned the paper for other articles of interest. He was curious to see if there was any more written about himself. Lower down on the front page, he found an article entitled 'General Douglas's Body Not Found.' The article described how it was initially believed that he may not have been on the train at all. It speculated that he had stayed in some posh hotel in Vancouver and was going to fly first class to Calgary, the tour's next scheduled destination. Then he was vexed to read how that question had been put to rest by some of the surviving passengers.

'Ya, the obnoxious bastard was definitely there. I heard him ordering everyone around,' confirmed one survivor.

'He's got to be alive,' another hypothesized, 'because there's no way that drunk could freeze with so much alcohol in his system.'

'He's probably still out there walking off a wicked hangover,' Sergeant Joe Longfellow was quoted as saying.

"I never trusted Longfellow," the general said. "But I always trusted you, Corporal."

Indeed, General Douglas trusted Corporal Patrick O'Neil like no other. While they were held together in captivity, O'Neil had become his trusted confidant. Two weeks had passed since the train's derailment and still their captors hadn't bothered to inter- rogate the general for information. Their attitude towards him sug- gested they considered him to be unimportant and it seemed that the only value they put on him was for making a prisoner exchange. He found that both demeaning and annoying.

"These idiots don't know who they've caught, Patrick. They're a bunch of amateurs."

"How so, sir?" Patrick yawned. "Just because of your rank?"

"It's not only my rank, although that should be enough by itself. It's because I know things they would love to find out. I've been privy to the whole game, you might say, right from the start."

"Things, sir?" Patrick asked as picked up a piece of black coal. He turned it over examining its unusual lustre. That annoyed the general who didn't like to be competing for the corporal's attention with a hunk of coal.

"Yes, things, corporal. Very important things. Things that you wouldn't understand," he snapped at the corporal, adding, "way more important than that nugget of coal you're ogling."

"I'm sure you're right, sir," O'Neil yawned again, tossing aside the nugget. "It's anthracite, sir."

"What?"

"That nugget of coal, sir. It's anthracite."

"What's anthracite?"

"It's mineral and harder than normal coal, sir. Harder to light too. And it burns with a clean smoke-free blue flame."

"WHO BLOODY CARES!" the general exclaimed.

Now, he was even more annoyed at the corporal for, not only had the coal captured O'Neil's attention more than he, the corporal had also demeaned him by addressing him like a student. Had the general been less concerned about the hierarchy of their relation- ship and given the corporal's observation more credit, he may have realized that, by finding anthracite, the corporal had given him a clue as to their whereabouts in the Canadian Rockies.

Instead, he let his mood govern and clammed up to sulk in silence. His eyes wandered around the walls of the cave. Bats huddled together overhead, drawing warmth from each other's presence and the relatively warmer air near the ceiling. He pulled the blankets draped over his shoulders more tightly around him.

Two crude beds had been given to them and their exit had been barred. Warm food and tea or coffee was served to them at mealtimes and, one by one, they were allowed out each day to use the toilet, wash up and get some exercise. They were limited to a guard escorted walk through the labyrinth of tunnels within the cave. The general had no doubt that he would quickly find himself hopelessly lost if he were ever to attempt an escape through the maze. Yet the idea that he'd played an important part in driving his captors into such a miserable place humoured him. What he didn't know was that each day the guards got out and mingled with the local community, only to return to rotate watch shifts with the other guards.

"Where are we?" he wondered, not realizing that that had been the whole point O'Neil had been trying to make when he talked about the anthracite.

"My guess is we're in the Rockies about 70 miles west of Calgary, sir," answered O'Neil.

"How would you know that, Corporal?"

"Lucky guess," he lied. "Calgary was to be our next stop, sir."

O'Neil had come to know the general's temperament and also how to massage his ego. He saw the general's demeanour begin to lighten.

"I think I get it, sir. You know about important things that affect the lives of lots of people."

"More than you can even imagine, Patrick."

"Secrets, sir?"

"Yes. Top secrets. Presidential secrets. Secrets that our enemies here would love to learn."

"I see," answered O'Neil.

"No, Corporal, you don't see. You have no idea what I know. Nor do these fools," he sneered as he pointed a thumb back towards the exit.

For a moment, Patrick deliberately chose not to respond. He knew it was best to leave the general in silence and let him feel superior. After the correct amount of time, he added, "Doesn't seem right, sir."

"What doesn't?"

"Odds are that I'll never get out of here, sir. Unlike you, I'm not worth anything to them. I'm just another mouth to feed and eventually, without you, what'll be the point in keeping me?"

The general nodded as the same thought had crossed his mind. He had seen how he'd been receiving better treatment and heartier meals from their captors than the corporal. He had tried to share his extra portions with Patrick, but the guards had intervened and had taken both their portions away, leaving Patrick even worse off for the attempt.

"Even if we both died here, sir, at least you'd die knowing the truth. Me, I'd die in the dark both literally and figuratively. With respect, sir, that seems un-American to me. In fact, I wish you hadn't said anything about it in the first place."

Over the course of the next couple of weeks what Patrick had said weighed heavily on the general's mind. He felt guilty for knowing what he did and it bothered him. He was gaining weight while Patrick appeared to become weaker. He was indebted to Patrick for having saved his life and now it seemed very probable that he'd never be able to make good his promise of ensuring that Patrick would be promoted.

Yet he couldn't tell the secrets he'd been sworn to keep. Patrick would have to figure things out for himself.

"You said you're from Flint, Michigan, Patrick?" he asked.

"That's right, sir."

"When were you first deployed to Canada?"

"Right after Fermi, sir. I've been with you right from the beginning, when you were a major. I was just a private then, sir."

General Douglas smiled knowing that they had both been together from the start. He recalled when an officer had recommended O'Neil as an outstanding candidate for his personal aide-de-camp to replace the previous one who had been shot by a rebel. The sniper's bullet had been intended for him.

"Those were heady days, sir. We almost made it to Niagara."

"Indeed we did. And we would have, Patrick, had we not been stopped by our previous weak-kneed president. This war needed a person like Kuhn."

"Well they do call it Mister Kuhn's War, sir."

"If they only knew the truth of those words, Patrick. If they only knew...."

~

'GENERAL DOUGLAS KILLED!' the headline of the Washington Post shouted. General Douglas couldn't believe his eyes and reread the article in disbelief. His death was the news of the day all across North America. He stared at the paper, trying to deny its meaning. But he couldn't. He'd been abandoned by the only man who had mattered to him.

'We don't negotiate with terrorists,' the President was quoted when asked to explain why he'd rejected the idea of a prisoner exchange.

"BULLSHIT!" the general exclaimed. "We've exchanged plenty of war prisoners."

"Then why not you too, sir?"

He didn't have a quick answer for that question. The article made it apparent that his captors had been trying to exchange him for some university professor named Hacker. In the general's way of thinking, Washington should have jumped at the offer. But they didn't and gradually he figured out why.

"They want me dead, Patrick," he admitted.

"Why you, sir?"

"I know too much," he said simply. "I'm just one of Kuhn's sacrificial lambs."

He could barely look Patrick in the eye. According to the news, he mattered less to the President than some lowly professor who'd been caught minting gold coins. He'd been humiliated in the eyes of the only person who now mattered, Patrick.

That evening, they were each brought a juicy steak, cooked perfectly to medium rare, and served with mashed potatoes, peas and butter. They washed the meal down with a fine bottle of red wine and finished it all off with dessert.

"Looks like we've been given our last meal, sir," the corporal stated.

"Looks like it, Patrick," admitted the general who'd come to the same conclusion. Mulling over that thought, an idea struck him.

"We're not dead yet, Patrick, my lad!" he declared, finishing the last drop of wine with a gulp.

"GUARDS!" he hollered.

~

"I'm worth more to you alive; way more than exchanging me for a lousy professor. I have information that will turn this whole war around," General Douglas claimed gleefully to his captors. He smiled knowing that they hadn't forced any information from him. Instead, Washington's betrayal of him had made it acceptable to tell all and he was almost bursting at the seams to let them know his true worth.

"You say that you have information that will favour Washington if it becomes public? Then we must kill you now!" Sydney joked.

But the general took her seriously.

"NO!" he panicked, adding quickly, "that's not what I meant!"

"Well your side is losing. So what do you mean by 'turn this whole war around?'"

"I mean it will be in your favour – Canada's favour."

"How?"

"I can prove that Canada was innocent. That it was all a setup."

"We are innocent."

"I know. But I have information that will prove to America that you are."

"How's that?" asked Sydney.

"He's just a windbag," declared a guard. "Full of bull. He'll drag it on and on and in the end, we'll have nothing to show for it."

"Fine," Sydney agreed and prepared to leave the room.

"We destroyed Fermi," he blurted out.

"Pardon me?" Sydney asked, coming back to the table.

"I said we destroyed Fermi," he repeated.

"I thought it was destroyed by that crazy kamikaze co-pilot, err, what's his name?"

"That Islamic-Canadian fella. Yes, he may have been Canadian on paper, but we made him who he was and we incited him to attack us."

For a moment, Sydney simply stared at him. Now she knew what evil looked like. She recomposed herself.

"Ok. Let's hear it then," Sydney replied calmly. Inside, she couldn't believe the horrific implications of what the general had just admitted. She turned to one of the guards.

"Hank, can you please go get the video camera?"

"Yes ma'am," he answered.

The general didn't like the direction this was taking. He'd seen too many videos made of captives who were killed afterwards when they lost their usefulness. Either way, such a betrayal ensured he was a dead man and he was not about to throw his life away.

"No. I will only speak to Anderson," he declared. He didn't know what made him say that. Perhaps it was that Anderson was the only name he could think of in the resistance. But once he said it, he dug in his heels for he knew that Anderson had a reputation for being humane and would not allow anyone to be tortured or publicly humiliated. Perhaps he would even protect him. He was proud of himself to have thought of the manoeuvre and decided to push for more.

"And Corporal O'Neil goes with me," he demanded.

"Very well," Sydney agreed, adding with a sneer, "General."

~

We've transformed ourselves into an army of snowmen. Gradually throughout the winter, we've learned how to dress properly for the relentless cold and, by doing so, have come to resemble snowmen. All one needs to do is add a carrot to our noses and two lumps of coal for eyes. Attired as such, we accidentally discovered how to avoid being detected by the enemy flying overhead.

Over our wool long underwear, we wear specially made tinfoil vests that trap our body heat and prevent it from escaping. On our heads we wear fur hats. We take the fur from whatever animal we get that'll serve the purpose. If it's a white rabbit it serves the double purpose of camouflage in our wintry landscape. Still we prefer

beaver, for that makes us feel we're sporting a proper
Canadian uniform.

We completely cover our faces, hands and feet too. Mitts
are better than gloves and layers of woollen socks and thick
felt boots are the best. Most of the men lack shavers
and have no option but to grow out their beards. This is
good in the north, as having a beard adds another layer
of insulation to their face, and one's face is where much
unchecked heat can escape. Being so clothed, we are invisible
to the enemy's heat-seeking equipment for we give off the
approximate heat signature of a partridge or a squirrel.
We often check our heat signature by seeing where the snow
melts on us. If it doesn't melt, we're insulated.

Lastly, we pull snow-white pants and overcoats over
everything. Now we are invisible in this landscape and
literally appear as snowmen in a snowy world.

— W. Anderson

"Attention, il y a une drone!" somebody shouted.

"Everyone down! Freeze!" shouted Will. Nobody panicked, but
all assumed their well-rehearsed positions. All were in place even
before he could finish his sentence. That order was their best
defence on open ground. By lying down, they didn't cast shadows
and they were undetected as long as there was no motion.
The most practiced landed on their backs so they could watch
the show.

"Freeze, sir? We're already frozen!" one jested. That got a few
laughs. Only a month or two before, a drone flying overhead would
have caused everyone to run in panic, but they'd all grown more
confident over the winter. It had been mostly by accident they'd
solved the problem of the drones. At first, they were easy targets
for their heat sensing cameras. So refined was the technology that
even a warm breath could be detected. It was a eureka moment

when they discovered that that same technology failed to sense them in their snow-caves.

They had dug the burrows into snow banks to protect themselves from the numbing cold and wind. Many of the snow-caves were right out in the open in the middle of a meadow. They were surprised to realize that a surveillance aircraft could fly directly overhead and not detect them. After this discovery, they quickly constructed numerous snow-caves as a sort of air raid defence shelter network.

Gradually they learned that they could also dress in such a way to achieve the same protection. With their clothes as their shields, the insurgents gradually became bold enough to remain outdoors and face their enemy. Now the freedom fighters shot at the drones for sport. Rarely, if they got lucky, they downed one, but more important was that they had learned the lesson that they no longer needed to fear their enemy.

On the other hand, it was devastating for the pilots' morale when they found bullet holes in the wings and fuselage of their aircraft. Their enemy had become invisible.

As a last ditch effort, the US strategy became one of mass. What couldn't be done with technology they tried to do with materiel. Right from the start the ill-fated Operation Polar Storm offensive was a disaster for it had to be delayed again and again due to inclement weather.

"GET GOING!" Kuhn ordered. "I DON'T CARE ABOUT THE WEATHER!"

The following day, they threw everything they had up into the air and into the storm to search for and destroy the insurgents. One out of ten didn't return and the New York Times declared: "Operation Polar Storm repulsed by a Canadian Storm."

Later, this time became known to the resisters as *the time of plenty* for the only thing the distressed aircraft shot at were large game animals. It was an unfortunate waste, but their kills became perfectly preserved carcasses, naturally frozen at those latitudes, and were found and used as food by the resisters. After a month of getting no conclusive results, the offensive was halted for it was too great an expense and a waste of limited fuel.

With the skies freed of the invaders, the insurgents ventured south to find and drive away their enemies.

~

The journey was going to be a long one. Two thousand miles of contested territory lay between Sydney and Will, but she was thrilled to be making that trip. She had an important job to do, escorting General Douglas to Anderson. Soon, she and Will would be together again and that motivation carried her forward.

"Use the waterways as much as you can, Syd," Will had advised her. "And be sure to disclose to nobody who you are," he added as a caution.

"Do you really travel so much by canoe?" Sydney had asked. It seemed impossible to her that he could cover so much territory by such outmoded means.

"I also travel by bike and on foot, Syd. But since you'll be travelling east from the Rockies, you'll find the Bow River to be the best option on the first leg of your journey. Expect the whole trip to take over two months, but it's the safest way," Will assured her.

"But it will take so long, Will," she complained.

"You'll be amazed how much territory you can cover in a day. Sure it's faster to try to drive, but the odds are against you to travel safely on the roads over such a great distance. There's no rush so be patient. Just remember, time is on our side in this war."

"I guess," admitted Sydney. She couldn't help but feel a little disappointed as Will seemed to have less a sense of urgency to see her than she'd hoped.

"Syd, it's more important to me that you make it here. For that reason alone, please don't rush. Think of it as an adventure. I just wish I could be there with you. I love you." Hearing that, Sydney put all doubts about Will out of her head.

Travelling eastward, they left behind the Rockies and descended through the foothills. Before them lay the prairies, a never-ending field of green, as vast as an ocean, which stretched off into the horizon. The general and Patrick travelled in separate canoes between two paddlers. It seemed ridiculous to the general how they travelled, but each day they covered a fair distance completely uninhibited by any road blocks.

'Who would have thought?' he mused. It gave him newfound respect for his adversaries.

Travelling in this way also gave the general a lot of time to reflect and prepare for his eventual meeting with Anderson. Instinctively, he disliked the man. It irked him that a non-military person had become such a thorn in their side and had gained widespread notoriety while he himself, a true-blue military man who'd come from a family with a long military tradition, had been cast aside and abandoned by his fellow countrymen. He had a high opinion of himself and fancied himself having similar qualities to the Civil War's General Sherman. But nobody else had made that comparison. To deepen the wound, he had heard others comparing Anderson to Brock and Tecumseh. That was another reason he disliked Anderson. General Douglas imagined there could be few similarities between Brock and Anderson. Brock was a refined English gentleman who'd been schooled in the best military tradition. He thought Brock would have been a worthy opponent, if only on the basis of his military background. On the other hand, Anderson was a nobody, a lucky bystander who'd been caught in events much larger than himself.

"But sometimes you can't pick your enemies," the general had once confided to Patrick. "Make them, yes. And we do that well enough, but to actually pick them, that's a little more complicated."

Thinking ahead to their eventual meeting, the general felt he'd have the upper hand and a scheme started to take shape in his head. He imagined intimidating Anderson with his superior rank and his power. As far as giving information, he decided it would be best to only divulge little bits and pieces of useless details. He imagined himself, with O'Neil's aid, turning the tables on Anderson. Possibly even capturing him. That would make him a national hero and perhaps even more powerful than Kuhn himself.

This strategy brought on a sly smile. He truly considered it a feasible plan to withhold anything really top secret from Anderson. He knew that Anderson had no heart for torturing the truth out of his prisoners. He snickered to himself at that thought. It proved Anderson was indeed an amateur in modern combat. He was on some sort of outmoded 'fight chivalrously' program, which made the general despise him even more.

"Anderson believes in fighting a gentleman's war, Patrick. That's why he's going to lose."

~

A couple of days into their journey, they made camp at the Stoney Indian Reserve on the Bow River about fifty miles west of Calgary. There, the two prisoners were reunited and left to themselves, locked inside their own cabin.

This setting provided the general the opportunity to discuss with Patrick what he had been thinking about all day. The question on his mind was how to strike the delicate balance between impressing his enemies just enough to assert his value, but not telling them too much so as to avoid being branded a coward and a traitor by his fellow countrymen later.

"That's a delicate balance, sir," the corporal commented.

Seeing that Patrick understood the stakes, he seemed perfectly suited as a sounding board. He trusted Patrick with his own life. Both of their lives depended upon keeping the things he knew a secret. He suspected that if their captors discovered his secrets prematurely, their lives would be of little value. And with such a long and dangerous journey ahead of them, why would they put themselves at such risk for no gain? Yet, in his mind, that risk did not include Patrick. Now they were alone. Having waited most of the day for this opportunity, the general was practically bursting at the seams.

"How's it going, sir?" Patrick inquired.

"Fine, Patrick, my lad. I've been doing a lot of thinking throughout the day and I've come up with a plan."

"GREAT! Are we going to escape, sir?" Patrick asked excitedly.

That question brought disappointment, for the idea of escape hadn't entered the general's head. The general was a man of words, not action.

"No, Corporal," the general continued. "My plan is more in the intellectual realm."

"What do you mean by that, sir?"

"Hummmm." The general had played and replayed his monologue many times in his head, but the corporal's line of questioning momentarily threw him off. He hesitated and drew in a deep breath.

As soon as he started again, he was in his zone. Patrick was, literally, a captured audience for the haughty general whose bombastic diatribe went on and on non-stop. In the general's mind, he held Patrick transfixed and he couldn't stop himself from telling him about all the intrigues he'd been privy to, trying to keep Patrick's interest from waning. It was a rare occasion for the general to hold someone so captivated and he took full advantage of it.

"You're kidding, sir," Patrick said, his glassy eyes revealing he was on the verge of becoming bored. "Are you sure we shouldn't just try to escape?"

Hearing this, General Douglas unleashed his greatest salvo.

"Corporal, you just don't get it. This whole war has been orchestrated. We provoked it. Even the plane flown into Fermi was masterminded by our own people!" he blurted out.

"Our people, sir?"

"Well, Kuhn's people," he clarified, distancing himself from directly playing a part in the scheme.

"That doesn't make any sense, sir," replied Patrick. "Why would we do that to ourselves? Didn't the investigation prove that it was an Islamic terrorist flying a Canadian airplane who was responsible for Fermi?"

"Yes and that's what we wanted everyone to think. It was the story that we produced and directed. We even picked the main character. With billions of dollars being spent on airport security, how do you think he slipped through the cracks? Who did you think incited him?"

"You, sir?"

"No. Not me personally. Kuhn's people did it all. I am, errrr, I was on his team. I was just following orders. Everything was spearheaded by Kuhn."

Douglas grinned with inner satisfaction. Betraying Kuhn, who had betrayed him first, felt just and gratifying.

"Kuhn made it all possible. In some ways, I guess I was just another one of his pawns," he conceded. "Kuhn was the king. It was all his idea."

"But why, sir?"

"The simple answer is that we had to address a problem that couldn't be solved."

The corporal looked perplexed so the general continued to explain.

"Our nuclear problem, Patrick. The power stations. Our weapons. Our navy. Heaven forbid that one of our nuclear subs or aircraft carriers ever sinks. We don't ever want another Pearl Harbour, do we now? But the most immediate problem is, err was, our nuclear power stations."

"Why's that, sir? I thought they were safe."

"SAFE! Are you joking? They're the most dangerous thing man has ever built. They're our Pandora's Box. And we've got them right smack in the middle of our population centres. Many constructed upon fault lines. How short-sighted is that? Didn't you see what happened at the Fukushima Daiichi nuclear power facility in Japan? The safety systems that weren't supposed to fail failed. We can't even safely store the waste they produce. And we know that some waste has gone missing, presumably into the wrong hands."

"Wrong hands, sir? And who would that be?"

"America's enemies, Patrick."

"Like Canada?"

"Maybe. Perhaps some wacko Canadian might try to use it against us – or maybe some wacko American for that matter, but we doubt it. It's not in either of our natures," he said disdainfully.

To that, Patrick looked interested, yet more confused, so the general went on.

"Patrick, here's a little history lesson. The Canucks were the only nation that came out of the Second World War with a nuclear capability yet decided not to develop nuclear weapons. How stupid is that? With their landmass and that might, they could have been a superpower. You see? It's not in their makeup. You've seen how they fight, Patrick!"

"Like a bunch of bloody gentlemen," Patrick piped in.

"Or women!" the general sneered. "They hide and come out of the woodwork only when conditions favour them."

"Sounds like how we fought the revolutionary war, sir."

"Well that was different. We were fighting for freedom."

"How's that unlike the Canadians, sir?"

"Well it is. We live in modern times and their methods are outdated. War is hell and we should use all the weapons we have at our disposal. I'm proud to say that we Americans are the only people on earth who've ever nuked anyone. Twice in fact! And we'll do it again, if…. or rather, when, we need to."

Patrick looked horrified.

"But back to my story, Patrick. The problem we faced was short-term because we knew it would only be a matter of time before one of those plants had a major leak, one many times larger than either Chernobyl or Japan. Everyone at the top in Washington has known about this problem for years, but nobody knew how to address it. Until Kuhn. The man is brilliant. A born leader. He saw it as an opportunity," the general admitted. Despite being betrayed, he couldn't help but still admire Kuhn. "So you see? Curse-shit was just a pawn."

"You mean Khurshid?"

"Who?"

"Khurshid, the terrorist who flew the aircraft into Fermi, sir?"

"That's right. But we called him Curse-shit. He was the perfect man for the job. He came to our attention as an Islamic-Canadian kid with a big chip on his shoulder from being picked on and bullied. We just continued the process and redirected his hate towards us."

"But how'd you find him, sir?"

"That was easy. We've been tracking Canadians for years. Under the guise of security, we got full access to the RCMP files. We know more about Canadians than they do. This kid had a record for committing minor offences, like unlawful possession of marijuana. Although all charges had been dismissed, we knew all about him. He had the perfect profile. Islamic. Grandparents, aunts and uncles still overseas. Parents devout. So, unbeknownst to him, we controlled his life. We paid bullies to beat him up. Then we planted friends who encouraged an interest in flying. We helped him obtain his private pilot's licence, then a commercial licence and eventually a job flying cargo planes. Ultimately we helped him get hired by Can-Air. Throughout the whole process, we inflamed his hatred of Americans. We destroyed his relatives' homes and businesses in Iraq. We continuously shamed his parents as well as himself at immigration whenever they attempted to cross over the border. We even caused his family to be laid off from their jobs at Chrysler and burnt down the mosque he worshipped at. In the end, all we needed to do was plant the idea of targeting Fermi in his head. We knew he flew over its vicinity all the time. The rest is history, Patrick my boy."

The general had stunned Patrick into silence. Suddenly it all made sense. The whole war with Canada had been orchestrated, as the general had said. They had manufactured an enemy and led him every step of the way to a tragic end. In the end, the poor bugger had been completely manipulated. Patrick felt chilled knowing that Washington would allow people to be sacrificed in such a way. Understanding the general better made him feel the immediate need to get away from him.

"GUARDS!" Patrick shouted. "UNLOCK THE DOOR AND LET ME OUT!"

That sounded like an order. And that didn't make any sense to General Douglas. Something wasn't right. Immediately, the door was unlocked and swung open. Fresh air and daylight streamed in.

"Patrick?"

Turning back to face the general, Patrick answered, "No. My real name is Owens, Captain Owens, Canadian Forces. And we've videotaped your statement."

The stunned look on the general's face told all. For the second time in a week, he'd been betrayed by the only people who meant anything to him. He seethed with hatred. Was there nobody he could trust anymore? If he had his finger on the proverbial button, he'd have pushed it.

~

"Did you get all that?" Owens asked.

"Yup, we got it all, York," Sydney answered. "Good job."

"I'm just glad it's over. I could barely stand another minute with that man. I guess there's no need to continue east, then?"

"I guess not," Sydney sighed in regret. The thought of having to abandon their trip saddened her. Once again, she wondered when she would ever see Will again.

"I said no *need*. But I still *want* to go. I miss Hana," York admitted.

"And I miss Will," she echoed.

"So let's go anyway. It'll be just the two of us so we'll travel lighter and faster."

"YES!" Sydney exclaimed.

Sydney and Owens would leave immediately.

After Owens had left him, the general had been thinking about his future too. He was now a desperate man who had no alternative but to act. The general's mind worked quickly. He knew only three other people remained in camp. The rest had gone into town to replenish their supplies, leaving behind only Sydney, Owens and a guard stationed outside the door of the general's cabin. By the time Owens and Sydney returned to his cabin to retrieve Owens' belongings, the general had come up with a plan.

As they unlocked the cabin door, it swung wide open, slamming right into Owen's face. The impact was so unexpected and sudden that Owens was knocked onto the ground. The general burst out from behind the door and, in one concerted motion, swung a board at the guard's head.

WHACK! The board resonated against the guard's head and he was rendered senseless. The guard's pistol still rested on the bench outside of the cabin and the general frantically grabbed it as he swung around to face Sydney and Owens. She froze just as Owens was getting back to his feet. Still dazed, Owens looked up to see the pistol pointing straight at them.

"SO YOU THINK YOU'RE SMART, DO YOU?" shouted the general at him. "WELL, YOU'RE NOT!" Taking a breath to calm himself, he continued, "I know who you are. You're that insubordinate asshole who stood in my path once."

"That would be me, and that was my job, you pompous ass," Owens countered.

"Well, maybe now you'll get a Victoria Cross too! GO TO HELL!"

With that, he pulled the trigger, followed by another four shots in quick succession. The final two shots went into Owens' lifeless body. Seeing the guard starting to come to, the general walked calmly over to him and dispatched him with one bullet into the back of his head. All the time he had kept a wary eye on Sydney, ready to turn his gun on her too, if necessary. With the other two dead, he now turned his full attention towards her, his final enemy.

"Where is that video, bitch?"

"Go to hell, you bastard!"

"I've got three bullets left," he threatened. "Now get me that video."

CHAPTER XXIII
O'er The Land
Of The Free

I am convinced you have acted wisely in abstaining from offensive operations, which in their effect might have united a people governed by public opinion, and among whom too much division exists, at this moment, to admit of its influence in promoting vigorous measures against us.

~

It was well into spring and the insurgents were getting anxious for duty. They didn't have to wait long for a target to present itself. Sydney's capture was now headline news, as was General Douglas' escape. The general had re-entered the world in a way that caused neither Kuhn nor himself any public embarrassment. In fact, Kuhn made the general's miraculous escape out to be a victory.

"The tide has turned!" he beamed while adding another star to the general's already heavily medaled tunic.

The general complained about those who had mistakenly reported his death to the President. He chastised them by saying that they were the voice of defeatism, whereas he and the President represented the voice of confidence and optimism.

Knowing the truth, Will followed the story with contempt and amazement. The whole situation reminded Will of what Brock had written about General Hull after the fall of Detroit.

He seems to be perfectly satisfied with himself, is lavish of censure upon his government, but appears to think that the most scrupulous cannot attach the slightest blame to his own immediate conduct at Detroit. The grounds upon which he rests his defence are not, I fancy, well founded, for he told us that he had not gunpowder at Detroit for the service of one day. Sir George has since shown him the return of the large supply found in the fort; it did not create a blush, but he made no reply. He professes great surprise and admiration at the zeal and military preparation that he has everywhere witnessed ... Hull seems cunning and unprincipled: how much reliance is to be placed on his professions, time will shew.

~

"I'm sorry to hear about Sydney, Will," said Renée, interrupting his thoughts. "When are you heading south?"

"Tomorrow," Will answered. "I plan to be in Washington by July 4th."

"Washington?"

It made sense. Washington was where both Sydney and the professor were being kept as prisoners. Will knew that imprisoning Sydney in Washington was Kuhn's strategy to lure him across the border, but he was going anyway. So far, the sequence of events for this war had followed those of the War of 1812. First Canada had been invaded, then Detroit had been attacked, and then Toronto. Now it was Washington's turn to experience the real war.

"I'm coming with you," Renée declared.

"No, you're not. Not this time."

"Why not?"

"It'll be only Hana and me. Your English is good, Renée, but you can't mask that wonderful Québécois accent. Hana and I were born and raised in the south, surrounded by the American news and media. If we choose our words deliberately, we can make ourselves sound just like them."

"Plus I need you here to coordinate the diversionary attacks, Renée. Washington will be expecting us to do something in response. Your job will to keep their attention in Canada. Hit them hard, hit them everywhere and hit them often. Comprends?"

"Oui. Je comprends."

Renée didn't like being left out, but she knew that Will was right. There was no point in arguing. She agreed that a diversion would be an important element of his success and would help to protect him. She nodded in assent.

On the other hand, Will couldn't refuse Hana even if he wanted to. After seeing Kevin imprisoned and hearing about York's death, she too had personal reasons to be drawn into the war and she would have gone Stateside by herself to avenge her loss. So for her protection, they would go together.

~

Despite the capture of Anderson's lover, time was quickly running out for Kuhn and he knew it. The opinion polls showed that his popularity had plummeted. All indicators pointed to a Democratic house being elected to Congress in the fall. Even the Republicans and Tea Partiers had merged and rebuilt their traditional base by returning to the ways forged by their predecessors. To turn it all around, Kuhn needed a final victory over Canada that summer. He needed the Canadians to lose their heart and accept the inevitable. For that he needed Anderson. If Anderson was caught Stateside, Kuhn could finally prove that the insurgents were a clear and present danger to America as he had portrayed them. It was Kuhn's last ditch hope that, by ensnaring Anderson, he would silence the American public's growing opposition to the war. At least until the elections were over.

Inspired by Brock's strategy up to this point in the war, Will had guided the insurgents to restrict their raids to Canadian territory or to minor nuisance raids just across the border. The cross border raids had proved a useful tactic in throwing the Americans on the defensive and had caused them to redeploy more of their troops back to the States, thinning their lines in Canada.

But Brock had never sent a force deep into the American interior. Will imagined that he may have eventually done so had he not been killed in action during the first year of the war. Lacking any guidance from Brock's diaries, Will still felt confident that he understood Brock's mentality so well that he knew what Brock would do in the face of this challenge. In a sense, this was to be his graduation from the schooling of Brock. With Sydney and the professor imprisoned in Washington and Kuhn being located there, his final objective had to be Washington DC.

In anticipation of Will entering the States, Kuhn had ordered the Homeland Guard to be put on highest alert, crimson red. This new colour had been added to the Homeland Security Advisory System to raise the level of alert to new heights. The old red had been so overused it had lost all sense of urgency. In the psyche of the people, red had become the old orange; orange, yellow; yellow, blue; blue, green, and green was never used any more.

The new colour, crimson red, didn't produce the desired effect. Years of scaremongering had numbed the public to any colour advisory.

"It's going to be mostly sunny today with temperatures rising to eighty-two degrees. A crimson red advisory is in effect so it would be a good day to enjoy the outdoors in wide open spaces," was a typical weather forecast. "But if your day takes you in or around public buildings and transportation systems, don't forget your flak jacket. Don't forget your umbrella either, as clouds are expected to form later in the day with a chance of thunderstorms. Today's lucky Minuteman Lotto number is J14A02Q92. This is Judy, the weather-person for the new CBC, Continental Broadcasting Centre news. Have a nice day!"

Hence, the strategy backfired on Kuhn and caused Washington to lose more credibility.

"Like our paper dollars, red has been devalued," one business-man quipped.

"We'll sponsor a burgundy red for the next peak colour," the Napa Wine Co. offered cashed-strapped Washington.

"What's next, Bloody Mary red?" a bartender joked. "Hey, that might sell, Charlie!" laughed a regular patron.

In the chest of most citizens, an independent, rebellious heart still beat. Each day, that beat grew in strength and intensity as more Americans became defiantly opposed to the heavy handed ways of Washington. That defiance was expressed by replacing the prescribed culture of paranoia with a new culture of openness and trust. In the second year of the war, fearing your friends and neighbours was no longer considered to be a wise security precaution; instead, it was thought to be un-American. Americans were recognizing that this pervasive attitude had offended most of the world and had created many enemies, both domestically and abroad.

This attitude shift was timed perfectly for Hana and Will. The night before slipping across the border, they'd slept in Fort Erie on the upper-end of the Niagara River. In addition to the Fort's close proximity to the States, Will had chosen the place because it held special meaning for him. Fort Erie was a fort which had figured prominently in the War of 1812. It had originally been built as part of a series of forts to help guard Canada against an American invasion. In the War of 1812, Fort Erie had been bombarded to smithereens, but had been rebuilt years later. Like Brock, the Fort symbolized for Will Canada's enduring spirit.

~

I returned three days ago from an excursion to Fort Erie—the Grand River, where the Indians of the Six Nations are settled—and back by the head of the lake. Every gentleman, with whom I had an opportunity of conversing, assured me that an exceedingly good disposition prevailed among the people. The flank companies, in the districts in which they have been established, were instantly completed with volunteers, and indeed an almost unanimous disposition to serve is daily manifested. I shall proceed to extend this system now I have ascertained that the people are so well disposed — but my means are very limited.

"Why am I not surprised?" Hana had said when Will had told her his plan.

To Hana, the old fort meant something as well. In their youth, Will and Hana had discovered it on a family vacation to Niagara Falls. Staying nearby, they had been more excited to visit the old fort than to see the Falls. To their temporary disappointment, he and Hana had found the fort to be closed for the season. But the high fortress walls just added another challenge to the adventure and so, pretending to be Indians, they'd snuck up to the walls, found a way to scale them and took the fort.

Once inside the fort, they were hidden from sight of others and spent most of the day exploring it in peace. Sitting astride one of its many cannons, they enjoyed a picnic of peanut butter and jam sandwiches. It was a typical childhood adventure for them that neither would forget.

Before their escapade into the States, the fort was still a safe place to hide. The resistance had covertly dug a tunnel from a neighbouring property through the fort's foundation to exit out of a large manhole drain in the middle of the parade grounds. Now instead of climbing over the walls, they crawled under them through the tunnel. Here they rendezvoused after many months apart.

"We'll wait in the fort until dark and catch a few winks under the stars," Will explained. "At midnight we'll leave through a second tunnel that goes under the main road to a hidden exit by the riverbank. From there, we'll canoe across the river to a small stream leading into enemy territory."

"How will we find it in the dark?" Hana asked.

"By GPS. We're not that primitive," he answered.

"Frankly, Will it wouldn't surprise me if you took a fix off the stars with your sextant to figure it out," she jested. It was something he'd learned to do as a kid and they both knew he was adept at using a sextant.

"I was thinking of that, but it would be difficult to do that while paddling," Will smiled as they exited into the parade grounds, adding, "We should get some sleep."

Under starry skies, Hana and Will found it hard to sleep with all their excitement. For Hana, it was almost like old times with her big brother. Will sensed her enthusiasm and hoped she understood the risk of their venture. It was going to be no picnic.

Lying there, gazing into the sky, Will felt the haunting spectacle of the ghosts of their brave predecessors surrounding them. To reassure himself, he glanced around but saw only the massive stone walls. A number of his men came to wish them 'bon chance.' As if to emphasize the meaning of the place and pay homage to Brock, they dressed in the traditional red-coated uniforms from that bygone era.

'What would Brock do?' was the persistent question that kept turning over in his mind.

Will woke to a nudge.

"It's time, sir," a red-coated officer told him.

"Thank you, Captain," Will answered.

He rubbed the sleep out of his eyes. Looking around and seeing the others and their modern weapons, along with Hana, launched his mind fast-forward two hundred years to the present. Once again he felt like a time traveller, a feeling that was happening to him more and more often.

"I made you some coffee just as you like it," said Hana, handing him a full mug.

"Thank you, Hana."

"No guns, sir?"

"No weapons of any kind, Max," he repeated. "Odds are they're going to capture us before we reach our target anyway. We don't want to give them anything that will be used to show we're armed and dangerous."

"But we are," Hana replied.

"True enough, but only to the enemies within our territory. Remember the red-wing. Once an intruder leaves the red-wing's territory, it returns to its nest. So we mustn't bring our guns. Plus don't forget, we've got lots of friends Stateside who are sympathetic to our cause. Let's not do anything now to turn them against us. Here, Max," he added, handing him his own 9mm pistol.

Will knew, from the reports he'd received from their Stateside friends, that a trap had been set for them. So, instead of carrying weapons, they armed themselves with harmless crimson red spray paint and stencils cut in the image of Xs and the Maple Leaf. If caught canoeing across, they'd play the part of harmless Canadian hoodlums crossing over to spray paint buildings in protest of the occupation. This non-violent form of protest was now happening so frequently that it got little press. It was also tolerated because many disgruntled American students had joined in on the act.

They hoped to canoe silently under the noses of the border patrol, but if they were caught, Will hedged his bets that they would just be scolded and escorted back to the border. This was the routine procedure of local and state police. Landing undetected on the American shore was only the first part of their plan. If they made it ashore safely, the second leg required them to take on the identities of Dillan and Angela who had given Hana their IDs for this purpose. Will was a dead match for Dillan and suspected most would not see the finer differences. Hana however had to alter her appearance somewhat so as to resemble Angela.

"Good luck!" were the last words they heard as they pushed off the Canadian shore.

As foreseen, the Niagara's current carried them swiftly downriver. If it hadn't been for their GPS, they would have undoubtedly passed the little river they were seeking to take them inland. Finding it, they paddled out of the swift current and headed up the tributary away from the heavily guarded border. As they paddled quietly upstream, they were alert to any noise that might spark a search light. Slowly making their way, their nerves began to settle and Will began to think about their next objective. They took the first right branch and continued until the GPS told them they'd arrived.

Will squinted and spied a red porch light on the right bank, signalling the location of their first safe house. Seeing it, he steered their canoe to the shoreline. All was quiet. After landing the canoe, they crept up to the house. Suddenly, a small dog began to bark.

"Down," whispered Will. Together, they dropped to the ground and froze. Visions of the Point Pelee ambush immediately came to mind.

"Hush, Bailey. Shhhhhhh," somebody said.

There on the porch rocker sat an elderly man wrapped up in a blanket. His motion had caught Will's eye as he reached down to give his dog a pat. After he did so he raised his head and looked directly at them.

"I do believe our northern friends have arrived, Bailey," he said with a welcoming voice.

With this reassurance, out of the gloom, Hana and Will approached the porch. Bailey stood beside his master happily wagging his tail.

"Mr Jackson?" Will asked, extending his hand.

"That would be me," he replied with a firm handshake. "And this ferocious dog here is Bailey."

"Hi there, Bailey," Hana answered, giving the beagle a little scratch behind the ear. "I'm Hana."

"And I'm William Anderson," Will said, "Best to call me Dillan though. And Hana is...." he hesitated. What he had to say didn't yet come naturally.

"Your wife, Angela," answered the woman who came out through the porch door. "Bienvenue."

The lady who'd come to Will's rescue had to be Mrs Jackson. He'd been told she was of Canadian descent, but hadn't realized she spoke a little French too.

"Merci, madame," Will answered.

"Please, call me Yvette. It's been a long time since I've felt comfortable in using my first name or speaking French with anyone. I'm not quite as bold as the young college kids," she admitted.

"Even so, Yvette's been waiting for your arrival so that she can brush up on her French, but let's go inside or we'll be inviting trouble. People still get uneasy when they hear foreigners," Mr Jackson explained.

Soon they'd been shown to their bedroom, where they stowed their bags, and then were soon seated comfortably in the family room with their hosts.

"How was your trip? Any problem finding our place?" Mr Jackson asked.

"None at all," Hana answered.

"The GPS made it easy," Will agreed.

"Here's a little something," Yvette said setting some cookies and tea before them. "And how are Dillan and Angela? The real ones, I mean. It's been ages since we've seen them."

Hana took out some photos and filled them in with all the most recent news. It was obvious how attached Hana was to the Gallaghers and their new baby. The fact that the Gallaghers had named their baby girl after Hana was a testament to how close they'd all become. Their intertwined relationships made the foursome seem like family.

"They look so happy," the Jacksons confessed.

Will's plan was to stay at the Jacksons' for two nights. They had a tight schedule to keep and being in constant motion was an important element of his plan.

"We appreciate that you are willing to let us stay here," Will told them.

"Is it a dilemma for you to support us Canadians?" asked Hana.

"Absolutely not!" replied Mr Jackson. "It's those buggers in Washington who are acting un-American. They don't represent me. I'm just fortunate to be one of the few who can still speak my mind."

"Why's that?" Hana prodded deeper.

"Well, I'm not in the Armed Forces or a public servant and I don't depend on their damned pension or handouts, so I can say what I like. I'm a rare breed nowadays, let's just leave it at that."

"Most Americans share our views," Yvette piped in. "They think of this conflict as more like a family feud than a war. Most would agree it's time to kiss and make up. They just aren't in a position to talk openly about it like we are. But I can assure you there's a lot of folks who think like us."

"It's almost becoming a sort of second Civil War," Mr Jackson asserted. "This conflict has not only driven deep divisions between the people, but it's divided the States into separate camps. The Northern States, Canada's closest neighbours, are mostly opposed to the war. Maine wants out immediately. It's only the Southern States that are generally for it."

"That's mainly because they don't want to give up the vacation properties they took from the Canadian snowbirds," Yvette explained.

"But you'll be travelling mostly through the north so you'll generally be amongst friends," Mr Jackson assured them.

"In a pinch you should be able to find another safe house," Yvette added. She gave them a list she had prepared of people they could safely contact en route who were part of what was becoming a modern underground railroad.

"Thank you," said Hana and Will simultaneously.

"So you're the notorious Anderson?" Yvette inquired, changing the subject. "Up close under the light, I'd say you look pretty harmless."

"He's dangerous if cornered," Hana assured her.

"I'm sure he is."

"Don't give up," Mr Jackson interjected.

"Funny you say that, sir. That's our motto: 'Jamais Capituler'."

Yvette smiled, comprehending the meaning.

"This fall," Mr Jackson continued, "there will be a whole new Congress elected and they'll put an end to this stupid war."

"Let's hope so, sir."

~

Yvette prepared a satisfying meal of eggs and toast for them. Seeing Yvette work in the kitchen, it was evident that the conflict had adversely affected their pantry stores for it was bare of all but the most basic essentials. With weak coffee, they all toasted one another 'to peace and friendship'.

After breakfast, Hana and Will were ushered to their room for a few winks. Hana was soon sleeping peacefully while Will's mind wandered back over the events of the day. Meeting the Jacksons and hearing them express their views validated the merit of their policies including fighting exclusively within Canadian territory. It wasn't difficult to imagine that the insurgents could have carried the war deep into America as well. The spray painters could have just as easily been laying explosives instead. Not having done so put them on the higher road in the eyes of Americans like the Jacksons. The good karma had paid off and the Jacksons provided a good reminder that many Americans still considered themselves to be Canada's friends.

~

The following day, Will and Hana laid low at the Jacksons' while Mr and Mrs Jackson were out gathering extra supplies for them and finalizing their arrangements.

"So what's next?" Hana inquired of Will. Will had deliberately kept Hana in the dark figuring that, if they were caught, the less she knew about their enterprise, the better. He planned to fill her in on a need to know basis.

"We're going on a week long bike ride," he said finally, "and we'll be tenting along the way."

"Perfect," Hana exclaimed. "I'm due for some exercise. So where are we going?"

Hana due for some exercise? The thought caused him to smile to himself. She was the perfect model of fitness and, like Sydney, the envy of most women. He also smiled because Hana obviously trusted him to work out the details of the plans without hesitation.

Will was glad to have Hana's company as her positive energy would help keep things light. That was important for he had a lot to think about. Foremost on his mind was his concern about how Sydney was coping with imprisonment. Freeing her from prison was his highest priority but, exactly how he was going to do that, he had yet to determine. It was going to be much more compli-cated than freeing Kevin from their small-town jail. Brock's diary couldn't offer him any guidance in this undertaking.

Much of Hana's day at the Jacksons' was spent watching TV. It was a luxury few Canadians had the opportunity to indulge in anymore.

"A large warehouse of fireworks, destined for Ottawa's Canada Day celebrations has been found and confiscated," a newsperson for the new CBC News reported.

"Did you hear that, Will?"

"I did, Hana. Hacker will be furious about that."

"Really? Why?"

"He and his friend Tadita were making those fireworks for a special occasion. They've been stockpiling them all winter," Will explained. "Renée will be really upset too. She wanted them for Ottawa's Canada Day celebrations."

Preparing for the July 1st Canada Day festivities had been one of the most effective diversions Renée had come up with. After the preceding year's event turned into a riot to protest the occupation, Washington had outlawed the national holiday and decreed that no Maple Leaf flags were to be seen and the Canadian anthem was not to be heard. Instead, all North Americans were expected to celebrate one day together, July 4th, Independence Day. Kuhn was trying to snuff out the last vestiges of Canadian nationalism.

Renée's efforts to encourage all communities all across the nation to unite and celebrate the forbidden national holiday had kept the occupation forces busy. Most communities rose to the occasion and soon the idea took on a life of its own. Ottawa's celebration was slated to be the main event and Renée had planned a national display of discontent.

Hordes of Canadian protestors were now descending upon Ottawa to take part in the massive anti-occupation demonstration. Their numbers were so large that, when they came upon a roving check-point, they simply pushed by it and all the guards could do was stand aside and watch.

Instead of enforcing the Restriction of Movement Decree, the occupation forces focused on controlling the size of the celebrations. This was why finding and confiscating the hidden fireworks had become national news.

"We'll be using the captured Canadian fireworks on July 4th in Washington!" Kuhn declared victoriously. It was his intention to have the largest display of fireworks in America's history and the fact that Canada had been deprived of using the fireworks for their own celebration gave more meaning to his plans.

~

Later that day, when the Jacksons returned, Hana had prepared a big meal of pancakes and maple syrup. Canadian maple syrup was considered contraband in the US since its sale was deemed to put money in the insurgents' coffers. Hana and Will had smuggled the syrup across the border to show their appreciation for the risk they knew their hosts had taken for them.

"This is such a treat!" Yvette declared.

"It's our way of saying 'thank you'" Will explained with a smile.

After the meal, the Jacksons dropped Hana and Will off at the University of Buffalo's northern campus.

"Thanks again," Will repeated as he lifted their bikes off the rack mounted on the car's rear bumper.

After exchanging hugs and well wishes, Hana and Will walked their bikes over to a large group of cyclists gathering across the road. At least fifty participants were busy packing their panniers and BOB trailers with food and gear and readying themselves for departure. Even more riders were anticipated to join the group en route. Hana and Will quickly intermingled with the crowd.

"Hello," somebody spoke to Will. "Have we met?"

Will exchanged looks with Hana. Although Will had grown a moustache, they feared he still might be recognized.

"Perhaps. I'm Dillan. Dillan Gallagher. And this is my wife, Angela," Will said.

"I guess not," the other answered. "I'm Jim," he said.

"Nice meeting ya," answered Will.

"Welcome riders!" shouted a person from the bed of a pick-up truck. "I'm Benjamin and this is Cathy," he motioned to the girl standing beside him. "We'll be heading off in about fifteen minutes. Before I tell you about today's ride, Cathy's got a few housekeeping items to mention."

"Hi everyone," Cathy started. "Like Ben said, we'll be leaving in about fifteen minutes. We have two support vehicles. This pick-up will drive ahead of the pack and arrive at our daily destination before us. You can throw any gear you won't need with you in the back of the pick-up or in the trailer it will be pulling. Your tents will already be set up for you by the time you arrive."

"That van there," she said, pointing at a large van capable of carrying a number of passengers and sporting a large number of racks on its roof, "will be our sag wagon. It will meet us at lunch so you can stow some light extras in it if you wish. Anyone having trouble doing the whole distance can ride partway in the van. Lastly, because we'll be taking trails as often as possible, we've got an ATV following us. It'll have tools, spare tubes and a pump," she concluded.

"Ok, thanks, Cathy," Ben continued. "Today's destination will be Salamanca, NY. It's sixty miles away. This will be our longest day and a good test to sort out the dreamers from those who are truly capable of doing the whole distance to DC. It will take us two weeks to do the full route. Today, the ride will mostly be on-road. After Salamanca, the next leg will take us to Pittsburgh, pedalling through the Alleghenies, both on and off road. From Pittsburgh, we'll ride on-road to Duquesne PA and then take the C&O trail, which parallels the Potomac River, for our final 184 mile leg down to Washington DC. Cathy's got a trip map for everyone once you sign the waiver form. Are there any questions?"

After Ben and Cathy fielded a few questions, everyone signed the waivers, got their maps, and got set to go.

"Welcome, Dillan. Welcome, Angela," Cathy had said when they signed in.

"You sound very organized," Hana said happily.

"It'll be a nice change to travel so light," Will admitted.

~

The whole journey felt surreal to Will. They were completely surrounded by their enemy, yet it felt as though they were living in peace amongst friends. The routine mode of travel and being among likeminded people put their minds at ease. Hana and Will tented together, making it appear as though they were a recently honeymooned couple in want of some privacy. To Hana, this only added to the fun and she enjoyed their little masquerade.

"Cheryl's off the back," Jim called as the main body of cyclists dropped another struggling rider.

The first day, they dropped over a dozen stragglers from the ride, but at each destination, they picked up even more who wanted to join them. Some joined just for the pleasure of having a good day ride. Others intended to stay on right to Washington. Upon reaching Washington on Independence Day, the group intended to hold an antiwar demonstration. What exactly they would do was yet to be determined, but having that as their purpose made Hana and Will feel that they were among friends.

Soon, they had nearly a thousand riders in their group and the line of cyclists stretched for miles. The number of riders, and the constant rotation of them, helped Hana and Will to maintain their anonymity. They tried to avoid becoming close to anyone, but that was difficult at times.

"Annie's flatted, Dillan," Ben reported to him.

This message had been relayed from Cathy, who had called them on her cell phone to report Annie's predicament. Being so accustomed to journeying independently on bike, word quickly spread that Will was the one to go to whenever a mechanical problem occurred. He felt it was a wise precaution to carry his own tools just in case he and Hana decided to go their own way. Consequently, he was often able to help others who needed some assistance. Most times, he could have a rider up and riding in a matter of minutes. Being a strong rider, Will could easily make up ground afterward and rejoin the company of those he'd been pedalling with.

"There's Annie," Ben said, as a rider came into view off to the side of the treed pathway.

"I'll take care of her, Ben," Will volunteered.

"I'll help," Jim offered.

"Do you need a hand, Annie?" Will hollered, riding up to her.

"Sure, Dillan," she answered with a thankful smile. "I've flatted again."

"You're becoming my best customer!" he laughed, dismounting his bike. "Careful, Angela's becoming jealous," he joked.

Within minutes, he'd taken her old tube out as she and Jim stood by and chatted.

"Maybe I'll give you a brand new tube this time," Will offered. "This one's had the biscuit." He held it up showing a number of patches on it already.

Despite their successful tactics to maintain their anonymity, Will was very relieved to reach Washington DC. As they readied themselves to part ways with the others, Jim, Cathy and Ben came over to say farewell.

"Thanks for all your help, Dillan," Ben said.

"Yes, you made things a lot easier for us," Cathy added. "And I especially enjoyed your company, Angela."

"Ditto," said Jim.

"We should do this again sometime," Hana piped in enthusiastically. "Let's exchange addr...," abruptly she caught herself as Will cast a warning glance her way. Her face flushed with obvious embarrassment. Not knowing what to say next, Hana froze. Unexpectedly, Jim came to their rescue.

"No need, Angela. Dillan has already given me your addresses," he lied. "I'll get everyone else's and make up a contact list and email it to everyone."

"Great!" Cathy answered.

~

"You gave Jim our address?" Hana asked Will a short while later, when they were alone.

"No, I didn't. He lied about that."

"I don't understand. Do you think he knows who we are, Will?"

"He must. That's the only explanation I can come up with." Will had been pondering that same question ever since Jim had come to their rescue. Will thought back to the day they first met.

"I think he's known all along, Hana. He thought he knew me right from the start."

"Shhhh…" Hana cautioned him as she saw Jim approaching.

Jim sensed their caution.

"I've spoken with Cathy and Ben and thought you'd both like to know how we're going protest the war," Jim stated matter-of-factly.

"Sure. Maybe we'll even join you," Will offered, "that is, if it fits into our plans."

"That may be a bad idea, Dillan," Jim cautioned. "We are going to stage a protest where the Canadian Sydney Hope is being held prisoner. She's Will Anderson's girlfriend. We're going to try to organize a massive rally calling for her release. Do you think Anderson will appreciate that?" he asked, looking Will directly in the eyes.

"I'm sure he will," Will answered.

"I'm glad you think so," Jim smiled.

"Why?" Hana asked him point blank. "Why would you do that?"

"Why? Because I served a tour of duty in Canada. My platoon was ambushed. We tried to fight back, but were surrounded and outnumbered. It was either surrender or be annihilated. I was wounded. Those who lived were taken prisoner and that included me. Anderson's band looked after me and, when I was healed, they released me on parole unharmed. That was when I first met Anderson. He shook my hand and wished me the best. That day, the war ended for me. Now, I must do everything I can to repay my debt. That's why I wanted to know if you," he said, looking directly at Will again, "think Anderson would be pleased if we tried to set Sydney Hope free."

"I know he will."

"Good. Every person captured and released from my platoon, and many others like them, their families, and their many friends feel the same way. We'll have a lot of support. So we don't need you two," he repeated the warning. "Just enjoy your time in Washington, see the parade and the fireworks."

Will held out his hand to the American, saying, "best wishes and good luck, Jim."

"Thank you, sir," Jim replied, gripping Will's extended hand.

~

Washington was abuzz with the preparations for Independence Day and nobody seemed to care about a couple of harmless cyclo-tourists pedalling around the city. Everything seemed peaceful, but in the news, there was the constant reminder that America was at war. Tension filled the media. Will smiled when he read the headlines of the Washington Post exclaiming that, despite the ban: 'Canadians Celebrate Canada Day!' Renée had done her job. Despite Hacker's fireworks being found and confiscated, the citizens had held enough of a celebration to mark the day and capture the headlines.

"Good job, Renée!" exclaimed Will to nobody in particular.

Despite the authorities clamping down on the festivities in Ottawa and the other garrisoned cities, all across the rest of Canada people celebrated. In small towns and remote rural places beyond the power of the occupation forces, Canadians celebrated in their own small way. The forbidden public celebrations were replaced by countless personal ones. It was a magnificent display of true unorchestrated national spirit. Some people simply dressed up gaily in the national red and white colours, occasionally a person whistled, sang or hummed O Canada and the now forbid-den Maple Leaf flags could be seen flying from every vantage point. Gardens, planted earlier in the season, now bloomed with red and white flowers. Yet the most enduring thing was achieved by those who planted the long living red maple trees. More than anything else these trees symbolized the Canadian connection to nature and the land. Many considered it to be the best Canada Day ever because it was celebrated privately and personally.

Before the war, the average American didn't know or care when Canada celebrated its national holiday. It only mattered now because of Washington's efforts to outlaw it. Despite the news, Kuhn tried to make the best of it.

"We've ripped the heart out of Canada Day," he boasted. "We're bringing the confiscated fireworks here for July 4th. Combined with our own, we'll light up the night skies over the Capitol like never before!"

"Good for them," Hana and Will heard one lady say, applauding the modest Canadian celebration. "How would we like it if somebody outlawed our Independence Day?"

That comment seemed to reflect the general reaction of the people Hana and Will came upon that day and it softened them even more towards their so-called adversaries. The people wouldn't be fooled again. Kuhn's boasting didn't reflect the popular sentiment. People had grown tired of the war and they were fed up with all the political doubletalk. Most people had come to Washington to commemorate the real meaning of Independence Day. Freedom-minded Americans publicly expressed their admiration of the Canadian resolve to uphold their own national holiday as well as their desire for sovereignty. Their words proved to the Andersons that the common founding spirit of independence united the two countries more than the politicians could divide them.

"These people don't want war either, Will," Hana concluded. "Makes you wonder who's running America, doesn't it?"

"Washington," Will answered.

Despite the general word on the street, the opinion polls still showed that almost half of Americans continued to support the war so Will knew they still had a job to do. He and Hana rode to the safe house address he'd memorized. Locking their bikes up to the stairway railing, they entered the front lobby. There Will buzzed Apartment 504.

"Yes?" answered a voice through the speaker.

"Hello, I'm Dillan Gallagher and I'm with my wife Angela. Are you Mr Leeside?"

"May I see some ID, please?"

"Pardon?"

"I need to see some ID. Hold it up to the security camera where I can see it."

Will did as he'd been instructed. Hana did likewise. A few seconds later, they heard the door unlock so they could enter. Hana's natural intuition put a worried look on her face as they exited the elevator, walked down the hallway and found the door of Room 504. Will knocked on the door.

"Stand before the peephole where I can see you," spoke the same voice from behind the door. Again, Will did as he was instructed.

"Where's the girl?" asked the voice.

"I'm here," answered Hana.

"I don't see your face." Hana gave Will a look of disbelief.

"Can't be too careful, I guess," Will shrugged.

"Are either of you carrying any weapons?"

"No," they answered simultaneously.

"I'm armed, so if you're lying, you'll set my scanner alarm off," he warned.

"We're unarmed, don't shoot."

"All right, I believe you. Come in."

They heard the door lock click. Opening the door warily, they entered the apartment. Looking about, Will could see baggage had been packed.

"Are you leaving?" Will asked.

"The name's Leeside. Now tell me, who are you really?"

This direct question was unexpected.

"I told you. Gallagher."

"No you're not. Under that moustache, I'd say you look more like Anderson."

Will hesitated for a moment then made up his mind.

"I am," Will admitted, "but how did you know?"

"A man showed up before you, claiming to be Dillan Gallagher. He knew using that name would get him in."

So that explained all the extra precautions, Will thought.

"He told me you'd be coming here using the same name. He told me only to speak with you if you could show me Gallagher's ID," the man continued.

That unexpected response threw Will for a loop.

"Who's the girl?" Mr Leeside asked.

"Christine, my.... friend," he lied. "Shit. Who was he?"

"He wouldn't say. He was about your age though, Canadian for sure. He was a lanky fellow and sickly."

"Why did he come?"

"He told me to give you a message."

"So what was it?"

"He wanted me to warn you to get the hell out of Washington before sundown, July 4th."

~

For many Americans, Independence Day that year had become a time to take an honest look at themselves. Washington DC provided the ideal backdrop for this solemn reflection on American values. There, the ghosts of those who had inspired, founded and solidified the nation and its ideals still lingered. All throughout the city, the many statues of the founding fathers reminded people of their noble purpose. The words inscribed upon public buildings took on new meaning. Large numbers of people were drawn to the Reflecting Pool to reflect upon their national journey from a newborn Republic in 1776 to a mature democratic nation. Will and Hana made their way there too.

Challenging questions were being asked. Would the founding fathers feel at home in America now? Would they even be allowed to voice their inner thoughts without being branded as revolutionaries and unpatriotic? And when did being a revolutionary become a bad thing in America? Would they have conceived of an America bent on conquest? How could Americans, in clear conscience, celebrate their liberation from British colonial rule, when they were now, in so many ways, acting like imperialistic colonizers themselves?

"We place no restriction on Her Majesty's prerogative
in the selection of her representative... The sovereign
has unrestricted freedom of choice... We leave that to
Her Majesty in all confidence."
— John A. MacDonald in a speech to the Legislative
Assembly of the Province of Canada, 1866

CHAPTER XXIV

Bombs Bursting In Air

It was a hot and humid day and people sought out shade wherever they could find it. Armed soldiers dressed in battle fatigues lined both sides of Constitution Avenue. Red, white and blue banners, fixed high up on every street light post, fluttered overhead in the gentle easterly breeze. Hana and Will pushed through the crowd in order to find a better position from which to view the parade. They were awed by the sight and by the crowd.

"How could we ever hope to hold back this vast population, Will?" Hana wondered. "There's so many of them."

"They are only ten times our number, Hana. Brock faced greater odds," he reminded her.

As if to reinforce the point, something airborne caught her eye.

"Look, Will," she pointed, "it's your red-winged blackbird."

"So it is," Will smiled. "That's a good omen."

As they watched, the bird swooped down from its perch to menace those standing around it. Down and down again it dove over the assorted heads in the crowd. Hands, holding baseball caps, waved in the air in an attempt to ward off these attacks, but the bird persisted undeterred.

"One against hundreds," Hana voiced what Will was thinking. "I wonder who will give up first?"

"I doubt the red-wing will."

Soon an empty circle had formed around the tree as the continuously harassed crowd grew tired of fighting off the attacks. Seeing the bird's victory restored Will and Hana's hope.

"If I were a Native, Hana," Will said, "seeing that would have much deeper meaning."

"Well, it moved me, Will."

The parade started with a Marine marching band playing *The Star-Spangled Banner*.

"That's fitting," said Will, remembering that the lyrics had been written during the War of 1812.

Out of habit, he mouthed the words, recalling them from the countless NHL hockey matches he'd watched.

"Oh, say can you see…"

"Pardon?" asked Hana.

"Old habits die hard," he replied.

"No, let's sing. I love their anthem."

Together they sang, just as heartily as they would have sung their own anthem. For a moment, doing so made them feel like they were back in the good old days, when they were at peace and friends with their American neighbours.

The volume of marching music rose as the parade came down the avenue. Will rose up on his toes to see over the heads of those crowded in front of them. Just after the Marine band came President Kuhn in a car completely surrounded by plain clothed security personnel. The President stood up in an open convertible, saluting the public, as if he was a man who had nothing to fear. But as he drew near, all could see it was not true for he was surrounded by bullet-proof glass.

With his hands in his pockets, Will felt their tickets to the President's reception after the fireworks. Mr Leeside had arranged that they would go as the Gallaghers to the reception representing the new North American citizenry from the Canadian territories. There, they would be in close personal proximity to the President and they would have a private introduction. Their meeting would be Will's first opportunity to meet Kuhn face to face. Even at this late hour, he hadn't figured exactly how he would do it, but his plan was to seize the President right in front of all of his security. It was an ambitious goal, but Will knew that unexpected guests had breached the highest level of presidential security before.

Again he fingered the tickets. It still bothered him that somebody had tried to warn them. Few knew of their plans to meet with Leeside. Will still wondered who that man was.

As the President's car passed by, the alert red-winged blackbird left its nest again and flew straight down toward the vehicle. Standing up in his car, Kuhn was the highest target for the bird. So close did it swoop that the President had to duck from the assault. Kuhn held his hand to his head as his aides quickly helped him to take his seat.

"Did you see that?" Hana exclaimed. "I think it actually pecked him!"

The crowd roared with laughter. Hearing that, Kuhn ordered that the roof of his car should be closed. Hidden from public view, he cocooned himself from further harm and ridicule.

"Safe at last, eh Kuhn?" someone shouted.

While all this commotion was taking place, something else caught Will's attention.

"Hacker's here," he said.

"Excuse me?"

"I said Hacker's here. And he's wearing a US army uniform."

"You're joking!"

"No, I'm serious. He's standing right across from us on the other side of the avenue."

Hana followed Will's gaze and saw him too.

"What's he doing here?" she asked.

"That's what I'd like to know," Will answered, "but it can't be good."

"Do you think he was the one who asked Mr Leeside to warn us?"

"That's exactly what I intend to find out."

Will's mind wandered through the possibilities. Hacker had been overseeing the manufacturing of the Canada Day fireworks. The ones that had been found, confiscated and brought here. Could he be intending to…

"Don't let him out of your sight, Hana. I must talk to him."

The parade went on and on and on. Finally it came to an end and, as it did so, the crowd swept into the avenue to follow on its heels. Hacker joined the crowd and Hana and Will, trying to keep out of his sight, followed him. They walked down Constitution Avenue until they came to 17th Street where the parade ended beside the National Mall. From there, the crowd dispersed in different directions for there were many events scheduled throughout the day.

"Look here, Will," said Hana pointing to a brochure she'd picked up. "It says here that there's a folk-life festival at the Smithsonian featuring music and dance performances, crafts and other activities celebrating America's birthday. This year's theme is Canada: Past, Present and Future. I'd like to go see that!"

"You do that, Hana. I've got to find out what Hacker's up to." Looking at his watch, he added, "Let's meet back here at 5pm so we can get something to eat before the concert and fire-works begin."

Most of the crowd carried their portable chairs and blankets toward the Capitol so they could claim their space on the west lawn. Hacker went in the opposite direction. Will nudged his way through the crowd until they were walking side by side.

"Hello, Will," said Hacker. "Didn't you get my message?"

"Hi, Hacker. Yes we got it. But what does it mean and what are you doing here? And why are you dressed in an American uniform?" Then, noting something for the first time, he added, "Are you feeling ok? You don't look well."

"I'm not. Nothing to worry about. It's not contagious."

"What are you doing here?" asked Will for a second time.

"Trying to win the war in my own way. Yours isn't working. Now, if you don't mind, I've got to go meet somebody. And you can't be there. I'll see you and Hana later."

"Fine," replied Will, deciding his best option was to show Hacker that he still trusted him. "You can meet us at 5pm by the security gates off Constitution Avenue near the Washington Monument. Promise you'll come."

"I promise."

Hacker made his way alone down Pennsylvania Avenue to the old Canadian Embassy where Sydney and his father were report-edly imprisoned. Reports indicated they were guarded by an elite Homeland security force led by their new leader, General Douglas.

Last night, the news had reported that a small group of bicyclists was camped outside the Embassy gates to protest the Canadians' imprisonment. The tone of the report was condescending towards the 'small band of tree hugging lefties', but it was obvious to Hacker that this group had now attracted to its cause Americans from all walks of life. Making his way through the crowd, he saw veterans, civilians, students, young and old. They had totally sur-rounded the building and were demanding the prisoners' release.

Hacker could hear the repetitive beat of a native drum being beaten as he squeezed his way to the barred gates. The drumbeat gave him courage.

"Here," said Hacker as he passed an envelope through to a private. "It's an urgent message for General Douglas. See that he gets it right away."

"Yes, sir." Hacker faded back into the crowd.

Looking down at the envelope, the private read: *Urgent and Confidential message for General Douglas from Corporal Patrick O'Neil, General Douglas' personal aide de camp.*

~

Unbeknownst to the crowd gathered at the Embassy, Sydney and the professor had secretly been moved overnight to a brig anchored in the Potomac near the Navy Yard.

"Ma'am. Sir. The captain says it'd be ok for you to come up on deck to watch the fireworks if you like," offered the naval officer.

"Please tell the captain we would appreciate that," replied the professor.

"Yes, sir."

A while later, the naval officer returned to escort Sydney and the professor onto the deck.

"It's a clear night. Should be good for watching the fireworks," noted the professor.

Sydney nodded, but her thoughts were elsewhere. The professor's love of history had inspired her to think about all things in a different way. To their south lay Virginia where the British first set foot in America to establish the colony of Jamestown. That colony wouldn't have survived if not for the generosity shown to the British by the Natives there at that time.

'Where are the descendants of those natives now?' she wondered. 'Did the Indians know it would end this way?'

"Excuse me, sir," she called to a midshipman standing nearby.

"Ma'am?"

"May I please have a pencil and some paper?"

The midshipman looked to the officer on duty who nodded in response. A few minutes later, she put pencil to paper and she wrote.

Did the Indians know it would end this way
When they walked the forests day by day?
With tall trees all around
With their ears to the ground
Did they know that this country
Would someday be found
By men who killed buffalo
Chopped down their trees
Changed rivers and mountains
Their quests to appease?
Did they fear for the animals
Wild and untamed?
Did they see the great waterways
Deadened and maimed?
Could they picture their ponies
Replaced by the wheel?
Did they dream of a tepee
Of glass and of steel?
Could they see their dominion
Crossed swiftly by air?
Did they see?
Did they know?
Did we care?

~

A number of pop artists played patriotic music throughout the afternoon and into the evening. At last, the final performer took to the stage to sing the National Anthem, after which President Kuhn was to speak. His speech was scheduled to end promptly at 9:10pm and the fireworks display would begin.

General Douglas had almost spoiled everything. Shortly after the conclusion of the parade, the general had found Kuhn and handed him a letter. At that particular moment, Kuhn was surrounded by the press, who were quizzing him about his reaction to the red-winged blackbird incident. The general's state of panic did not go unnoticed by the reporters which further irritated the President.

Annoyed as he was, Kuhn simply took the letter from the general and, without reading it, stuffed it into a pocket.

"But, Mr President, that's an imp…" The President silenced him by putting up his hand. He did want to hear any more bad news.

"Later, General, later," Kuhn said.

For the remainder of the day, Kuhn avoided the general. He wanted the spotlight to shine only on himself today and not on the pompous general. While listening to the performances, Kuhn reached into his pocket and felt the letter. Knowing that the cameras and the public's attention were focused on the performance on stage, he decided the time was right and pulled it out of his pocket.

The outer envelope was addressed to General Douglas. It had been opened and all that remained inside it now was a sealed inner envelope. Kuhn surmised correctly that it had originally contained a note for the general, worded to ensure he would immediately deliver the envelope to Kuhn. He looked at writing on the inner envelope:

Enclosed is an urgent message for President Kuhn to be read before 9pm July 4th. Barry Hacker

It was amateurish to send the President something this way, but the name Hacker, the same surname as the prisoner being held in the brig on the Potomac, raised Kuhn's curiosity. He looked at his watch. It was 8:49pm. As inconspicuously as possible, he carefully tore open the sealed envelope.

Mr President:

At precisely 9:10 pm, we will launch Canadian fireworks which contain highly radioactive nuclear dust which is extremely carcinogenic if inhaled. The fuses are under my sole control and I will launch them unless you pledge in your speech tonight the following: First, to immediately cease the occupation of Canada; second, to immediately release all the prisoners, including Professor Hacker (my father) and Sydney Hope; and third, to return all confiscated lands to their rightful Canadian owners. Should you fail to do so, it is with deepest regret that I will have no alternative but to launch the nuclear rockets.

I beg you to do the right thing, Barry Hacker.

Unperturbed, the President tore up the letter into tiny bits and pieces and then carefully dropped them over the edge of the VIP platform. The letter hadn't told him anything he didn't already know. Border control had already discovered that the Canadian fireworks contained radioactive materials and had immediately reported that fact directly to him. Under the guise of not panicking the general public, Kuhn ensured that the information was declared Top Secret and Confidential. Then, with great fanfare, he facilitated delivery of the fireworks to Washington. He knew the explosions of the contaminated fireworks wouldn't cause any blast damage, but their radioactive contents would be transported into the atmosphere and dispersed by the breeze. That's why he was happy to note the wind was blowing away from him.

Tomorrow, the radioactive particles would be found all over Washington and would be traced back to the Canadian fireworks. That news would cause instant panic and people would start fleeing the irradiated city. Even if radiation levels were not too high, the time and expense of clean-up would be enormous.

Canada would be blamed and an infuriated public would call for revenge against Canada. Hitting their cities with nuclear bombs would be as palatable and justifiable as it was in 1945. All he had to do was listen to one more song, deliver his speech, and leave. That night, he looked forward to sleeping better than he had slept in a long time.

A nine year old schoolgirl, Terra Wolfe of Maine, had been chosen to sing the National Anthem. At precisely 9 pm, she proudly climbed the stairs and took centre stage. The crowd fell silent.

'This is perfect,' Kuhn thought. Tomorrow, people will remember that children had been subject to the fallout too.

Terra stood looking out at the huge crowd. The cameras zoomed in close so that millions more could watch the event from their homes. For a moment, her head spun due to the excitement and immensity of her job. She closed her eyes, controlled her breathing and counted slowly to ten.

'Nine, ten,' she thought to herself. When she opened her eyes, she had gathered the confidence to sing.

In a soft voice that betrayed the strength of her singing voice, she spoke, "This goes out to my father, the one who protects me."

'Perfect,' Kuhn grinned.

Then in a clear voice, Terra started to sing.

"Oh, say can you see, by the dawn's early light, what so proudly we hailed at the twilight's last gleaming…."

Her pure voice, without the aid of instrumental accompaniment, enchanted the crowd.

"…does that star-spangled banner yet wave…," she sang.

Kuhn smiled knowing that victory was soon to be his.

"…O'er the land of the free and the home of the brave," she concluded.

As she sang her final note, the audience roared in applause. Kuhn beamed with confidence. Now it was his turn to take the stage.

As he rose to make his way to the stage, he noted that Terra hadn't stepped away from the mike as planned. The eyes and cameras were still on her. To quiet the applause of the audience, she held up a hand. She looked directly at the stunned President.

"This is for my mother, who takes care of me," she announced.

Disconcerted, Kuhn retook his seat.

Again, she began to sing, "O Canada! Terre de nos…"

Shouting from the crowd momentarily drowned her out, but through all the clamour, she continued to sing. Kuhn smiled. She had turned the crowd against her and he could not have asked for a better scenario.

As she continued to sing, an opposing chant began to drown out the protestors.

"Let her sing! Let her sing!" they demanded. A famous American entertainer mounted the stage and motioned for the crowd to be quiet. Turning to Terra, she placed her hands on the girl's shoulders and whispered something in her ear. The audience watched in silence as the two gave each other a hug and the celebrity turned back toward the audience.

"She's going to start again," she announced, clapping her hands together.

This time the audience listened in respectful silence as Terra sang the entire Canadian national anthem.

"…O Canada, we stand on guard for thee."

Once more, after her last note was sung, the audience erupted with applause.

Some in the audience began the chant, "President Kuhn, hold the fireworks, no more bombs, end the war with Can-a-da!"

More people joined in until most of the crowd were shouting it out. Kuhn realized he'd lost control of the citizenry. All his plans for the evening had been spoiled. He left without speaking.

Will saw a tear streak down Hacker's face as he snapped his cell phone closed. The number he was about to call would have caused the fireworks' fuses to be detonated.

"Hi, Hacker," said Will.

Hacker turned to look at him. It took a moment for him to connect Will with their surroundings. Then his eyes cleared.

"It's over, Barry."

"I know," he answered.

"Let's go," said Will, waving Hana over to join them. "By the way, who were you calling?"

"Nobody and it doesn't matter now."

~

CHAPTER XV

Beneath Thy Shining Skies

Will was dreaming of birdsong.

"Wake up, Will. Wake up!" Hana shook him again. Startled out of a dreamy sleep, Will immediately opened his eyes.

"What is it, Hana?" he asked, propping himself up on one elbow. He was now wide-eyed and fully alert.

"Relax, Will. It's good news!" she said. "Barry's got a copy of today's paper. Guess what the headlines are saying?"

"That peace broke out?" he joked. "That the young girl who sang both anthems last night softened their hearts?" Actually, he had hoped exactly for that, but didn't expect it would ever happen.

"Not quite, but you're almost right. Peace is breaking out," she said, thrusting a copy of the newspaper in his hand.

Taking it from her, he glanced at the headline.

'KUHN ACCUSED OF WAR CRIMES!' it proclaimed.

"You're kidding!" he stated incredulously. "Am I still dreaming?"

"No, you're not dreaming, Will. This is for real."

Looking back at the paper, he read:

President Kuhn was taken into custody earlier this morning charged with a number of federal criminal offences including inciting the war with Canada and election fraud. "We have obtained credible evidence that Kuhn masterminded the whole affair," Chief Justice Leroy King said, referring to both the kamikaze style attack on Fermi as well as the freighter's destruction of the Ambassador Bridge spanning the Detroit River into Canada.

"I simply gave the public what they wanted," Kuhn protested, referring to the thirty-four percent of the voting public who commanded a sufficient electoral majority to put him into the White House.

General Douglas, who himself faces court-martial charges for his role, was also taken into custody for further questioning.

"I've got no comment about that Benedict Arnold!" Kuhn replied when asked by reporters to comment on the statements made on video by General Douglas, the President's former right hand man.

"They're completely credible statements made without duress. Frankly, they are not surprising," Justice King stated, commenting on the video the Justice Department received from an undisclosed source. "[That video] is just the final piece of evidence we've gathered in a lengthy investigation."

"I was just following orders!" the general said to reporters in his own defence.

More arrests and charges can be expected as more witnesses from Kuhn's administration come forward.

~

Will had just finished the important parts of the headline article and was just about to scan the paper for more details when Hacker came running into the room and turned on the TV.

"Watch this, you guys," he said excitedly. They all turned their eyes to the TV screen to watch the latest breaking news.

"... and here from the White House is the Vice-President," the anchorperson announced.

My fellow Americans:

I speak to you from the Oval Office as your President. Moments ago, I received word that President Kuhn has been declared mentally unfit to continue to act as the Chief Executive and Commander in Chief of the Armed Forces of the United States of America.

As second in command, I have just taken the oath of office and assumed those responsibilities left vacant by the President.

My fellow Americans, after reviewing the evidence given to me this morning by the Justice Department, I, in performing my first duty to the Republic as the Chief Executive of the Military will recommend to Congress that the war with Canada be terminated.

I will also recommend, as a gesture of good faith, that all Canadian prisoners of war being presently held should immediately be released 'on parole' and furthermore, that our soldiers within the Canadian territory cease and desist any further military activity while we await Congress' assent.

Prince Arthur has given me his assurance that the Canadians will discontinue any further military activity as well.

My fellow Americans, it is time that this inconceivable war with Canada, a war that should have never have happened, is concluded. The war is over.

Thank you. God bless you and God bless the United States of America.

Aboard a ferry crossing the Detroit River back to the Canadian side, Hana, Sydney and Will stood looking up at the beginnings of the new Ambassador Bridge. Only three weeks had passed since Independence Day and already the foundation had been laid.

"Do you think it will be done by Christmas as the Prince promised?" asked Sydney, squeezing Will's hand a little tighter.

"I do," he answered. "With the parliamentary elections not being held until this fall, I think the Prince will see to finishing it before Ottawa gets in the way. And the States are doing their part," he added, nodding back to the construction taking place on their side.

"It's amazing what can be accomplished when nobody stands in your way," Sydney acknowledged.

"True, but as we know from the experience we just lived through, that can also be a bad thing. No person should have too much unchecked power."

"Do you think Barry will live long enough to see the bridge completed?"

Will stared blankly out towards Canada. He too had been thinking of Barry, who was now fighting for his life because of the radiation poison that contaminated his body from manufacturing the fireworks. Both he and the professor had remained Stateside where he was now receiving the best medical treatment available. The new President had seen to it that, under the extenuating wartime circumstances, all charges against him had been dropped.

"I hope so," said Will.

"So what do you think will become of the ruins of the old bridge?" Sydney wondered. Together their eyes sought out the wrecked old bridge, damaged beyond repair.

"I don't know," answered Will.

"Well I hope they leave it as it is," declared Hana. "It will remind us never to take anything for granted again."

"We can only hope," agreed Sydney.

The ferry pulled up to dock on the Canadian side where a crowd waited to welcome them home. Amongst the crowd, they could see Grant and Sophie Anderson.

"There's Kevin too!" exclaimed Hana, pointing at a man standing with them in priest's attire.

High up in a tree, Will spotted a red-winged blackbird. 'There you are, my friend,' he thought.

As they crossed over the gangplank, the crowd spontaneously broke into singing the National Anthem.

"O Canada…"

"Our home and native land....," sang Hana, Sydney and Will as they stepped ashore. The nightmare was over.

The End

CPSIA information can be obtained at www.ICGtesting.com
Printed in the USA
LVOW060329300911

248458LV00001B/14/P